DEVIL'S PLAGUE

AN IAN MACRAE NOVEL

JON P WELLS

Publisher: Jon P Wells
email: jonpwellsauthor@gmail.com
website: jonpwells.com

A catalogue record for this work is available from the National Library Of Australia

Creator: Wells, Jon P., 1962 – author.

Title: Devil's Plague / Jon P. Wells

ISBN: 9780994418333 (paperback)
               9780994418340 (Kindle ebook)

Subjects: Terrorism – Fiction
               Biological warfare – Fiction
               Conspiracy theory - Fiction
               Suspense – Fiction

Thank you to Carol, Ollie, Chrissie, Matt & Rene for your encouragement & support as this story came to life.

CONTENTS

PROLOGUE

Village of Hebra, Syrian desert
6th February 1986

Dr Lachlan Pike shuddered involuntarily as the fever coursing through his body relentlessly destroyed his red blood cells, the last line of his body's defences. He clamped his teeth shut hard, stifling a sob of self-pity as he shuffled through the devastation of the tiny village clinging for survival on the edges of the desolate wasteland of the Syrian desert.

A moan drifted through the humid air from a hut nearby. My God, there was still someone else alive. He half-turned towards the sound then stopped himself. What good could he do? Most of the villagers were already dead, decomposing corpses lying covered in flies. The stench of death hung heavy in the air.

All his colleagues were dead. An entire medical team, the best trained and equipped in the region, flown into the village only two days earlier when the news of the illness had reached the local medical centre. Within hours of encountering the infected villagers the first medical team member had displayed symptoms of the disease. Her decline into a coma had been frighteningly rapid. The rest of the team quickly followed. He felt the terrifying inevitability of his own death approaching.

But they had called for help, and the call had been answered. Even if he was the only survivor at least someone would be able to tell the world about this horrendous situation. He tried to stand, but even the effort of supporting his own body was too much and he slumped back down to sit on the hot red soil.

His breathing slowed to a shallow rasp as the disease tightened its grip, his eyes gently shutting as he prepared to fall into unconsciousness, a blessed relief from the horror engulfing him.

Then, through his fevered mind he heard the sound, bees buzzing in the distance. But it was getting louder...it was the sound of engines, vehicles. It must be the rescue team. A last ultimate effort of will and he shook himself awake, forcing himself to rise to his feet to meet his saviours.

The convoy of half a dozen Landcruisers snaked it's way around the final few sand dunes surrounding the settlement and entered the village, the tension showing in the faces of the vehicle occupants as they drove slowly between the ancient stone and mud houses, parts of the village dating back to biblical times. The scene greeting them indeed looked like a apocalyptic vision of revenge from an all-powerful but savage being.

The first of the vehicles pulled to a stop with a screech of the brakes to avoid driving over a body lying across the road, already decaying in the sun.

'Motherfucker, it's worse than I thought.' A man in his late fifties with a thick German accent stepped from the vehicle, medical coveralls and mask obscuring his face and body. 'I don't think anything can be done for these poor devils.'

Twenty five more men dressed similarly followed him silently through the village, the horror of the scene written on their faces.

'Jesus Christ, this was meant to be a drug trial that would save lives,' barked a man with a South African accent.

'Well I guess they got it wrong then didn't they?' the first man responded.

Then from the far side of the village they saw him, Pike, the leader of the first medical team. And from the state he was in they didn't want him anywhere near them.

'Get the guns,' the German called to the youngest member of the team, a fresh-faced scientist, barely out of university.

He stood still, not understanding the command. 'But there aren't any rebels near here are there?'

'Just do it.'

Within moments the entire team were armed, watching as Pike stumbled closer.

The German checked his weapon, chambering a round, then walked forward to meet Pike. 'This isn't how I want this to end either, but it can't go any further than us today.' He glanced around the men, meeting the eyes of each of them for a moment.

'Does anyone have a problem with that?'

The men were all suddenly acutely aware they were a long way from civilisation, with a very dangerous man. No one said a word.

In the blink of an eye he raised the weapon to his shoulder, and with a practised ease, aimed and fired, hitting Pike in the chest and killing him instantly.

Pike collapsed to the ground silently.

No one else moved.

The German turned to face them, assault rifle swinging gently in his arm. 'Now we do all of them, make sure they're all dead. No witnesses. We make it look like a rebel attack, then we burn the bodies where they lie okay?'

He swung the weapon in an arc over their heads, spraying bullets into the buildings, the explosion of gunshots shocking the men into action.

The group broke up, working its way through the village, the sound of gunshots echoing through the desert air. But the young scientist stood frozen next to a vehicle.

The German approached him, deciding what to do, then led him with an arm around his shoulder into the cool, dark interior of a house, following the rasping sound of breathing to a woman lying in the corner. He cocked the scientist's weapon for him, then pointed him at the forlorn figure.

'It gets easier after the first.'

The scientist looked at the woman, helpless before him, then at the German, fidgeting with the trigger of his own weapon.

He knew that he had no choice.

He'd never fired a gun before. He pointed the weapon at her face, shut his eyes, and pulled the trigger.

~

One hundred metres away at the crest of a sand dune, a pair of dark brown eyes stared in horror at the nightmare unfolding below.

The fourteen year old boy lying prone in the sand froze, his mind racing as he tried to think what to do.

He watched as the German and the young scientist emerged from a building, the younger man seemingly in a daze.

A small mound of sand pushed against the boy as a huge scorpion scuttled past, tail and claws raised menacingly on the never ending search for prey. The boy jumped to one side, then froze again as the men in the village jerked their eyes towards him, searching the endless dunes for the source of the movement.

He felt his heart pound as the German scanned the dunes, then abruptly turned, raising his weapon again, and walked into another hut.

The young scientist waited though, eyes scanning back and forth across the dunes. Then he paused, staring directly where the boy lay motionless, trying to sink down into the hot sand. The boy fought back the panic rising within him, the desperate urge to get up and run. He stared back into the eyes of the scientist, sure they were reading each other's minds.

A shout from a hut echoed up from the village, startling the scientist and the moment was broken. A last long look and he too raised his weapon and headed into a hut.

~

The boy waited until all the men were out of sight then ran at a crouch to a hut at the end of the village. He crept around the back, keeping low. No sounds from inside, the men must still be elsewhere. He peeked around the corner, then ducked inside the gloomy interior, kneeling down beside the motionless figure of his father lying on a canvas cot. He leaned forward to see if he was breathing then jerked upright at the sound of voices outside the hut, throwing himself under the bed with not a second to spare as they entered. He watched two pairs of boots walk around the hut, holding his breath in fear of discovery.

The men stopped right next to his father. There was silence then a searing pain in his leg as the first of the bullets tore through his father's body and into his own.

The boy clenched every muscle to stop from crying out, watching as the men walked back out into the sunlight. He lay there, the only sound his breathing through gritted teeth, then he wrinkled his nose from the acrid stench of gasoline, tossed over the hut from a fuel can by the men. He fought against his rising panic as he realised what was about to happen.

Then the soft *whoomph* as the gasoline was ignited from a casually thrown match and the hut was engulfed in flames.

~

CHAPTER 1

MONSTERS

Hobart, Tasmania, Australia
Present Day

The crowd of mourners shivered in the relentless freezing drizzle, the grey skies overhead heavy, oppressive, giving a Shakespearean sense of doom to the funeral. The twin eight year old girls huddled together under the umbrella held by their father and aunt as they listened in silence to the burial rites mumbled by the ageing priest. They comprehended nothing from his words of comfort as the empty casket representing their mother was slowly lowered into the cold, dark earth.

~

The young woman in the hospital bed watched her own funeral alone in her sterile hospital room. She's unsure where the room is, an isolation room at the Hobart City Hospital or maybe a private hospital, maybe even the Institute?

She had tried the door a day ago...or was it a week ago when she felt a little better, still had the energy to consider what else might have been. It wasn't a total surprise that the handle didn't work from the inside, and that was when she finally accepted she would never leave. But then that was the deal anyway, that she stay in the room until the end. She stifled a sob.

If only she could stand under the blue sky, the sun, a tree one last time. She so loved nature, the smell of the wet ferns after the rain, the sounds of a creek gently tracing it's path through the bush. That's why she had chosen the life of a biologist and medical researcher in the Tasmanian wilderness. Then she got infected. Had she been careless, or just plain unlucky? It wasn't meant to be able to cross the genetic barrier between species. No one knew how the cancer, the facial tumour disease, had come to infect Tasmanian Devils out of nowhere in 1996, and there had never been any indication it could cross to humans, until now. I guess there is always a first time for everything, she smiled ironically to herself. She absently raised her hand and touched the obscene growth now covering half her face.

She sobbed again. She had been beautiful once. But this was the deal, and the blessing. Her children would be looked after with her life insurance, never have to worry about a roof over their heads. And they would never have to see the hideous creature their mother had become.

The door opened silently, a nurse entering the room, completely covered in protective medical gowns, a cap and face mask. *Was it for their protection, or to hide their identity?*

The nurse never spoke but she was sure she knew them, how they walked, their breathing. She was familiar with it now.

The nurse checked her chart, oblivious to the funeral being shown in real time on the monitor at the end of her bed. Their finger tapped noisily on the tablet touchscreen as they made their notes. Then they turned and for a moment their sleeve was pulled up slightly, revealing the familiar small scar on their wrist...that same scar she was sure she had seen on the wrist of a professor at the medical school all those years ago when she was a student.

But she had to be wrong. How could they be involved in this evil arrangement? Her eyes drifted back to the funeral. She thought she was about to cry.

She didn't see the tight smile form on the lips of the nurse as they understood the implications of the data they'd gathered from the monitoring equipment. She was improving. The deadly tumours could be halted, perhaps even eliminated completely over time. They had invented the perfect disease.

The nurse went to the complex array of drips feeding her decimated body with experimental chemicals to control the disease, checking the rate of flow of the various powerful drugs. They found the one that was halting the growth of the tumour in its tracks.

Then they turned the flow rate to zero.

They had proved what they could do to a human.

Now it was time for Dr Khan to die.

~

Brilliant light flashed across the room, forcing its way through the woman's eyelids, tearing her from her tortured sleep. For a moment she couldn't breathe, then a gasp as her primal instincts forced her body to keep living, even for just a little bit longer.

She opened her eyes, mildly surprised that she wasn't dead yet, and saw another flash of light across the room. Her muddled brain struggled to understand what was happening. Then she remembered... Dark Winter, the strange, pagan arts festival that descended upon Hobart in the depths of winter each year was underway, and she recalled there was some kind of lighting installation this time.

She lay in silence for a moment longer, no sounds from the corridor. Could she risk it? Surely it couldn't jeopardise the deal now, after the funeral? She choked out an ironic laugh. What would they do, kill her? It was worth a try, just to feel alive a little longer.

She swung one leg off the bed, then the other, tentatively touching the floor. Would they support her weight? God knows she didn't weigh much anymore. Then she was across the room, dragging a chair under the tiny window high in the wall. She wobbled as she stood on her tiptoes, clinging to the wall, and froze as she looked out to see the night sky criss-crossed with lasers reaching kilometres into the heavens in beautiful, frenzied patterns.

A smile broke across the one side of her face she could still control. Then she slumped down onto the chair, exhausted. Her last thought as she took her final breath was that at least it had been worth it.

~

Two hundred metres away on the twelfth floor of the Holiday Isle Hotel, Lucy Wei was also enjoying the spectacular light display playing out over the darkened city. Her bohemian parents came down from Sydney to Hobart each year to immerse themselves in what was now the country's biggest winter arts festival, but at ten years old this was the first time they had brought their only daughter. Apparently they felt when she was younger she may have been unsettled by some of the "disturbing" material on show, whatever that means. More likely she just cramped their style.

But at least she'd conned them into buying her a guilty present for dragging her along. They were downstairs in the bar and she was meant to be asleep. But the light show was too good. She swung the barrel of the brand new telescope across the city again. It was so cool to look inside people's windows at night if they hadn't shut the curtains properly.

Another flash of light; then movement across the city caught her eye. She zoomed in on a tiny window high up a weird looking building. It was a woman's face, she was pretty. Then she moved the lens slightly and caught the other side of her face, and fell backwards with a scream. She folded down her telescope and shut the curtains. Her parents had lied to her when they said there was no such thing as monsters. She's just seen one.

~

CHAPTER 2

VILLAGE

The sound of children's laughter peeled through the thick humid air in the tiny African village. Gentle wind gusts sent mini-tornadoes of red soil dancing around their feet as they wandered between the huts to the small medical centre on the other side, nestled in the shade of the Baobab trees. Three pale, sweaty white faces amongst the one hundred and fifty or so shiny dark faces of the villagers.

Ian MacRae couldn't help but smile as he saw the excitement of the children with the arrival of the strangers to their village. But he was still very aware of the imminent danger spreading through the northern regions of Nigeria as the militant Islamic group Boko Haram brought terror and death to the defenceless villagers.

Here the Nigerian army was under siege, not enough resources, intelligence, weapons or men on the ground. Boko Haram seemed to be able to strike at will, killing anyone in their path for the sake of proving that they could. And that was why MacRae was here, persuaded to come to this God-forsaken place on the request of old friend Evan Holgate, a doctor from Tasmania who volunteered with Medecins a Travers Les Frontiers for a week each year, trying to improve the health and lives of those in the most desperate need.

MacRae usually conducted his security assessments from the controlled environments of the bigger towns and regions in trouble spots around the world, gathering and analysing intelligence from the various security services in country to develop a risk assessment and security plan for the businesses and Non-Government Organisations (NGOs) providing aid on the ground.

His company, HRS or Human Resource Solutions, got most of its work by word of mouth. He had a reputation for providing fast, accurate assessments and then advising on who could provide the best on-the-ground assets to protect workers in some of the most hazardous locations across the globe.

But this one was different. His friend was refusing to leave, despite the horrendous security threats all around. He had asked MacRae for help in keeping the medical centre open, but MacRae was really only here to try to persuade his friend to leave.

The third man in their group was the Belgian, Thierry LaBruge. He had something of a murky past, but MacRae knew he was solid, reliable and would be there for the client if the need arose. Unlike many of the local security forces.

MacRae knew LaBruge was ex-special forces, French Foreign Legion a long time ago according to the gossip, and MacRae suspected he had worked extensively as a mercenary. Then it was rumoured he had an unfortunate attack of conscience, found God, and had become a security contractor for NGOs around the world. He didn't talk much, but MacRae had used him once or twice in the past, and when he'd made the spot decision to fly into the medical centre without the time for the usual security arrangements he'd been relieved it was LaBruge who had met him at the airport and would be watching his back.

MacRae turned and gave him a nod that said *Everything okay?*

LaBruge shrugged, his eyes constantly scanning their surroundings. His finger stroked the trigger of his AR-15 Bushmaster assault rifle.

MacRae knew LaBruge wasn't happy to be here. The risks were far too high to himself, MacRae his client, and the doctor. But he didn't lack courage...he had made peace with his God and he knew they would perhaps be just a little bit safer with him there.

The doctor chatted excitedly to MacRae, explaining how his work was saving so many lives from diseases that would be unheard of in the civilised world. He led them into the dark, cool, interior of the corrugated iron shed that served as the clinic.

Metal cots were lined up along one wall of the building, a couple of them occupied with sleeping patients. A nurse stood silently at the foot of one of the beds making notes on a pad. She glanced up and smiled at the white men as they wandered through the shed. A battered rattan fan turned lazily on the ceiling, a gentle *whoosh whoosh* making glistening dust particles dance in the rays of sunlight sneaking in through the gaps in the steel wall cladding.

A giggle of laughter as two tall and slender girls ran into the building and up to the men.

Dr Holgate smiled as they ran up to him. 'Daluchi and Hassana, come and say hello to Mr MacRae and Mr LaBruge, they're here to help protect us apparently.'

The girls stopped in front of the men and extended their hands.

'My name's Ian MacRae, pleased to meet you,' MacRae said, shaking them in turn. He felt the roughness of skin used to toiling in the earth.

'They're sisters,' Holgate said looking from one to the other. 'Twins, as if it isn't obvious. In fact the name *Hassana* means twins, just in case they ever forget. And they are both studying hard, hoping to be doctors or lawyers one day.'

The girls beamed and nodded at Holgate. MacRae reached into his back pocket, pulling out a battered wallet, *IM* etched into the front. That wallet had shared a lot with him over the years. A flick of the wrist opened it and MacRae pulled out a plain white business card, looked at the girls, then pulled out a second.

'Well your country always needs more good doctors and lawyers, so I hope you study hard and do well.' He placed a business card in each outstretched hand. 'And if you ever make it to Tasmania in Australia, come and look me up and I'll look after you.'

The girls tucked the cards into their pockets, grinning shyly at MacRae.

'Thank you Mr Ian,' one said, before the other corrected her.

'It's Mr MacRae.'

Then with a giggle they skipped off across the room.

Holgate sighed. 'Part of what I try and bring to them here is hope and ambition, the self-belief that they can achieve anything if they try hard enough and don't give up. That is the only way the people in these third world countries have any hope of improving their lives and the lives of their children.' He waved his hand vaguely around the room. 'How many damaged bodies can I try and mend before society changes and makes the lives of these people better? This country should be so wealthy with all its oil and mineral wealth, but so much of it is redirected, the wealthy get richer and the rest stay poor...' His voice trailed off.

MacRae smiled. 'Evan, you shouldn't feel responsible for trying to fix the problems of the world. You've spent your life helping others, maybe it's time to slow down, let some others shoulder the load.'

Holgate frowned as he wandered over to check on a patient. 'What are you trying to say Ian? That I'm too old for this?'

MacRae joined him beside the cot, looking down at the emaciated child sleeping fitfully. He touched Holgate's shoulder. 'Evan...'

Holgate shrugged off MacRae's hand and turned to face him. 'I appreciate your concern Ian, but I didn't ask you to come here and tell me I shouldn't be here.' He waved a hand expansively. 'I've lived a lucky life, we all have in the west. We have every opportunity, and then I see this.' His shoulders slumped. 'I just can't stop yet. Can you see me retired, sitting in the back yard watching the roses grow as I wait to die?'

MacRae frowned, then his face creased into a grin. 'No I guess not. But I just don't think there's any way to guarantee your security working in these places. Sooner or later things just might go wrong, and it's only got to happen once.'

Holgate leaned forward, slapping MacRae's shoulder. 'Hey enough of the gloom and doom talk. I was born lucky. Come on, I'll show you around some more.'

A single bead of sweat worked its way down MacRae's cheek as he walked: he wiped it off distractedly with the back of his hand.

'Okay, show me what it is you really do here, apart from enjoying the climate and...'

The roar of a light truck interrupted his thoughts, the engine racing as it tore through the tiny village. Then more vehicles, three... more? MacRae froze. Then gunfire, automatic weapons punching supersonic bullets through the stifling air.

MacRae moved in front of Holgate, instinctively protecting his old friend while his eyes scanned the room for LaBruge. He was gone.

'Shit,' MacRae cursed under his breath. 'Where's Thierry?'

Surely he hadn't bolted on them?

The vehicles came closer, then the screech of brakes as they slewed to a halt in the dust outside the medical hut.

MacRae grabbed Holgate's arm, pulling him away from the main entry. 'C'mon, time to go. Is there another way out?'

Holgate jerked his arm free. 'I'm not going anywhere.' He planted his feet defiantly, staring at the door. 'These are my patients, my responsibility to keep them safe.'

MacRae took another step towards the back of the room. In the gloom he could make out the patients, terror etched across their faces. 'Please Evan, you can't help anyone if you're taken hostage by these guys...or worse.'

'I have no choice,' Holgate growled. 'This is what I do.'

MacRae hesitated a moment longer, then moved to join him.

'Okay you stubborn old bastard, I guess we do this together.'

Screams echoed across the village. MacRae moved to the doorway and quickly scanned the village, assessing the situation. Gunmen dressed in a ragged assortment of tattered military jungle camouflage and urban street-wear jumped off the back of utility vehicles, brandishing battered-looking AK-47 assault rifles and glistening machetes. They looked around wildly, then ran after the villagers, rounding up the men and boys. The women and young children huddled in groups, trying to blend in with the village huts, the children screaming in terror.

MacRae turned as he heard the patients in the hospital getting agitated, raising their voices, uncertain what was going on. Holgate moved quickly amongst the rows of beds, offering comfort and reassurance where he could, trying to calm the terrified nurses.

Then he saw the young girls he had met earlier, holding hands, backs against the wall at the far side of the room. Holgate moved to them, touched their shoulders. MacRae saw them nodding frantically then crouch down...and they were gone.

A huge hand slammed into MacRae's back, throwing him into the room, stumbling to one knee. He twisted to see the light from the door blocked by a hulking figure.

'We are Boko Haram and we're here to save you'. The figure stormed across the room swinging an assault rifle in a wide arc.

'Who's in charge here?' he spat in broken English.

MacRae got to his feet and stepped in front of the man. 'I am. What the hell are you doing here? This is a medical facility.'

The man stopped in his tracks. 'Who are you? Your accent, you are American?'

'I'm Australian. Dr Ian MacRae.' He thrust his open hand forwards in a greeting.

The gunman jerked back in surprise, then levelled the gun at MacRae's face. 'I'm the one in charge here. Do I have to shoot you to prove it?'

MacRae stood his ground, and spoke calmly. 'There's no need to shoot anyone. You're in charge.'

The gun lowered slightly. Then without warning the gunman leapt forward, screaming, 'Don't tell me who's in charge, now I kill you.'

The barrel swung back up to MacRae's eye level. This was it.

'I'm in charge. He's nothing,' Holgate shouted as he strode across the room towards the men. They both turned.

'Let me introduce myself. I'm Dr Holgate.' He waved his hand around the room, 'And these are my patients.'

He flicked a finger in MacRae's direction. 'He's just my driver. You want to talk to someone, talk to me. You want to shoot someone, shoot me.'

The gunman hesitated, unsure what to make of the old man challenging him. Then the moment was broken as half a dozen teenage militants surged into the room, shouting as they dragged a couple of the young village men by their hair.

The gunman turned from MacRae and Holgate, snarling at the young militants. 'Who have you got here then, some spies for the government?'

The militants threw the villagers to the floor at his feet.

'Or maybe we have some new recruits for our Army of Freedom?'

He crouched down, his face millimetres from a young man.

'Well? Are you a spy or are you one of my new soldiers?'

The man shrunk back, confusion all over his face. 'I, ummm...'

The gunman leapt up, then slammed the butt of his assault rifle into the man's face, smashing teeth with a spray of blood.

'You don't know? You must be a spy.' He screamed at one of his teenage soldiers. 'Take him outside and show what we do to spies.'

The soldier grinned maniacally and grabbed the young man's hair again, dragging him out of the building.

The gunman turned again to Holgate and MacRae.

'So what am I to do with you? The doctor and his driver.'

He stepped closer to MacRae. 'The old man might be worth something...maybe a ransom from the government or an aid agency. But you? A driver? You're worth nothing.'

His hands tensed around the assault rifle, his eyes burning into MacRae's. Not for the first time MacRae wished he had brought a weapon on this trip. He knew that carrying a firearm could be more trouble than it's worth in a place like this. But right now...

More child soldiers ran into the room, maybe six or seven, yelling and screaming. This time they were dragging terrified women behind them. Except they weren't women, they were girls. To MacRae's horror he realised they were the two young twins Holgate had introduced MacRae to only a few minutes earlier.

The gunman grinned. 'Now this is better. We have enough young soldiers for our cause. We have another better use for these fine young girls.' His eyes wandered over the girls pausing at the promising curves of their maturing bodies. 'Yes, they'll be a fine addition to the cause.'

The child soldiers threw the girls down in front of the gunman.

They stood up straight, side by side, eyes blazing with defiance.

He took a step forward reaching out and grabbing Hassana by the hair, pulling her close. 'And I think this one will be the first to know my kindness.'

He swung his assault rifle over his shoulder and grabbed her breast with his other hand.

Holgate bristled with anger. 'Get your hands off her, she's only a child.'

The gunman turned. 'She's now a member of the Army of Freedom, and she'll do what I say for the cause.'

He grabbed her blouse and ripped it to one side, exposing her chest. The girl wriggled herself free from the gunman's grasp, then spat in his face, hurling abuse at him in African.

The gunman snarled and smashed the back of his hand across her face.

Holgate couldn't contain himself, hurling himself at the gunman. 'Leave her alone you animal.'

The gunman thrust out a huge hand to Holgate's chest, stopping him in his tracks. Then in the blink of an eye a young soldier stepped forward, training his assault rifle at the old man. He grinned crazily, eyes darting from Holgate to the gunman.

'I kill him for you boss?'

MacRae caught the child-soldier's eye. His pupils were massive... the kid was stoned, his tongue flicking his lips between words. Yet another terrible consequence of these civil conflicts in isolated places. The only way to turn innocent children into fearless killers for the cause when they were pressed into an guerilla army was to get them addicted to any number of drugs. It numbed their senses and over-rode their morality.

MacRae knew there would be no arguing or pleading with this out-of-control youth.

No-one spoke.

Then the gunman's shoulders shook as he roared with laughter.

'Not today. A live doctor is worth far more than a dead one, my young warrior eh?'

The child soldier's face drooped with disappointment as he lowered his weapon.

Then the gunman shouted. 'But no-one tells me what to do. Kill him.'

The child-soldier's face lit up again as he swung his weapon back at Holgate, his finger tightening on the trigger.

A scream, then a desperate plea echoed across the room.

'Please protect us Mr Ian.'

It was Hassana.

For a brief moment the militants were distracted.

MacRae threw himself forward, reaching for the barrel of the gun, his fingertips coming into contact with the blued steel and pushing it sideways. Then it fired, the crack of the discharging bullet bursting through MacRae's ear. He grimaced with pain and grabbed the barrel, pulling it from the grasp of the child-soldier, his fingers reaching for the trigger as the room descended into chaos.

He heard a scream from behind him. Someone's been hit. Then the weapon was his.

He scanned the room, assessing the most immediate threat... the gunman charging towards him...swung the barrel of the AK-47 around and pulled the trigger.

Bullets sprayed across the room, then one found it's mark, slamming into the shoulder of the huge figure. But it wasn't enough, he kept coming, careening into MacRae and throwing them both to the ground in a tangle of arms and legs.

Blood from the gunman's bullet wound oozed onto his shirt as he pressed MacRae to the floor, ripping the weapon from MacRae's grasp.

MacRae punched hard twice at the bleeding wound, grinning as the gunman grunted with pain and rolled off MacRae, his other hand dragging a bush knife from a sheath on his chest.

MacRae pulled himself to one knee and prepared to throw himself at the man again when a shot was fired from behind him by a child-soldier.

MacRae felt a searing pain in his side as the bullet ripped through his torso. His vision swam, then a blow to the back of his head from a rifle butt sent him sprawling to the floor.

As his vision cleared he realised he was looking into the face of Dr Holgate. But he wasn't moving, his eyes vacant and glassy.

Then MacRae saw the pool of blood around his head.

Holgate was dead.

Thirty metres away LaBruge adjusted his prone position on the thatched roof of the village hut. His Kevlar ballistic vest cut uncomfortably into his chest as he positioned the Bushmaster in his shoulder. He pulled the weapon closer, squinting as he peered through the small telescopic sight. The barrel of the weapon moved almost imperceptibly as he panned across the brown dirt of the village centre, stopping as the figures just inside the hut came into view.

He smiled, a thin-lipped grimace of satisfaction. He knew he shouldn't get satisfaction from this, but it was the only thing he had ever been good at. And at least now he understood it was his life's work, and he was doing it for God.

He'd heard the sound of the approaching trucks long before it had been picked up by MacRae and the others. He'd always had a nose for trouble and figured the best place he could be was outside assessing the threat, but the rebels had swept through the town so quickly they were on all sides before he could return to MacRae.

A quick look around and he'd realised he had few options to avoid detection and protect the principle. He didn't like it but he had no choice than to make his way onto the roof of the hut.

He watched the scene inside the medical centre and saw the girls being dragged in.

The chaos in the village around him receded as he focused on the shot...the one shot he'd get before he was discovered and all hell broke loose.

One of the girls did something that angered the gunmen. Then he saw the old doctor leap forward and MacRae tussling with a child-soldier. A gunshot and the doctor fell to the ground, while MacRae grabbed the weapon. Fuck, the principal was down. Then a confused mess of arms and legs as the gunman and MacRae wrestled on the ground.

LaBruge felt his heart rate rise, took a slow breath to steady himself and focused on the shot. But which target?

MacRae groaned as he was hauled to his knees by the child soldiers, the bullet wound in his side oozing a bright red river of blood.

Then he was facing the gunman, one arm hanging limply to his side, shattered by MacRae's bullet, the other gently waving his bush knife towards MacRae. He moved the knife slowly in an arc back behind his shoulder, pausing for a moment before slashing it forward to MacRae's throat.

LaBruge watched as MacRae was dragged to his knees, then saw a flash of light as the bush knife moved to end MacRae's life, and in that split second had his target, paused his breathing, and squeezed the trigger, sending death into the hut at over a thousand metres per second.

MacRae jerked back as the knife came towards him, the gunman grinning...then the man's face shattered as LaBruge's bullet found it's mark.

The knife dropped from the gunman's limp hand and clattered to the ground.

Time stopped and no-one moved, then chaos as LaBruge's bullets found more marks, dropping militants to the ground, the rest panicking, firing wildly into the village.

MacRae grabbed for a militant, his fingers wrapping around the man's assault rifle but the man twisted hard and swung the butt of the weapon into the side of MacRae's head before dropping the weapon.

MacRae felt his knees buckle, his vision blur, watching the soldier run from the building. He staggered to his feet and lifted the assault rifle to his shoulder and releasing a burst of fire at the fleeing figure, a flash of satisfaction as the man fell to the ground.

Two steps and he was outside, the brilliant sunlight in his eyes, and he was surrounded by more men. But these weren't the terrorists, these were government soldiers, their weapons levelled at MacRae, screaming for him to drop his gun.

He froze, and slowly leaned forward to place his weapon on the sun-baked dirt. Then the world went black as he slumped to the ground.

CHAPTER 3

GLUTTONY

The tinkle of silver cutlery on fine china plates echoed around the room as Magnus Crane ate. It was the same at every table in the busy lunchtime restaurant in downtown San Francisco. An exercise in gluttony. Plates piled high with food, mostly meats, being consumed by mostly white middle-aged businessmen, almost to a man overweight or obese.

This was the epitome of the problem. Ridiculous, unnecessary, obscene consumption of the world's limited, and dwindling, resources. It made him sick.

What the fuck was wrong with the human race? Why was too much never enough? Why did everyone feel the need to prove they had more than everybody else, even if they didn't need it?

Crane hated these lunch meetings, exercises in small-talk and ego stroking. But it was a necessary evil in the world of business, making contacts, keeping the wheels of commerce turning, even between the pharmaceutical industry and agriculture.

He delicately cut a small piece of steak from the edge of the enormous slab of meat covering his plate. He was looking at enough protein for a family for a day, and most of these meals would probably end up being thrown away.

'Best piece of steak you'll find this side of the bridge Magnus,' drawled the man across from him.

Crane smiled and nodded. "Big Bill", as William Rison was known, came from Texas cattle country. Hell, he was the epitome of Texas cattle country, owning vast tracts of land to graze cattle, and some of the biggest feedlots in the world for fattening the animals before they were sent for slaughter, most of them destined to end up as hamburgers being flipped in fast food restaurants. And he loved nothing better than half a cow draped across his plate, barbecued to within a whisker of incineration, just like back home.

'I'm sure it is Bill,' Crane smiled and chewed at the same time. 'And I'm sure the planet is thanking us all for eating it.'

Rison spoke through a mouth full of steak. 'What're you talking about?'

'Well in a world of finite resources, western society chooses to focus on a high protein diet, which we know causes massive decimation of the forests in developing countries, and uses huge amounts of water, feed and chemicals. Ultimately the resources will run out and what happens then? Just the same as always happens when resources run out. War. Plague. The death of civilisations.'

Big Bill adjusted his waist band to fit in more steak and leaned back in his chair. 'That's bullshit. We get more and more efficient at production...more and more beef for less resources every year. It's what we do. And the more efficient we are, the more profit we make.' He grinned broadly. 'God bless capitalist America.'

Crane wiped his steak in some sauce, then paused. 'Well answer me this, what kind of society, what kind of humanity lets population growth continue unchecked in the capitalist endless pursuit of economic growth by increased consumption? Babies being born into poverty, starvation, death and disease...how is that the face of civilisation, humanity?'

Rison's face clouded over. 'That's sounding like the words of a hypocrite to me, coming from the man who supplies the drugs, a heck of a lot of drugs I might add, to me to help me grow the cattle to supply the increasing consumption as you put it. I think this system has made you very wealthy, and what have you done to solve the problems of humanity and overpopulation?'

The other conversations around the table stopped as the exchange between the two men caught everyone's attention.

Crane's eyes narrowed, then he erupted with laughter, waving his fork at Rison. 'Ha, got you there didn't I?'

Rison wrinkled his brow, then grinned. 'You sure did, you son of a gun. For a minute there you were sounding like one of those bleeding heart environmentalist sons of bitches.'

Crane shook his head and, still smiling, focused back on the task of cutting his steak, while Rison chatted happily through a mouthful of meat to his business partner across the table.

Crane was glad to be out of the small talk for the moment. It gave him the opportunity to think. And his mind was always back on task instantly. What have you done to solve the problems of humanity and overpopulation, Rison had asked?

Rison, like pretty much everyone else, had absolutely no idea what Crane had done. As the head of Medici-Royal, one of the biggest and most powerful medical corporations in the United States, indeed the world, Crane had a very public persona. Benevolent, responsible and dedicated to making society a better place through innovation in medical and sanitary technology, and healthcare. Parts of his company were involved in every continent and almost every country in the world, either directly or through business partnerships. Corporate social responsibility was ingrained throughout the organisation and its staff and was integral in every decision that was made.

Except for Crane.

He was the visionary, one of the few. A philosophy that started developing a long time ago in the horrific mass gas poisoning in Bophal, India in December 1984. There, as a young scientist working for a US corporation, he witnessed a world split between the wealthy west and the poverty stricken developing countries, the west exploiting low wages and lax standards to build factories that would never be allowed in the west.

A series of mistakes in maintenance and oversight and the factory released a deadly cloud of gas over a crowded slum. Up to sixteen thousand deaths, and many enquiries later, and life goes on having scarred many lives for ever, including his own, even if he didn't know it at the time.

And it was people like Big Bill Rison with his guiltless greed that had convinced Crane that Bophal and events like it was the future of a planet with unchecked population growth. More people competing for less on an increasingly polluted and uninhabitable planet. It was already happening, tensions between nations over shared water resources. Mineral rich nations being eyed off by desperate neighbours.

But Crane and other visionaries in his circle...some had worked with him from the very beginning...had been pondering possible solutions for years. Then, over time, planning and executing numerous programs with the singular goal of giving the human race and the planet, the best chance of survival, even thriving, by controlling population growth.

A shrill guffaw of laughter from Rison's wife, a masterpiece of modern science with her extensive Botox and plastic surgery, snapped Crane from his thoughts. He glanced at his watch. He'd done his duty, and it was time to get back to his real work, the one project that would achieve all his aims.

~

The bright yellow taxi swiftly merged into the traffic as Crane settled back into the sagging rear seat. He'd made his excuses to leave the lunch early, and to be honest the way the alcohol was going down at the table they probably wouldn't even notice he'd gone. It felt good to be out of there, no longer playing a character.

Crane barely noticed the city flashing past as they drove. He retrieved his laptop from his bag and checked his email, before opening the latest summary of current projects overseas, smiling with satisfaction as he read that the project in Africa was finally getting underway.

The driver glanced back at Crane in his rear view mirror for a second, then looked away.

Crane's mind wandered back to the lunch and Rison.

Damn right Crane sold a vast quantity of drugs, mainly antibiotics, to the agriculture industry, and made huge profits. But the medical science community was only just catching on to the end result of supposedly increasing productivity by keeping livestock disease free.

They were finally realising that the drugs passed from the animals along the food chain to humans, exposing our microscopic natural enemies, bacteria, to low doses of the very thing that was meant to protect us when were sick. And instead of killing the bacteria, it gave them ample time to adapt and mutate into what was terrifying those at the front line of disease control. Super-bugs. Bacteria resistant to all known antibiotics.

Crane smiled. Hospitals around the world were losing the battle, with patients coming in for minor treatments and then dying from Golden Staph infections they caught in the hospital. And the scourge of Tuberculosis, previously a killer of millions each year and once on the decline, was now spreading across the world again as new strains resistant to all but the newest and most powerful drugs of last resort.

This kind of research was fascinating, and yielding some promising results. But ultimately it was too slow to halt the continuing population explosion. But now he was tantalisingly close to perfecting the tools he needed to finish the job properly and pave the way for a brighter future. Yes, the price would be high for many, but it took a true leader to make the difficult decisions necessary for the greater good.

The cab swung sharply to the left, the laptop sliding across his knees. Crane looked up to chastise the driver, then frowned. This wasn't the usual route from the restaurant to his office. Instead of the bumper to bumper traffic at the intersection he was watching groups of young men milling around entrances to run-down buildings. Cars were few and far between and weeds sprouted along the sidewalks. Shit, he was being ripped off.

He leaned forward and spoke to the driver. 'Why are we taking this route? I know how much the fare should be you know.'

The driver spoke. 'I'm doing you a favour Sir. My GPS showed a traffic accident a few blocks ahead on the freeway, we would have got stuck for a while.' He shrugged. 'We'll be back on the freeway around 51st Street in a couple of minutes.'

Crane looked around, the streets were now pretty much deserted. 'Okay, but no more diversions.'

The driver nodded. 'Sure thing.'

Then the taxi stopped dead.

Crane leaned forward. 'What's the problem now?'

The driver turned to face him. 'There's a dog in the middle of the road.'

Crane opened his mouth to speak, just as the passenger door opposite him was yanked open from outside, and a wild eyed young woman crawled onto the seat next to Crane, shoving a snub-nosed revolver into his face.

'Gimme your money. Gimme your wallet and phone right now.'

Her breath reeked of cigarettes and dope as she snarled at Crane.

She waved the gun downwards. 'And your laptop too, asshole.'

Crane hesitated. His laptop contained detailed records of many of the secret projects he'd been working on. The files were encrypted but with the right expertise who knows how secure they were? Plus he'd spent most of his life travelling the world for his career and never been robbed. It sure as hell wasn't going to happen now.

The woman struck his jaw with the butt of the gun.

'NOW ASSHOLE.'

Crane flinched, then acted on survival reflexes honed over the years. His left hand shot out grabbing the gun and twisting it towards the woman. She tightened her grip, inadvertently squeezing the trigger.

The boom of the gun discharging was deafening in the confined spaced, Crane's ears ringing as the bullet tore through the woman's face and exited the open car door behind her head.

She slumped to the seat, then slid backwards half onto the road.

Crane heard another sound, shouting, as the ringing in his ears subsided. The cab driver screaming at him.

'Why'd you kill her? You didn't have to kill her.'

He reached for his mobile phone in the bracket on the dash.

'I've gotta call the police.'

Crane's mind raced. He didn't cause this, she did. It was self-defence by any measure. But who could predict how this would pan out in the courts? He was so close to finalising his plans for the most ambitious eugenics experiment in history. He didn't have time for this.

His hand was still wrapped around the woman's hand and the gun. In the blink of an eye Crane jerked it up and squeezed the trigger twice.

The cab driver didn't even flinch as the bullets hit home, then he fell backwards to the steering wheel and breathed his last.

Crane lowered the weapon and wiped away his fingerprints with the woman's shirt, before placing her fingers back around the stock and trigger. He looked around the street, it was deserted, then took out his phone and used the camera as a mirror. Shit, he was spattered with blood, his face, hair, clothes. He couldn't be seen by anyone in this condition. Well, almost anyone.

He flicked through his phone contacts and called a number tagged *The Russian,* and waited. Was he available? This was one of those times it was advantageous to be the CEO of a billion dollar corporation. You had access to resources most people didn't. In this case a personal bodyguard cum fixer, someone who was always there when you needed them, and never asked the wrong questions.

An emotionless voice answered with a hint of a Slavic accent. 'Yes?'

Crane replied. 'I need to be picked up at...' He checked his location on GPS, reading out the address. 'And I'll need a mess to be tidied up immediately. Can you do it?'

'Sure. I'll be there.'

Crane ended the call. Sometimes he wondered just how much he really knew about the Russian and his past. He wasn't even sure of his real name, he said it was Korshov, but who really knew. The Russian said it was better this way. Perhaps it would catch up with him one day.

Crane walked over to the recessed doorway of an abandoned shop where he could watch the street unnoticed. Fading painted signage on a sagging awning declared it as a dressmaker. He was buzzing with adrenaline. He hadn't killed anyone in a long time. It was nice to feel so alive again.

Maybe it wasn't such a bad day after all.

CHAPTER 4

AWAKENING

MacRae groaned as he opened his eyes, squinting in the bright sunlight flooding the African hospital room. It took him a moment to realise where he was...the stark white walls, smell of disinfectant, muffled sounds, the occasional cough. He started to lift his head then stopped as disjointed memories started coming back, the hut in the village, Dr Holgate. He'd seen Holgate murdered in front of him. Then fighting with the terrorists, a knife coming at his throat, and...nothing. Was he hurt?

Slowly he went through his body, moving each part. Aches and pains but nothing seemed too bad. He lifted his head...a sudden explosion of pain. He'd obviously caught a pretty serious blow to the head. Slowly he lifted his head again, not too bad this time, and raised his body to sit up, swinging his legs off the bed. Then a bolt of pain through his side. He peeled back a bandage to see a small hole with stitches. Obviously there was more. He scanned the room...a pretty standard hospital room, signs in English and most of the other patients around were African. Presumably he was still in Nigeria.

A roar of laughter echoed across the corridor followed by a growl of annoyance. He recognised the voice. LaBruge?

He gingerly stood up, pausing to make sure his legs would support him...all good so far...then stepped across the room towards the voices, wandering down the corridor until he heard more laughter spilling out a partially open door. He raised his hand to knock, then walked straight in.

A group of men, crowded around a figure on a bed. MacRae couldn't make out who it was, they were lying on their side facing away from the door. Then one of the men turned.

'Ian, you're up...' A familiar Deep South Louisiana drawl greeted him. It was Rafael Simpson, another security freelancer working in Nigeria. He'd crossed paths with MacRae here and there on jobs over the last few years. A likeable bloke, but prone to speak first and think afterwards, MacRae recalled.

The other men turned towards MacRae, looking at him with curiosity. He didn't know all of them, but now he could see who the patient was. He was right, it was Thierry LaBruge, and he was naked except for a hospital gown pulled up to his waist, and a huge bandage over his butt.

MacRae approached the hospital bed as LaBruge turned towards him, wincing with pain.

'Boss, good to see you're up and about.'

MacRae looked at him with concern. 'What the hell happened to you Thierry? I'm struggling to remember what went down at the village, the militia...' Then more memories came flooding back. The militia, the girls. Holgate's murder. 'I thought we were all dead, then gunfire and they started going down. Was that you?'

There was a long silence while LaBruge tried to find the words. Then Simpson spoke broke the silence. 'He got shot in the ass. That's what happened.' A nervous chuckle went around the room, but this time it didn't sound so funny.

'Yes it was me.' LaBruge swallowed hard, then met MacRae's eyes. 'They took the girls boss. I couldn't stop them.'

~

Tendrils of steam floated up into MacRae's face as he sipped the hot hospital coffee. The taste was terrible. It was instant coffee powder. How could they serve this in a country that produced some of the best coffee in the world?

MacRae looked back to LaBruge. Two hours had passed since the other visitors had left, and MacRae and LaBruge had been able to talk about the village, filling in each other with the details.

He hadn't missed much, with the village quickly being taken back by the government forces, as the militants seemingly melted back into the surrounding jungle, taking a dozen of the young boys and girls with them. LaBruge had played a pivotal role in disrupting the militants until the government soldiers arrived, but it hadn't taken them long to figure out where he was shooting from.

'I'm so sorry boss that I couldn't protect you and the doctor.' The anger and guilt was written across his face. 'And those little girls. If only I'd...'

'There wasn't anything else you could have done Thierry.' MacRae touched his shoulder. 'It's a miracle we weren't all killed.'

LaBruge's fingers fidgeted, drumming on the side of his cup.

'The Lord was with us boss. It's always his will, even if we don't know why.'

MacRae smiled, it's really hard to know why much of anything happened in his life lately.

~

A rapper thumped out his message about life in the 'hood from the speakers above the bar at the Smooth Criminal Cafe and Club. MacRae, LaBruge, and the other security contractors lounged around a fire pit in the small rear courtyard, beer bottles lazily swinging from their hands as they laughed and joked.

MacRae's faced creased into a smile. These were some of the toughest men he had ever met...some he had worked with before, some he knew by reputation...and that wasn't always a good thing depending on who they chose to work for. The only thing they had in common was that they all risked their lives to keep others safe. And as they drank and shared stories tonight that was enough.

The clink of empty beer bottles being tossed onto a pile in the fire echoed around the walls of the courtyard as the evening grew late. It had been three days until MacRae and LaBruge were given the okay to leave the hospital, and inevitably the conversation turned to the militant attack in the village. Everyone wanted to know how it unfolded, hoping to learn something that one day may save their own life.

'It was a bad day, couldn't have seen it coming.' LaBruge gazed into the embers. 'The fucking militants strike anywhere they want, and they'll keep doing it until the government gets it together with the army, and maybe starts giving a bit of the country's oil money back to the people who own it.'

A murmur of agreement went around the group. Then a voice from across the fire from MacRae. 'Hey, the conflict pays all our bills, doesn't it? If the world was a fair place we'd all be out of a job.' It was Simpson, the freelancer from Louisiana, his voice slurred by the liquor. 'And you're all a bunch of hypocrites if you pretend you're here for any other reason than the money.'

It went quiet, the silence only broken by the crackling of the embers burning in the fire pit.

Then LaBruge spoke, his voice low, his words measured.

'Some of us live, fight and are prepared to die for more than money.' The words hung in the air, the tension clear between the two men.

MacRae knew where this was going. LaBruge had a past, everyone here did. But he had taken a path unlike any of the others, and for his own reasons Simpson didn't buy it.

Simpson spoke. 'You think you're better than the rest of us, but it all comes down to the same thing, the excitement, the money, the kill. Once you've had a taste the hunger never leaves.'

LaBruge stood, his voice icy. 'Not everyone is cut from the same cloth, not everyone has a heart of stone.' He sighed. 'I used to think like you, be like you. But some people change, find other reasons to fight, it's not always about yourself. Maybe some of us hope to leave this world with a lighter heart, a clearer conscience.' He shrugged, his face betraying his internal conflict. 'That's all I have to say about it.'

MacRae breathed a sigh of relief. He'd seen LaBruge and Simpson go down this path before, and it never ended well.

'Just keep out of my way, and I'll make sure I never depend on you to watch my back.' The disdain dripped off Simpson's lips.

MacRae tensed. Simpson wasn't going to let it go this time.

LaBruge's voice was calm, measured words spoken slowly. 'If you fought with honour I would watch your back, but instead you and those like you are more the disease than the cure in this world.'

Then it was on. A blur of movement and Simpson vaulted the flames and was in LaBruge's face, his hand scruffing his shirt.

'That was my friend that died that day you piece of shit.'

LaBruge was momentarily taken off guard, Simpson's body crashing against his chest. He resisted, then relaxed his upper body, twisting sideways as he gripped Simpson's shoulders and throwing him onto the ground, followed by his own body collapsing on top of him.

Simpson thrust an arm down to break his fall, then he was on his back. LaBruge moved lightning fast, his hand down the side of his boot then at Simpson's throat, a glistening combat knife poised ready to strike.

Simpson screamed. 'No...' But all he could see was the cold disconnected eyes of a professional killer about to do his work.

Then a hand reached between the men. MacRae with a vice-like grip around LaBruge's wrist, muscles tensed to arrest the action of the knife.

'Thierry, no. Don't do this, it's not worth it.'

Silence around the fire as the seasoned soldiers watched, waiting to see how this would end, the crackle of the flames the only sound punctuating the air.

Then LaBruge relaxed, his shoulders slumped and the knife eased back from Simpson's neck. He pushed himself up, then he was standing, leaving Simpson on the ground. LaBruge held Simpson's eyes in a long stare, opened his mouth to speak, but instead turned and walked out of the bar.

A sigh of relief went around the fire pit as Simpson got up, then the buzz of conversation as the men chewed over the fight.

MacRae went after LaBruge, catching up with him in the poorly lit street. He threw a hand out and touched LaBruge's shoulder. LaBruge spun on his heel, flicking MacRae's hand to the side, and driving his fist towards MacRae's face.

MacRae didn't flinch. He felt sure LaBruge would stop short... and he did, millimetres from MacRae's jaw. MacRae looked into the Belgian's eyes, saw the pain, the confusion.

MacRae spoke. 'I've heard the rumours, the stories. It's eating you up. Isn't it time you talked about it?'

LaBruge looked away, staring into the distance, then walked a few paces away before stopping. 'Okay, but you're buying the drinks.'

~

A woman stroked the keys of a shiny black piano, the jazz music floating through the room. LaBruge glanced around, soaking up the atmosphere of the up-market bar. Not the kind of place he'd usually be found. The barman slid a sparkling crystal glass of whisky to him, and a beer to MacRae.

'I used to be like him, you know,' LaBruge started. 'A cliché. Messy childhood, running wild, looking for adventure. Next thing you know I'm travelling the world with the Foreign Legion.' He chuckled. 'It sure gave me the structure and discipline I was looking for in life. But then as time goes by you see too much, do too much. You get hard.' A sideways glance at MacRae. 'Know what I mean?'

MacRae took a mouthful of beer and shrugged. 'You certainly get to see too much of the bad in people.'

LaBruge swirled the toffee coloured liquid around his glass.

'Yeah, then you realise that maybe you could be doing the same dirty work for a lot more money as a contractor. What does it matter? It's always about the money, government wages or private.'

He took a sip, the whisky burning down his throat.

'So I went private. The big money was in minerals and oil exploration, protecting companies exploiting resources in poor countries.' He looked around the room. 'Like this shit-hole. It should be one of the richest countries in the world. I guess it is for those that control the oil rights.'

'So what changed?' MacRae turned to face the man.

LaBruge sighed. 'One job too many, clearing villagers from their fertile farmland to a barren hillside to live so the oil company could drill. They resisted. One rushed a contractor. He panicked and shot him. The air was electric, no-one knew what was going to happen next, then a woman, the guy's wife started beating on the contractor, it looked like it was about to turn into a tribal fucking war. The guy knocked her down, put his gun to her head. Everyone was screaming.'

Silence. Then LaBruge continued. 'Then God told me this had to stop. Right then and there. It scared the shit out of me. I heard his voice, like I'm talking to you, okay?'

MacRae nodded.

'So I shot him, a bullet right through the head.' Another shrug.

MacRae sat in silence, listening intently.

'He was a friend of Simpson's. Anyway, after a bit of a stand-off between me and the other contractors we left the village, just got out of there. Not that it mattered. The government covered it up. The villagers got relocated. I got fired.'

MacRae sat back on his stool.

'Security is the only thing I'm good at, so I stayed in the industry. But now I only take jobs God tells me to.' He drained the whisky glass. 'That's why Simpson hates me. And why not many people will hire me.'

His eyes met MacRae's. 'But you do and for that I'm grateful.'

MacRae knocked back the last of his beer. 'Maybe we're not that different Thierry. And I know I can rely on you when it matters.' He toyed with his empty glass, lost in thought, then met LaBruge's eyes. 'And something tells me we're going to be working together again before too long.'

LaBruge nodded, then spoke. 'So what's your plan now?'

MacRae shrugged. 'I'm flying home to Tasmania in the next couple of days to try and console a good woman who has lost a remarkable man and husband, and try and explain how I was there to protect him, and instead watched him die.'

His voice took on a hard edge. 'I'm not going to let this go Thierry, for the sake of Evan, and the girls who were taken.'

Then he relaxed, holding up his empty glass to catch the attention of the barman. 'Buy you another?'

~

CHAPTER 5

BANJOS

The pump hummed rhythmically as Kane Murdoch filled his car with petrol, the fumes filling his nostrils.

'Christ it's cold,' he muttered to himself. He didn't mind the cold, but it always took him by surprise when he was heading into the Tasmanian central highlands in winter to shoot footage for the wildlife documentary. He was well equipped for today's outing, from the expensive waterproof walking boots to the multi-pocketed bush jacket filled with camera equipment.

He jumped as the shop's door slammed shut behind him. Two thick-set men sauntered across the concrete forecourt, the steam from their takeaway coffee cups curling upwards in the frosty air. Murdoch met their eyes, then looked back to the petrol pump as it juddered when the tank filled, triggering the shut-off valve.

'Hey Rambo, you off to kill some gooks?' The shorter of the two men chuckled as passed.

Murdoch glanced up again, smiling. 'The only thing I'm shooting today is photographs.'

The man stopped, staring at Murdoch with cold blue eyes.

'You'd better be careful what you photograph out there in the bush, some people like their privacy.'

Murdoch held his gaze, he guessed the accent was northern European, maybe Russian?

'The only thing I'll be photographing today is wildlife, and they're not too precious about that.'

The other man reached over putting his hand on his friends shoulder. 'C'mon we've got work to do.'

He grinned at Murdoch before he turned away. 'I'll be seeing ya.' Then they were gone.

Jesus, there were some weird characters out here in the backwoods...you could almost hear the banjos playing. Murdoch chuckled at his joke. Not that the violence played out in the film *Deliverance* was anything to laugh about.

He screwed the petrol cap tight with his right hand, his left hand absently drifting to the bush machete slung in a sheath across his chest. When anyone asked, the machete was to hack his way through the sometimes almost impenetrable bush. But it's real purpose was more serious. He was often alone in very isolated places with a small fortune in camera equipment slung on his back. Experience had shown him that not everyone you came across in these places was your friend, but anyone planning on causing trouble thought twice when they saw the size of the blade on his chest. And something in his eyes told them that he wouldn't hesitate to use it.

~

The black mud from recent rains squelched under his boots as he walked at a slow but steady pace across the lightly forested plain. Murdoch was a very patient man. No-one expected that when they first met him. He had a wild, bubbly exuberance that dominated any room he was in. Women wanted him and men wanted to be like him. Or at least that was what he said with a laugh. It had been a very long journey to get him to where he was today, and he could never have predicted where he was going to end up all those years ago growing up in the middle class suburbs of Guatemala City.

He arched his back to adjust the weight of the backpack filled with bush survival equipment and a hugely expensive digital movie camera. A smile creased his face. Yes, tramping through the isolated and inhospitable, but stunningly beautiful and eerily silent Tasmanian wilderness to get the last few shots of the legendary Tasmanian Devil was a million miles from his sheltered schooling followed by military college from the age of sixteen in Latin America. Just a few more close-ups and he'd have everything he needed for a rough edit to sell his documentary to the Wildlife Channel, the biggest, and most respected independent producer of wildlife documentaries in the world. Then he'd have made it. No more Kane Murdoch, stable, reliable, chartered accountant. He could already see his name in the credits, rolling down millions of TV screens:

Producer: Kane Murdoch

The last thick stand of Tea Tree pushed back hard against him, then he was through to a clearing. A place he and his friends the Tasmanian Devils knew well.

He glanced at his watch then the sky. The time was almost right, they should be coming through here very soon, foraging for carrion, anything that has died recently and could be ripped apart to feed the adults and young. A spatter of rain hit his face, it looked like the weather was closing in; that meant wrapping the camera in waterproofing for the shoot. He lay face down with his stomach flat on a patch of Tussock grass, the wiry blades cushioning his elbows, hiding his silhouette. He could feel the wet coldness of the mud beneath the grass started to soak into his body, drawing the heat from him. It didn't matter, he wouldn't be here long this final time. The 400mm zoom lens stretched out in front of him, now all he had to do was wait.

Murdoch snapped out of his doze when he heard voices. He brought the camera up to his eye, peering through the viewfinder to get a closer look at the group as they strode across the grassy plain, the brown tannin-stained ground water splashing over their boots. They didn't seem to care about the delicate alpine environment, or about panicking the family of Tasmanian Devils that had been approaching Murdoch.

It took Murdoch a moment to count them as they were bunched together, two girls and two, no three guys. Then they abruptly fanned, encircling the devils, herding them towards the Tea Tree and grassy clearing. He instantly recognised two of them, the men from the service station earlier that day.

He carefully adjusted the camera, the zoom lens pulling them closer, like they were almost standing with him. The way they moved was kind of familiar, but he couldn't quite put his finger on it. Then it came to him. They had that bearing of guys who were fit, pretty tough, used to using their bodies. Boxers maybe? Then he saw them checking their surroundings, eyes lazily flicking around, watching their quarry, but also watching the other people in their team, then scanning the landscape. Shit, they were military, maybe ex-special forces. Not the kind of people he really wanted to run into in the middle of nowhere.

Murdoch checked his position, satisfied he was pretty well concealed, then settled in to watch as the group surrounded the animals. The larger of the carnivores went back on its haunches, snarling and hissing at the men. Murdoch suppressed a chuckle. These little critters were ugly as hell, smelly, made a hideous noise, and ate rotting meat. No wonder they were called Tasmanian Devils by the white early settlers in Tasmania.

Then a net was thrown by one of the women and the devil was caught, a writhing ball of anger. A man stepped in and scooped it up. But he was careless, one hand too close to the vicious teeth, and the devil latched on, fastening the man's fingers in a grip shaped by evolution to strip flesh from bone. He jerked back with a scream then swung the devil down hard onto a rock, smashing it's head. The jaws slackened and he was free, the devil dying at his feet. The woman leapt forward, yelling in the man's face. Murdoch couldn't make out what she was saying, but it obviously intimidated the man. He moved back, holding his bleeding hand, face seething.

Murdoch's eyes narrowed. What the hell were they doing here? He adjusted the zoom lens to fit the whole group and took a photo, then sent the picture to his mobile phone. He'd soon find out who these people were. Moving very carefully he reached into his jacket pocket, and pulled out the phone. Wrong one. It was his business phone. This was personal. He reached in again and swapped phones and checked the photo storage, satisfied that the image was there, added it to a text and pressed *send*...and nothing happened. No signal, probably to be expected in the middle of nowhere. It would have to wait until he got closer to civilisation.

Raised voices drew his attention back to the group so he zoomed back in, watching as they as they grabbed the devils one by one, this time more carefully, and examined them, measuring, photographing, long needles extracting blood. Murdoch could see some of the devils were diseased, their faces hideously deformed by a cruel and deadly affliction. Maybe they were scientists researching the devastating Tasmanian Devil facial tumour? But the cruelty didn't suggest that they liked the animals.

Then he heard it...or did he just sense it...a footfall behind him. His time in the military with the Engineers, digging in the sand and soil for hidden anti-personnel mines had given him an unsettling ability to feel danger. Sometimes a blessing, sometimes a curse.

Murdoch flung himself over and to the side, the camera and his phone landing in the mud with a thump, gently settling into the black ooze. His hand instinctively reaching for the machete strapped across his chest, and with one smooth movement it was out. His eyes met those of one of the guys from the service station. Where the hell had he come from? And why was he rushing at Murdoch with an evil looking military-style knife in his hand?

Murdoch swung his arm back and grunted as he threw the machete. The blade glistened as it turned through the air then found it's mark, slicing into the side of the man's body in a splash of blood, giving Murdoch time to scramble to his feet. Then from the corner of his eye he saw movement at the edge of the stand of Tea Tree. It was the other guy from that morning, the Russian, a dull black pistol extended in his hand.

Murdoch was half a second too slow as his mind desperately sought a way out. With a grim smile the man squeezed the trigger, the bullet punching through the bush jacket and penetrating deep into the left side of Murdoch's chest. With a sigh of disbelief Murdoch sunk to his knees then toppled forward into the mud.

The man with the gun stepped forward cautiously, weapon still trained at Murdoch's centre mass, paused as he stood over him, and knelt down in the mud beside him, checked his vital signs, then stood, satisfied he was dead. Next he turned his attention to his companion, crouched over on one knee, pressing hard on his side, trying to stem the flow of bright red blood coming from the gash in his side.

'Jesus, he almost finished you off.'

'Yeah, but almost isn't enough.' The words came out with a grimace as he watched the Russian pull a field dressing from his day pack, before reaching into the injured man's jacket to press it to the wound, the injured man not realising that the Russian had given serious consideration to whether it would be easier to just kill him too, and bury both bodies in the same grave.

The men turned to the sound of voices behind them as more of the group pushed through the Tea Tree.

A woman spoke, staring at Murdoch's body. 'Do we know him?'

The men shook their heads in unison.

'He was very quick though.' The man with the gun spoke, throwing a glance at the injured man, then back at Murdoch. 'So what about the body? Someone will come looking for him.'

The woman smiled. 'You really don't know where you are do you? This is the Tasmanian bush, some of the most isolated and inhospitable wilderness in the world. The weather can change from stifling heat to snow within hours, and parts of the mountains have never been fully explored. Pretty much every year someone goes walking out here and dies, or just disappears, either an unprepared tourist who dies of exposure, or an experienced walker who gets lost, or falls down a cliff. They're often not found for years...if ever. And even then by the time the devils and whatever else have finished with him there won't be much to identify him.' She grinned. 'He'll be a news story for a day or two, then there will be search and rescue, and that will be that.'

She reached down, pulling his camera from the mud and inadvertently stepping on his phone, pressing it further below the surface. 'So let's move him.'

CHAPTER 6

WAVES

The beige walls, fake stained glass windows and piped music of the funeral parlour and crematorium could have been anywhere in the world. A cookie-cutter off-the-plan franchise selling the product of helping people pass their loved ones from this life to the next.

MacRae stood at the back of the packed hall, squeezed in with the other mourners. All the seats had been filled an hour before the service, but MacRae preferred to be at the back. He hated funerals at the best of times, he'd been to far too many over the years. He flexed his shoulders in the tailored black suit, cut by an old and skilled tailor, an immigrant from Hong Kong a long time ago. He didn't wear it that often and it was feeling a little tighter across the chest than he remembered.

First world problems. He snapped back to the moment. At least this one wasn't a depressing religious ceremony, Holgate's widow Alicia choosing to honour and remember her husband and his remarkable life with a celebration.

Still, as the slides of Holgate's life, his adventures and friends, passed over the huge wall mounted screens to the sounds of his favourite music, MacRae could think of nothing but watching him die, and breaking the terrible news to his wife over the phone from Africa, then accompanying his body home to Tasmania as a mark of respect.

Alicia took to the podium, standing with her shoulders back, a picture of dignity. She was reading from notes held in a shaking hand when she broke down, the words spilling out, jumbled and wretched as the pain of her loss overwhelmed her.

MacRae felt his emotions rising with hers, then forced them back down, turning and silently weaving through the crowd to the exit.

~

The late afternoon sun glowed on MacRae's skin as he sat on the balcony outside the latest place he was calling home, at least for the immediate future. The last of the clouds drifted from cotton balls into nothing, forcing MacRae to squint in the harsh light before he put on his sunglasses. He reached out a hand for the crystal glass Sarah handed him, a slosh of gin and tonic spilling on the table from the overfilled drink as he took it. Maybe he'd had too many already, but what the hell, this was one time too many wouldn't be enough.

Sarah laughed. 'Don't waste it, it's my own special recipe you know.'

MacRae grinned as Sarah's dog Bruce threw a floppy paw onto the table before lapping at the clear liquid with a long pink tongue. 'I know journalists have a reputation for hard drinking, but their dogs as well?'

Sarah waved a hand at Bruce. 'Shoo you bugger.' The chocolate brown Labrador took a last lick and dropped to the floor at her feet.

'So how are you feeling Ian?' Concern punctuated her words.

MacRae shrugged, letting his gaze wander over the railing of the balcony to the waves gently breaking on the beach fifty metres to the north, then taking a long draw at the drink. Time was flying by too fast, the weeks since he'd returned from Africa a blur of emotion and activity.

He was having trouble accepting what had happened to Holgate and the girls in the village, and it had been difficult to return home without being able to make things right. But in the end events had overtaken him again, and after one of the most heart-breaking phone conversations in his life to Holgate's wife, MacRae had arranged to accompany Holgate's body on the flight home to be cremated.

MacRae took another sip of the drink. 'I don't think I'll ever forget the haunted look in Evan's wife's eyes at the memorial service this morning. I know it wasn't my fault but I still feel I failed her.'

Sarah nodded silently. She'd known MacRae for a long time, and had felt close to him from the first time they met as travellers in Europe when they were both barely out of school. They were almost cut of the same cloth. He'd become an idealistic police officer, determined to save the world one villain at a time, whilst she'd followed a different path by trying to save the world through the eyes of the media as an international journalist. But what they had in common despite their different journeys was that they both really cared about people and were trying to do what they could to make the world a better place.

And they also shared the bond that came from facing death many times by following their convictions.

'We both know that we try our best Ian, but sometimes life just isn't fair, and our fate is out of our control.'

A chill went down her spine as she flashed back to the terror she faced years ago at the hands of a militia army in Africa, and how MacRae was instrumental in bringing her to Tasmania to recover and find some peace. The flashbacks didn't occur so often anymore... even the worst experiences faded slowly over time. But occasionally they were just as vivid as if she was there, and it was terrifying all over again.

But when she was with MacRae, she felt safe, maybe even something more than that.

She suddenly realised she was staring at him, worry etched across her forehead...and he was looking back at her, a slight smile dancing at the corner of his mouth. She felt herself blush. Damn, he did this to her sometimes, seeing inside her mind. And they'd agreed a long time ago that they were best as friends. The closest friends.

She turned on her heel, back to the refrigerator in MacRae's rented beach-side apartment. 'Better get some more lime.'

MacRae stood, leaning on the railing to enjoy the view of the waves sparkling as the sun slowly sunk to the horizon. He loved this place. It was the right place for the right time in his life. He turned and watched Sarah working in the kitchen, deftly wielding a knife to cut perfect wedges of the bitter fruit. She looked toned and fit, the outdoor country life and keeping horses still suited her, and her eyes always sparkled when she smiled at him. Once again he felt the confusing mix of a warm friendship and attraction.

Maybe one day he'd share a house, a kitchen, a life with a woman again. Sarah liked to talk about fate. Could she somehow fit into his life in that way?

He thought back to the frightening times when they'd been caught up in the terrorist plot to reignite the nuclear terror of Chernobyl with the Devil's Breath weapon. It had almost cost them both their lives. But they were also instrumental in stopping a plot to end the human race in the name of religion. But his beloved house on five acres in the country hadn't felt the same after the events that unfolded there for him and Sarah. Besides he'd always wanted to live in an apartment near the sea, and this one in nearby Blackman's Bay had become available to rent just as he'd put his property up for sale.

Melancholy settled back on him like a grey cloud. The Devil's Breath plot had cost him so much in love, and betrayal. Then there was Ritchie, Sarah's friend in England, someone he'd never met, a computer hacker instrumental in changing the course of history, only to disappear without a trace.

He jumped slightly as Sarah touched his shoulder, then they clinked glasses as Sarah spoke the words MacRae was thinking.

'Here's a toast to one of the good guys, Dr Evan Holgate. Whenever he passed away it was going to be too soon.'

MacRae smiled. 'Cheers, to Evan.'

A comfortable silence descended on them as they relaxed with the drinks, until the persistent buzz of MacRae's phone vibrating on the kitchen bench behind them broke the mood.

Sarah was closest, so she reached over to grab it, glancing at the screen as she passed it to MacRae.

'It says it's Brad...is that Brad Schneider?'

MacRae pressed *accept* to take the video call. 'Sure is.' He shrugged. 'I thought I might as try and enlist the help of the CIA to try and find some answers about what happened in Africa.'

Sarah smiled. They all had history together. MacRae had known CIA agent Brad Schneider for a long time, going way back to MacRae's time as an anti-terror cop liaising in the middle east, then when he'd sent a desperate plea for Schneider to use his CIA resources to help to get Sarah out of Africa after her worst nightmare as a freelance reporter had come true. The last time being when they'd been caught up in the Devil's Breath plot, and all three of them almost killed. But times had changed. Maybe they'd all moved on and Schneider couldn't or wouldn't help.

MacRae positioned his phone in front of them as Brad's face filled the screen. Schneider still had his boyish good looks, and had grown his hair longer. He looked a little older, but then no doubt so did MacRae.

MacRae grinned. 'Good to see you haven't changed much, the Agency must be treating you well. Still riding a desk nowadays?'

A brief delay as the signals travelled across the Atlantic to the US, then Schneider replied. 'Yeah, and you haven't got any better looking either have you?'

He chuckled, then noticed the figure in the background.

'Sarah? Are you still hanging around this guy? He's trouble you know.'

Sarah leaned over MacRae's shoulder. 'Unfortunately so Brad. And for all the wrong reasons as usual. It's good to see you.'

MacRae broke in. 'Okay now the reunion is over Brad, do you think you can help me with Africa?'

Schneider got back to business, recalling the brief conversation they'd had over the phone just before MacRae had left Africa with Holgate's body.

'Yeah, look as I said at the time, the reach of the CIA is limited in plenty of places around the world, and Nigeria is one of those, particularly as politically we seem to be more inward looking in recent times. You know how it is, the politics is never ending. It's all about internal security nowadays.'

MacRae broke in, frustration edging into his voice. 'Yeah I get that Brad, but you've got eyes in the largest, best resourced spy organisation in the world, surely you can get me something to follow up with the Nigerian army operations against Boko Haram, or where it's likely they may have taken the hostages?'

Sarah sat silently, watching the exchange between the two men.

MacRae pushed harder. 'You're telling me that the US has no strategic interest in Nigeria, the biggest oil producer in the continent, and a country getting plenty of attention from emerging powers in the region like China?' He shook his head. 'Maybe the conspiracy theories have something to them, and the CIA is covertly backing Boko Haram to keep pressure on a Nigerian government that's unfriendly to the US and other western colonial influences.'

Schneider bristled. 'What the fuck? You know that's just bullshit put about to smear the US.'

It was MacRae's turn to stay silent. Then with a rush his last memory of Hassana flooded through his mind, her desperate plea.

Please protect us Mr Ian.

He'd failed her, just as he'd failed Holgate, and he'd do whatever it took to make amends.

Schneider saw the pain etched across MacRae's face.

'Okay, I'll ask some more questions, see if anyone on the ground has some background that can help. But I can't make any promises, you know that, right? And if there are any active operations I can't share any details.'

MacRae knew that was as good as it was going to get. He leaned forward to disconnect the call.

'Much appreciated old friend, It's always great to get co-operation from our *cousins across the ditch,* as they say in the Bond movies.'

'Yeah I'll do what I can. I know this has been a tough time for you.' Schneider smiled. 'Maybe you should consider a different line of work.'

Then he was gone.

MacRae leaned back, fingers tapping his drink.

Sarah spoke. 'So, fingers crossed then?'

MacRae took a sip, the bite of the lime hitting his tongue.

'Yes. It's not much, but it's all we've got for the moment.'

He pondered Schneider's words. *Maybe he should consider a different line of work.* But what else could he do? Perhaps he was just like LaBruge and all the others, and after so long this was all he was really good for.

CHAPTER 7

AID

The vibrations from the helicopter's rotors rattled Doctor Marion Weatherill's teeth as the chopper lowered itself gently down to the flattened bush grass landing area. She grimaced as she noticed her hands; knuckles white, fiercely gripping the sides of her seat. It didn't matter how many times she flew in choppers she never felt completely safe. But she loved her work so much it was worth it. In this business you never knew what to expect, where you'd be working, how safe or dangerous the job would be.

In her old life in an inner-city doctors practice she'd become jaded with medicine, dealing with the often self-inflicted illnesses of the modern western world...diabetes, obesity, cancer. That was until she volunteered with the Royal Flying Doctor Service, working in the remote "outback" parts of Australia, and found her real calling with indigenous people, harsh conditions, even harsher diseases. Real medicine. It was almost beyond belief that it was occurring in a first-world economy.

Eventually she'd become worn down by the bureaucracy of working with government agencies and their constantly changing policies depending upon their elected master at the time. So when she was offered a three month contract working with a United Nations emergency medicine response team she'd jumped at it.

That was six years and thirty seven countries ago. She'd seen a lot and helped many people since then, and been in some pretty dangerous situations. And as much as she didn't like having hired security along, if things went wrong you really appreciated it. But today she was on her own.

She mentally went over the briefing at the clinic in town again. It had been prompted by a garbled radio call from an army unit that stumbled across a Boko Haram camp in the bush. From what they could gather there had been a firefight and the rebels had taken off, leaving the camp to the army. It got a little confusing after that. The lieutenant in charge had said there were a bunch of civilian bodies in tents, all women and all mutilated. No, that wasn't the exact wording...he'd apparently described their faces as *deformed like demons*, whatever that meant. And there was one surviving female. He'd requested a medical response team, but given that there appeared to be only one survivor and the situation was unclear, she'd been dispatched to advise if a full response team was needed.

The screaming engines fell silent as she took off her headset, and the pilot, a grizzly unshaven man in his fifties, opened the door for her, extending a hand to help her out. She smiled and waved it away...she was pretty good at looking after herself... grabbing her medical backpack from the seat next to her and stepping into the harsh Nigerian sun. She wrinkled her nose at the pungent smell of burning. The pilot had commented on the smouldering fires in the clearing as they approached to land, but they hadn't been able to make out the source from above. Now she knew. It was burning flesh. She hoisted the bag onto her back, turning away from the chopper. A flare of sunlight caused her to squint, then a figure in military fatigues appeared in front of her.

'You're the medical team? Where are the others?'

Marion saw the insignia on his shoulders. It was the unit commander.

'I'm it, Dr Weatherill.' She thrust her hand forward.

The lieutenant ignored it and turned on his heel.

'Come this way while there's still something to see.'

He led the way through the camp, Marion close behind stepping around the bodies of rebel fighters.

'We killed most of the rebels. They were just as surprised as us when we stumbled on their camp. A few escaped further into the bush.' The lieutenant nodded his head to the left side of the camp.

They wandered past soldiers in groups of two or three, toying with their weapons nervously. Fires burned around them, acrid smoke drifting through the camp.

'What's burning in the fires?' Marion said.

The lieutenant stopped walking. 'The hostages' bodies.'

Marion blinked in shock. 'All of them? Why? How can I examine them?'

'They were all dead, and their faces, deformed. My men aren't afraid to fight, but this is different. Maybe it was an infectious disease. I tried to stop them, but it wasn't worth my life so I let them burn them.'

Marion's face clouded over. 'And you don't have any prisoners to say what happened here?'

The lieutenant shrugged. 'The rebels are either dead or gone into the bush.'

'You didn't go after them?'

'The bush is their territory, their advantage. Besides my men didn't want the same thing to happen to them if they were captured.'

Marion started walking again. 'But there's a survivor?'

'Yes,' the lieutenant said. 'My men thought she must be the same as the others. They wanted to burn her too, but I managed to stop them...so far. She's over here.'

On the far side of the camp one tent still stood, a lone young woman sitting in the dirt outside watched closely by a soldier. She turned to look at them as they approached, her face brightening as she saw Marion, another female.

'This is Hassana, she wants to show you something. It's the last body,' the lieutenant said. 'She says it's her sister.'

Marion knelt down to greet the woman, offering her hand. 'Hassana is it? I'm Dr Weatherill. You'd like to show me something?'

Hassana nodded, taking her hand and leading her into the tent. The soldier was a footstep behind.

For a few seconds Marion couldn't make out anything in the gloom, just the shape of a body on a mat on the ground, then her eyes adjusted. Despite everywhere she'd been and everything she'd seen over the years, she couldn't suppress a gasp of horror as she saw what was left of the young woman's face.

She breathed deeply and slowly to calm her racing heart as she focused on the figure before her, reminding herself that this was a patient...no...a person, no matter how disfigured.

She glanced over her shoulder. The soldier was watching her suspiciously. A crackle of gunfire in the distance startled her. *I'm getting jumpy in my old age.*

The lieutenant's voice came from outside the tent. 'It's okay, this is government territory now. That was just some soldiers celebrating our victory. Probably.'

Marion knew the protocol for this situation. At the very least she should be in full protective clothing to do an examination, then when she had a better idea of what they were dealing with she should quarantine the site until she could make a report and get the full support team in. But she knew there was no time for that in this volatile environment. She reached into her bag and pulled on gloves, a mask and eye protection, then leaned in close to examine the body.

The face of the patient, or should she call her a victim, was covered with some kind of growth, possibly infectious, but what was the nature of transmission?

'Hassana, do you know what happened to your sister and the other women?'

Hassana spoke quietly. 'When we were taken they gave us injections. We thought they were to help us, but then these things started to grow on their faces.'

'How long ago was that?' Marion said.

'A few months ago. I don't really know how much time has passed.'

Marion looked around the victim's face, making mental notes.

The disease obviously progressed incredibly rapidly, leading to total destruction of the eyes, nose, mouth, and moving inside the jaw cavity, inevitably resulting in death. It seemed to operate like a cancer, but the rate of growth was extraordinary, and affecting so many victims?

She took out her phone and took a series of photos from different angles around the face.

'Did it affect them anywhere else?'

Hassana shook her head. 'I don't think so. After a while if they hadn't already died from those things, they couldn't eat and so they starved.' She reached her hand out to Marion, grasping her arm. 'Is this going to happen to me?'

Marion hesitated, she knew she shouldn't do it, but acting against all protocols she took Hassana's hand, squeezing it for reassurance. 'I'll do everything I can to find out what happened here and keep you safe, okay?'

She went back into her bag, extracting a scalpel and sample tubes filled with preservative liquid.

'It's probably best if you go outside while I get some samples from your sister.'

Hassana backed out of the tent, and Marion leaned in to remove some of the infected tissue.

'No, don't touch her,' the soldier behind her shouted. 'It's the Devil's work.'

Marion opened her mouth to reason with him, but he continued shouting, taking her arm and dragging her from the tent. The noise had drawn the attention of the other soldiers. The lieutenant barked orders for them to stay back, but it was too late, as guns were levelled at him, Marion and Hassana.

He stood his ground, then shepherded his arms around the women, guiding them through the soldiers and back towards the helicopter.

'What are they doing?' Marion shouted.

'They're going to burn the body.'

'I need samples. Can't you stop them?'

The lieutenant took Marion's shoulders with both hands. 'You saw their mood. Just be glad you, me and Hassana aren't being burnt too.'

Marion stood fixed in place defiantly, glancing back through the village as the soldiers threw petrol over the tent and lit it with a flick of a match. A soldier saw her watching and gestured wildly towards her.

'Okay, let me take Hassana with me?'

The lieutenant nodded. 'Just get out of here, okay?'

The helicopter pilot had heard the exchange and by the time they reached the chopper the rotors were accelerating. He ushered them in as the soldiers started heading their way.

Marion let out a sigh of relief as the chopper lifted off, and was waving to the lieutenant when she felt pressure against her side. Hassana had slid over the seat to hold her arm. Marion stiffened then let Hassana relax against her.

Hassana's eyes pleaded at her as she spoke. 'Is it over now? Are we safe?'

~

They rode in silence for a while, Marion starting to recognise the scenery as they neared the town again. Hassana had dozed against her briefly, but now was wide awake and looking out the window with curiosity, taking in the view and the sensations of the flight.

'I've always wanted to go in one of these.'

Marion smiled. 'It's an interesting experience isn't it?'

Hassana looked at her quizzically. 'Your voice, your accent. Where are you from? Is it Canada?'

'No, I've spent time in Canada.' Marion said. 'I've worked all around the world, but my accent is mostly Australian. That's where I was born.'

Hassana shuffled away across the seat, reaching into the pocket of her dress, pulling it inside out, then slipping her fingers into a hidden pouch in the lining. She carefully extracted a tattered white business card with her fingers and held it out to Marion.

'Then you must know my friend, Mr Ian. He's from Australia.'

Marion laughed. 'I know everyone thinks we all know each other in Australia, but it's actually a very big country.'

She took the card from Hassana and read the name, then for a very long second her head was spinning and she was thrust back in time to the middle east when she'd desperately needed a security escort at short notice to visit a remote, disease-ravaged village in war-torn Iraq. That was the first time she'd met the man named on the card. Exasperating, charming, incredibly competent, and possibly the love of her life. Ian MacRae.

~

The city of Hobart stretched out before MacRae, looking magnificent bathed in morning sunlight, the River Derwent glistening in the background. He didn't get up to the top of Mount Wellington, Kunanyi as the original inhabitants called it, often enough. I guess being a local you took it for granted, leaving it for the tourists. But since he'd been back he'd felt the need to reconnect with his home, and what better way than to claw his way to the top of the imposing rock on his mountain bike.

His muscles had burned with the exertion, sweat covering his back, as he slowly devoured the thirteen hundred metre climb, exploring new trails and occasionally crossing the twisting road hacked out of the dolerite by hand to ease the unemployment crisis of the Great Depression engulfing the world in the 1930's.

He was out of practice, and didn't really have the fitness this demanded. But still he pushed himself, throwing the bike around corners, jumping rocks and logs, knowing he was at the limits of his skill, but driven to go faster to keep his mind focused on the moment and not what had happened in Africa.

MacRae had seen a lot of death and sadness in his life and career, from his time as a young idealistic police recruit, to the tours of foreign lands and conflicts when serving as an anti-terrorist police specialist. Even now his career as a security adviser for corporations, mainly non-government aid organisations, undertaking projects in dangerous locations around the world, showed him both the best and worst of humanity.

But somehow this was different. Holgate was special, so were the people, the young girls he had met in the village so briefly. And now they were gone. He was there to help them, the so-called expert. His advice and presence hadn't been requested, he'd chosen to go there against Holgate's protestations. He'd even taken a fucking mercenary, a hired gun, professional muscle just in case something went wrong, and it had been for nothing. A good man had died and MacRae now lived with the responsibility of trying to make sense of it to his grieving widow.

MacRae arched his back and slowly breathed in, the cool mountain air chilling his lungs, making him feel alive. A brisk breeze came up the face of the rugged cliff face known as The Organ Pipes, swaying MacRae back as he stood, his feet firmly planted on a huge boulder.

For the thousandth time he went over how the events had unfolded; what could he have done differently? But his logical analysis kept returning to the way Holgate chose to live his life, pursuing his passion to help those no-one else would, in some of the most high-risk places on the planet. Maybe it was inevitable how Holgate's life would end, and perhaps that's how he expected it. *Better to live one day as a tiger, than a lifetime as a mouse* as he used to say.

But the two girls?

MacRae had spent days after his release from hospital in Nigeria enquiring about them. It seemed the Nigerian army had chased the militia with their kidnapped hostages from the village, but had either lost them in the nearby bush, or didn't want to risk another firefight on the militia's territory. The end result was the same, the girls had disappeared without a trace and there was little government will, or resources, to look for a few more missing children in the midst of a vicious conflict.

MacRae had even tried to pull together a team of contractors... mercenaries in layman's terms...at short notice to chase down the militia, but it seemed there was more lucrative, and less dangerous, contracts to be had locally. And the consensus was that there was no chance of ever recovering the girls alive anyway.

Voices approaching from behind snapped MacRae from his thoughts. A group of half a dozen tourists, probably from the huge bus with its engine idling in the car park, wandered towards the lookout to his left, pointing out landmarks as they went, then pulling their jackets close as they encountered the chilly wind at the edge of the mountain. It had been a long time since MacRae had relaxed on a holiday, been to a foreign country for pleasure rather than the business of life and death.

He jumped off the rock and opened his backpack slung over the handlebars of his mountain bike, pulling out a black helmet and gloves. A tingle of excitement went through him as he prepared for the ride back down. This was just what he needed to clear his mind, help him figure out what came next for him. Perhaps it was time for a change from the life he'd lived for so long, as Brad had suggested, *consider a different line of work.*

But then what could he do that gave him the same sense of fulfilment, and if he was completely honest with himself, the adrenaline?

A last look at the view and MacRae mounted the bike, swinging the front wheel to the start of the steep track back down. Then he felt the vibration of his phone in his pocket. He stayed poised to go, foot on the pedal, the phone stopped. Then it rang again. They weren't going to go away, so he pulled it out and hit *answer...*and listened in disbelief to the voice he knew so well from the other side of the world and a previous life, saying words he thought he'd never hear.

'Ian MacRae? This is Marion.' She paused. Did he recognise her? It had been a very long time. 'Dr Marion Weatherill. I'm in Nigeria with a young woman who's just been rescued from Boko Haram. She says she knows you. Her name is Hassana.'

~

CHAPTER 8

LAB

The buzz of conversation faded as the last of the students wandered from the acoustically dampened lecture theatre into the twisting, echoing corridors of the Merton Institute Research Centre building nestled in the Hobart city centre. Professor Laura Edison smiled as she pondered the last few curious enquiries from students keen to pick her brain.

She was pretty good at spotting who was trying to leave a good impression with the lecturer, and who was genuinely seeking the insight to achieve their best. She glanced at the clock mounted on the wall behind her. The room was free for another half hour or so, so she took a moment to tidy her lecture notes, before opening her laptop to check emails.

The screen reflected her face as it started up, her dark brown eyes sparkling as she smiled. Cropped red hair wrapped around her face in a bob, and perfect teeth, the product of much time and expense, gave her an almost too good to be true look. She looked so youthful, nothing like her fifty five years. Surprising, given what she'd had to achieve to get to her position at the prestigious research facility.

Maybe it was like the classic tale, *The Picture of Dorian Gray*, and somewhere along the way she'd made a deal with the Devil, and all the bad things she'd done had been transferred to another image of her somewhere, her corrupted soul one day waiting to be released back into her life to make her accountable. But then all acts by everyone could be viewed in different ways, depending on your point of view. At least that's what she told herself when doubts crept in, and the faces from the past, like Dr Khan, haunted her at night.

Her finger rolled the mouse wheel silently, scrolling down the email list, ignoring most, pausing briefly on others to assess their priority. So much work to do, so much responsibility. And would it ever be enough for him to give her the recognition, the position, and the money she knew she deserved?

Her phone pinged on the desk next to her, demanding her attention. A quick glance showed what she expected, another notification of a special offer from an online gambling service. She felt her stress levels rising, and along with it the familiar desire, no, she knew it was actually a need, for a drink and the thrill of the bet.

Her thoughts drifted, longing for the release of the cool glass of wine in her hand and the bright, exciting lights and sounds of the poker machines in a gaming room. Laura Edison was an extremely bright and disciplined woman, and even though she knew it was an addiction, the gambling encouraged and reinforced by a faceless organisation of experts in how to keep you playing and losing, she still couldn't stop. And now it was getting to the point where she wasn't sure she could hide the demands for debts to be paid from her husband any longer. She just needed more money and time to make it right.

Her mind wandered to the messaging group she'd joined on the Dark Web, and as much as she tried to resist the idea, it was becoming more appealing as she became more desperate. The illegal trade in human organs was extremely risky but also extremely lucrative. The nature of her work and her position in the organisation gave her access to some highly sought after human body products at times, and the Dark Web had all the information she needed to connect with buyers who would do anything for a last chance at life, no matter the cost to others.

She pushed the thoughts from her mind, focusing back on her job as Director of the Institute, and the research programs she was running. She loved her work, and she knew Tasmania, as an island, was the perfect place for so much of what she did.

Isolated from the rest of Australia by three hundred kilometres of ocean, it had a relatively static population of around half a million. It also had the descendants of an ancient indigenous population, once again separated from the rest of the country, and many of the current residents were linked back to the unwanted criminals of England in the eighteenth century, the dregs of society transported to serve out their sentences for often minor crimes, and then settling to develop this Godforsaken outpost of the British Empire. It was the ideal gene pool for genetics research and her speciality...disease and population health for both animals and humans. And of course being an island it was easy to close the borders and keep people either in or out if there was an outbreak of a deadly disease within the island population or in the outside world.

But there was constant pressure to get results, justifying the government grants, the university support and the medical industry partnership funding. And then there were the other projects, the privately funded ones that had led her here, and of course the devastating disease afflicting the native Tasmanian Devil population.

She'd almost finished reviewing the emails when another appeared, instantly catching her eye. He was chasing her for another update on the Africa Project, the most promising and fascinating work they'd done in a long time. She smiled; a good result on this was hopefully her way back up the corporate ladder. She deserved it. She'd been with him since the early days at Bophal in India when the chemical leak happened, killing thousands of innocent people, how they'd seen the greed, corruption and misery before and after the disaster, and how it had helped shape their thoughts and future, even if they didn't know it at the time.

She smiled as she remembered the many humid Indian evenings spent in hotel bars with him and the other amateur philosophers, or visionaries as she liked to think of them. Mostly westerners, professionals in a variety of fields of industry discussing how to make the world a better place for future generations. She'd enjoyed the spirited debates on population control the most. Would the world be a better place if human breeding was controlled, say by race, or geographic location? Or perhaps only people of certain blood types should be able to reproduce?

Then there were the discussions on the Nazis and their fixation on an Aryan master race, ethnic cleansing across history, and the Chinese one-child social engineering experiment. But the debates always seem to end with religion, and that ignited such passion...it was easy to bait zealots, and Edison's pet subject was contraception. She'd find out who had strong religious beliefs and then challenge them to show moral justification for religious policies dictated by mostly wealthy old white men in western countries that forbade contraception, when it meant millions of people each year born into a lifetime of poverty and disease, a far cry from their privileged existence.

And finally, when the hours were late and the drinks had flowed, the conversation sometimes turned to what could be done about it. Some of the ideas were suited to a spy novel, like the suggestion to assassinate the pope as an ardent opposer of contraception in third world countries. He was elderly and had frequent visits to hospital, so perhaps a particularly virulent variety of Golden Staph bacteria could be administered? It was already rife in hospitals, and no-one would suspect anything. But then they would simply elect another pope, probably just as conservative. And so the ideas to save the world at that time remained as just ideas.

But now he was at the top. Magnus Crane, once her colleague was now a corporate leader, and somehow she'd been left behind even though they shared the same vision, goals, and secrets.

Voices from approaching students in the corridor startled her, her finger stabbing at the mouse to hide the email. She snapped the laptop closed, and gathering her things, strode out the door, nodding as a couple of enthusiastic young women entered the lecture theatre.

The lobby of the building was emptying as the next sessions of lectures and tutorials commenced. She smiled at the young security guard behind a high white counter waving directions for a small group of students to the Tasmania Devil facial tumour research program display to his left, then she headed down a corridor leading to the research wing, and the two swipe card actuated elevators.

She watched the LED display count down the floor numbers as the elevator approached, and her mind wandered back to the Africa Project. It had certainly exceeded all expectations, possibly a game changer for how they were approaching things, and the daily updates from the in-country medical contractor running the operation over the relatively short period since they'd obtained the human test subjects had been nothing short of startling. But the flow of update emails had abruptly stopped yesterday, and that made her nervous. Very nervous.

The elevator pinged its arrival, disgorging it's chattering contents of post-grad research students into the corridor next to her, then she was alone again, listening to a pleasant female voice count back up the floor numbers as they passed. Her security card had told the elevator where to take her...a restricted access floor not shown on the control panel. A floor very few people even knew existed.

Her mind wandered again. Humans were curious things. Why did we all like to be told what to do by technology with female voices? Elevators, supermarket checkouts, car GPS systems all giving instructions in a soft but sexy female voice. A man-free zone in a world still mostly controlled by men. It'll be interesting to see where the balance lies when the world population is disrupted and we all have to start again. Maybe the balance should be skewed? If we get the techniques right we could change the male to female ratio and really put women in charge. She smiled to herself; after all, with the advances in IVF research the male of the species could be redundant in a few more decades, genetic relics of an outdated reproductive model, just a few kept around to ensure genetic diversity.

A gentle jot and the elevator doors slid open revealing plain white corridors in both directions. Her eyes barely noticed the signs:

THIS IS A RESTRICTED ACCESS ZONE
AUTHORIZED PERSONNEL ONLY

Security cameras watched the corridor with unblinking eyes as she wandered past locked laboratories, bio-hazard levels displayed in warning signs on their doors. She paused, peering through a glass panel in an airlock-isolated door at the staff in bio-hazard suits working inside. A man wearing thick over-gloves held a diseased Tasmanian Devil test subject down firmly as a colleague slid a long needle into its torso, before returning the animal to a row of cages along the wall. She shook her head. These people had no idea what they were actually doing, what the research was really going to be used for, how it was already being used.

Then it was her turn. Room 508. One of the few carefully located research laboratories that couldn't be seen either inside or outside on the building security monitors. A nondescript door belied the sinister nature of the project she was undertaking in the highest bio security level BSL-4 rated laboratory.

Another swipe of her security card and she was in the ante room, stowing her laptop and personal clothing, then she passed into the first airlock, and was facing a rack of sanitised bio-hazard suits, the door automatically locking and sealing with a quiet hiss behind her.

Expert hands quickly pulled on and sealed the coveralls, helmet and gloves. She connected an isolated oxygen supply, opening a valve to inflate her suit and check for leaks, then she passed into the lab, sealing the final door behind her.

Instantly her mind was focused on the research, a thrill of excitement running through her as she approached the equipment storing many of the most dangerous...and illegal...pathogens the world had ever seen.

She still marvelled at how he'd been able to access some of them, supposedly strictly controlled in only a couple of government research labs around the world. But here they all were.

She logged into the laboratory computer, fire-walled from the rest of the research institute network, and opened her research database, categories flashing up on the screen:

Ebola
Bubonic Plague
Smallpox
Spanish Flu
SARS

Swine Flu
Hendra virus
MERS
Measles

A real who's-who of plagues to terrify the conservative old bureaucrats at the World Health Organisation and US Centre for Disease Control. And here she was with the state-of-the-art technology to study them, pulling them apart, discovering their secrets. And then using the latest gene splicing technology to modify them in highly illegal Gain of Function research, customising them to become targeted, picking and choosing who they would kill based on race, gender or any number of other criteria. And just as importantly, perfecting their ability to spread undetected.

Edison's mind wandered again. Ebola was a wonderful killer, terrifyingly efficient with up to a ninety percent death rate for those infected. But there was no disguising who was infected and dying a hideous death, so it was relatively easy to isolate and control. Other diseases, like many influenza variants, spread almost undetected, the infectious being blissfully ignorant as they moved around the community and showing no initial symptoms, but with a low mortality rate.

But she'd got the mix just right, a disease with a two week incubation and infection time to spread without showing symptoms, a reproduction rate of R6.2, so each carrier infected six others, then finally the masterpiece of an almost more than ninety percent death rate, matching the worst of the known Ebola outbreaks. This was a true Armageddon disease, death far beyond biblical descriptions. Any biological warfare laboratory in the world would have been proud of her.

She thought of her boss and mentor. There was no doubt Crane was a genius, and his vision combined with her research would make them the worst enemy, or as she preferred to see it, the best ally for the survival of the human race. She ran her finger over the touch screen and electric motors whirred into life, a robotic arm selecting a vial of pathogen from a cryogenic freezer and delivering it to be viewed under an electron microscope. She truly had the potential power of life and death over millions with this work, in fact sometimes she felt like a God in her job.

~

Four hours had passed by the time Edison finished her research work for the day. She'd decontaminated herself, and after retrieving her laptop and securing the laboratory again, continued along the corridor, turning to the left at the end.

As always she glanced along to the right, to the unmarked laboratory door where the hapless, or perhaps she'd been careless, Dr Khan had been kept as the Devil facial tumour disease had taken its course and she'd passed away. It had been a chilling reminder to the few that knew about it, including Crane when he'd visited, how dangerous this work could be.

She swiped her card to gain entry to her own private research office, and sat at her desk, leafing through beige project folders, but her mind was drawn back to the Africa Project, the real life trial of the modified-for-humans facial tumour, and her ticket out of here. It couldn't go wrong. She reached into her desk drawer, taking out a bottle of whisky and a small crystal glass, pouring a measure, then after a brief pause filling the glass to the top.

Her phone pinged to announce the arrival of an email. She smiled, it was from the Africa Project contractor, finally. A swipe of her thumb and it was open, her eyes flashing down the lines of text as she realised the nightmare was coming true. The project had been compromised, raided by the army, and the contractor had pulled out, leaving Edison the mess to clean up.

And as much as the thought unsettled her, she'd have to tell Crane sooner or later.

~

CHAPTER 9

REUNION

MacRae sat across the rickety white plastic table from Dr Marion Weatherill, taking in her face. It had been a long time since they'd spent time together, but the years had been good to her. He instantly knew why he'd been drawn to her, the chemistry between them was as strong as ever, and she was just as beautiful; high cheekbones, sparkling eyes and smile always playing on her lips. She was dressed for the climate, jeans, open toed shoes and a white blouse. Cool but discreet, whilst giving a hint of her femininity. MacRae smiled, reflecting on their past, how close they'd been, the intensity of their passion.

A gust of wind swirled along the dusty road next to them, bringing MacRae back to the present...sharing a late breakfast at a street cafe in a bustling suburb of Lagos in Nigeria, with a Medecins a Travers Les Frontiers international aid doctor and a young woman just rescued from the horrors of captivity with the Boko Haram militia army for nearly three months.

Tasmania seemed an awfully long way away, although it had only been thirty-six hours since MacRae had answered Marion's phone call atop Mount Wellington or Kunanyi. He'd listened as she explained the situation, then booked the first flight over.

It had been an intensely emotional moment when he'd joined them in the hotel late the previous evening, seeing Hassana safe again, and Marion after what seemed like a lifetime. The flight had been gruelling though, and a good night's sleep had been his first priority. Now it was time to get up to speed with the situation.

He watched as Marion speared pieces of yam on her fork, savouring the flavour as she chewed. She said nothing, hoping that MacRae couldn't see her inner turmoil from seeing him again after so long.

She glanced at him from the corner of her eye. He seemed to have barely aged since she'd last seen him. He had such a strong physical presence, and she was still drawn to his blue-grey eyes and the warmth of his smile. Her eyes drifted subconsciously to his left side as she remembered the scar on his torso, a knife wound not far from his heart, the legacy of intervening in a domestic dispute when he was a young police officer. That incident had set him on the path of law enforcement around the world, and without it they would never have met.

'It's a miracle she survived her ordeal,' MacRae said, breaking into Marion's thoughts.

She nodded. 'She's one tough young woman. God knows what she was subjected to, and having to watch her sister die so horribly. She hasn't opened up about it at all really.' She brought another piece of fruit to her lips, then paused looking quizzically at MacRae. 'She wanted to wait until you were here.'

MacRae glanced inside the gloomy interior of the cafe, watching the outline of Hassana in the shadows at the counter, ordering food.

'So how did she come to be in your care?'

Marion smiled grimly. 'The military focus here is solely on eliminating Boko Haram so they're never much good at looking after their victims, especially when they've all died of some horrible disease.'

'All except one,' MacRae said.

'So by the time we were called in to assess the medical situation the soldiers who'd discovered the camp and killed the militia had totally freaked out.'

MacRae pulled out his phone, and opened the file of photos Marion had sent him, flicking through them one by one, shaking his head at the horrible facial deformities. 'Not surprising given the state of the bodies.'

Marion peered over to see. 'Yes, I think there was a fair bit of superstition in it too. It's easier to blame something like this on the Devil or witchcraft.'

'That's why they torched the place?' MacRae asked.

'Yes, by the time I arrived they'd destroyed most of the evidence of what had been going on.' She shuddered. 'I had to be very careful trying to intervene, they were seriously spooked. So I only really got the photos and not much else.'

MacRae looked around as Hassana approached, a tall glass full of fruit and ice in her hand. 'Well, you did manage to save one extremely valuable thing.'

Marion spoke quietly to MacRae. 'Only just. Some of the soldiers thought it was the work of the Devil that she was the only survivor, and maybe she should be killed too. Luckily calmer heads prevailed until I got there, and the army were glad for her to be taken away and released into my care. Even the medical clinic weren't interested in her as there was no medical evidence from the camp, and Hassana seems to be perfectly healthy.'

Marion turned towards Hassana as she sat next to MacRae, placing her hand on her forearm. 'But she only wanted to talk to you about what had happened, didn't you?'

Hassana grinned shyly at MacRae, huge brown eyes blinking at him, nodding her head as she took a long sip of the drink through a brightly coloured straw, then she spoke. 'You promised me you'd look after me. You said it to Dr Evan.'

The words hung in the thick heat of the African air, a promise being called in after the most terrible events.

MacRae sighed, his heart heavy, the death of Holgate still haunting and raw. He met her eyes. 'Yes, I promised, and now I'll do what I can to look after you.'

A few flies buzzed lazily around the table looking for a chance to settle on their food, then giving up to pursue a cart of live chickens being carted along the road next to them.

'So Hassana, are you ready to tell me what happened after the militia took you and the other children from the village that day?'

She lowered her eyes, focusing intently on sucking the chilled liquid up the straw, then nodded, steeling herself to relive the nightmare. 'I so missed this when I was...' She paused, searching for the words. 'Away.'

She grimaced as the cold attacked her sinuses, giving her an ice-cream headache. 'We'd all heard what happens to children taken by Boko Haram, the boys made to fight and die for the cause, the girls sold for ransom, taken as wives, or used as slaves for the men. And at first that's what they did.' She shuddered. 'But nothing prepared us for what happened next.'

MacRae and Marion listened in silence.

'We saw the boys being trained, taken into the bush with guns, coming back beaten if they didn't do what they were told. Sometimes the boys were made to hurt us.' Tears formed in her eyes. 'I knew them, they were my friends, but if they didn't do it they were hit with sticks. One boy fought back and the man got a knife...' Her words caught in her mouth.

Marion reached over to touch her arm.

Hassana recoiled at the act of tenderness, tension etched across her face, then she relaxed. 'Then one day the boys and some of the men were gone, off to fight the government I suppose. We thought maybe things would get better, maybe the government would pay a ransom to get us back. But then the doctors came.'

She sucked her straw noisily around the bottom of the almost-empty glass.

'We were so excited to see the clean white cars come into the camp, and the men and women in doctor's coats come to see us. Surely they were here to help us? We were happy to go into the tents and be checked and measured, even for the injections they said were to keep the diseases away. But then we...' she paused to correct herself, 'They started to get sick, and their faces changed, those things growing on them.'

Marion nodded, taking notes on her phone as Hassana described the symptoms of the advancing disease, interjecting occasionally with a question, or for clarification.

'...And one by one they died, everyone I knew, but so horrible I didn't even recognise them anymore. I hated them, they were so ugly, even my own sister.' Her eyes moved from Marion to MacRae, imploring forgiveness, tears forming. 'How could I hate my own sister as she died in front of me?'

MacRae moved around the table, placing an arm around her shoulders as she sobbed. 'It wasn't your fault.'

'Why was I the only one to live? I didn't even feel sick, while they died.'

'Did they treat you differently to the others?' Marion said.

Hassana blew her nose noisily into the handkerchief MacRae offered her.

'No, they gave me the same injections from the same bottles, and every time they came and visited us to measure us, take our blood, they questioned me. It was like they were angry that I wasn't getting sick too.'

She held up her empty glass, looking at Marion with a hopeful, toothy grin. 'Can I have another one?'

'I think that should be okay.' Marion smiled as she pressed some coins into the outstretched hand.

MacRae watched as Hassana ran into the cool darkness of the cafe, then leaned back in his chair letting out a long sigh.

'What the hell were they up to? It's not unusual for the militia to take kids from villages they attack, as child soldiers or sex slaves, but medical experiments? That's something new to me. I don't get it.'

Marion's fork clinked against her plate. 'Me neither. Maybe it was a way of raising money for the militia, they provide services for illegal medical tests in exchange for funding their cause?'

She frowned. 'There's always been a history of dodgy medical trials in third world countries where the standards are lax or non-existent, and away from the prying eyes of the western regulators.'

'This was something else though,' MacRae said. 'Who conducts trials where all the participants develop the disease and die, and why only the girls, no boys?'

He shuddered as he recalled the photos again of the victims, the mutilated faces making them barely recognisable as human.

'All the participants died except one,' Marion pointed out, checking to see where Hassana was, still inside the cafe. 'From what she described it seems they knew what was going to happen to the subjects, they didn't try to arrest the process, let alone reverse it. In fact they were frustrated that she didn't die as well.'

MacRae watched as a couple of heavily armed soldiers sauntered past them on a cracked and broken concrete footpath, boots kicking up little swirls of dust with each step, assault rifles slung across their chest, a reminder of how dangerous this place could be. One of them met MacRae's eyes. MacRae briefly held his gaze then looked away. Trouble was never far away here.

'So I guess that makes her pretty special, if there's an experiment that kills all the female subjects but despite their best efforts she survives.'

Marion nodded. 'And people don't usually like to lose something special, something like Hassana that they've obviously invested a lot of time and money in.'

Something was niggling in the back of MacRae's mind. What else made her even more special in this situation? He thought back to when Holgate had first introduced them, then it came to him.

'There's something else that I think may be significant. The name *Hassana* means twin, presumably she was the second born.'

'So?' Marion gave him a quizzical look.

'Well, twins are often asked to participate in health studies aren't they? Or forced into sadistic experiments like those done on Jews in the Nazi concentration camps in the Second World War.'

'Yes.' Marion nodded slowly. 'Twins are genetically identical, it causes problems in DNA testing. It's even led to law enforcement not being able to identify who's responsible for a crime based on DNA evidence. So science is always intrigued by their similarities and differences.'

'Well in this case two identical sisters have been treated exactly the same way in the same environment, yet one has been unaffected by the experiment...'

'...which makes her extremely special.' Marion said.

'So we'd better take really good care of her until we find out what's going on,' MacRae said.

His face broke into a smile as Hassana emerged into the sunlight, a frosty bottle of cola in her hand. 'But with all the evidence destroyed by the army, I'm not sure where we start looking for the truth.'

'Well you could start with the hire car company that the doctors were using.' Hassana sat back at the table, joining the conversation. 'I mean, who except the Road Runner, calls a car company Acme Car Hire.' She broke into laughter.

'Sorry?' Marion wrinkled her brow.

Hassana, smiled patiently. 'When we were little we loved to watch those American cartoons with that crazy coyote always chasing the road runner bird across the desert. And everything was always called *Acme.*'

Marion nodded.

'Well, the cars the doctors came to visit in were all plain white, but you could see where the car company name stickers had been peeled off and left a shadow from the sun where the letters used to be. Acme Car Hire, the name always made me smile. And one of the car number plates made me sure God was telling me I'd see you again.' She looked at MacRae. 'It started off with ROO, just like your Australian kangaroos. And I was right,' she said triumphantly.

MacRae grinned at her. 'Well aren't you observant? Now this is something for me chase.'

~

MacRae leaned forward in the front seat of the sweet smelling taxi, a scented plastic pineapple swinging from the sun visor dangerously close to his eyes as he peered at the names of the shop fronts and businesses as they drove slowly past. He'd left Marion to take Hassana shopping for some new clothing, and hailed a taxi to take him across town to look for the hire car company.

The taxi driver glanced at a blue marker dot on his phone GPS tracker, the cracked screen sparkling in the sun and obscuring the location every now and then. 'Don't worry boss, it's around here somewhere.'

Then MacRae saw it, a neat but modest glassed shop front nestled amongst rows of cheap clothing retailers. 'There it is, pull over here.'

He took a handful of notes from his wallet.

'Would you like me to wait?' The driver asked hopefully. It had been a quiet morning so far. But MacRae was already gone.

~

He wandered down the footpath, checking out the bustling businesses. This city, despite facing all the issues of a growing metropolis in a developing country, had an energy, a vibrancy of people doing their best to build a better life. The colourful clothing worn by the women suggested a hopefulness despite the obstacles of overpopulation and poverty.

Laneways full of motorcycles squeezing past each other and pedestrians led off either side of the main road. MacRae headed down the first to his left and his hunch was proven correct. There was an access to a rutted car park full of cars and small trucks ready to rent. The wire mesh fence surround was too high to climb easily, but he was able to see most of the number plates, but none showing the letters ROO. Time to talk to the management.

The air conditioning was a welcome relief from the rising temperature outside as he entered the office, and he was greeted enthusiastically by *Roger, Assistant Manager*, as described on the name tag pinned to the front of his immaculately pressed white shirt, his face in a fixed broad smile as he anticipated some good business coming from this well dressed foreigner. But the smile slowly dropped as MacRae politely but persistently asked questions about the cars being rented to a private medical company.

'I'm sorry sir, but all rental agreements are confidential between us and the client, as I'm sure you would like yours to be if you choose to rent from us.'

MacRae pressed a little harder.

'The company renting from you has been involved in possibly illegal activities. I'm sure you'd prefer to not be caught up in any kind of police investigation?'

Roger flinched at MacRae's words. 'We conduct all our business in good faith. So if there's nothing else I can do to help you...'

'Well perhaps there is, let's go and see what vehicles you have available in your yard to rent me...' MacRae pulled out his wallet as he walked, ensuring Roger could see the thick wad of notes, '...and see if we can come to an agreement.'

~

MacRae smiled as he drove the small white sedan out of the yard, heading for the address across town the assistant manager had given him. This was one very expensive car hire for a day, as the man had kept silent about the medical company's details until MacRae had passed him more US dollars than he'd usually earn in a month. But finally it had been too much of a temptation, apparently client confidentiality wasn't so important anymore, and a company name, probably false, and local address had been scrawled on the back of MacRae's business card.

MacRae wove the car carefully through the chaotic traffic in streets where the only road rule seemed to be don't hit anyone else, with cars, trucks and motorcycles alike threading their way between gridlocked vehicles with only millimetres between them. But he'd experienced this in many places his work had taken him around the world, and soon settled into the rhythm, taking twenty five minutes to find the right street.

He drove past the address, noting an absence of any signage or identification, pulling over to park a few shops further down. This was very much more a light industrial area. Fewer people wandered the footpaths, and many of the building frontages were shuttered, seemingly deserted. He drew a few curious glances from street vendors hawking anything from fruit and freshly cooked meat skewers, to sunglasses, as he wandered back to the address he was interested in, and wondered if his hire car was going to be okay where he'd left it. But then he'd probably paid enough with the bribe to replace it anyway, even without the insurance.

Up close the building didn't reveal any more than he'd seen from the car. A two story brick building, faded yellow render desperately attempting to cling to the walls, small windows on both the ground and first floor covered in a rusty steel mesh. No signage or anything else to identify it. The rental car company had been given contact details for the client at this address, but apart from that all the arrangements had been made online from overseas, including the payments, so there were no leads to follow there.

The front door to the building was recessed in a small alcove. MacRae stepped off the street, turned the handle and pushed, but the lock held. The fierce African sun had cast him in deep shadow, and a quick glance back into the street showed he was concealed. A half step back and he thrust his right boot hard into the door near the lock. It moved slightly with a sharp crack, and flew open on the second kick.

He checked the street a final time and hadn't attracted any attention, and despite an unsettling feeling in his gut that this was all too easy he slipped inside, pushing the door closed behind him.

Fifty metres down the street, the assistant manager from the car rental company smiled. This was indeed going to be a very profitable day. First this man MacRae bribes him for the name and address of a client, and now he was following the client's instructions to inform them if anyone enquired about them, so he was going to collect handsomely from them as well. He settled back in the seat of his car, the engine idling to keep the air conditioning running, and watched to see what Mr MacRae would do next.

~

He was too late, that was the unfortunate conclusion. The more MacRae looked the less he found. This organisation must be good at operating with a minimal footprint. Rent a space, use the least equipment possible, and be ready to clear out on a moment's notice. Like when your operation is unravelled by the army.

The power had been disconnected and despite the bright morning sunshine it was gloomy inside. He went from room to room methodically, starting on the ground floor then moving to the first floor via a rickety wooden staircase, checking out all the cupboards and drawers, empty filing cabinets and office desks. Nothing. So he dropped a level. Most people, even trained operators, get lazy sometimes, no-one likes crawling around on their knees, and that is sometimes their only mistake. But it had become a habit for MacRae when he travelled, always taking that last moment to look underneath everything in a hotel room before he vacated, and more than once he'd found something important that either he or someone else would wish they hadn't left behind.

It was a slow process as he went around each room again, examining the edge of each piece of carpet, under the furniture, peering into the darkness with his phone light for illumination. Then, as he neared the end of the final room, cursing to himself that it was going to ruin the knees of a good pair of pants for nothing, he saw it, the corner of a small piece of paper projecting out of the back of a drawer in a small desk. Too much had been stuffed in by the previous occupants, and this had slipped down the back unnoticed.

He lay on his side and reached under the desk, fingers feeling for the texture, then gently pulling it free. It was a shipping receipt, printed out automatically and attached when items were shipped.

His eyes scanned the document. Half of it was missing, but there was enough to spark his interest. It was for a case of syringes, shipped across the continent from a medical supplies company in Sweden. The address matched the office in Lagos, but there was no company name. However with the date, address and consignment details it might just be enough.

MacRae placed it on a table near a window and took a photo with his phone, attached it to a text message and clicked *send*, then folded the document and placed it in his pocket. He spent another ten minutes finishing his search, then satisfied that he hadn't missed anything, went back into the brilliant sunshine in the street, pulling the shattered door gently shut behind him.

He was pleasantly surprised to see his rental car was untouched where he'd left it and climbed in, opening the windows to flush the stifling air before he drove out into the traffic back to the hotel, oblivious to the car at the end of the street slowly pulling out into the traffic behind him.

~

Across the world at her cosy home in the country, Sarah glanced at her phone as it pinged with the new message from MacRae. She pondered his request, keeping her hot cup of coffee at her lips, softly blowing air across the steaming surface, then opened the attached photo and noted the key details.

She liked her life now, freelancing as a journalist, choosing the stories and deadlines she wanted. Master of her own fate she liked to think. And it was certainly less dangerous or distressing than travelling the world in war zones, or famine afflicted African nations watching children die of starvation or disease.

But then there was the side projects she did for MacRae. No job was ever the same, finding out obscure information for him to assist in his work as a security adviser. And she had to admit this was the exciting stuff.

She fired up her laptop, searching for medical supply companies in Sweden, and found the one she was looking for.

She'd done this many times in her career as an investigative journalist, so she sat straight at her work desk, closed her eyes, getting into character, took a deep breath, and dialled the number.

She subconsciously drummed her fingers on the desk top as she waited for the number to connect, wondering about the person in Customer Services who'd take her call. Hopefully they were in a cooperative mood. No matter if they weren't, she rarely failed to get the information she was after when she made pretext calls.

Then it was on, a male speaking English with a strong Scandinavian accent.

'Good afternoon, Beauman Pharmaceuticals, this is Larson, how may I help you?'

Sarah launched into him. 'Larson is it? How do you spell that?... never mind. Well I'm hoping you're the one that can finally answer my question, as I'm sick of being passed around your customer services department like a piece of refuse.'

'But madam, my records indicate I'm the first to take your call...'

Sarah grinned to herself. She actually quite enjoyed the game.

'And doesn't that say it all about the efficiency of your customer services systems? You're the third person I've spoken to in the last thirty minutes and I'm just about to escalate my complaint formally to your management...' She let the words hang, giving him time to digest her tirade, waiting for the desire to help kick in.

'Please accept my apologies. If you'd be kind enough to explain your problem rest assured I'll do whatever I can to resolve it.'

Bingo. Sarah spent the next ten minutes explaining how a consignment of syringes had been delivered to one of her company's field offices in Nigeria but they'd been damaged. She'd been trying to enter the loss in the accounts but there was confusion around which subsidiary had originally ordered the equipment.

Larson had hesitated. 'I'm not sure if I'm able to release the information over the phone.'

'Even though I've provided the delivery address and consignment number?'

'Our company procedure states...'

Sarah changed tack, allowing a hint of panic into her voice.

'Look Larson, the truth is it was partially my mistake for confusing the order, we've got so many field offices around the world, so many contractors, and I'm worried about my performance review next week. This will really help me out, and our business relationship of course.' she added hastily.

There was a long silence at the other end then, 'Well okay, I guess if it's in the interests of our business relationship...'

Sarah looked at the company name she'd jotted down. Not one she was familiar with, but she was sure she'd soon know a lot more about them.

CHAPTER 10

GONE

E dison took a deep breath of the fresh sea air, soaking up the warmth of the morning sun on her face. This was indeed a lovely location to work, an Antarctic marine research organisation sited in a converted warehouse on the working docks of Hobart. It's a shame the conference she was attending on population trends and global warming was so boring and predictable. But then she accepted she had a responsibility to fly the flag for her organisation locally as well as at the conferences she attended in more exotic locations like Paris and Hawaii.

But thirty minutes break between presentations was barely enough to refresh outside the dull interior of the lecture theatre and the droning voices accompanying the endless slide presentations.

She was munching a chocolate coated muffin hungrily while balancing a coffee cup on a saucer with her other hand, when her phone rang. The climate scientist chatting in her face shot her a barely disguised look of irritation as she excused herself with a wave of her hand, placing the saucer on a shiny black bollard at the edge of the wharf to retrieve her phone from her purse. It must be important as she gave out this number to virtually no-one.

'Edison speaking.'

The voice at the other end didn't identify itself, but she instantly knew it was the African contractor.

'I believe we have some information that may be beneficial for you regarding the recently compromised project in Nigeria. Can you talk?'

Edison barely contained herself. She'd been worried sick about how she was going to resolve this. She glanced around. No-one was within earshot.

'Sure, go ahead.'

'We've been contacted by a local source to advise that the sole surviving female subject from the project has been located, still in Nigeria.'

'Can you be sure?' This was almost too good to be true.

'I'm sending you through a photo of the girl now.'

Edison's phone pinged as she received the picture in a text message.

'She's in the care of a female western aid worker and a Caucasian male named Ian MacRae at a hotel. Forwarding their pictures now.'

Another ping on Edison's phone.

She opened the texts, taking in the face of the African girl, then the pretty but serious looking woman, and finally the man. He was well built, a steely look caught in his eyes by the discreet photographer in a hotel lobby.

Could she dare hope for too much? She took another look around her. A couple of young female scientists walked past her eating fruit, engrossed in an animated conversation.

'Can you recover the girl? She's uniquely valuable to us at this point.'

There was a long silence at the other end.

'Anything can be organised for the right price.'

'Money isn't an issue. Make it happen.'

A beep and the call went dead.

Edison enjoyed the sun on her face a moment longer, ate the last bite of muffin and wandered back inside, distractedly leaving her coffee perched on the bollard, seagulls circling above it curiously. Things were looking up. Maybe she'd even enjoy the rest of the conference now.

~

Roger, the Assistant Manager at the hire car company couldn't help feeling nervous as he walked out of the floating slum area of Lagos in his shiny suit. This was not his world, but in Nigeria everyone knew someone who could arrange to get things done, legally or otherwise.

The Area Boys ran the streets in gangs, informally acting as police, vigilantes and tax collectors, depending on the day and their mood. The real police and military generally turned a blind eye to their activities as long as basic law and order was kept...and the right share of the money raised went to the right people in power.

But then there was the other side of their activities that he was paying for today. Well not him, but the contractor he'd been in contact with about the man snooping around asking questions.

It had obviously been a smart move, following the man to his hotel. For a few US dollars slipped in the hand of the hotel duty manager taking a smoking break around the side of the hotel, Roger had been given the mystery man's name and room number and told he was staying with two women, one foreigner, one local. God knows what he was up to, and why the contractor was so interested, but the information was apparently valuable. When Roger had included photos taken in the lobby on his phone as they walked past, the contractor had been very generous indeed.

But he had to admit it was with a mixture of excitement and fear that he agreed to the request to engage some locals to arrange the local girl's kidnap and delivery to the contractor.

He knew everyone was doing their best to make their way in the bustling, growing but still corrupt developing African nation, but he also knew he was crossing a dangerous line.

His childhood friend on the fringe of the Area Boys world had made the introduction, and he'd passed on the details as he'd been instructed by the contractor. He stepped off the last of the floating walkways onto the dusty gravel industrial wasteland where he'd left his car, physically and mentally leaving the shanty town behind him.

Now it was out of his hands, and suddenly returning to the boring world of hire cars seemed safe and desirable.

~

The two rough looking men in their early twenties cautiously entered the hotel corridor from the service passage door next to the elevators. The white bell-boy jackets were too tight for their muscular frames, and they'd only pass a cursory inspection by the security staff stationed throughout the lobby.

They'd been let in a side entrance to the hotel laundry at the back of the building as arranged, and had been told they could leave the same way unchallenged and unobserved.

They quickly found the door they were looking for, and after pulling his jacket straight, the shorter of the men stood in front of the peep hole, smiled broadly, and knocked three times.

'Room service.'

Inside the room Marion was drying her hair after a shower when she heard the muffled voice outside the door. She initially thought it was MacRae returning from the shops, but then realised there was a deeper tone, and before she could say a word she heard Hassana squeal with delight as she ran to the door.

'I've never had room service before...what are they bringing?'

Marion called out, 'Don't open the door, we haven't ordered anyth...'

But it was too late, as Hassana unhooked the security chain and released the lock. Instantly the door swung open and the two men charged inside, the first pushing Hassana up against a wall, sliding a small revolver from his belt and holding it to her face. The second man's eyes flashed around the room and spotted Marion in the bathroom. He rushed over and jammed a foot in the door just as she tried to slam it shut.

~

The rattan fan swirled lazily overhead as MacRae walked through the hotel lobby. He nodded and smiled at the reception staff as he passed, putting a bag of groceries down briefly as he waited for the elevator to arrive. An elderly couple shared the ride up with him, getting out on the third floor, one before his. He chuckled to himself at their matching sandshoes, cargo pants and rain jackets, all displaying the correct expensive logo for the well-heeled senior traveller. Maybe he'd end up exploring the few parts of the world he hadn't already visited for his work one day with a partner, looking just like them. But he doubted it.

His footsteps were silent on the plush carpet as he walked along the corridor to their room, muffled voices coming through the door as he swiped his electronic key card. Things were finally looking up. Another few days for the girl to recuperate, sort out the formalities, and then they'd be out of the country to help her start a new, and hopefully better and safer life.

He pushed the handle down with one hand...it was unlocked... and used his shoulder to open the door, still holding the shopping bag. He looked across the room to Marion standing with her back against the window, arms crossed behind her, a bright halo of sunlight shining through her hair. He was having trouble reading her face in the shadows. She looked angry, or was it frightened? Then he followed her eyes to Hassana being held against a wall to his left by a man holding a sleek black revolver, and his companion hurtling across the room at MacRae.

Time seemed to freeze as he took in the situation and prepared to act. But in reality a lifetime of dealing with danger had finely tuned him to react in milliseconds.

MacRae jerked his arm upwards, spraying groceries into the face of the man coming at him, a can of tomatoes colliding with his teeth with a sharp crack. The man swung a lumbering fist at MacRae's face, or at least where it used to be, but MacRae had already stepped to the side and forwards, throwing an elbow into the man's nose, snapping him backwards to the floor in a spatter of blood.

MacRae barely slowed with the impact as he ran at the man holding Hassana. The man seemed shocked to see his companion fall, then keeping one hand pinning the girl he swung the gun wildly at MacRae, trying to get a clear shot. But he was too slow as MacRae barrelled into the side of his chest, shoulder held low.

The man slammed backwards into the wall, releasing his grip on the girl, the gun falling from his other hand. MacRae had also landed heavily against the wall, both men winded, struggling to recover. But it was the man on the floor behind them who was first back up, spitting blood as he charged into the fray, throwing his weight onto MacRae's back, linking his arms around him.

MacRae was fit, a body used to the tough routines of cross-fit training, but he struggled to break the man's grip, so he swung sideways flipping his hip up and dropping his upper body as he moved backwards, throwing the man over his shoulder against the wall.

Marion screamed as she pulled against the cable ties binding her wrists to the window lock.

Hassana saw her chance, running to where the gun had slid under a cabinet, fingers searching for the weapon as MacRae turned to face his foes. This time they moved in unison, darting to either side of him, not giving him the opportunity to tackle them one at a time in the confined space of the hotel room. The shorter man threw his arms around MacRae again, whilst his companion lashed out with a kick to MacRae's solar plexus.

MacRae pushed away the pain and leaned forward, the man behind him leaning with him. Then MacRae stamped down hard on his foot, lifted his arms up and out sharply, breaking the man's grip, and flicked his head backwards into the man's already bloodied nose. He then twisted sideways, driving an elbow into the man's kidney, the man's face creasing in agony as his knees buckled to the floor.

To the left, Hassana's fingers had found the revolver. She squealed triumphantly as she pulled it out and turned to face the room...straight into the arms of the bigger man. A push of his hand to her chest sent her flying back into the cabinet, but not before he'd snatched the gun from her grasp.

MacRae readied to throw himself at the man with the gun, but it was too late, the weapon held in a steady hand pointing at Marion's face as she struggled to break free.

'That's enough,' he barked, everyone in the room stopping in their tracks, the sound of the combatant's panting the only noise breaking the silence.

The shorter man approached MacRae, moving gingerly to protect his bruised kidney and pulling a plastic bag of cable ties from his pocket. He pointed at MacRae's hands.

MacRae stared into this eyes, then the bigger man's voice boomed across the room. 'Do it.'

MacRae put his wrists together and moved his hands forward. The shorter man grinned, knowing they'd won. He wiped the blood from his face with a dirty shirt sleeve, then stepped forward and drove a hook punch into MacRae's jaw, snapping his head sideways into unconsciousness.

~

Marion leaned in to check MacRae's pupils as his eyes fluttered open. He tried to raise himself from the hotel room floor, but his head swam, Marion gently pressing his chest back down until he recovered.

Another minute or so and his vision cleared enough for him to see the other figures in the room. The hotel manager spoke to the head of hotel security, his arms waving in agitation as he sought to understand how guests could be assaulted in the rooms of his fine establishment. From the snatches of conversation he seemed more concerned about the hotel's reputation than the well-being of the guests.

A couple of bored-looking police officers consulted their phones, then noticed MacRae was getting to his feet.

Marion steadied his arm as he spoke.

'Where is she?'

Marion was silent for a moment, tears welled in her eyes.

Then the words he was dreading. 'They took her, Ian.'

The police officers came over, their first question making it clear how this was going to go.

'So Mr MacRae, what is a white Australian man doing in a hotel room with an under-age Nigerian girl?'

~

CHAPTER 11

BEACH

The gentle sound of waves lapping on the golden sand washed rhythmically over the consciousness of Magnus Crane as he reclined on the cane banana lounge. A historical novel was held open by the fingers of his left hand, whilst he raised a frosted cocktail glass carefully to his lips. He smiled as the crisp melon scent filled his nose, anticipating the first delicious sip of Midori whetting his lips from the Japanese Slipper.

This was always a favourite cocktail, introduced to him by a well-travelled journalist who brought his love of the drink back from an assignment in Japan, back when it was only known in its country of origin. He always associated the taste with late nights discussing the state of the world, often followed by a hangover. He placed the glass on the table to his side, freeing up his hand to adjust his hat against the harsh ultraviolet rays from above.

He frowned, looking down at his naked stomach. He looked after himself pretty well, a rigorous and regular exercise routine over the years had given him a lithe and muscular body, carrying virtually no body fat. Hell, at a pinch he could run a half marathon in a time to put many men ten years younger than him to shame.

But he had a weakness for a tan. And he knew you have to be careful as you get older, can't take your health for granted anymore. He'd seen friends die an awful death from skin cancer, starting as a freckle subtly changing colour after a few too many youthful days lying in the sun, then spreading undetected throughout their bodies until it was too late.

Then there was his personal brush with the horrors of cancer, his beautiful, perfect daughter taking an agonising year to wither and die from a rare brain tumour before she even reached her teens. And always in the back of his mind that it may have been caused by him unknowingly passing on a genetic mutation to her...a genetic mutation caused by his exposure to the poisonous chemical cocktail filling the air in Bophal all those years ago. It was another demonstration of what an over populated and polluted world could do to humans, a species with an already plummeting fertility rate. The face of his wife drifted into his mind. It had aged her so, watching their daughter die. Ultimately their marriage hadn't withstood the tragedy, but it had given him the reflection and focus to return to the research and goals he now pursued with such a passion.

Then his smile returned as fond memories of vacations in breathtakingly beautiful coastal resorts and towns came flooding back. He was a privileged man indeed, and despite the tragedy had lived a life that would be the envy of most.

Beyond the beach and sea, the sun was slowly sinking to the horizon. A glance at his watch, he still had time to work on his tan a little longer before getting back to work, but the sun was losing its heat. He leaned sideways, his hand groping around, then fingers wrapping around a sleek silver remote control next to his cocktail. A press of a button to activate voice control, then he spoke, his voice clear and crisp. 'Climate control...reset time to midday.' A pause. 'Make it the Caribbean. And no waves, but a gentle breeze please.'

A brief flash and the wall-length screen in front of him changed from the Pacific Island scene to a secluded beach in Jamaica, the sun high overhead. At the same time the ultraviolet lights mounted on the ceiling adjusted to provide the appropriate levels of brightness and radiated heat, and concealed fans whirred into life sending cooling gusts of air across his toned body. He listened with satisfaction as the wave generating pumps went silent. Yes, he was privileged indeed to have his own personalised artificial beach environment, in the safety of a hardened underground home that would withstand a nuclear attack. Or, he chuckled, a zombie invasion.

His eyes flicked across a few more pages of the novel as he absorbed the story and characters, enjoying how the plot was advancing. He'd always loved the power of books, whether paper or ebooks, to share storytelling and transport the readers to another place or time, perhaps challenge their beliefs, or even arouse them. It also never ceased to surprise him that the characters, the people, their wants and needs, their vulnerabilities, and their greed and aggression towards each other never changed. Fiction truly mirrored real life.

A purring noise sounded from his phone. He glanced at the screen, it was Edison, the manager of the research facility in Australia, requesting a video call. The last time they'd spoken it had been about the Africa Program, and she had not given him good news, no detail, just that it had been raided and closed down. He closed the book, dropping it to the table beside him with a grunt of frustration. Now the spell was broken, he was thinking about work again, so he might as well get on with it.

A swipe of his finger and Edison's face filled the screen. Edison spoke quickly, her image crisp and clear, a testament to the quality of the communications systems Crane had installed in the bunker.

'Hi Magnus, I've got some good news for you on the devil facial tumour program.' The words tumbled out, eager to please. 'An army unit stumbled across the militia camp in Nigeria and we thought we'd lost our most important subject in the human trials...' She paused a moment, leaning forward so her face filled the screen as she tried to peer behind Crane. 'Are you on the beach? I thought it was late evening in the US.'

Crane sighed. 'Maybe I'm not in the US at the moment.'

It was none of Edison's fucking business where he was, and he certainly wasn't going to let Edison in on the facilities he had on hand at his underground bunker. Lack of focus, that was the trouble with Edison lately. And it was becoming a problem Crane was going to be forced to address before too long.

'You were saying?'

Edison snapped back as though she'd been slapped.

'Yes, well the army went in in their usual heavy-handed way and made a nice job of destroying all the evidence of what had been going on in the camp, saving us the grief of trying to organise a cover-up. It seems their superstitions went into overdrive when they saw some of the diseased subjects.' Her mind wandered again. '... awful deformities. So they just torched everything, the bodies, the labs, everything.'

Crane grunted. 'Did we have records of the research completed before they were overrun? This program has real promise.'

Relief washed across Edison's face, Crane didn't seem too angry. 'Yes, I've kept the contractor at best practice, uploading all the results to the cloud as they record them.'

Crane shook his head. Typical, the best portable medical research and communications technology on the planet in the hands of a terrorist organisation, and yet all that matters to them is money and power, sought by any means possible, including ancient Soviet AK-47s.

Edison's voice broke through again. '...so the army didn't think the girl was anything other than an ordinary hostage and released her into the care of an NGO medic on the scene.'

Crane jolted upright. 'The girl with immunity to the tumours survived? But she's back in the community? Jesus, we can't afford to lose her, she could be the key to us controlling this entire new disease.'

Edison knew she was on to a winner. 'Well everything has a price in Nigeria, so I put the word out for anyone enquiring about the research contractor or the army raid and got lucky. A man was snooping around asking about the cars the contractor leased, so the car hire rep followed him.'

Crane was interested now. 'And...'

Edison looked down, consulting notes. 'The man went to the office building the contractor had been using until the camp was raided and had a poke around.'

'Did he find anything?'

'I don't think so. We use them because they're discreet, and nimble. As soon as they got word the operation was busted they were out, all the documents, stripped everything that could identify them.'

Crane was relieved. 'Yes, they are good. That is why we use them.' One thing Crane did was reward competence and loyalty. But God help you if you let him down.

Edison's image froze as the internet connection lagged for a moment, then she continued. 'Then the man headed back to his hotel, and this is where it got interesting. The hire car rep had a chat to the manager and got the man's name, Ian MacRae, and...' Edison paused for effect, '...found out there were also two woman staying in the same room, one of them a local.'

Crane smiled at this stroke of good fortune. 'He's got the girl staying in a hotel in the city?'

Edison nodded enthusiastically. 'The rep hung around for a while and got a glimpse as they went out the lobby, took photos on his phone. It's grainy, but definitely her. I'll send you the photos.'

Crane chewed it over. 'Can you get resources on the ground to get her back?'

This time Edison really savoured the moment before answering. 'Already done. She's back in our care as we speak.'

Crane smiled. Edison had strung him along, but she obviously still could do good work. Maybe he should keep her around a bit longer after all.

⁓

Crane waited patiently after they ended the call for the photos to arrive, and was rewarded with the ping of an email notification. He opened the first photo, zooming in to focus on the two white faces in the hotel lobby, then googled their names. There wasn't a lot to find about the woman, other than an online employment profile detailing her time as a contract doctor with extensive experience with NGOs in trouble spots around the world. Crane's search on MacRae immediately brought up MacRae's business website, and within

minutes Crane felt he'd learned all he need to know about the man...
more than enough to wonder how he'd got involved in the Africa
Project. This was someone worth watching.

CHAPTER 12

CONFERENCE

MacRae and Marion arrived at the foyer of the office building in the city at the same time. Marion wore a light jacket pulled tight against the morning chill.

MacRae smiled. 'Not quite the weather you've been used to?'

Marion rubbed her hands together. 'No, not quite the same as an African morning.'

MacRae scanned the building directory and led the way to double glass doors on the left, a colourful logo painted down one side. He could see Sarah waiting inside as they approached.

She brushed her swipe card at the security lock and held the door open for MacRae and Marion, waving to the tattooed receptionist focusing on a fashion magazine as they entered.

MacRae took in the muted buzz of conversation from the occupied cubicles in the light and airy open plan space.

'So this is your official address for your contract journalism?'

Sarah talked over her shoulder. 'Sure is. I could work from home, but it's sometimes nicer to work from a funky building in the centre of town.'

She waved a hand towards the workstations to one side. 'It caters for anyone who needs either the facilities or company that a shared office offers. And you can hire space by the month, week, day, or even hour if you like.'

A bearded hipster in a cubicle decorated with black and white photos of landscapes made a noisy video call on his phone as they passed.

Sarah continued. 'You know what being your own boss can be like Ian. It's the same for me, freelance writing and research can be lonely, but here I enjoy the energy of the wannabe entrepreneurs and artists struggling to get their big break, but unable to afford their own office.'

She stopped at a door and swiped her card again.

'I usually work from a hot-desk, but today I've organised a conference room. I think we'll need the space and privacy.'

Sarah set up Marion and MacRae with WiFi linked to a big screen on the wall and an electronic whiteboard, then left them to it while she hit the kitchen to organise a pot of coffee.

An awkward silence filled the room between MacRae and Marion. MacRae had returned home to Tasmania a few days before Marion had arrived, and this was the first time they'd caught up in person.

'So how does it feel to be back in Hobart after such a long time?' MacRae said.

Marion unzipped her laptop bag. 'It's not quite the circumstances I would have expected to bring me back here, but it's nice to be staying with Stella at her apartment in the city.'

She placed the bag to one side.

MacRae had heard of Stella Coats, as an immunology scientist at the government research labs sometimes quoted in news stories, but they'd never met.

'When we became friends at the conference in New York years ago, we always said we'd catch up. So despite the circumstances I'm glad I've come.'

MacRae took off his jacket, folding it over the back of his chair. 'I'm glad you've come too. I think it's the only way we're going to make some sense of the events in Africa.'

Marion shrugged, looking at her laptop as it fired up.

'Yes, getting out of Nigeria was pretty awful, wasn't it?'

MacRae tried to meet her eyes. 'Less than ideal.'

Their departure had been rushed and frustrating.

'We had no choice, Marion. Whether it was deliberate or not, the local police seemed more intent on finding a reason to throw me in jail than finding who took Hassana.'

Marion knew he was right. She looked up. 'I felt so helpless, you being interviewed at the police station for hours on end, day after day, neither of us able to leave until they released our passports.'

'I know,' MacRae said. 'So much valuable time lost when maybe we...or perhaps they...could have made real progress in tracking her down.'

Marion's eyes narrowed. 'Incompetent assholes.'

She threw a pen hard onto the table, watching it bounce onto the floor. 'The only reason we got out at all was because I'd meticulously documented the course of events since we found Hassana with my boss at Medecins a Travers Les Frontiers. If they hadn't weighed in with their political muscle you...and our passports...might never have been released.'

MacRae retrieved the pen, passing it to Marion.

She took it back, then spoke, choosing her words carefully.

'How did they even find us Ian? I would have thought the police officer instincts that have always seemed so important to you would have sensed something was wrong?'

MacRae caught the change in tone. This was about more than what happened in Nigeria. It seemed they had unfinished business, but this wasn't the right time or place.

He opened his mouth to speak, just as the door swung open. Sarah placed a tray with cups, sugar and milk on the table, pushing the door closed with her foot. She sensed the tension.

'It seems a little chilly in here...maybe I should turn up the heating?'

MacRae laughed. 'I think a hot cup of coffee will do the trick.'

Sarah smiled at Marion as she poured. 'It's great to finally meet you Marion. Ian's told me a lot about you, it's just a shame we're meeting this way.'

Marion glanced at MacRae, her voice deadpan. 'It always seems to be challenging circumstances when we catch up.' Then she relaxed.

'He's told me a lot about you too Sarah, you've had quite a history together I believe?'

MacRae grinned sheepishly as he looked between the two women.

'Sugar anyone?'

An hour passed, then another, as they collated as much information as they could from the events of the last few months.

Sarah sighed. 'It doesn't seem to make much sense, any of it. Has Brad come up with anything?'

MacRae shook his head. 'We've had a bit of contact. I filled him in on Marion finding Hassana and then her being taken again at the hotel. He thinks she must be extremely important given the lengths they're going to keep her. He said if she's being kept in the country there's not much hope of finding her, but he's put an unofficial alert out for her with Interpol. It's a bit of a long shot but she might be flagged if someone tries to take her across a border.'

'It looks like we're pretty much on our own then.' Marion said.

'It seems so,' Sarah said. 'But maybe there's something you're missing because you're too close to everything. Let me approach it as an outsider.'

MacRae nodded. 'Sure. Go ahead.'

Sarah used her skills as a journalist, questioning Marion and MacRae's recall of how things had unfolded, then collating the information, trying to find leads to explore, breaking it down into topics on an electronic whiteboard.

'Okay, the key questions seem to be...'

The felt tip pen squeaked as she wrote bullet points.

'One. Who's running a drug trial that kills all,' She corrected herself. 'Almost all the participants?'

The pen squeaked again.

'Two. How did they track you down and arrange the kidnap in the hotel?'

Another dot point.

'Three. And where would they take the girl, given her apparent value?'

MacRae shifted in his seat, leaning forward, elbows on the table. 'Unfortunately I think the only conclusion we can draw is that it was probably me trying to track down the drug trial company that alerted them to where Hassana was. Presumably enquiring at the hire car company started things.'

His face clouded over. 'If we hadn't ended up being targeted by the local police I'd have had a chance to go and have a little chat with the hire car guy.'

Sarah smiled. She'd seen the kind of conversations MacRae had with people when he needed information. They didn't usually enjoy the experience, and they always told him what he needed to know.

'Well I think that horse has bolted. And I doubt the local police will even follow him up, despite what you told them, and it wouldn't be very smart to go back there for another go.'

Marion spoke. 'So if that's a dead end, do we have any other leads on the drug trial contractor?'

Sarah nodded. 'I've done some detective work with the consignment note Ian found in the rented offices in Nigeria, and I think I'm making progress. This company has a brief but interesting history, and I'm starting to uncover some curious links to other medical companies around the world. I'm not sure what to make of it all just yet. I've tried to contact them, but they're registered in an off-shore tax haven and I'm not getting anywhere.'

'What have you got so far?' MacRae said.

Sarah scrolled through some notes on her phone. 'There's a bit of online info suggesting they do contract work for some of the big pharma companies; a few years ago they were linked to anti-malaria trials in Malaysia for a company called Medici-Royal. Anyone heard of them?'

'Medici-Royal is one of the biggest multi-national pharmaceutical companies, based in the US I think,' Marion said. 'They've got a good reputation.'

'In an industry that at times has a pretty dubious reputation,' Sarah said.

'How so?' MacRae said.

Sarah leaned back in her chair. 'Well, my understanding is that developing drugs and therapies is a hugely expensive business, and the majority of drugs that show promise end up struggling to prove their efficacy and being approved for sale. So the drug companies have to make a profit on the relatively small number of drugs they develop that actually work.'

'So they minimise their development costs by sometimes outsourcing the drug trials to contractors.' MacRae said.

'That's it,' Sarah said. 'I came across a whole lot of stuff about drug trials gone wrong. Some run by big companies, some off-shored to places with lax regulation. And the crazy thing is that the drug companies don't have to report the failed drug trials to anyone, so a drug can fail a dozen trials, then be successful once, and the one successful trial is all they need to publish to market the drug and recoup their costs.'

'So there have been other trials like this one?' Marion said.

'Plenty of drug trials have ended badly. I came across a trial in the nineties for an anti-cancer drug, nothing special. The participants were a mix of community minded volunteers and those looking for an easy dollar. It was outsourced to a third party to run, and they were meant to increase the dosage over the first day to check for reactions, but they screwed up and gave the full dose first up. Within hours all the subjects were unconscious with total organ failure. They survived...just, but many had ongoing medical issues and they sued the contractor.' Sarah said. 'But nothing quite like this.'

'So this is pretty unique,' MacRae said. 'Is there anything I can do to help you with the research?'

Sarah shook her head. 'Not at the moment. I want to spend a little more time collating information, then let's have another look at it.' She turned to Marion. 'I think I'm going to end up with a list of names and corporations. Perhaps you can help me with background on them, given your experience in the field over the years?'

Marion nodded. 'I'll do what I can. I have plenty of contacts I can use for information too.'

MacRae stretched his arms over his head. He was starting to get antsy, too much talk, not enough getting done.

'It looks like there's not much I can do to help at the moment then. But there's something bothering me.'

Sarah looked at him curiously. 'Yes?'

'The photos Marion sent me from Nigeria when she'd first seen the trial subjects. It was hideous what the disease or whatever it is, had done to those girls.' He shuddered. 'They reminded me of the effects of the Tasmanian Devil facial tumour disease. It came out of nowhere here a few years back, spreads like wildfire in the native population, and deforms the devil's face so badly that they can't eat, and they starve to death, if the cancer doesn't kill them first.'

Sarah nodded. 'Yes, I've covered a few stories on it over the years. Pretty distressing stuff. When it hits them the growth rate is phenomenal, and it's highly infectious.'

'It makes the international press now and then,' Marion said. 'The Tasmanian Devil is a bit of a star, well at least the American cartoon version of it. And no-one likes the idea that a species can be taken from thriving, to the edge of extinction, in the space of a couple of years by a previously unknown disease.'

'So I'm wondering if there's anything we can learn from it, if there are any parallels in what happened to the girls in Nigeria, and why Hassana is so special,' MacRae said.

'It's a long shot, but worth pursuing,' Marion said. 'There have been numerous diseases appearing in humans that are thought to have originated in animals, jumping species somewhere along the way, SARS, AIDS and MERS to name a few, and humans have no natural resistance to them.'

'Well I've still got the contact details of the woman running the research program,' Sarah said. 'I'm pretty sure she's the director of the institute now. Let's get some background on the program, find a reason for you to pay her a visit.'

Marion's chair scraped the polished concrete floor as she stood. 'Oops, sorry for the noise. The restrooms are to the left?' She smiled sheepishly as she left the room.

MacRae's eyes lingered on her, then he bent down to sip his coffee. He wrinkled his nose as he tasted the tepid fluid, and glanced up to see Sarah watching him, a smile playing at the corner of her lips.

She looked back down to her keyboard, tapping *Tasmanian Devil facial tumour* into a search window.

'You really like her don't you?' She said without looking up.

'Is it that obvious?'

'I guess it is if you're looking.'

MacRae shrugged, tapping the top of his cup. 'We had a bit of a thing a long time ago, not sure if you'd call it a relationship. It didn't work out.'

'Do you mind if I ask why?' Sarah said.

MacRae chose his words carefully. He hadn't talked about this for a long time and the strength of his feelings had caught him off guard. 'We were both working all around the world, I was seconded to law enforcement agencies doing anti-terrorism work, Marion was mostly with NGOs doing aid work. It's funny how life throws people together sometimes, if there's a God perhaps she has a little joke now and then.' MacRae chuckled. 'Let's give two people intense chemistry, then make it impossible for them to make it work.'

Sarah smiled.

'Whenever our paths crossed we'd catch up, it was pretty intense, you know, living fast and dangerous, all the cliches.'

'So what happened?'

MacRae glanced across to the door, no sight of her returning yet.

'We started to try and plan our contracts so we could spend more time together, but it ended up compromising work for both of us.' He shrugged. 'She said she could see a future for us. Maybe I could too at times. But then I was offered a twelve month post in Iraq right when the violence there was at its worst, the insurrection after the American invasion was in full swing. I felt it was important for me to help keep things there together, for their country and ours. We had words about what was most important.'

'And you went?' Sarah said.

'Yes, I suggested she came too, do humanitarian work and we could be together. There was a huge need with the civilian population, but she was already committed in Haiti and said she couldn't, or wouldn't break her contract, so we called it quits. We swapped phone calls when we could for a while, but that was it.'

Sarah nodded, then gazed out the window, watching the wind blowing autumn leaves into flurries of golden brown on the city streets.

Silence filled the air, both of them lost in their thoughts. MacRae knew she was thinking the same thing, that Sarah had also been close to him, more than once. It was a long time since they'd met as travellers in Europe. She'd been on a ferry getting unwanted attention from a bunch of young guys...until she peeled a piece of fruit with a huge folding knife. He smiled at the thought. They'd travelled together for a while, even tried some drunken passion, then both realised they were best as friends. Then years later she'd found herself in serious trouble working as a journalist in Africa, and MacRae, with the help of Brad Schneider and unofficially the resources of the CIA, had got her out of the country. Sarah had come to stay with MacRae in Tasmania to recuperate, and ended up settling in the state. Then a couple of years ago they'd both been caught up in the terrorist plot to detonate a horrific weapon called Devil's Breath.

It was unspoken, but they had each other's back, a special bond, a rare friendship. He watched her for a moment, then as though she could sense his gaze she met his eyes. They both smiled; they knew some things are just as they are meant to be.

'Am I interrupting something?' Marion shut the door behind her and sat back down. They hadn't noticed her returning.

'Just reminiscing.' MacRae knocked back the last of his coffee. 'Right, let's get into this.'

'This is interesting.' Sarah said, the results of her search filling the big screen.

MacRae scanned the list. 'Mostly scientific papers...'

Sarah scrolled the screen down. 'Yes, but check these out.' Her mouse cursor highlighted a group of links to local news articles.

Now MacRae saw what had caught her eye, the eye of a journalist, always suspicious, looking for a different angle in everything.

TASMANIA DEVIL FACIAL TUMOUR RESEARCH SCIENTIST LOST IN FREAK MARITIME ACCIDENT.

'Okay,' Marion said. 'That's unusual but these things happen.'

Sarah read from the article out loud. 'Most experienced researcher...huge loss to the program.'

'No body was recovered...funeral to be held in the coming weeks for Dr Khan. Deepest sympathy to her young daughters and husband from Program Director Dr Laura Edison as a colleague and friend.' Marion added. 'Why has this sparked your interest?'

MacRae was way ahead of her. 'It's not just this article.'

He pointed at the screen lower down the list. 'It's this one too isn't it Sarah?'

'You got it Ian.' She hovered the mouse over another headline.

WILDLIFE PHOTOGRAPHER AND FILM MAKER MISSING IN CENTRAL HIGHLANDS.

This time MacRae read out loud. 'Kane Murdoch, known for his work documenting the secret life of the platypus and the Tasmanian Devil was reported missing by his wife when he failed to return from an expedition last week.'

'That's just a coincidence isn't it?' Marion said.

Sarah looked at MacRae. 'Journalists and ex-police officers don't like coincidences do we?'

MacRae picked up his phone. 'What's Dr Edison's number Sarah? I think it's time I paid her a visit.'

~

CHAPTER 13

INSTITUTE

Dr Laura Edison checked her watch as she sat in her office at the institute flicking distractedly through a pile of scientific papers she was supposed to be reviewing.

She was normally a calm and measured person, but this meeting had her intrigued, and if she was completely honest, a little worried. The work at the Institute often had a high profile, usually created deliberately to raise funds and garner support for the programs being undertaken, so it wasn't unusual to receive requests for interviews to discuss the research, particularly for the Tasmanian Devil facial tumour. It struck a chord with the local community, even though most of the population had no closer contact with the animal than an occasional two minute clip on the evening news.

So Edison's first reaction to the message taken by the reception downstairs, asking for an appointment to discuss the program with her, had been to refer the caller to the media unit. After all that was their area of expertise, they had all the right information packages, and their time was certainly a lot cheaper than hers.

But then she'd seen the name.

She read the message in her mailbox one more time.

Ian MacRae.

Initially it had seemed no more than vaguely familiar, perhaps someone she'd met socially recently, then she remembered. Nigeria. When the contractor had located the girl in the hotel after she'd been rescued by the army, they'd sent Edison a photo of the people she was staying with. The hotel reception had identified the man as Ian MacRae.

She'd given him little thought since then...until now. She tapped out the internet search for him again. There was only one MacRae matching the contact details so it must be him, a security consultant based here in Hobart and offering services for companies and organisations all around the world. His resume was impressive, ex-police, an anti-terrorism specialist with an extensive international client list. Interesting.

But then curiosity got the better of her. What the hell was he doing in Nigeria, and how had he linked her with the project? Surely it was just a coincidence. There was only one way to find out, so she'd called him back and arranged the meeting with him...she checked her watch again...in just a moment.

MacRae was also checking his watch as he approached the medical research institute. Dead on time. He cast his eyes over the building for the hundredth time, it never ceased to intrigue him, cladding a building so it looked like a living human cell.

He wasn't exactly an expert in architecture but I guess it was a form of art, and he knew what he liked, and this was okay. Being unusual, it had sparked a healthy public debate, and the community seemed equally divided on whether it was a monstrosity of architectural indulgence, or a creative masterpiece.

For MacRae, different was generally good, and maybe this type of expression was reflective of the people working inside. He was about to find out, and judging by the unexpectedly enthusiastic response to his request for a meeting with Dr Laura Edison...she'd called him straight back after he'd left a message and agreed to meet him the next day...he suspected this would be the case.

He entered the foyer, an echoing expanse of white walls and varnished timber, and headed straight to the reception desk. A portly security officer in a black uniform seated behind a glass screen looked him over with disinterest.

'How can I help you?' His tone suggested he didn't really care.

MacRae beamed back at him. 'I'm here for an appointment with Dr Edison, can you...'

He was interrupted by a voice across the foyer. 'Mr MacRae?'

A tall woman was approaching, her posture, demeanour, and the way the security guard suddenly sat up straight, suggesting she ran the place.

'I'm Dr Laura Edison.'

MacRae smiled and extended his hand. He was right, she did.

She led the way towards the elevators, past the glass display cabinet outlining the devil facial tumour program. A bleached devil skull mounted on stainless steel spikes, one eye socket eaten away by the disease stared at him.

MacRae slowed his pace, taking in the assortment of artefacts labelled with locations and dates, all linked to a chart along the top of the cabinet showing the timeline of the discovery and spread of the disease up to a couple of months ago.

Edison slowed with him, following his gaze. 'A little display showing some of the work we undertake here. I believe this is your area of interest for today's meeting?'

'Yes, I'm fascinated by the work you undertake here, and perhaps how it can help me in my consultancy work. And this is of particular interest to me, probably like everyone else here, because it's so close to home.'

Edison spoke as she walked, leading past the elevators, along a corridor then swiped her security card to gain access to a suite of rooms. 'Please come in. This is our media centre. We use it to co-ordinate the distribution of information about our work, as well as a learning centre for school groups and the like.'

MacRae entered a spacious room. Flexible dividers were pulled to one side, maximising the space. Offices lined the walls, one looked like it may be sound proofed for use as a recording studio. Banners, posters and framed photographs covered the walls, and various pieces of laboratory equipment were set up along a series of benches to his right. Display cabinets showcased samples of the type of projects undertaken by the institute.

'Nice setup.' MacRae said.

'Thanks,' Edison said. 'You've found us at a quiet time. It can be very busy in here, especially if there are forty or fifty primary school students mixing colourful chemicals.'

She took him into a lounge area, directing him to a couch, then pressed a series of buttons on a chrome-plated coffee machine at the side of a kitchenette, before sitting opposite him.

'Coffee?'

MacRae nodded. 'Thanks.'

'So Mr MacRae, how can I help you?'

'Firstly, thank you for taking the time out of what must be a very busy schedule to talk to me.'

She smiled. 'I try to make time to talk to the public when I can. It keeps me grounded.'

The coffee machine coughed and sputtered in the background.

MacRae leaned forward. 'I'm in the business of providing security advice to individuals and corporations in high-risk environments around the world, how to keep their staff and operations safe when providing services in hostile environments. I'm aware that the nature of what can be considered risks is ever changing, depending upon the activities being undertaken and the location. Do you follow me?'

Edison came over from the coffee machine, placing two steaming cups on the low table between them.

'I'm with you so far. So what does that have to do with the work we do at the Institute?'

'The risks I am generally assessing relate to, for example, volatile political situations, or perhaps physical risks such as terrorism and insurgencies. My clients are often non-government organisations providing aid to refugees, or supplying essential services in remote locations affected by natural disasters.'

He took a sip of his coffee. 'Not bad for a machine.'

Edison nodded. 'Go on...'

MacRae continued. 'It's become more apparent that as humans push further into isolated and sometimes little explored natural habitats we see an increasing risk of exposure to previously undiscovered pathogens, disease or whatever. While they may be naturally occurring on the animal populations, if they are able to be spread to humans they can be devastating to populations with no natural immunity.'

Edison agreed. 'Yes. I assume you're referring to diseases like Ebola in Africa?'

MacRae nodded. 'As well as the more recent outbreaks of the flu-like viruses SARS and MERS that affected the Asian region over the past decade or two.'

He drained his cup, leaving a line of froth around the rim. 'So I'm wondering if you can advise me on the best way for me to build this kind of potential threat into my risk management planning strategy for my clients?'

Edison reached for MacRae's cup, returning it to the coffee machine, leaning against the bench. She still couldn't decide if there was more to it than he was letting on.

'I'm sure I can point you in the right direction for developing some kind of risk rating framework. I can put you in touch with some people that specialise in this kind of disease risk assessment if that would help?' She looked at him curiously. 'So is the devil facial tumour program of particular interest to you in this context?'

MacRae smiled. 'Well, to me as a non-scientist, this disease seems to be the perfect example of a new disease infecting a particular species with devastating speed and mortality. It's the kind of thing that would be equally devastating to a human population if they were to encounter it unexpectedly if it jumped species.'

An unsettling feeling crept over him. Edison was watching him intently, scrutinising every word. His police instincts were kicking in. Should he show her the pictures from Africa? Not just now.

Edison walked across the room to a display, beckoning him over. 'You're exactly right. As you can see we've done a lot of research into this particular disease.'

MacRae took a moment to take in the display information. It was an expanded version of the display in the foyer.

'Although we're only slowly unlocking it's secrets, one thing I can say is that this is extremely unlikely to ever jump the species barrier and be any kind of threat to humans. It's just not that kind of disease.'

MacRae wandered amongst the displays, then paused at a photograph of a smiling young woman carefully holding a healthy Tasmanian Devil while an older man took measurements with a tape.

He peered in to get a closer look. 'Isn't that Dr Khan, the researcher who had an accident at sea not long ago? An awful situation. Her body was never found was it?'

Edison came to stand next to him. 'Yes, very sad. A great loss to the Institute, and her family of course. I wasn't close to her personally though.'

That wasn't the impression MacRae had got from the news articles. He was getting the feeling there was more to Edison than he'd thought.

'And you've also lost another resource for the program recently I believe?'

'How so?' Edison said.

'Kane Murdoch, the wildlife photographer is missing, isn't that right?'

Edison shook her head slowly. 'I'd heard something about that. But he only worked with us sporadically on contract. I do hope he is okay though. He did exceptional work...for many organisations. He was a very talented photographer.'

MacRae wandered further along the display. Why had she referred to Murdoch as *was*, as though he wouldn't be found?

He paused at another photograph. A group of suits stood in a line, smiling for the camera, Edison in the centre next to a serious looking man with silver grey hair, each of them holding one end of an oversized cheque, ***$1 MILLION*** - handwritten on it.

Edison looked over his shoulder. 'We have many very generous benefactors, both private and corporate who assist in funding the various programs we run.'

'I'm sure joint ventures and co-operation with industry for the development and commercialisation of your research is a vital part of your business strategy,' MacRae said.

Edison shrugged. 'Research is always the poor cousin of the medical sciences, and everyone gets less and less government funding nowadays.'

MacRae nodded and glanced at a clock on the wall. 'Speaking of funding, I'd better get to my next appointment to make sure I can keep funding my business.'

Edison felt the opportunity to scrutinise MacRae slipping away. 'Well I'll email you some contact details, people who may be able to help you with your business planning.'

She made one last attempt to determine if his visit was simply a coincidence. 'Oh, are there any regions that you're particularly interested in? Asia? Africa perhaps?'

Again MacRae felt Edison scrutinising him. Perhaps it was his turn to look for a reaction.

'Well, part of the reason I was prompted to look into this more closely was that I came across some pretty distressing photos of diseased kids in Africa recently. The trouble is you can never tell if the photos are genuine or not nowadays with digital manipulation. The disease reminded me of images I'd seen of the Tasmanian Devil disease, so it did get me thinking.' He shrugged. 'I know you've pretty much discounted any likely connection between diseases like this, but would you like to see them anyway?'

'Sure, sounds fascinating.'

MacRae found the photos on his phone, holding it over to her.

She felt a surge of adrenaline as she recognised the subjects and the disease instantly. 'I see what you mean. At first glance there does seem to be some similarities in presentation of the pathology of the infection.' She expanded an image. 'But there are a multitude of diseases that unfortunately can present in this manner.'

She looked up from the phone, heart pounding. 'So is this outbreak being fully investigated, is there any information I can examine to give you a more informed view?'

But he'd seen enough. Her pupils had dilated the second she'd seen the images. She was hiding something.

'I don't think so. Apparently the outbreak was first encountered by a military force. They panicked when they saw the victims, and burnt the bodies before medical teams could intervene and mount an investigation. These photos are pretty much all that remains.'

He slid the phone into his pocket. 'So unfortunately there's no way to prove whether the images, or even the disease is real or not.'

Edison breathed a sigh of relief. There was no evidence left apart from the girl, and MacRae was here only on a whim.

'This unfortunately is often the case in this era of fake news, Mr MacRae. Who knows if the truth will ever be uncovered about your pictures from Nigeria.'

Now it was MacRae's turn to hide his surprise.

'So has the Institute been involved in any projects in Africa?'

Edison paused too long before answering.

'We're one of the biggest research institutions in this country, with connections and partnerships with other similar organisations around the world, so we've got indirect involvement in projects in every continent. But I'm sure we're not running any projects ourselves in Africa at the moment, although I can certainly check, if it would be helpful?'

She led the way from the room. 'Let me show you out.'

'Thanks, that would be great, and you've been most helpful already Dr Edison,' MacRae said.

~

MacRae watched as Edison walked back into the building. He'd arranged the appointment with her on the off-chance he could learn something about the disease in Africa. But he'd been shocked when she'd inadvertently identified the photos of the diseased children as originating in Nigeria, something he was sure he hadn't mentioned.

Now he had the strong feeling that he, Marion, Hassana and Edison were all involved in something more far reaching than he first imagined.

He retrieved his phone and ran two searches for contact details, the first for the grieving family of a scientist, the second for a missing wildlife photographer. There was very little to find for the scientist, other than the original news reports, and the funeral notice asking for the privacy of the family to be respected during a difficult time. He considered following it up further, then decided against it...for the moment. It was different for the photographer. Within seconds MacRae had the business contact details, and this time the news reports included a plea from the photographer's wife for any information that might help find her husband. MacRae dialled the contact number.

Time to head further down the rabbit hole.

CHAPTER 14

NUMBERS

Numbers, places, names floated around Jake Welsh's head, too much information, manifesting itself in a dull ache in his left temple. Medical Statistician, why had he ever thought that sounded like an interesting, even exciting, profession?

He leaned back in the shiny chrome office chair, a loud squeak coming from the hinges. It felt good to arch his back, stretch the underused muscles. He used to be fit; regular jogging, tennis on Sundays. It kept him strong. But now he lived a pretty sedentary lifestyle, most of his time was long hours shackled to a desk. He caught his reflection in his computer monitor. Tired, sore eyes looked back at him, slumped shoulders, sagging skin. Fuck. What was he turning into?

Years of medical school to become a doctor then the shock surprise that he actually found sick people quite depressing. So a jump sideways into research before an uncanny knack for maths and pattern recognition came into play and *bingo!* he was a highly paid and sought after Medical Statistician, sorting through vast amounts of dry medical research and historical data.

He raised a hand to the side of his head, gently massaging in circles to work away the headache.

But medical research was so boring, and often misleading. Sorting wheat from chaff, that's how he saw it. Many of the studies were meticulously detailed, documented to within an inch of their lives and actually useful. But others were basically fakes, a scam, produced using money supplied by a corporation to prove it's dubious product actually worked. It was extraordinary that in most jurisdictions there was no obligation for any of these studies to be released, so if a study was conducted, and as happened so many times, it failed to produce any evidence that a product actually worked, the study was quietly shelved, never to be seen again. But the company still flogged the product to unsuspecting consumers. And who could blame them? Millions of dollars spent developing something that didn't work... they had to recoup the money somehow.

And that's where he came in, a medical private investigator for hire, helping governments or medical organisations or whoever decide whether some highly priced cure-all was actually worth paying for. But it was so boring. Some days he looked at those pimply adolescents serving junk food at some drive-thru, and even their job looked more appealing. Except for the money.

The ski holidays, cruises in the Mediterranean, upgrading his car every year, almost made his work bearable. And a large part of that money came from one particular client, someone he'd been contracted to for many years now, so long in fact that he felt they'd moved past simply a business arrangement to more of a friendship. Magnus Crane. And that's what was making all of this more difficult to understand or accept.

Part of his job for Crane was to assess which of the vast number of products his companies produced were of most value, both in efficacy and profitability. To this end he'd been granted extensive access to the corporation's computer network and data files. And in what he could only assume was an error on the part of the IT and security department, he now had access to a vast trove of confidential information on what appeared to be secret drug development projects and tests around the world. And there was only one conclusion he could draw from the data...that Medici-Royal through its subsidiaries, either with or without the knowledge of its CEO was at the least reckless and incompetent, or at worst criminally culpable for a series of extremely dangerous and morally corrupt practices.

His eyes drifted over yet another series of charts. The data was collected from such a variety of sources that it should have been meaningless, and yet there seemed to be a correlation.

Suicide was the common outcome, the inevitable end to the terrible spiral of depression that appeared to be taking over the modern western capitalist society. For the first time in history humans had far more than they needed to survive and thrive, but instead of a happy and healthy society we were ending our lives at a spectacular rate. And it seemed to be across all levels of society, rich, poor, old, young, single, married. Life was too great a burden to carry for so many people. And the question was, why? Psychologists and psychiatrists the world over were trying to find the cause and cure in what was to some a pointless, disconnected, consumerist society. Some theorised it was largely due to our desire to live in lonely isolation in our own houses as soon as we could afford it, destroying the very social connections that humans have always needed, further exacerbated by the loss of faith in organised religion and other social structures.

But Jake R Welsh felt there was more to it. And now he was sure it was to do with the avalanche of chemicals we bombarded ourselves with, in our food, water, everything we touched or consumed. Again, for the first time in history, we were actually filling our bodies and brains with things humans were never meant to be exposed to. And perhaps now we were paying the price.

And then in front of his eyes the number, codes and words of products, places, and timelines gelled and he could see it. Surely it couldn't be, could it? Something modern western society had introduced for the good of the population into water supplies decades ago was now driving them to end their own lives in horrifying numbers?

And he'd identified it.

And his biggest client was involved in the manufacture and sale of the additive, as well as the myriad of drugs now being used to treat depression. Drugs that often had a fifty percent success rate, no better than a placebo. He mustn't be aware, after all no-one else had reached this conclusion before. Maybe the data hadn't been so readily available before, or maybe there hadn't been the means to collate and interpret it. Or perhaps it had needed the right brain to see the patterns.

His eyes flicked between the other five screens arrayed across his desk. But it was the other research that was even more disturbing, all identified by its spectacular success rate.

He re-opened the document he was compiling, cutting and pasting screen shots and spreadsheets in with his own notes, carefully removing anything that might be traced back to him.

He skimmed through internal memos describing the success of research around the world including projects undertaken for the Defence Department for genetic modification of various pathogens to enhance their infection and mortality rates, and targeting them to specific genetic codes. These modified pathogens were more infectious that the worst flu epidemics, and deadlier than Ebola. He shook his head. This Gain of Function research was highly illegal.

Then there was the mess of the centralised distribution networks implemented by Medici-Royal. Was it all about efficiency and cost cutting that meant pretty much everything they produced passed through the same nodes in each country? But from what he was seeing there was widespread confusion and mix-ups in re-routing, with pathogens intended for US government facilities being instead shipped to countries like India alongside fluoride treatments for water supply.

He rubbed his temple absently. The headache was intense now. But through the fog of the pain more numbers swirled, names and dates of studies and trials, drugs, manufacturing and distribution networks around the world. And without even trying, his mind started to see more patterns emerging, real or imagined. And the picture they painted was terrifying. With this technology, manufacture and distribution system you could remove an entire race from the planet.

He couldn't keep this to himself, he'd have to inform someone of what he'd found. But who would even listen or care?

Then he recalled the conversations he'd had with Crane about the conspiracy theorist who seemed determined to destroy Crane and everything he'd achieved. He remembered that Crane had sued him and eventually shut him down. Maybe the guy had been right after all. Now all he had to do was track him down.

~

CHAPTER 15

GRIEF

Children's laughter muffled by the thick timber door echoed from inside the house as MacRae pushed the doorbell. He stepped back, casting his eyes over the other houses in the street. Great expanses of glass pointed at the views, alongside interesting roof angles and colours. The touch of architects evident everywhere. A quiet leafy, neighbourhood it looked like a place for achievers, those with money.

He waited patiently, recalling yesterday's phone call to Carol Murdoch about her missing husband. She'd sounded exhausted, her disappointment obvious that his call hadn't been the one from the police telling her that husband been found alive and well.

He was jerked from his thoughts by the sound of footsteps, heeled shoes on a polished wooden floor, and the door swung open. MacRae was greeted by a woman in her forties, olive skin, piercing blue eyes, long dark hair pulled into a neat ponytail. They shook hands and she led the way into a living area. Two children, a boy and a girl, maybe six or seven years old peeked curiously around a doorway at MacRae before Carol shooed them away with a wave of her hand.

The sun warmed MacRae's face as he sat on a leather couch, eyes drawn to the unbroken view over the river through the massive plate glass window along the entire length of one wall. Carol sat opposite him dressed in a tailored business skirt and jacket, legs crossed to one side.

'I'm sorry Mr MacRae, I don't have long to talk, I've got to get the kids to school and I'm due at work soon.' She tried to smile, then dropped her eyes to the floor. 'My job's pretty demanding and life must go on as they say, despite everything else.'

She met his eyes again, searching for some insight. 'Why do you think you can help find Kane when the police haven't been able to? And why do you want to? You don't even know him do you?'

MacRae leaned forward, forearms on his knees. 'I used to be a police officer, and I understand the processes they'll go through, but sometimes they think too rigidly. I'll take a different approach and do what I have to do.' He paused, choosing his words carefully. 'You're right, I don't know Kane. I run a company that plans security for people, mostly aid organisations, working in dangerous places around the world. Recently some people I care about got hurt and I'm trying to find out why. It's a long story but I was following up a hunch with some possible links to Tasmanian Devils and the facial tumour research program. A Google search bought up the news story about your husband going missing recently, and that part of his work involved photographing the devils in the wild.'

He tried to smile reassuringly. 'I don't know if there's anything to all this yet, it doesn't make any sense so far, but I've learned to trust my instincts, and I can't help feeling it's something I should be following up.'

She studied his face, then made her decision.

'Okay, I'm going to trust you. My husband is the most capable man I've ever met. We've been together a long time and I've never seen him in a situation he can't handle, so I don't believe he's just gone missing, or tried to disappear as the police have suggested.' Her eyes blazed with anger for a moment. 'Kane's devoted to me and the kids.'

She leaned forward and grabbed his forearm with both her hands, knuckles white. 'You promise me you'll do whatever it takes to find him and bring him home?' She released her grip, sitting back shocked by her anger and desperation. Her voice shook. 'Where do we start?'

MacRae stood up, looking over the beautiful wildlife and landscape photos mounted on the walls. 'Let's start with the work he's been doing photographing the devils and the facial tumour research program. Talk me through it, what he's done, where and when he's been working.'

Carol sighed. 'I'd better call work, tell them I'll be late.'

For the first time since he'd got there, MacRae heard hope in her voice.

~

An hour had gone by as they'd checked out her husband's graphics computer in the study, clicking through the directory systems and files, looking for patterns, information, anything that could help. Murdoch's photography and videos of the landscape and wildlife were stunning, he was truly a talented man, passionate about capturing nature in all its glory, and bringing it home to the rest of the world.

'Kane sells the images all around the world to nature and travel magazines and websites.' Carol explained. 'But his dream was...is,' she corrected herself, 'to shoot enough video material to produce a documentary on the devils that would be broadcast on TV networks all around the world.'

MacRae had to stop himself being distracted from the task at hand by the sheer beauty of the images he was looking through. Some locations MacRae recognised, others identified by Murdoch's wife, or from file names or notes.

Then MacRae blinked in shock. Image after image of diseased and deformed devils in the wild filled the screen.

Carol saw his reaction. 'Yes, this is the confronting stuff. The paid work for the facial tumour research program.'

She scrolled through the images. 'They do a lot of the work in the research centre, but apparently it's just as important to have a catalogued photographic record of how they're performing in the wild, you know, devils that have been treated, how the infection spreads, that sort of thing.'

She kept scrolling. Now the images were from above, some long distance, others looked so close you felt you could almost touch the creatures.

'Kane used a drone a lot, but he always said there was nothing like being there to capture the best images.'

She smiled warmly, MacRae seeing a glimpse of joy in her face. 'I think he just loves crawling around in the mud and snow in these remote locations for days at time. You should see him...and smell him when he gets home after one of these trips. The kids think it's hilarious, all the...' Her voice trailed off with a sigh.

'Anyway, he travels all over the state to get these shots and that apparently is making it hard for the police to know where to focus their efforts. And I think they've got it completely wrong.'

MacRae's curiosity was sparked. 'How so?'

Carol swivelled her chair and pointed a finger at a large map of Tasmania mounted on the opposite wall of the study. Coloured pins dotted the surface, some with numbers and letters tagged to them on tiny pieces of paper.

'These are the locations of most of his shoots, the green ones are current shoots, places he's still working on.'

She rolled on her chair across the room and stabbed a finger at the middle of the map.

'See here?'

MacRae joined her, leaning in and nodded.

'This is where the police found his car, reported by local bush walkers. So this is where the search has been concentrated. But look,' Her finger moved in a circle. 'There's no current pins nearby. I'm sure he'd pretty much finished working there, so I really can't see why his car was found there.'

Her fingers drummed the arm of the chair. 'Plus the police checked out his mobile phone records, the logs from the transmission towers that pick up the signals from all the mobile phones. The last signals weren't anywhere near that location, they were further north. They said reception is pretty bad up there so the signals faded in and out, then stopped completely, but nowhere near where his car was found.'

'So what did the police think of your view?' MacRae said.

'They listened but didn't act on it. I guess they have their procedures to follow, like you said.'

MacRae sat back. 'So where would you be looking?'

Carol's finger stabbed the map. 'There. It's a plateau in the Central Highlands. He had a secret spot, said it was the best place for filming the baby devils. He called it his goldmine, it was going to make him rich and he only needed a few more shots.'

'Okay, that sounds promising. How do I find it?'

'The same way he did. Drop into the local pub and ask for Eileen...something.' She leaned over and opened a contacts list on her husband's computer. '...Killop. She's a local tour guide, runs fishing and hiking trips. He said she knows the Highlands like the back of her hand.'

~

MacRae sat in his car outside the house sifting through the information Carol Murdoch had given him. It seemed like a really long shot that he'd find Kane Murdoch at all, let alone alive. And the whole disappearance might not have anything do with what MacRae was involved in anyway. Maybe the police were right, most people disappeared because they choose to, a fact proven time after time. Is that what happened here? Then he remembered her words. *the most capable man she's ever met, devoted to her and the kids.'*

He picked up his phone and dialled a number. Time for a motorbike ride, and a guided tour of the Central Highlands. And this might be a good chance to spend some relaxing time with Marion by showing her a lovely part of the state.

~

CHAPTER 16

SPEED

MacRae lifted his foot onto the chair in the garage and reached down, pulling the zip up the side of the black leather boot. He loved the feel of the motorcycle boots, they were old but over time had stretched to fit his feet perfectly. He flexed his shoulders into the leather riding jacket, the reinforced protection zones hard against his elbows, then pulled on the red and black helmet. It always felt a little tight, but putting it on gave him a tingle of anticipation for the adrenaline rush to come. He wriggled his fingers into the leather gloves...always the left one first...then swung his leg over the motorcycle seat.

He nodded to Marion and she settled herself on the seat behind him. MacRae smiled. Marion looked good in motorcycle gear, even if it was a little big for her. He had to admit he'd felt a little nervous when he'd called to invite her along for the ride to the Highlands, a kind of high school nervousness like inviting a girl you liked out for the first time. But Marion had jumped at the chance for a motorcycle adventure.

A twist of the key, press of the starter, and the engine roared into life, quickly settling to a low rumbling idle. A tap on the gear lever with his foot, then a twist on the throttle as he flicked the clutch out, catapulting the racing-tuned motorcycle onto the road.

Within seconds he worked up through the gears and wove his way through the traffic to the highway that would take him to the east coast tourist road. It was the long way to get to the Central Highlands but well worth the detour. He smiled in anticipation of the tightly twisting road that lay ahead. Wrapped around the cliffs and beaches with spectacular views for a hundred kilometres, the perfectly maintained strip of asphalt was a motorcycling paradise.

He concentrated hard, avoiding careless motorists changing lanes without indicating, and overtaking lumbering camper-vans. Then he was free, no traffic in any direction, and relishing the ride up the hilly and twisty road that hugged the hills bordering the ocean. He knocked back the motorcycle two gears, revelling in the scream of the engine as the maximum power was transmitted from the tires to the road.

MacRae felt his heartbeat jump as he threw the machine into the hairpin bends, braking at the last possible moment, the foot-pegs briefly scraping the ground and sending a shower of sparks behind him as he laid the bike over to one side, then accelerating hard as he left the corners. Marion's arms tightened around his waist as she settled into the motion of the bike, leaning left and right into the corners with MacRae.

Although he was concentrating intensely, he was overtaken with a sense of calm. It was curious how the body and mind reacted to the thrill of being pushed to the brink of disaster. All the physical senses tingled, hyper-alert, trying to process the data flooding in to keep the body safe. The heart rate increased, pumping more oxygen-rich blood around the body, powering up muscles to cope with danger, yet constricting blood vessels in the extremities to cope with possible breaches and loss of blood. Pupils dilated for best possible vision as adrenaline levels surged, the brain hyper vigilant. This was a primitive fight or flight response, the ultimate human response to physical danger.

Yet to MacRae this was meditation, mindfulness, being totally alive and focused. Now his mind was clear, the memories of Holgate came flooding back.

It had started as a flash of red when the rear brake light of the motorcycle in front of him braked for a corner. That was the first time he had crossed paths with Dr Evan Holgate, almost 15 years ago. Holgate was a member of the Ulysses Club, for supposedly older, wiser and more sensible motorcyclists. At the age of fifty-five

Holgate was anything but that, as MacRae was about to learn. The two riders had duelled for almost ten kilometres, one seeing a chance to undercut the other, then the lead swapping again, until MacRae had finally pulled ahead, arriving at the cafe in Orford moments before the other motorcyclist.

The two riders had parked next to each other and MacRae had blinked in surprise when Holgate had taken his helmet off, revealing silver-white hair. Over coffee they'd shared riding stories, near misses, dicing with death, pushing their machines further, harder than they should, and MacRae had developed a deep respect for this ageing doctor who insisted on tackling everything in his life with one hundred and ten percent effort, to the dismay of his wife who dreaded the visit from the police to advise her of his death in a motorcycle accident.

Holgate was a man of passion, and that's why when he felt there was more he could do for humanity than in his city medical practice, he had decided to spend his vacations volunteering for short-term overseas charitable postings. He seemed to have no sense for the risks he sometimes took, and MacRae had taken it upon himself to use his business experience as a security consultant to at least advise Holgate on the best ways to perform his work in trouble spots whilst staying relatively safe.

But MacRae had failed, and it had cost Holgate his life. Everyone had told MacRae that it was not his fault, that Holgate had put himself in harm's way, but MacRae couldn't shake the sense of guilt. And he would never forget the look of exhaustion and despair on the face of Alicia, Holgate's wife of almost fifty years, when MacRae had sat with her in the beautiful house overlooking the River Derwent describing, at her insistence, the last few moments of his life, as always trying to help others, in the clinic in Africa.

He snapped out of the melancholic mood, focusing back on the twisting black road unfolding ahead of him.

~

MacRae sat up straight in the motorcycle seat, arching his back, twisting his shoulders then flexing his fingers and forearms one at a time to ease the cramp that was setting in from the long ride. The engine was a muted growl, easily eating up the kilometres, seemingly waiting for a chance to be let loose and show what the bike could do.

The last hour or so had gone in a bit if a blur as they'd cut across the dry grassy midlands to their destination. The flora changed as the altitude increased, leaving behind the pastures and lush forests, now turning into smaller trees and tough strappy grasses and bushes. He felt the air temperature start to drop, and from the corner of his eye he caught glimpses of the famous trout fishing lakes.

Privately owned shacks peeked out from between the trees in the distance, some of them a hundred years old or more, built or shipped in by hardy souls looking for holiday escapes from the more civilised parts of the island state, or a last refuge for post-war European migrant workers.

Then his destination was in sight, the Lakes View Hotel, an isolated refuge from the biting blizzards that closed in without warning any time of the year.

He felt Marion move against his back, peering around his shoulder to get a clearer look at the imposing structure. Her voice crackled slightly through his earphones. 'That's a curious mix of construction materials...native stone, timber and corrugated steel cladding.'

MacRae nodded, he'd done some research before they'd headed up.

'Yes, the accommodation and bar has been built in stages, getting bigger each time from the early 1960s. Apparently an earlier version dating back another 50 years burnt to the ground; rumour had it torched either by the owner for the insurance money, or as an extortion threat that went too far.' He slowed the bike to negotiate a last corner, the engine briefly growling as he changing down through the gears with a flick of the throttle. 'Some of these remote areas have a reputation for tough and colourful characters who live by their own rules, and visitors weren't always welcome.'

'Okay. Sounds interesting,' Marion said.

'Throw in conflict over the years between the miners and loggers, and environmentalists trying to preserve the wilderness, and you've got a pretty complicated place.'

MacRae steered the bike into a sheltered corner of the gravel car park, the *ping* of the cooling motor the only sound as he pulled off his helmet and gloves, stretching his arms back over his head to get the blood flowing again. Marion did the same, then ruffled her hair to give it some life after hours in her helmet. MacRae couldn't help but notice her curves in the biking gear. He smiled, she somehow managed to always look great, even after hours on a motorcycle.

'That was a lot of fun Ian, and such beautiful changes of scenery from the coast to the Highlands.'

MacRae smiled. The scenery wasn't the only beautiful thing he was noticing.

～

Marion led the way into the building, pushing through a heavy timber door with smoked glass panels into an unattended reception area. Varnished timber lined the walls, a faded *Please Ring For Service* sign leaned up against a tarnished silver bell. It took a moment for their eyes to adjust to the artificial light.

'This way.' MacRae pointed to a swing door to the right labelled *Public Bar.*

The buzz of conversation drifted through the door as they entered. It was mid afternoon but the bar was busy. Mostly men leaned on the polished bar running the length of the room. A dozen tables were spread in a grid on dark blue carpet, empty glasses and beer bottles collecting in their centres.

MacRae tilted his head at them. 'Too many customers and not enough staff.'

She wrinkled her nose. 'Yes, and nothing like stale beer as a change from the crisp fresh air of the Highlands.'

Faded photographs in dusty frames lined the walls, images of untouched wilderness interspersed with group shots of rugged characters in earlier days clearing the bush for mining or logging, curly moustaches and long beards, dressed in coarse woollen jackets against the bitter winter cold.

'We're a bit early, would you like a drink while we wait?'

Marion cast an eye around the room, nodding at an empty space at the end of the bar. 'Over here?'

MacRae couldn't help noticing the heads turning to watch her as she headed for the bar, eyes taking in her tall, lean figure. Then he felt the eyes on him, wondering who a woman like this would be travelling with.

He ordered drinks then checked his phone for messages. Eileen Killop had tried to call him while they were riding. He hit the call button and waited.

The barman leaned over from pouring a beer. 'Cell phone reception is crap in here, the signal drops out. You'll have to go outside.'

MacRae nodded and hung up, sipped his beer then turned to Marion. 'I'd better call her back. Are you okay in here?'

She grinned. 'I've worked with Ebola victims in Africa and refugees in war zones, and you're concerned about me in local bar?'

~

The cell phone signal shot back up to four bars as soon as MacRae left the building. Eileen Killop answered in a broad Scottish accent on the second ring.

'Sorry for the delay, I couldn't get off the phone, just been confirming a booking for a big group of tourists wanting the full wilderness experience, I'm still another fifteen minutes away.'

MacRae felt a chill wash over him. The sun was setting and the temperature was dropping quickly. He turned as a noisy SVU motored past him. The car park was filling up.

'We're in the bar, the two people that look a bit out of place.'

There was a pause on the other end. 'Maybe it's easier if you come straight to my place. Besides, because I run eco tours in a logging region I'm not always the most popular person in the bar.'

MacRae slipped his phone back into his pocket and squeezed through a group of drinkers inside the door of the bar. Across the room he saw Marion room talking to two men. Her jaw was clenched and she pointed a finger at the bigger of the two. Heads on either side were looking over curiously as the voices became raised. MacRae felt a familiar tightening of his muscles.

Grinning broadly he stepped in next to Marion, placing an arm around her shoulders. 'Hi sweetheart. You've made some new friends?'

Marion glared at the man in front of her. 'Something like that. We seem to have a difference of opinion about some conservation issues.'

The men sized up MacRae. The one to his left, taller than MacRae and lean, hair cut into a mullet, looked fit, pointed at the *Sea Shepherd* badge sewn onto the shoulder of Marion's jacket.

'She doesn't have any friends up here. We've lost too many jobs to the greenies, always wanting to save something. Everything except our jobs.' Beer on his breath wafted into MacRae's face.

Marion bristled with anger, she was itching to respond. MacRae touched her forearm gently. 'I'd love to join the conversation but we've got an appointment to get to.'

The other man joined in. 'You people come up here buying up the best land, locking it up so no one can use it. Building your crazy bunkers.' He slurred his words slightly, looking MacRae up and down. He was shorter than MacRae, but stocky, body hardened by a life on the land and in the bush.

MacRae took a step to the side, gently guiding Marion past the men by her elbow. 'Nice talking to you guys, but we're just passing through.'

He moved his body between Marion and the men as they moved from the bar, then felt an arm brush his elbow as the tall man reached out and grabbed Marion's wrist.

The shorter man moved across to face MacRae. 'Maybe she'd like to make her own mind up about that.'

MacRae glanced at Marion, her face confused then angry as she tried to jerk her arm free.

Then MacRae reacted, locking his hand onto the tall man's wrist on Marion's arm, thumb underneath pressing into the nerves. His other hand went to the man's elbow, lifting it up and around sharply, the man doubling over, releasing his grip on Marion with a snarl of anger and pain. MacRae lifted the wrist up between the man's shoulder blades and pushed his face onto the bar.

The shorter man jerked into action, grabbing MacRae by the shoulder and pulling hard. MacRae released his grip on the tall man's elbow, keeping pressure on his wrist with one hand, then swung his other arm in a loop under the shorter man's arm and lifting up hard, trapping his elbow and bending the joint backwards. The man shrieked, standing on the tips of his toes, then stopped resisting.

MacRae kept the tension on both men, increasing the pressure if they tried to move. 'We're going now, and I'm going to release you.' He upped the pressure. 'I haven't hurt you...yet. But next time I won't hold back. Do you understand?'

The tall man hissed through clenched teeth, cheek hard against the bar. 'Okay. Just let me go.'

His friend glared at MacRae, but said nothing, so MacRae increased the pressure on his elbow again.

'Arrghh... okay alright.'

The barman appeared in front of them, a battered baseball bat in his hand, and roared. 'No fighting in the bar.'

MacRae couldn't read his expression, a mix of anger and fear?

The bar fell silent, every eye in the place on him.

Marion seemed calm but concerned. MacRae knew why. She'd been around violence too many times.

'C'mon Ian, let's go.'

MacRae slowly released the two men, leaving them to rub their arms, humiliation and rage written on their faces. His eyes flicked between them, waiting to see if they'd let it go.

Marion weaved a path across the room, patrons stepping aside to let her through, MacRae close behind. Then they were outside.

Marion spoke first, her voice quavering slightly. 'Jesus Ian, that got out of hand so quickly.'

MacRae looked at her in the dying rays of the sun, one side of her face shrouded in the shadows. Dammit, she was such a gentle soul, devoting her life to helping others. He'd forgotten that underneath her tough exterior she was as vulnerable as any other woman.

A couple of steps and he was there, arms around her, pulling her in close. She was shivering...was it the cold or the adrenaline?

'Isn't that sweet.' The voice between them and the motorbike dripped with sarcasm.

MacRae gently released Marion and turned. It was the tall guy, stripped back to a dirty singlet, a tire lever in his hand hanging loosely down his side.

Then another voice came from behind them, the shorter guy.

'You're a long way from home buddy. This is our world, and you and your bitch are about to learn what that means.'

MacRae caught a flash of light in his hand. A knife?

MacRae took a step sideways, moving Marion away from the men.

She spoke quietly. 'I'll call the police.'

The tall guy stepped closer, lifting his weapon. 'The nearest cop is stationed an hour's drive away.' He grinned at them. 'He won't be here in time to help.'

MacRae slowed his breathing, his heartbeat settled in to a gentle rhythm, all his senses sharpening. A grim smile crept over his lips. 'You're right about that.'

He crabbed sideways, ensuring the two men stayed in his field of vision and neither was behind him, and waited. From the corner of his eye he saw a small crowd of drinkers had come outside to watch.

Then all hell broke loose.

The tall man growled and charged at MacRae, raising the tire lever over his head. MacRae darted forward, raising his arm and arresting the swing of the tire lever. The man stopped, shocked that MacRae was so close, then it was too late as MacRae drove the palm of his other hand twice hard into his unprotected face. He shrieked, trying to stagger back as his nose streamed with blood, but MacRae had his fingers locked around his forearm near the tire lever. The shorter man rushed forward swinging the knife upwards in an arc at MacRae's back.

MacRae twisted, wrenching the tall man's arm with the tire lever behind him...straight into the wrist holding the knife. A sharp crack echoed around the car park, the shattering of the man's bones, then the sound of the knife bouncing along the ground at MacRae's feet.

The short man froze, stunned at the pain shooting up his arm, giving MacRae all the time he needed. He stamped down hard behind the tall man's knee, dropping him to the ground with a final palm strike to his face, then turned to his other attacker.

The short man's face seethed, his eyes scanning the ground for the knife. MacRae took a couple of quick steps forward and unleashed a boxing combination...a jab followed by a vicious hook to his jaw. The man's head snapped sideways as his eyes rolled up and he crumpled to his knees, then slumped to the ground.

MacRae straightened up then heard the shuffle of feet off to the side, turning his head to see the tall man rushing towards him holding the knife. Then a blur of movement as Marion rushed at him, motorcycle helmet swinging in her hand before a loud crack as it connected with the side of his head. He staggered wildly to the side, collapsing to the ground and was still.

MacRae smiled at Marion and shook his head. 'Remind me not to ever upset you.'

She shrugged, holding the helmet to her side. 'I just hope I didn't damage the helmet.'

The two men on the ground weren't moving. Marion went from one to the other checking vital signs. 'They'll live.'

MacRae looked across the car park at the small crowd, starting to disappear back into the bar now the excitement was over. One figure, an older woman, a hard life etched across her face wandered over, stopping in front of Marion and MacRae with hands on her hips. She looked at the two men on the ground for a long moment, then looked from Marion to MacRae.

'They had it coming. They've been terrorising locals and visitors alike for a long time, picking fights, bullying people. Just watch out, you might not have seen the last of them.' She grinned and walked away. 'Oh, and when the police get here I think they'll find no-one saw anything.'

CHAPTER 17

GIN

It was almost fully dark by the time MacRae eased the motorbike up the gravel road the last kilometre to the modern stone house. Warm yellow light spilled out the windows welcoming them in.

Eileen met them at the door, taking a moment to size them up. 'Welcome to my humble house, an uneventful trip up was it?'

MacRae and Marion swapped a glance, Marion spoke first.

'It's always a bit of an adventure on a motorbike.'

Eileen smiled and led them through to a huge kitchen, where two German Shepherds dozed lazily on the warm terracotta tiled floor near a blazing wood heater. She bent down and grabbed a huge log from a pile, hefting it effortlessly onto the pile of embers in the wood heater. Years of guiding walking tours through the bush had kept Eileen fit and lithe. Her practical short cut hair showed a hint of grey through the red as she approached forty. Pale skin and sparkling blue eyes gave a clue to her heritage.

The hot gin toddy she offered them, combined with the wood heater, quickly spread warmth through MacRae and Marion. Eileen sat in an old armchair, listening closely as MacRae explained about his visit to Kane Murdoch's wife, and their interest in the Tasmanian Devil facial tumour research program. She blew softly across the top of her cup, tendrils of steam twisting upwards.

There was a long silence, unbroken except for the wheezing of the bigger dog as it slept. Then Eileen looked up, eyes piercing into MacRae's. 'But there's more to it than that isn't there?'

MacRae held her gaze, then spoke. 'Yes, there is. How did you know?'

Eileen shrugged, holding up her phone. 'We might be on the fringe of the world's most amazing wilderness here, but we still have social media. Have a look.'

MacRae and Marion leaned in, squinting to watch the video of the confrontation outside the Lakes View Hotel unfold, the crowd, the brutal action, then them leaving on the motorcycle.

'Nothing stays secret up here for long, and there are plenty of people who are glad to see what happened to those pricks,' Eileen said, placing the phone on the arm of her chair. 'People like you always have a good reason to be somewhere.'

She smiled. 'Been wondering about my accent? Glasgow, Scotland. Where I grew up people, mainly the men, fight as readily as drink a beer,' She drained her glass with a touch of irony. 'It's a tough world, lots of poverty despite being in one of the most sophisticated countries in the world. Some people don't know any different.'

MacRae's eyes searched hers. Was she a domestic violence survivor? He'd seen the consequences too many times as a young police officer, bruises, broken bones, or worse. Or the less obvious damage caused by years of psychological abuse. His hand moved subconsciously to the faded scar on his side, his permanent reminder of intervening in a domestic dispute on duty a long time ago.

Eileen pointed a finger gently at MacRae. 'But you? You fight because you have to. And then you fight to win.'

She leaned back, peering in her glass for a last drop. 'Ex-military?'

MacRae tipped his head towards Marion. 'Something like that. Marion's the hero, the life saver. Me? Trouble just seems to find me wherever I go.'

Marion reached over, touching his knee. His hand absently dropped onto hers. He sat his drink in his lap and leaned back. 'So this is why we're here...'

⁓

An hour passed, then Eileen smiled grimly. 'Well that's a hell of a story. Now we're friends let's see what we can do about this?'

She cleared the big oak dining table in the kitchen, laying a detailed map across the middle.

MacRae's eyes flicked across it, picking up the grades and elevations from the contours. 'There are some pretty serious climbs here...' His finger traced a path to a group of close orange lines, a cliff. '...and you don't want to slip here.'

Eileen nodded. 'These are the areas I took Kane, much flatter territory, best for the devils.' She stood back, a finger tapping her chin. 'He was most interested in their breeding grounds, where he said he could guarantee the best footage.'

'So if you were to bet, where would you say he went for the final vision for his documentary?' Marion said.

Eileen stabbed a finger at the left of the map. 'There. It's relatively accessible but not the most popular destination for tourists. Not many people know it's special and the devils love it. They can bunker down and do their thing without being interrupted, generally.'

MacRae chuckled. 'Funny you should say that. The guys in the bar were complaining about outsiders hunkering down in the Highlands just before our little altercation. I guess they weren't talking about the wildlife.'

'Were they now?' Eileen raised an eyebrow. 'Yeah, there's a bit of a history of people coming up here to do crazy stuff. I reckon they're taking about the Americans buying up the big property over here.' Her finger tapped the map again. 'Some corporation fenced it all off a few years ago and put a huge building in the middle. Apparently it includes an underground shelter. Some local guys were hired to do part of the construction work, had to sign confidentiality agreements.' She laughed. 'But they're not worth much after a few beers in the pub.'

'Survivalist kind of stuff? Marion said. 'Is that what they've built?'

'Who knows what they do with it.' Eileen replied. 'Maybe they know something we don't.'

'Well it kinda makes sense to me,' MacRae said. 'If the end of the world is coming, Tasmanian is probably about the safest place to be.'

'Damn right,' Eileen said, topping up their drinks. 'That's why I'm here. I got sick of feeling the whole of Europe was a nuclear target for someone. Throw in scares like Mad Cow disease affecting the entire British population, not that you'd notice if they all went mad.' She laughed. 'I looked for a long time for somewhere to live isolated from all that. The clincher for here was the beautiful wild landscape and temperate climate, just like home.' She passed the steaming cups back to them. 'And here I am.'

They pored over the map for another hour, watching the occasional flurry of drizzle drift past the window, until Eileen felt they'd exhausted the options of where to look for Murdoch.

Marion's eyes felt full of sand. She rubbed them with the back of her hand, trying to keep alert, and placed her empty cup on the table. She glanced at MacRae, he smiled and nodded.

'Well Eileen, I think we know where we have to look. We'd better be heading back to the hotel.'

Eileen glared at them. 'I really don't think staying there is the best idea. Do you?'

MacRae shrugged.

'You're staying here tonight, and I'll come out with you tomorrow to look for Kane. And I won't take no for an answer.'

~

The room Eileen offered them was cosy and warm, part of the accommodation for her guided walking groups. She'd assumed they were a couple and the room was furnished with an enormous king-sized bed.

Marion broke the ice as Eileen left the room. 'That looks comfy sweetheart.'

MacRae smiled with fond memories. 'Well it wouldn't be the first time. I'm sure we'll make it work somehow.'

They unpacked their clothes in comfortable silence and MacRae turned the lights low as they got ready for sleep, taking the left side of the bed.

Marion smiled. This was all too familiar, a routine they'd developed over their time as lovers before. The king-sized bed seemed cavernous, a physical and emotional gulf between them as Marion killed the lights.

They lay in silence. MacRae gazed at the outline of Marion's face in the gentle light of the three-quarter moon. She was every bit as beautiful and alluring as he remembered. The room was warm, and she was only covered with a sheet, the material clinging to the soft roundness of her breasts as they moved with each breath. She was an amazing woman, so strong, fiercely protective as she'd shown in the fight at the pub, yet vulnerable and ever so sexy.

He pushed the thoughts from his mind, stretching out to sleep.

Marion felt him move as he settled. She lay still but her mind swam with images of MacRae. She didn't want to picture him in his leathers on the motorcycle, or the tense explosive power of his body as he fought to protect her in the bar, then again outside. Half the things that she was so attracted to were the things that meant they could never have a normal life together. And the last image was his body as he stripped down for bed. A body she knew so well, and had loved so tenderly and ferociously. She forced the images away and turned to sleep. But somewhere in the gulf between them their hands met. And the surge of energy between them electrified the room.

The years fell away as they moved together, hands exploring slowly at first, then with an urgency that neither of them could control, the shapes of each other in the moonlight as they kissed, her curves and softness opposed by his muscled hardness, driving their unstoppable lust for each other. The sex was a blur of two bodies as they devoured each other, Marion lying back with her hands over her head giving MacRae permission to take her as he wished, savouring every thrust of his body over hers. And then almost too soon they reached the heights of their hunger and both released together, collapsing into each other's arms and a spent slumber.

~

MacRae woke first at the tiniest flicker of sun over the horizon and lay quietly, one hand gently caressing Marion's face, stroking her hair back, tracing a line from her neck to her chin, touching her soft, full lips. The fingertips of his other hand followed a path between her breasts, the touch of a feather, down her stomach to her navel. How had they ended up here again? Sharing a bed, the linen sheets cool against their bodies.

Just like now, they had been lovers so many times before, always unexpected, thrown together by circumstance, their passion burning with an exquisite intensity. Neither of them could explain the electricity between them, deliberately restrained in public, but often noticed by those around them, and when they were alone like this, desire overwhelmed them.

His fingertips moved lower, her body slowly moving to welcome his touch as she woke from her slumber. She lifted her chin, lips parted in invitation until his lips caressed hers.

The world fell away from around them. He sensed more than heard the pounding of rain on the roof above them as he felt the beating of her heart next to his. He bathed in her scent, the softness of her skin. How long had they been lying in each other's arms? Seconds, minutes, hours? Time had no meaning.

He traced a line along her cheek with his palm and looked into her eyes, her face radiating beauty and desire, her breath on his face in almost imperceptible gasps.

Then he saw it, deep within her eyes, under a layer of tears, her love for him, so strong and powerful. But she had hidden it behind a wall, a barrier he could no longer penetrate. He hadn't honoured her love a long time ago, and now he had lost her.

That was when he knew things could never be the same between them.

~

They rose early, keen to make the most of the day. MacRae and Marion wore their walking clothes to breakfast, ready to go. They'd both slept well, exhausted by the previous day, and the renewal between them.

MacRae looked across the table at Marion as she crunched into her toast. He wasn't sure how it had happened, how they had gone from being just friends again in an instant. He hadn't felt such passion, the warmth and connection of being with a woman he loved, for so long.

A flash of sadness swept across him. It seemed an eternity since he'd been caught up in the deadly battle to stop the detonation of the Devil's Breath weapon, and the intense but ultimately heartbreaking relationship that was forged in those desperate days.

He saw Marion glancing wistfully at him as he stirred his coffee and cursed to himself. Why was it always so complicated when she was in his life?

Eileen smiled at them cheerily and checked the weather forecast on her phone. 'We've got a bit of a hike ahead of us and it may get pretty cold up there. We'll take some wet weather gear in case we need it.'

She packed a couple of day packs for them, throwing in extra food and water, a first aid kit, and a GPS tracker each in case they got separated or lost.

'We'll check the most likely spots first, if we don't find anything I'm not sure there's any point looking any further.' She looked across the sky. 'No-one would survive more than a couple of days up here in this weather.'

~

For a few hours MacRae was able to forget why they were here, walking in silence through some of the most beautiful and isolated wilderness left in the world. The sun warmed their backs and the smell of the wildflowers drifted across the plain in waves on the gentle breeze. They'd got into an easy walking rhythm, keeping an even pace as the ground changed from muddy path, to grassy plain, to light forest. The most challenging path was over huge boulders at the base of a three hundred metre cliff, seemingly thrown in random patterns from above.

Eileen glanced at her watch. The bright orange digits displayed 3:22 pm. They'd been walking for over seven hours, and had checked out all secret devil breeding locations she'd shown Murdoch except one, taking the time to first search for anything left in the hides he'd made, then walking out in concentric circles for any hint that he'd wandered in any particular direction. Each search had yielded the same result. Nothing. She could see fatigue, and disappointment setting into Marion's face.

'We're almost there.' She pointed across the plain, tussock grass swaying gently like ocean waves in the breeze. 'Just through that bunch of Tea Tree. This was his last resort location, so fingers crossed for us too.'

Eileen led the way into the dense copse of Tea Tree, pushing branches aside to squeeze through, then gently letting them go so they didn't snap back onto Marion and MacRae. She cursed occasionally as a twig pierced into her skin through her trousers or shirt. Abruptly the trees ended, opening out into a small clearing.

'This is it,' she declared.

MacRae stepped past her, taking in the space, then swung his day pack from his shoulders to the ground. 'Okay, let's see what we can find.'

His years of training as a police investigator kicked back in effortlessly, scoping the scene, breaking it down into zones, assigning resources, searching for the unexpected, the sign of something that was hidden, perhaps not meant to ever be discovered.

Marion and Eileen had learnt the basics quickly on the previous search sites and moved with silent, focused efficiency over the moist grass, eyes scanning for clues that Murdoch had been there, or might even still be close by.

They searched for ten minutes, pausing to discuss their progress then stretched it to fifteen.

Eileen voiced her frustration. 'I don't think there's anything to find here. Perhaps the police were right, he'd have to be near his car, the mobile phone ping up this way was a red herring.'

MacRae stretched his back, sore from bending down to look at things that always turned out to be nothing. But that was the nature of police work. So was the gut feeling he had that they were so close to finding something. 'Maybe you're right. But I'm not ready to quit just yet. A few more minutes?'

Eileen smiled. She'd needed the reassurance that they weren't wasting their time. 'Sure, let's keep going.'

A hideous snarl behind her startled Marion. 'What the hell was that?'

She turned to see MacRae and Eileen laughing.

'You're about to meet your first Tassie Devil in the wild.' Eileen crouched low, moving toward the edge of the clearing where some Tea Tree had been carefully cut aside to give an uninterrupted view across the grassy plain. 'Come over here, very quietly.'

Marion followed Eileen's lead, crouching, then as she neared the edge of the clearing lowering herself to her hands and knees. They shared the narrow gap, waiting silently, then movement in front of them as three devils wandered into view, backs arched, snarling and snapping at each other's scruffy fur.

'Not the prettiest of creatures are they?' Marion whispered.

'And not the sweetest smelling either.' Eileen wrinkled her nose. 'It goes a long way to explaining why the early white settlers called them Tasmanian Devils.'

MacRae joined them, smiling at the animal's antics, seemingly totally oblivious to their observers' presence. Then the lead animal turned, staring fixedly at their location, nose twitching as it tried to analyse their scent, but struggling due to the tumour covering one side of its face.

Marion gasped. 'It's even out here.'

'Yes, its devastated devil populations right across the state. The spread of the disease seems to be unstoppable,' Eileen said.

Then with a final snarl the lead devil turned and scampered off, followed by the others.

Marion went to stand, pushing up with her hand, then stopped, peering into the dark brown mud by two tall Tea Trees.

'What the...' She crawled forward, reaching into the mud, then stood, a mud encrusted rectangle between her fingertips.

MacRae leaned in. 'Is that a phone? What the hell's it doing out here?'

Marion scraped away some of the mud with her sleeve, handing it to MacRae. He sealed it in a zip lock bag, tucking it inside his day pack.

'Hopefully it's still working.'

They resumed their search and finished working across the clearing in another couple of minutes, then MacRae called them together.

'I think we've done the best we can. It looks like there's nothing more to find here, and we can't waste any more time without any proof that we're even looking in the right place. Let's just hope the phone has something that might help, otherwise we're at a dead end.'

He took a last look across the clearing, satisfied they hadn't missed anything. 'Time to head home?'

Eileen looked at her watch, then the sky. 'We've got a bit of time before its dark. There's is one more thing we could do that might make your trip worthwhile... if you want to see what the guys at the Lakes View were talking about. The big property with the bunker is only half an hour over there.' She pointed in the direction of a large hill. 'The National Park we're in stretches for a hundred kilometres in most directions from here. But that side borders on to private land. It used to be well hidden from the hill by the bush, until the big fires last summer. Now you get a pretty good view.' She laughed. 'It must really piss them off that they're not so secret anymore...at least until the bush grows back.'

MacRae and Marion exchanged glances, then curiosity got the best of them. Marion spoke for them both. 'Let's go.'

~

The final part of the climb was steep and slippery, the loose stones of the path moving randomly under their feet, unsettling when the hill dropped away sharply, leaving a twenty metre drop down a cliff to one side. Then they reached the crest and the view of the burnt bushland unfolded in front of them, charred hundred year old tree trunks reaching forlornly into the sky. A carpet of green undergrowth thrived at the base of the trees as the forest regenerated.

MacRae let out a low whistle. 'It really ripped through the place didn't it?'

Eileen nodded. 'It was one of the biggest bush fires in the history of the state, devastating huge tracts of ancient rainforest before they got it under control. And it revealed a lot more of this place than the owners wanted.'

She reached into her day pack, pulling out sleek grey binoculars, handing them to MacRae. 'Check out the hollow up the back to the left.'

MacRae sat on a rock, bracing his elbows on his knees to steady the optics and scanned the property, coming to rest on a cluster of low buildings. A twist of a dial and the scene came into focus, a couple of big houses, outbuildings and sheds, then behind them a wide low concrete entry into the side of the hill.

'Ah, so their little secret isn't so secret anymore,' MacRae said, passing the binoculars to Marion.

She braced herself against MacRae and scanned the property, stopping as movement in the foreground caught her eye.

'They have deer?'

'Yes, they can be a bit of a problem up here,' Eileen said. 'They were first bred for hunting, then farming. But it wasn't well regulated, so there's a lot of feral deer.'

Marion panned the binoculars along the boundary fence. 'So is the electric fence to keep the deer in...'

MacRae thought out loud, '...or unwanted visitors out?'

'Interesting you should ask,' Eileen said. 'Would you like to find out?'

~

It took another fifteen minutes to scramble down the far side of the hill through the light bush along twisting paths made by the wildlife, then they were at the base of the three metre high wire mesh fence.

MacRae noticed other hardware along the fence, plastic lenses, sensors and transmitters.

'This seems a bit of an overkill to keep deer in. Motion detectors, infra-red scanners?'

'Don't know what they are, but something interesting happens if you get too close,' Eileen said. 'Step closer if you want to find out.'

Marion was the first to move. A couple of quick steps and she was there, feet almost touching the base of the mesh. A startled deer jumping away into the nearby bushes.

She waited, then turned back to them. 'And?'

Eileen grinned. 'Wait for it.'

A minute or two of silence, then a high pitched whine from the direction of the buildings. They all looked up, MacRae spotting the small white drone first as it reached the fence fifty metres to their south, pausing before accelerating along the fence line towards them.

Eileen pulled up the hood of her coat, casting heavy shadow on her face. 'I'm sure they record what the drone sees, so if you want to stay incognito you might want to do the same. I've run into people from the facility once or twice in town. They know who I am, but never seem too friendly.'

MacRae straightened his shoulders, looking directly at the approaching craft. 'Sometimes it's good to let people know when you're around.'

Marion joined him, staring defiantly as the drone hovered a few metres above the fence, a strange modern day version of a Mexican stand-off. Then with a final angry buzz the drone shot up vertically, spun around and disappeared back to the buildings in the distance.

The walk back to Eileen's house was mostly silent, each lost in their thoughts. MacRae chewed over the events of the last twenty four hours. But now he was immersed in the almost spiritual experience of the untouched wilderness, a sometimes brutally inhospitable place the indigenous Australians had managed to live in harmony with for forty thousand years. But a day earlier he'd yet again seen the worst of humanity. Brutal and cruel. And yet again he'd drawn on his primal instincts, as well as his modern training and skills, to defend someone he cared about.

He looked at Marion walking at an even pace in front of him, boots carefully sidestepping mud and rocks. She's devoted her life and training to saving lives, relieving pain and distress. What did she think when she saw him destroy another man? Or two? Did she see in him what sometimes he caught a glimpse of in himself...the warrior in combat, the adrenaline and excitement that came from being totally focused in the moment in a fight for survival and dominance? If she knew, would she be proud of him or horrified by what stirred inside him?

He shrugged off the thought, focusing on what came next. Did the phone still work, and would it reveal anything about Murdoch's disappearance? Even if it did, would that mean anything in their search for Hassana?

~

The security guard was bored. The pay was good, but was it really worth it living in such an isolated place, keeping an eye on a company property that was rarely used? His eyes wandered over the monitors as they flicked between fixed surveillance cameras monitoring entry points to the property and the buildings. He toyed with his phone, tempted to play a game. There was a house decorating one that always drew him in. He felt sure it gave him the opportunity to prove he could have been an interior decorator in another life. But he'd been caught on his phone at work before and it almost cost him his job.

The most exciting thing that had happened all day had been when a motion detector had been triggered along the southern boundary fence a few minutes earlier. Even then he'd only got to sit back and watch as the automated drone had sent itself off to investigate, covering the hundreds of metres in seconds, locating the activity and recording the curious bush walkers peering through the perimeter fence.

His fingers danced over the keyboard as he brought up the stills from the drone, zooming in to each face in turn, shaking his head at the woman with a hoodie obscuring her face. Probably that bush walking tour guide again. Then an attractive younger woman, glancing disinterestedly up. He zoomed in to the final face, a man, maybe late thirties. He wanted to be seen, staring directly into the camera. The guard was drawn to his eyes, piercing blue grey. A shiver went down his spine. This wasn't a man to mess with.

He made a judgement call. Most curious walkers glanced at the property and moved on. Very occasionally they showed more interest, and that was of interest to the management. He picked the clearest images of the three walkers, copied them into an email and clicked *send,* then leaned back in his chair, putting his feet up on the desk and settled back into watching screens where nothing ever really happened.

The email flashed instantly across the world through a network of servers, satellites and undersea cables to a data storage facility tucked away in the majestic forests of Norway. Home to a sizeable chunk of the data generated every second through the world on the internet, mainly on mobile phones, this private data warehouse also sorted vast amounts of shared information for its clients, mostly to be on-sold as marketing information. This was the new world currency, personal details about every aspect of the lives of pretty much everyone on the planet.

What was hidden deep in a complex corporate structure however was that this company was also owned by the Medici-Royal pharmaceutical corporation, and was an invaluable source of information on population patterns across the globe. And in this modern world of outsourcing, the facility also stored and analysed information for government agencies as diverse as the British intelligence agency MI5, and the US government Centre For Disease Control.

But at this moment the facility was utilising its processing power to compare the images of MacRae and Marion with a database of more than a billion faces illegally harvested, categorised and stored for facial recognition.

Silently and within a millisecond they were matched. Artificial intelligence software then applied a risk rating algorithm to their profiles, compiled it into another email and sent it off to two email addresses. The first to Laura Edison at the Merton Research Institute, the second to Magnus Crane in the US.

~

It was late as Crane headed for home after the charity dinner. He couldn't suppress a belch as his meal repeated on him. Damn. He was usually very measured in how he ate. The body was a temple, and should be respected. At least his body anyway. He was somewhat less concerned with those of the mostly obese and lazy people he encountered in the business and pharmaceutical world. The UberX driver drove carefully, not wishing to risk his perfect rating by throwing this important looking passenger around the back of his beautiful new Tesla.

Crane checked emails on his phone. He had a pretty good filtering system for his work flow, otherwise he'd be swamped with information, most of it irrelevant for a man in his position. The company more or less ran itself nowadays, and so it should with over ten thousand employees around the world, so he could indulge himself by focusing on his philanthropic work. As well as the population control research projects he had running in a dozen different countries.

He chuckled at the innocuous looking titles for the emails: *Pesticide genome splicing and enhancement program, Bolivia*

This was a very promising project, demonstrating how easy it was to modify the common bacillus thuringiensis bacterium, a pesticide used for eliminating mosquitoes, so it could be rapidly mass produced and distributed. He'd been a scientist most of his life, but it still amazed him how quickly technology was advancing because of the way information was shared nowadays. Techniques like this that once required a fully equipped government laboratory could now be done in a high school classroom. Only a trusted few in the entire program knew that this virus was almost identical to Anthrax, and the techniques were directly applicable to one of the most deadly bacterium known to man. Perfect if you needed to reduce a large urban population quickly through airborne dissemination of the spores. And the company already had the chemical factories set up for mass production.

He briefly opened then closed a half dozen more emails, satisfied that all were progressing smoothly and didn't need his personal attention. Then:

Tasmanian Devil facial tumour program, incident report:

Crane's eyes flicked across the email about bush walkers snooping around the highlands facility in Tasmania, and he frowned as he stopped on a name. Ian MacRae. Crane recognised it from Edison's report on the project in Nigeria. He was popping up in a bunch of unexpected places associated with the work. Maybe this MacRae needed some encouragement to mind his own business. He mentally ran some names of who could get there quickly, then smiled. He knew just who to call.

~

The last of the light was fading when Eileen, Marion and MacRae arrived back at Eileen's house, huge Eucalypts casting long shadows across their paths as they walked.

Eileen sighed with relief as she eased her walking boots off in the porch. 'That was quite a walk in the end.' She rubbed one aching foot, then the other, before going inside.

MacRae sat at the table and took the plastic bag from his backpack, retrieving the phone and cleaning it with a damp cloth. Then the moment of truth as he tried to turn it on. Nothing. Perhaps it just had no charge. He plugged it into his phone charger and waited ten minutes before trying it again. This time the screen glowed blue, but was covered with gibberish.

He put it down on the kitchen bench. 'I think it's ruined.'

'Let's try another way,' Eileen said, leading them through to her office.

Her laptop hummed quietly as it started up, then Eileen slid it across the desk to MacRae.

'Try plugging it in.'

MacRae spent the next thirty minutes working on the laptop, trying different programs to recover information, but it kept coming up against error messages.

Marion leaned against the wall, warming her hands with a mug of coffee. 'I think we'll need more technical expertise than we've got.'

'I think you're right, and I know just who to ask,' MacRae said. 'Let's get packed up and head home.'

Eileen shut down the laptop. 'You're not riding home now, it's too dangerous for a motorcycle on these roads in the dark, there's far too much wildlife. You're staying here again tonight. Okay?'

It was a statement, not a question.

Marion and MacRae swapped a glance, then both shrugged.

~

'Which side of the sink do you like your toothbrush?' Marion called from the bathroom, tapping a glass.

'I'll let you decide, honey.' MacRae smiled at their brief illusion of domestic bliss.

Marion wandered back into the bedroom, towels wrapped around her head and torso fresh from the shower. It had been a tough day's walk, they'd all felt the stress, both physical and mental from the search.

'Do you think we achieved anything today?' She rubbed her hair vigorously, lost in the towel.

'It's hard to say. I think it's quite likely the phone is Murdoch's, but whether or not it has anything that might help us on it, or if we can even view it...' MacRae felt his eyes being drawn to Marion, her naked legs strong and smooth from an active life.

She finished her hair, dropping the towel and looking over to see MacRae watching her. She smiled, taking in the face she knew so well, the kindness and gentleness she'd know as his lover, and the determination and toughness to do what he felt had to be done when necessary. It had been years since she'd seen him like this and she was pleased to see his body was still toned in his T-shirt. The memories of being held in his arms as they made love came flooding back.

MacRae met her eyes and time stopped for them both. MacRae could feel the desire stirring in his body, the pull to be with her again so powerful. And he could see the hunger in her eyes too, as her breaths became shorter with passing seconds. MacRae moved slowly across the room towards her, pulling his shirt over his head and dropping it to the floor. Marion gasping as her eyes wandered over his tightly muscled torso. Almost without realising, she dropped the towel from her body, MacRae soaking up the beauty of her naked form.

Then she saw the scars. Not the old ones she knew so well from long ago when she'd explored every part of his body. These were new reminders of many battles, violence, fights fought and won since they parted long ago. Nothing had changed for either of them.

The spell was broken as she remembered why they were here, and why they had torn apart from each other long ago to stop the pain of their impossible love.

She looked away and picked up her towel, self-consciously covering herself up.

'Well we haven't got any time to waste to find Hassana. God knows where the poor kid is or what's happening to her.'

She headed back into the bathroom with a last glance at MacRae as he stood in the centre of the room. They were sharing the bed again tonight, but couldn't let anything happen between them again no matter how strong their feelings for each other.

It was going to be a long night.

~

CHAPTER 18

PING

MacRae and Marion loaded the motorcycle up early the next morning and said their goodbyes before headed back south. It was a chilly but clear morning, the sun sparkling on the dew-covered leaves. MacRae quickly relaxed into the rhythm of the ride, approaching shady and winding sections of the road cautiously, looking for the invisible hazard of black ice.

He slowed as he approached an intersection, casting a quick glance at the white SUV pulled off to the side. A man in the driver's seat leaned down reading something. Then he felt Marion's arms grip tighter around his waist as he accelerated hard onto the main road.

Inside the SUV Vlad Korshov looked up as the motorcycle sped past. He smiled and stretched his shoulders before starting the motor. He liked this kind of job, scare someone off, or worse if he felt it appropriate. This guy MacRae had already made an impression, turning up where he wasn't wanted. Then facial recognition had traced him back to security cameras at the local hotel where he'd been involved in a fight, before leaving on the motorcycle that just went past.

Korshov took his work seriously. Years in the Russian internal security forces had taught him to do that, and from what he'd seen of the bar fight on Facebook and the background information Crane had sent through, he knew to take MacRae seriously.

The electric window hummed quietly as he wound it down, tossing his cigarette out with a shower of sparks. Then with a spray of gravel from the tires, the turbocharged engine hurtled the SUV on to the road in pursuit of MacRae and Marion.

~

MacRae's eyes adjusted to the change in light as he entered a line of trees, then the road swung to the left. He glanced in his rear viewmirror before he touched the brake, a good thing as the SUV he'd noticed earlier was approaching rapidly from behind them and might not have expected him to slow. He accelerated out of the corner, glancing again in the mirror. The car had closed the gap between them. MacRae frowned. Too close for comfort. He opened the throttle, the bike leapt forward with a roar, Marion's hands gripping hard around his waist. Another glance in the mirror, he'd opened the gap but could see the car was also accelerating hard. He couldn't pick the make, must be a European sports model, some of those are built more like racing cars than anything else. Jesus it was quick. MacRae's stomach tightened as he realised it was the car by the side of the road he's seen earlier...they'd been waiting for him. What was he playing at?

Marion's voice crackled through on the intercom. 'What's going on Ian?'

He could hear her concern. 'Not sure, it seems we've picked up an unwanted tail.' A quick glance in his mirror. 'Maybe it's to do with the trouble at the hotel.'

Marion glanced over her shoulder. 'Do you think it's those two guys? Can we lose them?'

MacRae checked his speed, he was still accelerating hard on the straight, up past two hundred kilometres per hour now...two ten... two twenty. The bike would have been fast enough if it was just him. But with Marion as well? And he knew that he was subconsciously holding back to avoid risking a crash with her on the back.

He felt his heart rate increase, a mixture of trepidation and anger coursing through him. The car was right on him, almost touching his rear wheel. MacRae could see the driver's face, a grim mask of concentration. It wasn't one of the guys from the fight. This was different, and he was trying to hit the motorcycle.

MacRae moved into a crouch, tucking down behind the windshield to take the pressure off his neck and lower the wind resistance, Marion tucking in behind him instinctively. He felt a tingle of sweat on his palms as he focused intently on the road. A sign flashed past...winding road ahead. The car could match his speed on the open road, but the bike should be able to brake and accelerate more quickly. Maybe this would give him the edge.

They flew over the crest of a hill, then the first corner approached at terrifying speed. They were going way too fast. MacRae waited, his mind screamed to hit the brakes, but the car was still so close. Who was going to blink first?

The car driver lost his nerve, suddenly falling back, the front of the SUV nosing abruptly down as the huge racing disk brakes bit. MacRae smiled and hit the motorcycle brakes hard almost as the bike entered the corner, throwing it over to one side, engine screaming as he dropped down through the gears, then opening the throttle with a roar as he exited the bend, the tachometer needle flicking up to the red zone with every gear change. He heard the scream of tires and saw the car in his mirror, rear wheels drifting around the corner behind him, closing fast. For the first time MacRae wasn't sure if he could shake him.

Another corner approached, a sweeping bend. MacRae thought it looked familiar from the ride up, but there was something about it he should remember.

He entered the corner fast, leaning over hard, the car closing behind him again.

'Jesus'. He swore to himself as it came to him. It was a spiral, rapidly twisting ever tighter, and he was going way too fast.

MacRae hit the brakes, the rear wheel locking up, skipping and bouncing on the road. The needle on the speedometer plunged, but he was still way too fast, he wasn't going to make it, the motorcycle starting to slide across the other side of the road...towards a huge drop over the embankment into the forest below. Then the screech of tires behind him as the car driver also realised his mistake and slid sideways across the road towards him, about to take them both over the edge.

In desperation, MacRae lifted the bike upright to stop the slide, and watched in amazement as the car slid past in a cloud of acrid tire smoke, missing his rear wheel by a hair's breadth.

The motorbike finally stopped, front wheel teetering on the edge of the drop to the forest below, rear wheel pulled around to the side. MacRae held the bike up with one foot on the ground, his gloves gripping the handlebars like a vice. A roar entered his head... he had the clutch and the brake gripped, but the engine was still revving fiercely. MacRae eased his grip on the throttle and relaxed.

He felt Marion release her grip around him. 'God, Ian that was way too close.'

Then he saw it. The car up ahead of him had also managed to avoid the deadly fall down the embankment and was starting to turn back towards him on the narrow mountain road. It looked like they hadn't finished yet.

~

Graeme Ashley had been a truck driver for many years and seen a lot of crazy behaviour on the roads, but even he'd been shocked by the street race he'd seen from his driveway as he approached the main road in his log truck. First a motorcycle, two-up no less, flashed past, engine screaming, riders lying flat on the tank, then a white SUV flying past in hot pursuit a split second later, must've been doing two hundred clicks or more. A shake of his head as he turned onto the road, working his way slowly up through the fifteen gears. It was going to end in disaster for sure.

~

'It's not over yet Marion.' MacRae's voice was icy cold in her headphones.

She looked down the road at the turning car and threw her arms around him again. 'What now Ian?'

The motorcycle was still sideways on the gravel shoulder, almost over the edge. MacRae yanked on the handle bars, pulling the machine backwards onto the asphalt road. He still had to completely turn the bike around though, and the SUV was now accelerating hard towards them. MacRae's muscles screamed as he straightened the bike up. It wasn't quick enough, the car's engine roaring as it hurtled towards them.

MacRae made a snap decision. 'Marion, get off the bike...now.'

She jumped to one side, MacRae leaned the bike on its stand, then took her hand, pulling her to the edge of the embankment.

'You wait here, he'll choose me first.'

Her eyes blazed. 'What are you doing?'

MacRae scanned the ground, finding what he needed, scooping it up into his hand, shooting her a confident grin. 'I'll be fine.' He stepped back over to the bike, pretending to try and start it.

Korshov watched the woman move to the side of the road then MacRae go back to the bike. Perfect, he'd take him out first then go back for the cute bitch. A bonus.

MacRae watched as the SUV veered straight towards him. His mind flashed to when he'd first met Sarah years ago in Spain, and they'd attended their first bullfight together. Now he was the Matador, with a huge steel bull trying to kill him. He looked down at the motorbike, waiting. This must be timed perfectly.

Korshov smiled as he tracked the last few metres to the motorbike. Too easy. Then at the last second MacRae looked straight at Korshov, and leapt to the side, swinging his arm at the car with all his strength.

Korshov cursed as his target jumped to safety, the car clipping the front of the bike with a grinding crash, sending it spinning in a crumpled wreck to the side of the road. Then his eyes widened as the huge stone thrown by MacRae speared straight at his face, punching through the windshield in a shower of glass.

He slammed on the brakes, bringing the car to a shuddering halt as he brushed pieces from glass from his face. Eyes blazing with a cold rage, he reached into the glove box, pulling out a dull black 9mm pistol. He glanced up to the rear view mirror to see MacRae running full speed at the car. Korshov pulled back the slide on the weapon, driving a round into the chamber.

MacRae caught a glimpse of the gun through the rear window of the car, his legs pumped with a new urgency to get there before the man could take a shot. But it was too late, the man swinging his legs out the door.

MacRae looked both sides, no obvious cover, and threw himself around the opposite side of the car...as the sharp crack of gunfire propelled a slug where he'd just been...straight into the path of a huge log truck rounding the corner behind them, air brakes growling as Graeme Ashley tried to arrest the massive vehicle.

Marion screamed at him. 'Ian...the truck.'

MacRae turned, as the truck juddered to a halt a mere arm's length away, the truck driver glaring down at him, shock etched across his face.

Korshov stood still, lowering the gun to his side, out of view of the truck driver. This was getting way too complicated. His eyes locked with MacRae's, they both knew they had unfinished business, but this wasn't the time.

Korshov climbed back into the car, keeping the weapon out of sight, and accelerated hard down the road away from them, glistening pieces of glass littering the road behind him.

The truck driver climbed down from the cab, his one hundred and twenty kilo frame thumping heavily on the steel steps, his voice a roar. 'You nearly made me crash my truck. And I could have killed you.' His eyes took in the wrecked motorcycle and Marion running towards them, the only sound the *ping* of the cooling motorcycle engine. His hands balled into fists, then he recognised the shape as a woman and his voice softened. 'What the hell do you think you were doing?'

Marion couldn't hold back, throwing her arms around MacRae as he pulled off his helmet. He helped remove hers, seeing for the first time tears streaming down her face.

'I thought he was going to kill you Ian.' Then came words she didn't want to say to him but couldn't hold back any longer. 'I thought I'd lost you Ian, and I can't stand the thought of losing you again.'

~

It had taken MacRae and Marion a while to convince the truck driver that the incident had started as a bit of fun, pushing the motorcycle to its limits along the country roads far from the watchful eyes and speed cameras of the police. Then they'd overtaken the SUV, enraging the driver. In an instant the morning's ride had become a life or death road rage attack.

The truck driver gritted his teeth. 'I still think you should call the police, the guy was crazy.'

MacRae and Marion spoke at the same time. 'No, not the police.'

'Why the hell not?' the truck driver said, hands on hips.

MacRae shot a glance to Marion. 'I haven't got the best driving record. I could lose my licence...' The truckie didn't look convinced. '...and my job.'

'So what happens now?' the truckie said.

Marion took the initiative. 'How about we load the bike onto your truck, you give us a ride back home, and we all forget this ever happened?'

The truckie sensed an opportunity. 'And why would we want to do that?'

'I can give you a hundred reasons to help us,' MacRae said, pulling out his wallet. The truckie looked away impassively.

Marion shook her head and sighed. 'Make that three hundred...' The truckie still wasn't quite convinced. '...and a case of beer.'

The truckie grinned broadly, displaying an array of crooked teeth, and thrust a meaty hand in their direction. 'You've got a deal.'

~

Korshov parked the SUV back at the compound where it would stay until he arranged to get the windscreen and damaged panel replaced. He'd have to file a report on the incident to the company. They didn't like loose ends. Neither did he.

He felt a prick in his back, lifting his shirt to pull out another piece of the shattered windscreen and grinned. This guy MacRae was something else. Most of the people Korshov was sent after to frighten or kill folded into frightened little balls when he confronted them. It wasn't a challenge anymore, just boring, not the same sense of excitement and fun he used to get exercising his power over others. But this guy MacRae, he had the spark. He wasn't someone who was going to go quietly, and this was exciting. Korshov would have to wait for further instructions, but his gut told him he would be finishing the job. Hopefully soon.

The security guard gave him a curious look as he'd entered the building, but knew better than to ask what had happened. The extent of his training was a few weeks with a private security contractor, mainly doing night club doors and late night commercial building patrols. But he could see The Russian, as he called him, was in a different, frightening league.

And there was a lot of stuff went on here he didn't ask about.

~

CHAPTER 19

THE BAY

The truck driver counted the money carefully when he dropped MacRae and Marion at MacRae's apartment. He stuffed the bundle of notes in a back pocket, then helped MacRae move the smashed motorcycle out of sight into the double garage. He cast a curious eye around the sleek timber and glass exterior of the apartment, struggling to reconcile the incident with the SUV and MacRae's sophisticated lifestyle by the sea.

'Nice place you got here.'

MacRae shrugged. 'I used to live in the bush like you.' His mind flashed back to his torture by terrorists at his property in the bush. He loved the property, but it was never the same after that.

'But a change is as good as a holiday as they say.'

The sound of surf crashing on the nearby beach was drowned out by the roar of the log truck's diesel engine firing back to life, and with a shake of his head and a wave the truckie headed back up north. MacRae and Marion looked at each other as the sound of the truck faded in the distance. MacRae walked over to the shattered remains of the motorcycle and gave it a gentle kick.

'Well that didn't go quite as I planned.'

Marion laughed. 'Well you certainly know how to give a girl an interesting time. But I think that's the last time I go on a motorcycle with you.'

MacRae pulled out his phone, dialling Sarah's number. Marion listened while MacRae gave her a quick rundown of the search in the bush, the drone at the bunker and the incident with the SUV driver, then he hung up.

'You make it all sound so matter of fact, us almost being killed. Is this just another day at the office for you?' Marion said.

Her words hit home. Had she just summarised his life...one incident after another? Was that why she decided long ago that she couldn't share this world with him?

MacRae turned away and hit the button to close the garage door. 'Sarah's coming over. Let's get some coffee on.'

~

Sarah walked slowly around the wrecked motorcycle while MacRae and Marion looked on. 'Holy shit. I think you're right, this was no accident. What's your gut feeling Ian, was it linked to the guys you took down at the pub, or something else, maybe the drone surveillance?'

'It was only one person, and he seemed pretty calculated about it. He was a damned good driver, the SUV was pretty new, expensive, he was armed, and it didn't look like he was going to quit, until the truck turned up.' He looked at Marion. 'I think we were pretty lucky it did.'

Sarah chewed her lip. 'It looks to me like you're starting to attract the wrong kind of attention.'

MacRae nodded. 'And the sooner we sort it out the better,' He passed her a plastic bag. 'So this is the phone we found. It might be nothing, but maybe there's something useful on it. I've had a go at accessing it without any luck. Either it's corrupted or encrypted, or being exposed to the weather has ruined it.'

Sarah turned it over in her fingers. 'I'll give it my best shot, run some diagnostics with hacking software I came across a while ago.'

MacRae grinned. 'I suspected this wouldn't be the first time you'd tried to pull data off a phone.'

'Investigative journalist or police detective, we're all trying to uncover the truth aren't we?' She slipped it into her pocket as she headed out the door. 'I'll let you know how I go.'

Marion checked the time. 'I'm off too Ian, try to live like a normal person for a while.'

MacRae felt slightly uneasy, unable to put his finger on why. Then he realised it was the silence in the apartment. He was used to being alone most of the time, but he'd enjoyed having Marion around the last few days. He shook off the feeling and sat at his dining table and fired up his laptop. Time to do some research on the devil facial tumour program, and the facility in the Central Highlands.

His mind wandered as he waited for search results to come up. Then, irritated that the unease with the silence lingered, he scooped up his laptop and left the apartment for the short walk to the cafe bar on the beach around the corner.

It was pretty quiet early afternoon and he took his favourite seat near the window. The staff all knew him and before he'd even ordered, a drink and snack turned up.

He barely noticed the place filling up as the next few hours passed while he worked. He started with the State Titles Office website, and for a few dollars downloaded the ownership records of the facility in the Highlands. He then cross-checked it with the local government office records for building and development approvals. It made interesting reading.

The property had originally been part of a huge land holding passed down through the generations from an early settler. The land was remote, inaccessible and not very productive, so had been broken up and sold in smaller parcels over time. This particular parcel being snapped up ten years ago by an overseas corporation, Landhaven Holdings, a subsidiary of the pharmaceutical company, Medici-Royal. The name seemed familiar. Then he recalled Sarah had found information suggesting the drug trial contractor in Nigeria had done work for Medici-Royal.

He searched the name. The Medici-Royal company was a huge corporation with interests around the world and run by an American, Magnus Crane. Crane, as the founder and CEO, seemed to be held in high regard, particularly for his philanthropic work in developing countries like India where, according to news reports, he was building water treatments plants across the continent to provide clean drinking water to millions of people, timing the project so he could personally commission the plants as a double celebration at the start of Diwali, their national festival of lights marking the triumph of good over evil.

The company had grown very quickly, largely by the astute acquisition of smaller companies, usually leaders in particular fields, or with undervalued assets that Medici-Royal had been able to leverage. Some of the smaller company's names seemed familiar, so MacRae spent some time researching their background. Some of them went back almost a hundred years and had very murky pasts, one German company accused of supplying chemicals to the Nazi concentration camps for poison gas production. Others, whilst manufacturing and supplying vaccines for third world countries had reportedly also held US Defence Department contracts for biological weapons research. MacRae flicked between news reports of company activities and official company denials. He leaned back in his chair and rubbed his eyes. It was hard sorting the truth from conspiracy theories nowadays as so much information reported as fact was unverified by any credible source.

He turned his focus back to Crane. The man's public persona seemed very well managed, always a consistent message focusing on the good works he did. There was very little on his private life, or his personal history, at least at the top of the internet search results. MacRae scrolled further down the list and started to find more obscure references.

It seemed it wasn't always smooth sailing for his companies. At one point a subsidiary had been accused of profiteering from a deadly flu outbreak, supplying millions of doses of a vaccine to western governments for front-line health workers if the outbreak got out of control, only for it to be revealed the vaccine was for a previous variant of the flu and would have been of little use against the current outbreak. A photo showed a sombre looking Crane assuring the media that it was an honest attempt to assist in a public health crisis but that of course all money paid for the vaccine would be returned.

MacRae took another approach on search results for Crane, clicking on the browser *images* tab. Hundreds of photos of Crane appeared. MacRae clicked on an image of Crane holding one side of a book, the other side held by a smiling man in what looked like hiking clothing. The photo was linked to an old website promoting a survivalists conference where Crane seemed to be endorsing a book on urban survival techniques. MacRae frowned. Not something he'd expected from a respected corporate leader.

Another picture caught his eye. It was attached to a press release announcing a funding package for genetics research. MacRae recognised it as the photo he'd seen in the Merton Institute media centre. Crane was standing next to the Director Dr Edison, as they held the oversized cheque for a million dollars. Medici-Royal obviously had ties to Tasmania, but was it all just coincidence?

He returned to an earlier search and checked out the development application for the property in the highlands where they'd been scrutinised by the drone. The application was for a dwelling, but the size of the building and materials to be used suggested another purpose. Much of the building was to be constructed in solid concrete underground, and the layout of the rooms, independent power and water supply suggested it could accommodate a lot of people almost indefinitely. Was it simply a country retreat for a large corporation or the bunker as speculated by the locals? He loaded an aerial photography website and found the area the bunker was located, zooming in to find more detail of the layout of the structure but the closer he zoomed the blurrier the image became. He frowned. A glitch in the software? He loaded an alternate mapping and aerial photography website, zooming in again, getting the same result. This was no glitch. Someone had arranged to have the location blurred for privacy or security reason. That suggested they had something to hide, and either considerable influence or plenty of money to buy influence.

MacRae became aware of the buzz of conversation around him as patrons filed in for dinner. Almost time for him to leave.

He toyed with the idea of the house in the highlands having a more sinister purpose. Time for one more search. He typed in *Magnus Crane* and *conspiracy* and instantly was rewarded with a series of news reports relating to Crane winning a defamation suit against a man, Elias Ali, a few years back, where Crane had been accused of being involved in illegal drug trials in third world countries and worse. MacRae read a few of the reports. There were no details of a settlement other than that the man had to apologise and retract numerous statements he'd made about Crane, and close down websites where he'd been publishing his views.

MacRae followed a few links relating to the story but all the websites were no longer functioning. The only active link was for a conspiracy theorist's forum. He'd come across these sites before, where believers swapped their stories of aliens amongst us, QAnon, and the world cabal trafficking children for their blood, amongst other things.

He searched the forum threads for *Crane* and *Elias* and spend another ten minutes reading through what must have been the basis of Crane's defamation lawsuit. Elias was accusing Crane of everything from running illegal drug trials for decades to being involved in the disastrous chemical plant explosion in Bophal, India in 1984. And unfortunately for Elias he seemed to be offering no actual evidence to support his claims.

MacRae sighed and closed his laptop. This was all very interesting, but all he'd really uncovered was a whole lot of information that could mean a lot, or nothing. He felt a brief rush of disappointment. Nothing could be described as a solid lead in his search for Hassana. He gathered up his things and headed out into the fresh evening air back to his apartment. But he also knew that sometimes you have to make your own luck, and the one common factor that seemed to keep coming up was the Merton Institute. He was sure Edison knew more than she was saying after letting slip about Nigeria, so it was time to see which of the two, him or Edison, was the best at bluffing.

He made two phone calls when he got home. The first to Sarah. She didn't pick up, so he left a message asking if she'd had any luck getting data off the phone, and that he was going to see Edison again, try and shake the tree a bit to see what fell off.

The second call was to Edison. She didn't pick up either, so he left a message asking for another meeting as he'd uncovered some disturbing information regarding the devil facial tumour program.

He smiled as he ended the message. The bait was out there, now to see if Edison would bite.

A few minutes' drive away at her house, Sarah was getting frustrated with her lack of progress in pulling data from the phone. The screen wasn't working and accessing it externally she couldn't get a coherent directory structure from the memory, although the hacking software told her there were recent files that had been sent to and from the phone. She suspected that the operating system was functioning but was locking her out as she hadn't accessed the phone with a password. This wasn't the first time she'd encountered problems with accessing locked phones, but in this case she might need some more assistance.

Her thoughts were interrupted as she heard her phone ringing in the distance. She looked around her. Damn, she must have left it somewhere else in the house. She pushed it from her mind. If it was important they'd call back or leave a message.

She opened the Tor web browser on her laptop and threw out a request onto the Dark Web for assistance in hacking a possible locked or encrypted phone, and as she waited responses came trickling in. She felt her heart rate increase as she looked through the proposals, comparing the payments requested and what they needed from her. Paying for services on the Dark Web always made her nervous. You never knew who you were dealing with, and what they might do it they got access to your computer. Then before she could pick one, a message appeared on the centre of her screen, an empty text box at the bottom.

You can't trust anyone you find here, do not give them access to your computer.

Sarah tapped her finger on the desk, then typed in the text box.
Who are you? And how else can I get access to the phone?
Another text box appeared.
I can get you access to anything, and you can trust me.
We've trusted each other before.
More words appeared.
You, me, Ian, Brad, Devil's Breath....it's been a long time.
Sarah sat back, stunned. Surely it couldn't be...?
With trembling fingers she typed a name.
Ritchie?

~

Sarah felt a jumble of emotions wash across her, shock that he'd got in contact with her after so long, and relief that he was alive and well...wherever he was.

She'd first come across Ritchie as a teenager years ago when he'd been caught up with a radical religious group in London. He'd almost gone to jail for his misguided involvement, but her work as a journalist had helped prove his innocence in their activities.

Thankfully he'd been given a second chance, because his extraordinary talent as a hacker, once abused by the radical group, had helped them when they'd been in desperate need with the Devil's Breath weapon, only for him to disappear without a trace immediately afterwards.

Even Brad Schneider with his CIA resources hadn't been able to shed any light on Ritchie's disappearance, other than to show them a grainy video of a police raid on a gloomy London apartment around the time Ritchie disappeared.

But just now in a flurry of messages he'd described how it was indeed him being arrested in the police video, before being extradited to the US to be charged with causing deaths in the US from his hacking. But the National Security Agency, the most secretive of the US spy agencies, had offered him a deal with a new identity and a job as hacker for them instead. Now he makes more money than he could have dreamed of in England, as long as he never goes home.

Sarah tapped the keys again.

Do you miss England, your mother?

There was a pause before he replied.

I missed my mother, but she passed a while ago. Cancer. As for England? I don't have any ties there anymore, and I don't miss the cold.

Two photos flashed briefly on her screen. The first was a shiny red open-topped Ferrari, the second an ocean view from a beautiful modern apartment, the foreground filled with shops and palm trees bathed in sunlight. Then they were gone.

I'm happy, although it does seem like a golden cage sometimes. What's the significance of the phone?

Sarah quickly explained about Hassana, MacRae's search for her and the missing photographer, and where they'd found the phone, then followed Ritchie's instructions to connect it to her computer.

She typed a message.

Are you sure you can get something off it, even if it's encrypted?

A smiley face appeared in the text box.

Despite what is said in the media or on the internet, nothing is truly secure with the right tools and skills.

Then Sarah watched as her screen was filled with data flashing from the phone to her computer then across the Dark Web to wherever Ritchie was working.

CHAPTER 20

SUB-CONTINENT

Magnus Crane waited patiently in the back seat of the hotel courtesy car as it went through the first of many security checks to gain entry to the water treatment plant in the suburban industrial park on the eastern fringe of Chennai. He was never quite sure why security was taken so zealously in India. Maybe it was part of the culture of keeping as many of the population employed in often duplicated services. Or perhaps it was the appropriate response to the terrorist threats, both interior and exterior that too often played themselves out here in shocking violence.

The first barrier gate lifted as the driver's papers were returned to him by the guard in an immaculate white uniform. Then they were stopped again at a second barrier and the underside of the car checked by another serious looking guard using a mirror on a long pole, presumably checking for a bomb.

The car pulled up under a steel and glass awning at the main entrance. A third guard opened the car door for Crane, checking his documents before directing him to the walk through a metal detector and into the building foyer, collecting his briefcase from the X-ray machine as he went.

'Welcome back Mr Crane,' beamed the plant manager, enthusiastically shaking Crane's hand. 'So glad to see you here for the final preparations for our wonderful joint venture.'

Crane nodded his head. 'It's always a pleasure to be in your country, working together to improve the lives of your citizens.'

He smiled to himself. No matter how complex their security, nothing would protect them from what he was about to unleash upon their population. In fact the manager, and the others like him that Crane was working with across the Indian continent, couldn't even have imagined the pivotal role they were playing as facilitators for his work, unknowingly inviting the Devil into their home.

The manager whisked him through the brand new, beautifully furnished office suites and out the back to the huge concrete and steel buildings of the water treatment plant. He spoke in a crisp English accent, giving an unintended sense of formality to his words.

'I'm so proud to be destined to be commissioning this wonderful new facility with much fanfare and celebration, as the new, clean water supply for up to fifteen million people across the region.'

Crane agreed. 'I also feel privileged to be joining you on such a special endeavour. And this is just one of the many to be commissioned remotely the same day across the length and breadth of your country, revolutionising the water supply, and hygiene, of much of India's population in one incredible day.'

He mentally zoned out as the manager gushed about the quality of the finishes of the construction, and the monumental efforts of so many local and multinational corporations, alongside the visionary Indian government, that had united to bring this to fruition. And of course the tireless efforts and generosity as both a business partner and philanthropist that Magnus Crane as CEO of Medici-Royal Corporation had devoted over the recent years to this milestone in the development of India as a nation, and indeed an international power.

For the next hour Crane and the manager went through the motions of inspecting the facility, checking the key stages and processes. Much of it was in fact a waste of time for Crane, as he already had a skilled team of project managers reporting to him at every step. Their advice was that despite the challenges of doing business in India, operating to the special rhythm of the Indian way of life, and the sometimes overwhelming bureaucracy and occasional corruption, everything was on schedule for the commissioning, a joint event with Crane and the Indian Minister for Development.

The manager tapped in yet another security code to exit the engineering side of the plant. Much of this had been designed and built by subsidiaries of Crane's organisation, and was of little interest to him...as long as it worked.

But now they were inspecting the equipment that was unique to these new modern water treatment plants...the systems to allow the addition of complex combinations of chemicals and agents to the water supply. This would enable the operators, and the Indian government, to make huge advances in public health through the distribution of vaccines, fluoride or a multitude of other desirable additives on a population level. It would also enable Crane to implement his own agenda completely undetected.

He listened intently as the manager took him through the flow diagrams and procedures for the operations of the equipment, nodding approval at the shiny stainless steel chemical storage and distribution equipment. The manager saw a perfect example of planning and construction, the plant rapidly nearing completion in front of him. Crane saw something else...a fine example of vertical integration, where his web of companies controlled every aspect of the supply chain, from the planning and design of the water treatment plant, to the manufacture and installation of the equipment, the chemicals to be distributed through it, and the software that controlled and monitored the entire process. And that was why he had been able to put together this complex and risky plan, by ensuring there was no outside scrutiny or third party involvement. Even within his organisation no-one except himself was across all the links of the supply chain.

In a masterpiece of organisational siloing, the researchers developing pathogens for the Defence Department didn't know the same pathogens were being produced in commercial quantities at another of Crane's facilities, and the distribution arm of the company had no idea what they were actually shipping at any time.

They climbed another set of stairs, shoes clanking on the steel mesh of the treads until they stood on a service catwalk overlooking the main operations floor.

The manager let out a slow breath, then turned to face Crane.

'It is indeed a powerful position to be in isn't it Mr Crane?'

Crane wrinkled his brow. 'How so?'

The manager waved a hand across the room.

'We are like Gods when we're in charge of something as powerful as this modern plant. Everything we do can affect the health of millions of people. In fact it is even more so for you, as you're doing this all across our country.'

Crane nodded. 'Yes, in some ways this is perhaps the boldest experiment in public health to be undertaken at such a scale. Perhaps it is even an experiment in social engineering, changing the health outcomes for a continent for generations to come.'

The manager's eyes searched Crane's.

'With great power also comes great responsibility, don't you agree Mr Crane? A facility like this in the modern world of terrorism could also perhaps be used to inflict great harm upon a great number of people.'

Crane's heart rate increased. What the hell was he talking about? Surely Crane hadn't slipped up, inadvertently giving a clue to his true intentions?

The manager turned away, leaning onto the narrow tubular steel handrail along the catwalk, gazing over the nearly completed plant.

Crane stepped silently closer to him. Now was not the time for the project to be questioned, or perhaps Crane blackmailed.

He glanced around the cavernous room. All the workers were on the other side of the space. And besides, no-one generally looked up unless they had a reason. The security cameras didn't seem to cover this area, it was too high. It would only take a moment to unbalance the manager and tip him to his death on the polished concrete floor fifteen metres below.

Crane made the decision and moved another step closer...just as the manager turned back to him and spoke.

'But we are so lucky as a developing nation to have men of your calibre working to give us all a better future.'

He reached out and grasped the hand that Crane had extended towards him to throw him overt the handrail, holding it for a moment in both his hands.

'Now what would you like to see?'

Crane relaxed, his heartbeat returning to normal.

'I'm happy for you to decide where we go next.'

~

The next hour passed quickly and they were done, the manager escorting Crane back to the foyer. He returned Crane's Visitor ID card to the reception desk and spoke.

'Once again I thank you for your visit, and the great work you are doing for my country.'

He paused, placing his hands in front as though praying, then continued. 'And it would be the greatest of honours for me if you had the time whilst you are here to join with my family for dinner at our modest home.'

The words hung in the air.

Crane was genuinely taken aback at this expression of generosity. From what he knew, the manager lived a relatively humble middle class life and this was not an invitation extended lightly to a man like Crane.

Crane replied with a smile. 'I'm deeply honoured by your invitation, and will see if there is an opportunity to accept, in the brief time I have left on this visit to India.'

Another round of handshakes and security checks and his driver was racing him out of the sparking efficiency of the plant and back into the bewildering chaos of the Indian roads.

He relaxed to observe the show as his driver, immaculate in his white suit complete with gold crested hat weaved his way through the traffic. Line marking and signs meant very little as the drivers of everything from bicycles, hand-pulled carts, overcrowded buses and three wheeled Tuk-Tuk taxis jockeyed for road space, weaving past each other with millimetres to spare, searching for the most efficient way to their destination.

Crane felt a rush of exhilaration as he always did when he was immersed in the energy and diversity of these developing countries. Deep down he knew he missed the excitement of his younger life crisscrossing the globe for work, rather than now with his time being spent mostly behind a desk in a modern city.

The car slowed at an intersection and an old woman approached his window waving pieces of fruit at him, hand outstretched for anything to help feed her and probably her family for the day. The driver opened his window enough to dismiss her, then the car was off again, passing a bewildering array of traders, food stalls and the occasional upmarket retailer crammed along the road side.

Crane's mind wandered.

The responsibility of what he was planning to unleash soon upon the people of India weighed heavily upon him. It hadn't been an easy choice. India or China. Each of them developing rapidly. Each of them with around fifteen percent of the world's population. And as it turned out with the rapid advances in genetic mapping, each with sufficient unique ethnic markers in their genome.

Yes it was true that there was only a tiny percentage of difference in the genetic makeup of all the races of the world, unexpected given how different the visual characteristics of the races appeared. But that was enough for the scientists employed across the vast range of companies under the umbrella of the Medici-Royal Corporation to be able to use these differences to tailor viruses to only be infectious to a specific race. And that was the breakthrough Crane had been awaiting for so long.

The shrill ring of his phone broke his train of thought. He checked the name before answering. It was one of his local project managers. Crane listened as the man gave his progress report, occasionally asking for more information as he struggled with the strong accent. Things were going well, as he'd expected. In fact he'd been surprised there was so little for him to sort out himself, perhaps a testament to the increasingly sophisticated Indian population, the younger generations well educated and motivated, hungry to compete in the modern international world of business.

The car slowed again, this time on a highway, as the cars in front manoeuvred carefully around the three sacred cows dozing in the centre lane. He shook his head. This country and its traditions never ceased to amaze him. Many of them were starting to fade now with the younger generations. Arranged marriages were often by consent, organised through dating websites, just with the parents involved. But superstitions still ran deep, and the caste system had yet to completely disappear into history.

But there was a dynamism, an optimism with the youthful generations building a first-world future of manufacturing and technology.

And this was what had made Crane's choice of country so difficult. He wholeheartedly supported the democracy of India over the communism of China, the right of people to choose their own future. But ultimately it was the poverty and pollution that continued to blight this nation that made his decision. In a world of diminishing resources and failing ecosystems, the elimination of the population of India would make the biggest difference. Plus he was certain that with China's more advanced technology they would no doubt have tried to appropriate his processes, perhaps removing him and his companies from the commissioning, and accidentally discovering what he was really planning.

The traffic snarled temporarily like an eddy of water caught in the corner of a river as everyone squeezed past the cows, Crane's driver sounding his horn, along with everyone else letting each other know they were threading their way through, almost touching. Crane turned to look as a motorcycle stopped briefly next to his window. The driver had his helmet perched backwards on the top of his head, a nod to the new laws requiring helmets to be worn. A teenage boy was squeezed between the driver and his wife behind, and a baby strapped to the mother's back blinked and smiled at Crane.

For the thousandth time Crane doubted his decision. He knew the hospitality that would have been extended to him by the plant manager if he attended his house for dinner. These were a mostly kind and generous people. But then like every general who ever sent men to their death in battle, he knew that someone had to make the decisions to sacrifice the few to save the many. Even if *the few* in this case were one point three billion people.

The traffic cleared and the next half hour on the highway passed without incident. The car turned down a rutted laneway, through a decaying concrete archway with fading text in gold. Another kilometre and the grey shape of the house loomed into view.

Crane watched the driver as they approached the building. He showed little interest in the modern steel and concrete structure. But then why should he? From the outside there was little to indicate that this was one of the most sophisticated bunkers on the planet, part of a series built around the globe with great discretion for those with the need...and financial resources...to own one.

Crane exited the air-conditioned interior of the car, surprised as always by the blast of humid heat outside, and thanked the driver with a generous tip.

As he walked to the door he cast his eyes over the tinted glass windows reflecting back the lush vegetation surrounding the house. He looked carefully for clues, but to the untrained eye there was nothing to suggest that with the flick of a switch the external walls actually slid over each other to completely encase the building in a nuclear blast-proof reinforced concrete sheath.

He tapped a code into the door keypad, whilst his hand print and eyes were being simultaneously scanned. The door swung silently open, granting him entry to a place that would protect him and those he cared about from the worst the world, and humanity, could throw at him.

~

CHAPTER 21

SPARE PARTS

D r Laura Edison stood outside the rear fire escape door, watching through a side window as MacRae walked up. Her finger jiggled keys in her pocket absentmindedly, then she realised she was doing it and stopped. She knew it was a habit that revealed too much about her.

But then she had been more than a little unsettled since MacRae had called insisting on another meeting. She knew from the surveillance email drone pictures that he'd been in the Central Highlands checking out the bunker, but what had he discovered that took him there? Things were starting to get messy and Edison didn't like that. The project had been getting back on track again recently. Was there still a loose end to tidy up?

She guided MacRae through the door and into the building without a word. She'd come a long way from the squalor of third world medicine, seen the effects of poverty, overpopulation, and the disease that inevitably followed. Now she was finally part of a nobler cause, something that would make a real difference to the future of the planet. And nothing was going to get in her way.

~

MacRae had felt slightly disorientated as he followed Edison along the twisting corridors, past the research laboratories, then up the lift to her executive office overlooking the city. He was a little surprised that this time Edison had met him at a rear entrance of the building, explaining it was a quicker way through the facility for their after-hours meeting.

The view from her office was quite spectacular at night, lights blinking from the nearby buildings, the green and red navigation lights of water craft on the river, and in the distance the glimmer of the houses across the river.

Edison waved MacRae to a chair opposite her desk, then took a seat herself. MacRae peeled off his coat in the warmth of the room.

Edison spoke first. 'Well I have to say I'm not totally surprised to see you here again. You seem very persistent.'

MacRae shrugged. 'The truth is important to me.'

'A noble sentiment,' Edison said. 'So what are you hoping for from this meeting?'

MacRae didn't waste time. 'When I first came to see you I was asking for background information on exotic diseases, and in particular the devil facial tumour disease, and you were less than truthful in your responses.'

'How so?' Edison said.

'Nigeria.' MacRae said.

Edison tried to mask her surprise.

MacRae pressed on. 'I asked if there was a link between the devil facial tumour and an unknown disease in Africa, and you named the African country.'

A smile touched Edison's lips. 'A lucky guess. Nigeria is notorious for disease, corruption and other unpleasantness.'

'Perhaps,' MacRae said. 'But a lot has happened since our last meeting.'

'And what has this got to do with me?' Edison was stony faced.

'A girl, a friend of mine, was kidnapped in Nigeria recently, and the more I look, the more links I'm finding between what happened there and this institute and the operations of Magnus Crane, head of Medici-Royal Corporation.'

This time despite her best efforts MacRae saw Edison flinch. It had been a long shot, but now he was sure he was onto something.

Edison looked down with a sigh. She hadn't planned for this to happen, but she was prepared for the possibility. Was it fate that had forced her hand in this way, making her solve a lot of problems in one go?

MacRae shifted in his chair. The room was too hot. Edison noticed his discomfort and leaned down to a bar fridge against the wall, taking out a timber tray with a pitcher of chilled water and a couple of glasses. She poured herself a drink and slid the tray across the desk to MacRae.

'Sorry about the warm room, I worked in India for years and got quite used to the heat. Help yourself.'

She watched as MacRae filled a glass, emptying it in one quick motion, before she spoke again.

'Ah, yes, Magnus Crane. We go back quite a long way. All the way back to when I worked with him in India in the eighties. It was quite a meeting of the minds in a lot of ways, forged in adversity and death. Bophal, have you heard of that? A terrible business. But our time there did help us decide on our future, our legacy.'

She formed a church spire with her hands on the table. 'You really should have just let this go.'

MacRae shook his head. 'Too many people associated with the facial tumour program have had bad things happen to them.'

Edison smiled and leaned back in her chair, curious about what drove the man in front of her.

'It's been a bit of a journey that's taken you here hasn't it? This isn't just about the facial tumour disease or this institute. You can't help getting involved in other people's troubles can you?'

MacRae shrugged, toying with his glass.

'I've had a pretty interesting life, met a lot of people around the world. Some good, some not so good. And some just need help. That's what I'm good at, so that's what I do,' His voice went cold. 'But people I care about are getting hurt, and its led me here.'

Edison gazed out the window. How much had MacRae figured out already? Did it even matter? Certainly not for MacRae. He'd already sealed his fate.

'You know this research institute started off as a private facility, funded entirely by a wealthy businessman who lost his daughter to cancer?'

MacRae shook his head, puzzled by the change in conversation. 'I didn't know that.' Then it clicked. 'Magnus Crane?'

Edison nodded. 'Sometimes all the money and medical resources in the world isn't enough, even for someone like him. He lost his only child and eventually his marriage.'

He felt his mind wander as he looked at Edison. She was a scientist, but also a polished businesswoman. Expensive clothes, maybe mid-fifties, well groomed, fit. She must take care of herself. Was that because she was a scientist, staving off the inexorable advance of the ageing human body, or just vanity?

Edison's voice broke into MacRae's distracted thoughts. 'It ran on a shoestring back then, before my time. It was built on the site of one of the first hospitals in the original penal colony, set up by a wealthy landowner called Merton. The irony being that now rather than being seen as a kind and charitable man, Merton's past is being viewed as that of a cruel and greedy colonist at the time of the genocide of the indigenous population.'

She waved a hand around the office expansively. 'Now look at it. As time went by they were getting such impressive results in cancer research they attracted industry funding, then a partnership with the university and the teaching hospital. Now the place is awash with money. Hundreds of staff from all around the world, massive buildings.' She laughed. 'In fact most of the people actually working here have no idea what they're doing. Can you imagine spending your working life thinking you're helping to cure diseases, or studying the spread of pathogens believing you'll save millions of lives, when you're actually contributing to one of the greatest experiments in human history?'

She paused to reflect, then continued. 'In fact the irony is they may well end up being the subjects of their own research.' A smug smile creased her face. 'But I'm one of the select few who has the overview, the big picture. I have the box with the picture of the jigsaw if you will. But you my friend, were starting to put the pieces together.'

The one thing they could do here was turn up the air conditioning MacRae thought, a bead of sweat forming on his forehead. How hot did she need it? He struggled to organise his thoughts. What was she telling him? He refilled his glass and took another sip, relishing the cold liquid sliding down his throat.

Edison watched MacRae's discomfort. 'Enjoying the drink?'

MacRae's eyelids felt heavy, his mind drifting in circles.

'It's very relaxing. I made it for you myself.' Edison leaned forward to observe MacRae, expert eyes noting the physiological reactions to the powerful muscle relaxant.

A moment of clarity flashed through MacRae's mind. He'd been drugged.

'I'm sure with your medical history you recognise the sensations of surgical anaesthesia, so no point fighting it, just relax and settle in for the ride. This organisation and those leading it, myself included, have worked long and hard to build a better future, and it's not going to be destroyed by you on your personal crusade. This didn't have to happen, you could've just walked away after our last meeting. But you went looking for Murdoch in the highlands didn't you? Did you know you were picked up by our surveillance drone when you were checking out our facility up there?'

MacRae desperately fought the chemical cocktail coursing through his blood stream, taking a grip on his muscles. He grasped the arms of the chair and tried to stand, willing his arms and legs to drag him from the chair. A grunt escaped his lips, then his mouth went slack, his mind reeled. What was happening to him?

'That's it, give it your best shot. You might as well relax, your body will anyway. But I'm sure you'll find the experience interesting, for a while at least, as I've only paralysed your body. The drug is used in surgery so the body can be relaxed but the patient remains fully conscious, reducing some of the risks when a patient is rendered unconscious.'

MacRae's eyes seethed with anger and frustration as his central nervous system refused to respond to the desperate commands his mind was sending to get up and fight.

Edison continued. 'Do you know the human body has a specific value based on the body parts that can be used for organ donation?

It varies of course depending on the country you're in, the quality of the body parts, the age and lifestyle of the donor.'

She opened a cupboard, pulling out an organ donation chart of the human body and spreading it on the desk in front of MacRae.

'We're all a veritable warehouse of spare parts for other sick humans.' She lifted the chart directly in front of MacRae and apologised. 'Sorry, I forgot you can't lean forward to look. I estimate in your condition...you seem pretty fit, clean living, non-smoker, light drinker...you're worth anywhere between two and twenty million dollars. For the right buyer just your heart is worth over a million, even on the black market. And to ensure the best outcome you'll be fully conscious as you contribute to our scientific research and funding by donating your organs. Oh, and paying off a few troublesome personal debts of mine.'

Edison walked around the table and sat on the desk next to MacRae.

'Unfortunately for you I won't be administering an anaesthetic to ease the discomfort of the organ removal process, as the chemicals can pollute the donated organs, reducing their value.'

Sarah was heading down Campbell Street towards the waterfront to meet a friend for a drink when she saw the SUV parked by the side of the road. She pulled over and walked around the car, looking for identifying marks, eyes squinting under the glow of the street lights. There it was, the scratch on the front wheel arch where a kid on a skateboard had collided with MacRae's SUV. She smiled, MacRae had been annoyed by the scratch, but grudgingly admired the jump the kid had been attempting.

MacRae had left a message on her phone earlier and said he was going to talk to the research centre director again, so maybe he was there now. She glanced at her watch. She wouldn't have thought he'd have been here this late. She flicked to his number on her phone and called, but the number rang out, finishing with MacRae's voice suggesting she leave a voicemail. She tucked the phone back in her pocket and tapped her finger on the car roof, looking up the road at the research centre. Something didn't feel quite right.

On impulse, she darted across the road to the research centre. The main entry glass door was locked, but when she spoke into the intercom a security guard's voice came back in a bored monotone. A shrill buzz and the glass door slid open.

Sarah entered the foyer warily and approached the security desk. 'I'm looking for a friend who had an appointment here this evening. Ian MacRae?'

The security guard glanced down at his visitor log, then shook his head. 'All visitors left by the end of business hours. And no MacRae signed in.'

'So he couldn't have come in after hours for a meeting with someone called Edison?'

'I'm the only one here at this time of night,' The security guard said. 'I'll buzz you out now if there's nothing else.'

Sarah wasn't ready to let it go so easily. 'Can you just check if Ms Edison is still here?' She gave a broad smile. 'Please?'

The security guard sighed, and checked his computer, then frowned. 'Ah, she doesn't seem to have left the building, must be working late.'

He looked up at Sarah, then pressed a speed dial number.

'Okay, I'll ask if she's seen your friend.' He pointed to a couch at the side of the foyer. 'If you could just wait there please.'

~

Edison pushed her arms through the surgical gown, wrinkling her nose as she caught the scent of her sweat. This had been harder than she'd thought, getting the dead weight of MacRae from his chair onto a surgical trolley, then taking him carefully though the corridors undetected to a surgical suite.

There had been an anxious moment as an overzealous researcher working late rushed into a corridor in front of them towards the lift on their way get home. Thankfully they hadn't turned around and seen them.

It had been a while since she'd performed surgery and she was relishing the chance to explore anatomy again. This time without the stress of ensuring a good outcome for the patient.

MacRae lay on the operating table, half blinded by the surgical lights above, unable to shut his eyes, watching Edison move quickly around him. He fought to hold down a rising panic as he watched the surgical instruments being arrayed on a stainless steel dish next to him. He'd been trying desperately to will some movement back into his motionless body without success for what seemed an eternity. A couple of times Edison had answered her phone but MacRae had been unable to utter a sound for help.

Edison leaned over MacRae, looking into his eyes, checking his condition, smiling with sadistic satisfaction.

'Well we're about ready to go I think. And when I've finished here, I'll reconnect the security protocols for the doors we've been through, and the security cameras for the rear of the building, before I dump your car and phone a long way from here. You'll be just another missing person, maybe someone who decided they didn't want to be found, quite plausible with your background.'

She stepped back from the table, checking everything was in place, then after a moment's consideration moved the patient monitoring equipment for heartbeat, blood pressure, brain activity to the side of the room.

'I don't think we need to worry too much about you staying alive today do we?' She smiled. 'This is going to be a very lucrative exercise for me. I'll think of you on my next ski holiday, one that you've helped pay for.'

Then her phone rang again. She glanced at it, then MacRae. 'I hope it's not my husband, he just won't leave me alone tonight. It's as though he thinks I'm up to no good.'

Edison hit the answer button as she left the operating suite. 'Yes...'

MacRae lay in a silence broken only be Edison's voice drifting in from the corridor, and the hum of the air filtration system.

Then it happened. His right hand twitched.

A glimmer of hope flashed through his mind. He instantly focused all his will power on his right hand, time stretching out while he concentrated. Then it moved again, his fingers opening and closing. The grip of the muscle relaxant on his body was weakening.

Edison hadn't bothered to hook him up to any monitoring equipment and hadn't noticed. He concentrated hard once again, this time on his upper body, and found he was regaining movement in his neck and shoulders. From the corner of his eye he could see the glistening surgical steel of scalpels, tantalisingly close to his fingers.

The door of the operating suite swung open as Edison strode back in, still holding the phone to her ear. 'So there's a woman called Sarah in the foyer, enquiring about a meeting this evening between a Mr MacRae and myself?'

MacRae's heart leapt. What the hell was Sarah doing here?

'No, I haven't seen him tonight. I briefly met with him a few days ago. Does she want to see me?'

Edison pressed mute on her phone and spoke to MacRae while the security guard talked to Sarah. 'I wonder how much she knows?' She leaned over MacRae peering into his eyes and smiled. 'She's important to you isn't she? Well if she decides that she must come and see me tonight, I think she'll be joining you on the operating table.'

MacRae seethed with the hopelessness of his paralysis, at the same time trying not to let on that with each passing moment he was regaining more and more movement.

Edison spoke into the phone again.

'No, she doesn't want to see me? Okay, that's fine. I hope she catches up with her friend.'

She ended the call and smiled at MacRae. 'Well I guess it's her lucky day. Maybe she should buy a lottery ticket.'

MacRae lay completely still as Edison walked around him checking one last time before commencing her work, praying that she wouldn't notice his changing condition. If he got out of this alive he'd owe Sarah and Edison's husband a debt of gratitude for keeping her talking on the phone, enough time for the effect of the muscle relaxants to start to lose their deadly grip.

Edison pulled her surgical mask over her mouth and chose a scalpel, checking the weight and balance in her hand, positioning it gently on MacRae's exposed chest.

MacRae could feel the cool metal of the blade upon him, the razor sharp blade making a tiny slice in his skin. He braced himself for the agony of his chest being opened as he watched helplessly.

Edison peered over to the chart she'd placed on the wall, confirming the sequence she'd perform the procedures in for the last time before making his first incision. Yes, heart would be good, nice and fresh, but that would lead to a quick death, possibly degrading the other organs to be harvested, and shortening the exquisite agony and horror her victim would experience.

She smiled, there was plenty she could do before ending MacRae's life.

MacRae knew this was his first and only chance to act whilst Edison was distracted. He visualised the location of the scalpels, feeling blindly before his fingers locked onto the handle of the instrument. He twisted his head...just enough to see Edison turning back to him...and swung his wrist sideways, plunging the slender blade through Edison's surgical gown and into the inside of her thigh, piercing her femoral artery....and opening the major blood supply to her leg.

Edison uttered a primal shriek as she staggered back, a mixture of shock and rage, eyes fixed in disbelief at the fountain of blood pumping from her thigh. She clamped a hand over the incision, trying to stem the flow, then with a cry of anger raised her scalpel over MacRae and lunged forward. The blade swung down in an arc at MacRae's heart...until Edison slipped in the growing pool of blood at her feet, throwing her violently over backwards.

MacRae watched in amazement as Edison disappeared from his field of vision, followed by a dull crack as her head hit the floor. Minutes passed as MacRae waited for Edison to regain her feet and finish her task, but the silence was broken only by the hum of the air conditioning.

Little by little MacRae could feel movement return throughout his body as the muscle relaxant lost its grip more rapidly. First his arms, then legs, followed by his upper body, until he felt strong enough to grip the sides of the table, swinging his legs off the bed and raising his torso to sit upright.

The sight greeting him was from a horror movie. Edison had been knocked unconscious, and was lying in a pool of her own blood. MacRae gingerly stepped to the floor, unsure if his legs would support him, then knelt next to Edison, checking her pulse. Nothing. Edison's wound shouldn't have been fatal...except the flow of blood wasn't stopped.

MacRae searched the room, finding his clothes and pulling out his phone. His fingers starting tapping out 000 for the police but stopped at the last digit. How was he going to explain what had just happened? He couldn't risk being charged with Edison's death, there was too much at stake. He slipped the phone back in his pocket and methodically went through the operating suite removing as best he could any trace that he'd been there. He thought about what Edison had said about rigging the security system. Presumably that meant it was still disabled.

He checked a closet in the corner of the room and found clean surgical gowns, pulling one over his clothes, along with a hair net and mask, in case he encountered anyone in the corridors.

He looked around one last time, eyes lingering on a cabinet with specimen jars containing dissected parts of Tasmanian Devils, unwitting subjects no doubt in the search for a cure to the terrible disease, and more props in the nightmare he'd found himself in. Then it hit him. What if all this wasn't about finding a cure for the disease? Instead it was about creating diseases? And then the question became why?

He checked the mask was covering his face, and with a last look at Edison he was gone, retracing his steps back to Edison's office. Once there he checked the room for signs of his visit, carefully wiping the spiked drinking glass Edison had offered him.

No alarms had gone off as he walked the corridors, so presumably as long as he stayed to the same route Edison had used he'd be undetected...for a while at least.

He walked around Edison's desk. A green light on the computer monitor blinked at him, so he moved the mouse and the screen flashed into life. Maybe he could get access to the computer? His heart sank as he was faced with a login screen. Should he bother? Not worth pushing his luck. He pulled out the desk drawers, searching each in turn. Nothing of interest there. Time to go. He looked up at the framed photo on the wall behind the desk. Smiling businessmen and women lined up, the picture of success. But what did their success really hide?

He retraced his steps again through the building, occasionally peering through glass panels in laboratory doors, wondering what work was done here. Then he was back at the rear entry. He opened the door carefully, anticipating the scream of an alarm, then he was out, the door closing with a *click* as it locked behind him.

CHAPTER 22

HACK

As soon as MacRae hit the cool night air his head spun and knees buckled. He knew he was close to collapsing in the street, probably the paralysing drugs still working their way through his body. He fumbled through his pockets, found his phone and made a call.

Marion answered almost instantly and listened in shocked silence as MacRae explained the situation, leaving straight away to pick him up, collecting Sarah on the way.

They met MacRae at his car and Sarah helped him into the passenger seat, before getting behind the wheel.

'Marion told me what happened with Edison. Jesus Ian, you're lucky to be alive.'

'When I was lying paralysed on the operating theatre bed, Edison said you almost came to join us,' MacRae said. 'She was planning to kill you too.'

A shiver went through Sarah. 'Let's work through all this when we get you home.'

Sarah pulled out into the light night time traffic, Marion following closely. MacRae slumped against the door as the car changed direction. Sarah glanced over with concern.

MacRae pulled himself upright with a grunt. 'Actually, I'd prefer to avoid my place at the moment. Any chance of staying at the holiday house for a day or two, give me time to think?'

Sarah smiled. 'Sounds like a good excuse for a break from work for me. I'll see if it's vacant. And Marion?'

'Let's see what she says.'

~

Sarah had checked online and the holiday house was vacant, so a couple of stops to grab some overnight essentials and they arrived at the ferry terminal as the first glimpse of morning light broke through the clouds.

There was no queue for Bruny Island so early on a weekday, and within minutes MacRae's car was loaded for the twenty minute trip across the channel. They sat in the lounge atop the ferry, sipping vending-machine coffee in reflective silence, the only sounds the rumble of the diesel engine below decks, and the slap of the swell against the hull.

MacRae was struggling to stay awake by the time they offloaded from the ferry for the drive across the island to the shack.

A comforting sense of normality settled on them as the timber-clad holiday home nestled by the rocky foreshore came into view. Friends of Sarah owned the shack, and she'd holidayed there for almost two decades. For a token rent they let her use it on occasion, and MacRae had joined her there once or twice.

Sarah lifted an old terracotta flowerpot in the porch and retrieved the front door key. She opened the door for MacRae and Marion then headed to town for groceries. MacRae and Marion settled in, lighting the wood fire and making a pot of tea.

MacRae sank into a tattered old armchair and within minutes his eyelids succumbed to gravity and he fell into a deep sleep, waking with a start when Marion shook his shoulder an hour later to offer fresh pastries and coffees brought by Sarah from the local bakery.

'How are you feeling?' Sarah said, offering a Danish.

MacRae shaded his eyes from the bright sunlight, took the Danish and walked out onto the deck overlooking the sparkling water lapping against the rocky shore a stone's throw away.

'Better, although I dreamt about being the subject of medical experiments for some reason,' he said with a shudder.

The food and coffee revived him, and after a third pastry he decided it was time to get back to reality, Sarah and Marion listening in silence as MacRae described the events of the night before, from the relatively civil conversation in Edison's office to the nightmare of lying paralysed in the operating theatre, waiting for an agonising death.

MacRae finished and waited while they contemplated his words.

Sarah broke the silence. 'There's no doubt now that Edison at least thinks, correction, thought you were getting far too close to something. Tie that in with the guy in his car trying to run you and Marion off the road, it must be something pretty important. I mean the events must be linked mustn't they?'

MacRae nodded. 'Her attitude changed when I mentioned Magnus Crane, the pharmaceutical company CEO. She said they go way back and it had shaped a shared vision for the future, whatever that meant. And the stuff about the staff having no idea what they're really working on,' MacRae said. 'Do you think the Merton Institute research could be linked to the other research around the world, not just studying diseases but...I don't know. And what does this have to do with Crane? Mentioning him was just a guess to see if I'd get a reaction,' MacRae said.

'It's fair to say you got one,' Marion said.

'Speaking of reaction,' MacRae said. 'Has there been any news about Edison or the Merton?'

Sarah shrugged. 'I haven't seen anything in the mainstream media or from the police yet, but there's rumours on social media about an unexpected death there overnight. They're saying she was found by a security guard, and there's speculation someone else was involved. Gossip spreads so fast.'

MacRae checked the local TV station news on his phone. The headline was a live report only minutes earlier about the death. He tapped the video and held his phone out for Sarah and Marion to watch. A sombre-looking young woman in jacket and skirt spoke to camera, the imposing bulk of the Merton Institute building behind her, a police car and ambulance parked to one side.

'Unexpected death of renowned researcher and Director of the Institute. She was a pioneer in ground-breaking research on the Tasmanian Devil facial tumour disease...no details released yet....devastating news for husband.'

The reporter waved over at the building.

'The police are appealing for witnesses and request anyone with information or in the vicinity overnight to come forward or contact CrimeWatch.'

MacRae closed the video and frowned. 'It's not going to go away but I think I covered my tracks. I don't need to be involved in a police investigation, at least until we know what's going on.'

'Where to from here then?' Marion asked, heading inside to make more coffee.

'Let's go back a step,' MacRae said. 'Edison mentioned the surveillance drone in the central highlands. Sarah, did you have any more luck with the mobile phone we found?'

Sarah bit her lip. 'I forgot to tell you, something freaky happened with that.'

Sarah described her failed attempt to get data off the phone, then being contacted by Ritchie on the Dark Web.

'It was really him, after all this time?' MacRae shook his head. 'We thought he was in some secret jail, hiding out somewhere, or possibly dead.'

'It's him,' Sarah said. 'He knows us too well.'

'Something good has come from this then. Even if he's in some covert government program, at least he's still alive, and enjoying the sunshine by the sounds of it.' MacRae smiled. 'Did he find anything on the phone?'

'Let's find out.' Sarah said, reaching into her bag for her laptop. She opened her email and clicked a link Ritchie had sent her. 'It looks like he got something.'

MacRae and Marion looked over her shoulder. Another click and the screen was filled with images.

'He said the phone was pretty much cooked, but he got through the password encryption and was able to recover some photos that had recently been sent to the phone, probably from a digital camera.'

'That's it?' MacRae said.

'Looks like it,' Sarah said.

'Okay let's see what we've got.'

Sarah scrolled through the images, beautiful photos of Tasmanian Devils in their natural habitat filling the screen.

Marion's eyes widened. 'The photos are stunning, the clarity and composition, and from the angle and proximity to the devils, they were taken from the clearing we found.'

'I think it's answered one question,' MacRae said. 'It fits with what Murdoch's wife told me about his work. It must be his phone.'

Sarah kept scrolling through the images, skipping through them faster, then stopped.

'Check these out, they're the last of the images.'

The three of them watched in silence as the images showed the devils being caught and abused by the research party.

MacRae pointed to a close-up of the researchers. 'Can you zoom in there?'

'Sure,' Sarah said.

The heads and shoulders of the research team filled the screen.

Marion stabbed her finger at a man at the rear of the party.

'That's him. The guy who tried to run us off the road.'

MacRae nodded. 'And I recognise the man next to him, the older guy. That's Magnus Crane, the drug corporation boss who goes way back with Edison apparently. He's a long way from home.'

'Speaking of Americans,' Sarah said. 'Did Brad Schneider get anywhere with his enquiries into Hassana and Nigeria?'

MacRae shrugged. 'I haven't heard anything but now's a good time to follow it up.'

~

MacRae adjusted his position seated on the smooth grey rock by the water's edge as he reached backwards then flicked the old fishing rod forward, sending the bait and hook into the sparkling water twenty metres out with a soft *plop*. He couldn't remember when he'd last taken the time to go fishing. Not that he ever caught much, but it was the enforced relaxing that he was appreciating.

He'd left a message on Schneider's phone, and hopefully he'd get back to him with some news because MacRae felt they were at a dead end, that circumstances beyond his control were now pushing him further and further into a corner, and he still had no idea why.

He watched the swells lapping gently against the shore then tensed as the fishing line twitched once, then again, before pulling tight as he got a bite. That's when his phone rang. It was Schneider. He held the phone with one hand and was trying to reel in what felt like an enormous catch when with a final jerk the line went slack and the fish was gone.

MacRae sighed and hit answer. 'Brad, you just cost me the biggest fish I almost ever caught.'

Schneider snorted with laughter. 'Do you want me to call back another time?'

'No, it's okay, there's plenty of other fish in the sea as they say, and we've got a lot to talk about.'

The men spoke for twenty minutes, MacRae starting with the trip to the Central Highlands and the attempt on his and Marion's life, the discovery of the phone with a picture of Crane, and finished with the death of Edison.

Schneider's was voice was slow and measured. 'Jesus Ian, not sure you should have told me about Edison and the Merton. I work for the government you know. I'm not sure what my responsibility is in this.'

'You don't work for my government, and I'm not sure I classify a CIA spook as a responsible government employee.'

'Good point,' Schneider said.

'So what have you got for me? Anything new on Hassana's whereabouts?'

'Well yes and no. I don't know if it'll be much help, that's why I haven't got back to you before,' Schneider said. 'It's all been unofficial so the usual resources haven't been available to me, but it looks like Hassana might have been taken out of Nigeria a few weeks ago. We don't have a confirmed border crossing, but there's a lot of people-smuggling in the area so it wouldn't have been too hard.'

'So why do you think she's left the country?'

'I've had a low-level travel alert out for her, and got a possible match through passport facial recognition checks on a medical charter flight out of Germany, so she may have been smuggled along the refugee route to Germany.'

'Where was the flight heading?' MacRae said, the tranquillity and peace of the fishing fading.

'It was logged to the US, San Francisco. But the flight plan may be bogus, as I haven't found a corresponding arrival at any of the local airports.'

Both men went quiet, then Schneider spoke again.

'So what's your plan?'

'I'm sure there will be an investigation into Edison's death, at least by the coroner, so it might be prudent to not be around for that,' MacRae said. 'And I know it's a slim chance, but your information on Hassana possibly being in the US is the best lead I've got at the moment. Plus this guy Crane just keeps popping up, linked to the Merton Institute, Edison, maybe the missing photographer, and the Nigerian contractor. And I'm intrigued by his interest in survivalists. Maybe he knows something the rest of us don't. Perhaps the best way to find out is to ask him.'

'I don't know what you think you're going to find with Crane. The guy runs a huge corporation, it's bound to be controversial. But hey, if you're over my way let me know and let's catch up if we can. It's been a long time.'

MacRae ended the call and gathered up the fishing gear. Schneider was right, he had nothing but hunches, but whatever he was involved in was enough to make him and Marion targets, and for Edison to risk everything to stop him.

Now it was time to talk to Marion and Sarah about the one that got away just now, and going to the US to find the one that got away in Nigeria.

CHAPTER 23

TOURISTS

San Francisco. MacRae smiled. He'd always wanted to visit, but never quite made it here before, and despite the serious nature of the trip as soon as Marion had said she was coming too it almost felt like a holiday. In fact as they basked in the morning sun standing on Torpedo Wharf at The Presidio taking photos of the Golden Gate Bridge, MacRae almost felt like any other of the tourists milling around.

He knew it was a long shot hoping to find some kind of evidence of Hassana arriving here, but then the reason to go directly to San Francisco took an unexpected turn when Sarah had done some more digging before their departure, and informed them that not only was Medici-Royal's biggest US manufacturing and research facility in nearby Silicon Valley, but that Crane's corporate headquarters was situated in the most prestigious building in the heart of the city.

Most of their time in the few days since they'd arrived had been spent driving around in their hire car, checking out the airfields in the area, large and small. Unfortunately access to most of them was restricted and they hadn't gained any useful information about incoming overseas medical flights. So they'd turned their attention to trying to meeting with Crane in between some sightseeing. But despite their best efforts to talk their way into arranging a meeting at his office, they'd been stopped by the perfect gate-keeper...a no-nonsense Executive Assistant who offered them nothing but the chance to leave a message for her boss.

So MacRae had decided to take a more direct approach. He figured that if the flight plan from Germany did involve Crane somehow, there was a fair chance he'd want to be around for whatever happened to Hassana next. They hadn't been able to find out Crane's personal contact details or home address so had resorted to more traditional means to track him down...hiring a local investigator to keep an eye on Crane's corporate headquarters.

Marion struck a pose, hand shading her eyes to look at the bridge while MacRae took a last photo, when his phone pinged. The message was succinct.

Subject has just been dropped off at his office building.

MacRae smiled. It was game time.

⁓

Marion sipped her fruit smoothie, sunglasses perched precariously on the end of her nose while MacRae flicked through a brochure describing the twenty best tourist attractions in the Bay area. From their bright red metal seats outside Jay and Ray's Deli on Market Street they had a clear line of sight to the office tower Crane had entered forty minutes earlier. The investigator assured MacRae that Crane was still in the building and now it was just a matter of waiting. MacRae had spent plenty of time on surveillance over the years and he quickly settled into the mindset, relaxing and enjoying Marion's company. His eyes flicked down to his watch. Ninety minutes had passed and the street was getting busier.

Marion read his mind. 'Do you think he's settled into the office for the day, or perhaps left by another entrance?'

MacRae was about to speak when a streetcar overflowing with locals and tourists rolled past, blocking their view of the building. When it was gone MacRae smiled and nodded his head towards the building.

'Neither Marion. He's here, let's go.'

Marion looked over to see Crane striding down the building steps, heading for a sleek black limo approaching the kerb.

MacRae dropped some dollar bills on the table and, taking Marion by the hand crossed the street, approaching Crane from the side. A street hawker selling snow globes of the bridge stepped in their path, blocking them for a second.

Crane paused at the kerb, seemingly checking his pockets, then abruptly turned and headed back up the stairs to the building.

'We're about to lose him, wait here Marion,' MacRae said as he skipped around the hawker and ran for the building, taking the steps two at a time.

By the time he got to the top, Crane was in the building and waiting for an elevator. They were only a couple of metres apart, but separated by a series of four electronic entry gates, a yawning security guard keeping an eye on the comings and goings from one side. MacRae considered his options. He could easily jump the gates, but was sure to be spotted and that wouldn't end well. There was only one other choice. He waited for a queue to form at one of the gates and joined the end, taking his hotel room security key out of his wallet. It was the best he could do, and at least it was the right colour. A couple of seconds shuffling forward listening to the scanners beep for each entry, and the man in front of him, dressed for business in a tight blue suit, scanned his card. The barrier swung sideways to let him through, then closed before MacRae could follow.

MacRae swiped his card and swore as a deeper beep came from the gate. He glared at the card. 'Shit, I've left my security card in the cab. I can't be late to this meeting.'

The man in front turned around, hesitated, then spoke. 'Yeah I know the feeling, did it myself last week.' He glanced over at the security guard, eyes shut in full yawn, then swiped his card again, the gate swinging back open to let MacRae through.

MacRae smiled. 'Thanks buddy, you're a lifesaver.'

The man turned to a corridor to the left while MacRae dashed forward as the elevator doors started to slide shut. He thrust an arm in front of the closing sensors, the doors swinging back open to the annoyed looks of the half dozen or so people inside, and then he was in, standing next to Crane.

MacRae grinned. 'Magnus Crane? The head of Medici-Royal?'

Crane wrinkled his brow. 'Do I know you?'

'Ah, probably not. I'm on holiday here from Australia. Tasmania actually.'

'Oh.' Crane smiled politely.

'So I was doing some research about a disease affecting one of our crazy local animals...the Tasmanian Devil...and ended up having a great chat to Dr Edison, the head of the research institute looking for a cure. Such a shame she died how she did.'

MacRae saw Crane's pupils contract. He had his interest. Had Edison's death made the news here, or was Crane advised personally?

'I'm sorry?' Crane said.

'The rumour is she was always working late, and died all alone.' MacRae continued. 'Anyway while I was at her office I saw a photo of you donating money to the Institute. She said you were a great benefactor and friend. So I looked up your company. You've got stuff going on all around the world.'

Crane smiled. 'Ah yes, Laura and I have done some good work together. So what brings...'

'So then here I am checking out the sights of San Francisco and see you across the road. I couldn't resist coming to say hi. Hope you don't mind.'

Curiosity was getting the better of the others in the elevator as they listened to the conversation. A loud ping and the elevator stopped, four people exiting to a plushly carpeted office suite. The door slid silently shut and the ride up continued.

Then it clicked with Crane. He'd felt the irritating stranger was familiar, but now he knew why. He'd seen photos of him, firstly at the Nigerian hotel, then again in the Tasmanian Highlands, checking out their property. What was his name...Ian MacRae? Fuck, he'd even caused trouble for the Russian, sent to dissuade him from his enquiries. This was no coincidence.

'Did you like Tasmania?' MacRae said. 'It's got some of the best untouched wilderness in the world, particularly up around the Central Highlands. It's one of the key habitats for the Tasmanian Devil so some of the disease research is being undertaken there. From what I've seen on the internet you're a bit of an adventurer. Did you get to see any of it?'

Crane sensed the question was loaded. What did MacRae know? Why was he here...and how the hell had he got into a supposedly secure building?

'Tasmania is beautiful, certainly the parts I saw,' Crane said.

MacRae smiled. They were both playing games.

'Beautiful, but also unforgiving. People don't appreciate how dangerous it can be. Only recently a famous wildlife photographer disappeared without a trace up that way. Did it make the international news?'

The elevator stopped again, disgorging another couple of people, leaving just Crane, MacRae and a young woman in a business suit.

'No, that's sad to hear,' Crane said, looking directly at MacRae. 'I suppose people do just disappear from time to time though. You've got to be very careful, don't you?'

'I guess so. The wilderness attracts all sorts, hippies, survivalists. Let's face it Tasmania is probably the right place to be if the end of the world is coming.'

The young woman shot them both a glance. The conversation was taking a weird turn.

The elevator stopped for a final time and the woman exited followed by Crane. A glass and stone reception desk spanned the foyer outside the elevator. Three receptionists were seated, spaced equally along the desk.

Crane turned to face MacRae, blocking his exit.

'Well it's been interesting to meet you Mr, ummm?'

'MacRae.'

'Yes, Mr MacRae. Please excuse me as I have an appointment. I hope you enjoy the rest of your time in our lovely city.'

MacRae smiled as he hit the button for the ground floor and the doors slid shut. 'Thanks. I'm sure there's a lot more for us to discover before we leave.'

Marion was waiting in the sun outside the main entry. She shook her new snow globe proudly.

'Winter in San Francisco apparently. So how did it go?'

'Not sure really, he didn't say much,' MacRae said. 'I certainly got his attention when I mentioned Edison's death though.'

'Did he admit he was up in the Highlands with the devils?'

'No, I got the feeling he was holding back, but he did acknowledge he knew Edison.'

'So what's next if he didn't give us anything new to follow up?'

'Well, apart from enjoying the sights of San Francisco as he suggested, I've got a couple of other ideas,' MacRae said, pulling out his phone. 'But first I'll try Brad again, maybe he has something for us by now.'

~

Back in his office, Crane twirled a pen around with his fingers. This guy MacRae was turning out to be more persistent than he'd expected. He had to admit that when he'd got over the surprise of seeing him here, he'd been intrigued to hear what he had to say. Not much as it turned out, except about Edison's death. Crane had been advised by the Institute as soon as it happened of course, but there were scant details, other than that she was working late at night when she had an unfortunate accident. Nothing more would be available until after the coroner had investigated. Did MacRae know something? And how the hell had he got through the building security? Crane made a mental note to review the surveillance camera footage. Someone was going to lose their job. And he'd better keep track of MacRae, and anyone else with him.

~

Marion squinted in the sun as she read the faded painted sign above the restaurant.

'The Pelican Shack. Are you sure this is it? It looks a little down on its luck.'

'Well only if you compare it to the other tourist traps,' MacRae said. 'But Brad said this is one of the last genuine seafood places left at Fisherman's Wharf. And let's face it, downmarket is kind of his style isn't it?'

He led Marion in and frowned as he saw the huge lunchtime queue at the cashier. Then a voice range out from the further in.

'Hey, Ian, over this way. I've saved you seats.'

The queue parted to let them through and MacRae spotted Schneider seated at the long marble counter with two empty seats next to him. It had been years since they'd caught up. Schneider still looked fit although his shirt was a little tighter around the waist than MacRae remembered.

The men grinned at each other for a moment, then MacRae wrapped Schneider in a bear hug.

'It's been a long time Brad. I couldn't believe it when you said you could swing by San Francisco for work and take time out for lunch with us.'

'It's great to see you.' Schneider slapped MacRae's back enthusiastically, then turned to Marion. 'And great to meet you Marion.'

Marion hugged Schneider. 'I guess we've both heard a lot about each other.'

Schneider waved them to seats. 'This place is the last of the best. All the rest have been bought out or gentrified, but here the food is simple, great and most importantly, cheap. Just how the CIA like it for their expenses claims.'

Schneider ordered, and within a couple of minutes a half dozen dishes appeared.

'This is what this place is famous for.' Schneider passed the food around. 'San Francisco Dungeness crab, Cioppino and local oysters, soaked up with freshly made sourdough.'

The food went down almost as quickly as the glasses of craft beer while they chatted, Schneider filling MacRae in on his wife and family, then laughing as MacRae described his preconceptions of San Francisco based on watching police cars flying through the air as a kid on the TV show, *The Streets of San Francisco*.

'Yeah, that was the old city.' Schneider wiped his bowl with a piece of bread. 'The new city is something else, all high tech businesses and money. Speaking of which how did your visit with Crane go?'

'It didn't really go anywhere unfortunately. Although I'm sure he recognised me, and it definitely threw him when I talked about Edison's death,' MacRae said. 'So have you got anything new for us on Hassana?'

'The medical flight is a dead end so far. All these companies have very complex corporate structures, often based offshore with little or no US assets, so even I can't get much background on them.' Schneider wiped his mouth with a paper napkin. 'What's your next move?'

'Well I could try and talk to Crane again.'

'I wouldn't advise that,' Schneider said. 'If he decided you were harassing or stalking him, an influential figure like him, and you in a foreign land? I can't see that ending well.'

Marion touched MacRae's arm, Schneider noticing the gesture.

'I think we want to avoid that. There must be something else.'

MacRae waved to their server to refill their beers. 'Well we can spend a few more days playing the tourist here, then maybe I need to talk to someone with a different perspective on Crane.' He turned to Marion. 'Remember those news reports on the defamation suit Crane brought against a conspiracy theorist... did they say where he lived? You know the old saying *There's no smoke without fire.*'

'I think it was Florida wasn't it?'

Schneider smiled. 'I hear Florida is lovely this time of year.'

~

CHAPTER 24

SURVIVOR

MacRae watched the leaves swirl around the legs of the bench at his feet. The boardwalk park alongside the River Beach Marina in North Palm Beach was mostly empty, not surprising as it was still early and a little cool despite the clear sky and Florida sunshine. A young man wearing headphones jogged by oblivious to his presence. Then two women with matching strollers sauntered past chatting animatedly, their strapped-in children reaching across to touch each other's fingers. It was nice to feel that sense of normality, even briefly, with everything else going on around him.

He checked the time. It was now fifteen minutes past the meeting time, maybe he wasn't going to show. Or perhaps this was just part of the drama, after all the guy was a conspiracy theorist and had come across as more than a little paranoid in their interactions so far. He thought of Marion back at the hotel. Was it too late to join her for the day checking out the city?

A shadow fell across him as a man walked past then paused at the far end of the bench. The man flicked a leaf off the seat, then turned and sat. He ignored MacRae, taking out a brown bag and reaching in to pull out a hand full of seed, throwing it on the black footpath in front of them. A couple of birds fluttered down and squabbled over the food. MacRae quickly took him in. Probably in his early fifties, dark skin, dressed smartly but casually in jeans and a sweater. Short cut curly black hair with flashes of grey framed his face. Then MacRae noticed it as the man turned his head...faint scarring down one side of his face the width of a hand from his ear to his jaw. MacRae had seen enough injuries to know the look of plastic surgery and grafted skin to repair serious burns.

The man's eyes flicked around, taking in everything around him, including MacRae. He fitted the picture MacRae had built, but he still couldn't be sure if it was him.

Then the man spoke, a deep gravelly voice, mostly American but a hint of something else?

'Ah, to be free as a bird. A wonderful life don't you think?'

MacRae nodded. 'Not a care in the world, particularly when there's free food.'

MacRae had followed the instructions he'd been given correctly. There was silence, then the man spoke again.

'Ian MacRae?'

'Elias?' MacRae replied.

The man nodded, then extended his hand, eyes still darting around to watch around them. 'Pleasure to meet you. Although I'm still not sure why.'

MacRae hadn't been mistaken when he'd sensed the man's reluctance to arranging this meeting. He was seriously paranoid. That explained the whole secret words about feeding birds charade.

MacRae wanted to set him at ease.

'I know my request must have seemed unusual, wanting to meet you on short notice, but I'd come across your blog researching something else, and felt sure there was more you could share with me if we met in person.'

'My blog's been around for years. Why are you so interested in my comments on Magnus Crane and his organisations now?'

He looked at MacRae with suspicion. 'You said you were a security consultant. Show me proof before we go any further.'

MacRae extracted a business card from his wallet and handed it across.

Elias read it out. 'Ian MacRae, Principal, Human Resource Security. Sounds impressive, but you've got to give me more than that. What do you actually do?'

MacRae pulled up his website on his phone, talking through the services he offered to clients from around the world, and examples of projects he'd been involved with.

'You're a bit of a white knight then are you?' Elias said.

MacRae shrugged. 'I was in various branches of law enforcement for a long time, but in the end didn't feel I was making much of a difference to improve people's lives. The work I do now keeps people safe while they provide aid to some of those most in need in the most dangerous parts of the world. I find it fulfilling.'

Elias pondered MacRae's comments, and handed the business card back.

'Why did this lead you to me?'

'I've been involved in a project in Africa recently and might have stumbled on illegal medical trials being conducted on local people with devastating results.'

'Go on,' Elias said quietly.

MacRae knew he'd struck a chord. 'So a bit of digging and a few too many coincidences led me to companies linked to Magnus Crane. That's where I came across the records of him suing you for defamation a few years ago, trying to shut down your blog about him and his operations.'

'The bastard certainly gave it his best shot.' Elias's face clouded over. 'But I'm still here aren't I?'

MacRae smiled, turning his face to the water to watch the reflection of the sun shimmering between the boats tied up in ordered rows along the jetties. The temperature was rising as the sun climbed in the sky.

A man walking a small dog stopped to lean against a lamp post twenty metres to their left. He took out his phone and tapped at the screen. MacRae glanced at Elias. They were thinking the same thing. Were they being watched? Or were they both just paranoid?

Elias stood. 'Do you like boats?'

The rumble of the supercharged marine engine settled into the background as MacRae relaxed into the rise and fall of the ten metre cruiser powering through the gentle swell.

Elias stood proudly at the helm, a smile playing on his lips as he steered the magnificent craft. MacRae sensed this was the man's passion. This certainly wasn't what he was expecting when Elias had suggested they go for a boat ride, maybe fish for a while whilst they talked. But MacRae loved that people often surprised him.

Elias saw MacRae looking at him. He looked over his shoulder. The shore was disappearing on the horizon. He eased back on the throttle and the boat dropped down from the plane to slowly motor into the gentle headwind.

'So you really want to know the truth about Magnus Crane?'

MacRae leaned against a white upholstered chair. 'I've come a long way find it.'

'Okay,' Elias said. 'Call me paranoid, but arms up please.'

MacRae lifted his arms for Elias to frisk him.

'Sorry, but I can't take any chances when dealing with that son-of-a-bitch.' He patted down MacRae's body. 'He's sent people after me before, investigators, trying to get dirt on me.' His hands brushed along MacRae's legs. 'They've tried to bribe me, then threatened me. Not the kind of people you want to mess with.'

He stood back satisfied. 'We're too far from shore for surveillance now, so let's talk.'

MacRae grinned. 'It's not the first time I've been frisked. And in my line of work I've met more than a few nasty characters, but I'm not intimidated very easily.'

Elias, disappeared into the forward cabin, then called to MacRae. 'I'll pass these up to you.'

MacRae leaned through the swing doors. Elias was reaching into a refrigerator in a kitchenette to the left of the cosy lounge area. A bathroom and shower were along the right side. Framed photographs of smiling people were spaced along the walls. Elias handed MacRae a six-pack of icy frosted beer bottles and a couple of packets of nuts.

MacRae took them to the rear of the cruiser and sat at a round table. He took in the long slender lines of the boat. She oozed speed and power. Elias joined him and they clinked their beer bottles together before drinking.

'You like her?' Elias said.

MacRae savoured the cool liquid before replying. 'She's beautiful.'

Elias smiled. 'My one indulgence, even though I could afford plenty more.' Then his mood changed. 'But this isn't about me, it's about you. And there's a lot more to it than you've said so far.'

MacRae washed a handful of nuts down with a mouthful of beer, then spoke. 'I was with a friend of mine, a doctor, in a Nigerian village a few months back when it was raided by local militia. My friend was killed and many local young men and women were taken from the village. We thought they were destined to be child soldiers, but it turns out it was much worse.'

Elias was staring at MacRae intently.

'The missing kids were found by the army months later, and they were all dead except one. As far as we can tell the militia was paid to use them for some kind of medical trial that either accidentally or deliberately took their lives.'

MacRae looked over the water, watching a large fish alongside the boat just under the surface.

'I was looking after the sole survivor, a girl, when she was taken again. There's something about her that makes her extremely important to whoever was running the trial.'

He caught Elias's eyes. 'So this is personal, and I'll do whatever it takes to get her back again. And if that means I'm taking on Magnus Crane and all his resources, so be it.'

He sat back, lost in his thoughts as the image of Hassana's face flashed through his mind.

Elias finished his beer then took the top off another two, passing one to MacRae. He took a sip, then disappeared back into the cabin, bringing back two of the framed photos.

He placed them on the table facing MacRae.

'As I said, I can afford just about anything most people seem to value in this modern world, but this boat is my one indulgence. I always find it curious how our lives are shaped, how we get to where we are. Don't you?'

MacRae drew on his beer. 'Sure. Life is half lottery...where we're born, who our parents are. And the rest is what we make of it.'

'Exactly,' Elias said. 'Sometimes the worst beginnings can lead to great strength.' He waved his hand over the boat. 'Maybe I have Magnus Crane to thank for all this.' He pointed to the photos. 'And these people's success is owed to Crane.'

'How so?' MacRae said.

Elias leaned back, not sure where to start.

'I was born in Hebra in northern Syria, and lost my parents when I was young. I ended up emigrating to the US on my eighteenth birthday as a refugee and threw myself into building a new life here.' He smiled, 'They said it was the land of opportunity, and for me it was. I started washing windshields at traffic intersections while I got my high school diploma, then expanded into car detailing, building a network of franchises. By the time I was thirty I was a millionaire, bought my house for cash.'

He held up a photo of himself with a pretty woman similar to him in age, and a young man. 'We'd been dating for five years so we got married and had a son.' Elias smiled with pride. 'They're the best thing that ever happened to me. He's just qualified as a lawyer.'

'And the other photo? Is that you with those young men?'

Elias nodded. 'Our son's birth was very difficult so we couldn't have any more children. But I invested my money like Warren Buffet, and we live in that same house we bought, just like Warren Buffet and we got wealthier. So we decided to foster other refugee kids, just like me. Some did really well.' He pointed to a tall slender young man in the centre. 'He's studying to be a doctor. Others were lost souls.'

He put the photos down. 'Now my wife works in healthcare, and I have a bit more time to spend on my other passions.'

'This boat?' MacRae said

Elias leaned into MacRae, stabbing his finger forward. 'And my work on bringing down Magnus Crane after what he did to me and my family. Mark my words I'll never rest until that bastard is destroyed.'

Another beer went down while MacRae listened to Elias describe the day when, as a fourteen year old boy, after visiting relatives for a few weeks he'd returned to his village in the northern Sahara to see it devastated by a hideous disease and everyone dying, including the doctors sent to help them. Then, as he hid atop a sand dune, he watched men with guns arriving to cover up the crime, shooting everyone who was still alive, and burning the bodies.

MacRae let out a slow breath. 'Surely there was an investigation into the massacre? People must have known about it? And how can you be sure this is linked to Crane?'

Elias smiled grimly. 'It's always the same in that part of the world. Money and corruption equals influence. Before I went to visit my relatives, my father had told me that the village was taking part in an important trial of new drugs that would help people across the world, and that the money we were being paid would help our village out of poverty. That's why they participated in the trial.'

But in the days and weeks after the massacre it was always reported as a terror attack by local militia, and no-one looked any further. I suppose it was in everyone's interests to cover it up...the government officials who must have got kickbacks to allow the drug trials to take place. No one wants to be held responsible. And the drug company no doubt just took their illegal drug trials to somewhere else they could get away with it.'

MacRae pressed him. 'You were so young then. Can you be sure it was what you think it was?'

Elias turned his face to MacRae, taking his hand and pressing it to his scarred cheek. 'This tells me I know what I know. I was burnt that day as I watched my father die, and my blood was spilt on the desert sand where I was shot. I lay hiding underneath his bed with my face on fire, holding back my screams because they were still outside watching the village burn.'

MacRae felt Elias's pain from the memory, and his anger that there was no justice. 'You're sure Crane was there that day?'

Elias nodded. 'I saw his face. He stared right at me as I hid on the sand dune, before he joined in the killing. How could I forget him?'

'When did you find out who he was?' MacRae said.

'Not until I'd been in the US for almost ten years. I guess he'd been building his career and his companies. Then suddenly there he was, all over the press as the kind and generous head of the medical corporation.' He sneered. 'He could build any image he wanted to the world, but I knew who he really was.'

MacRae thought it through. He knew cover-ups occurred frequently in developing countries. But this scale of medical conspiracy?

'And you're sure it wasn't some kind of local terror group involved?'

'There were too many white men involved.'

'Mercenaries?' suggested MacRae.

'Maybe,' Elias said. 'But not working for local militia. Not with the guns they had.'

'What do you mean?'

'I'd seen terrorists and militia raiding villages before. They always had Russian or Chinese weapons. Cheap and easy to get AK-47s or SKS rifles. These men had M16s, every one of them. Western guns, used by white men and paid for with western money. Just like the cover up by the medical trial company.'

The similarities with the Nigerian medical trial were striking to MacRae. Surely this pattern of research and testing wasn't still continuing?

The swell was increasing now, the boat rocking side to side.

Elias pointed over the bow at grey clouds gathering in the distance. 'Looks like the weather's going to close in.' He drained the last of his beer and resumed his seat at the helm, easing the throttles open.

The engine growled back into life, lifting the nose of the cruiser onto the plane as Elias turned back towards the marina.

MacRae joined him, holding the side of the cabin as the boat bounced over the growing swell, a fine spray mist peppering his face.

He'd never spent a lot of time on the water, but he knew that every time he did something like this he'd toy with the idea buying a boat of his own for a while, but then came to the same conclusion he always did. That he was never home long enough to use, and it would just sit in the water and rot. Maybe if he'd had a more normal life, settled down with someone. Marion's face came into his mind.

He snapped back to the present, raising his voice above the roar of the engine.

'So you made a whole lot of claims about Crane and his companies on your blog. How much of it have you been able to prove?'

Elias kept looking ahead. 'Nowhere near as much as I'd like. When you're dealing with a powerful and successful person like Crane, people are reluctant to talk to someone like me. I guess they figure it's not going to change anything.'

MacRae persisted. 'I came across some really unexpected connections to Crane recently. Do you think there's more to him than just an unscrupulous businessman?'

Elias checked the storm behind them, they'd put a bit more distance between it and them. He eased off the throttle, the roar settling to a growl, so they could talk.

'I don't know how people like him think,' Elias said. 'Are there any limits to what they'll do to make money? I found links between charities his company was donating to and anti-vaxxer organisations. What's that about? Maybe he's trying to discourage vaccinations so he can supply the expensive drugs when there are disease outbreaks, like that measles outbreak on the Pacific Island recently that killed a bunch of babies. But this is the kind of thing that doesn't actually prove anything.'

A large swell loomed in front of the boat. The air pressure from the approaching storm was stirring the sea into steadily increasing swells and waves, the rising wind whipping white froth from the top of the waves. Elias spun the wheel into the swell and the boat climbed the face, briefly reaching into the air at the crest before crashing down the other side.

MacRae grinned. 'Are your boat rides always so exciting?'

Elias smiled back. 'It reminds me to respect the sea and the weather.'

He spun the wheel back to the shore and increased the throttle again, outrunning the waves behind them.

'So maybe Crane is just about profits,' MacRae said.

Elias shot him a glance. 'What really does drive people? I've chased the history of his company back decades. Did you know one of its many acquisitions was a German pharmaceutical company used by the Nazis to develop and manufacture chemical weapons and poison gas for the concentration camps? Very dubious morality if nothing else.'

'True,' MacRae said. 'But it's a depressing fact of human nature that there's always someone willing to benefit from the misery of others. The US government was among many others that made deals with Nazi scientists after the war for their knowledge of nuclear weapons research, and the research for the V1 and V2 flying bombs launched against London was used by the US in the space race against the Russians.'

'This piece of human garbage,' Elias spat the words. 'Is in a different league. You know one of his early career moves was as chief scientist with a business subcontracted to supply chemicals to a US company with a plant in a little place in India called Bophal. Heard of it?'

'Sure, the site of possibly the worst industrial accident in history.'

'That's it. You can say it was a western company providing industrialisation and jobs in a developing country. Or was it a western company avoiding stricter environmental and safety laws in the US, to manufacturer cheaply in India? Does it matter? The official investigations blamed it on poor maintenance practices causing a leak of toxic gas, but whatever the reason the outcome was the same. Ten thousand dead as a result of a deadly cloud drifting over densely populated slums, and ongoing illnesses for many more over the next few decades. And ultimately no-one held to account.'

MacRae could sense the man getting agitated. Was this where he turned from being credible with insight into Crane, and instead became just another obsessed conspiracy theorist?

Elias trimmed the boat so it stayed just on the plane, then spoke. 'I'm not the only one who's trying to expose Crane you know. I've got a secret source.' He nodded conspiratorially to MacRae. 'They sent me data files about Crane's operations, things he's developing, where he operates around the world.'

'And you think it's credible?'

'Sure,' Elias said. 'It fits with stuff I already know. But I reckon they're an insider from what they're sending me.'

'Can I see it?' MacRae asked.

Elias looked at MacRae long and hard. 'Not sure if I trust you yet. I'll think about it.'

MacRae watched the blurry horizon clear into the shape of beaches and buildings as they headed back to the marina.

Looks like this visit was coming to an end. MacRae was disappointed it hadn't revealed much concrete information. At least the boat ride had been fun.

'Well I appreciate you taking the time to talk to me about Crane. I'm sure you'll get enough to bring him to account for what he's done sooner or later.'

Elias shrugged. 'I'll never give up. But I can't even publish half of what he's done. Not until I'm sure what it means.'

'Like what?'

Elias backed off the throttle a little as they approached the marina, watching the trailer boats and luxury cruisers weaving carefully around each other. He shot a glance at MacRae.

'Like why does a successful western businessman want to visit an abandoned Cold-war Soviet biological warfare facility on an island in the middle of Uzbekistan of all places?'

'How do you know he did that?' MacRae said, watching as Elias reversed his cruiser back into its berth, skilfully using the bow thrusters to counter the swell and wind gusts being whipped up by the rapidly approaching storm.

Elias called instructions to MacRae. 'Can you throw that rope over the bollard and pull the bow in close?'

MacRae did as he was asked, and Elias cut the engine.

Elias looked around, no one was nearby.

'So if you look it up on the 'net you'll find publicity photos of Crane in Uzbekistan a couple of years ago, the western philanthropist helping the local government work out how to bring the old dead lake back to life for the sake of the local population.'

'Okay, take a step back,' MacRae said. 'What dead lake.'

Elias signed and sat on the edge of the cruiser.

'Back when the Soviet Union was in full swing they felt they were dependent on western cotton and should develop their own cotton industry for textiles. So in typical Soviet fashion they threw everything into creating a new industry, one that unfortunately needs lots of water. So they redirected the feeder rivers for the Aral Sea in Uzbekistan to irrigate the new cotton fields, and within forty years had almost completely drained the fourth largest inland sea in the world, turning it into a huge desert called the Aralkum Desert, complete with rusting ships left high and dry from the now-dead fishing industry that used to thrive in the region.'

'Another example of us looking after our environment,' MacRae shook his head. 'But what's that got to do with bio-warfare labs?'

Elias leaned closer. 'Crane was there for almost a week between press conferences and it got me thinking. Why would he spend so much time in a shit-hole like that? I checked out the region and discovered that the only other interesting thing about it is that the Soviets set up a secret biological weapons research station called Aralsk-7 on Vozrozhdeniya Island in the Aral Sea just after the Second World War. They built a whole town for the workers and their families, and used to develop bio-weapons and perform open air dispersion tests, tying up animals then releasing clouds of pathogens into the air to see how effective they were. They had a few accidents too, scientists died, and a ship was once found floating aimlessly in the Aral Sea nearby, all the sailors dead. Apparently there was one incident where fifty thousand antelopes on the steppes nearby mysteriously dropped dead within a couple of hours.' He shook his head. 'I mean what the fuck were they doing there?'

'Doing what governments do it appears.'

Elias nodded then continued. 'Anyway Aralsk-7 was abandoned in the nineties when the Soviet Union collapsed, and they apparently didn't do much of a cleanup, leaving the place contaminated with all kinds of weaponised diseases, mainly Anthrax.' He was silent while he recalled. 'Yes it must be the Anthrax. The Soviets shipped it from another of their research sites, Compound-19, after a series of accidents that killed over a hundred people. They turned it into a slurry, packed it into steel barrels and buried a couple of hundred tonnes of it at Aralsk-7. That's the real reason Crane was there...to see if he could get his hands on it.'

MacRae thought about it. Sure, there were many questions about Crane. But going to an abandoned bio-weapons site to recover weaponised Anthrax, or anything else for that matter?

'Can you prove he went there?'

Elias hesitated. 'Not exactly, well kinda. I found out that back then it was really difficult to get there. I mean who the hell would want to go somewhere like that? But I know he went, and he must have had a local guide.'

MacRae was sceptical. 'So what did you do?'

'I didn't know how to follow it up at first. I mean it's easier to get to there now...it's even getting onto the adventure tourism circuit like Chernobyl...but I didn't know how to find who might have taken someone there years ago when it was still secretive and illegal. So I went where you find all the good illegal stuff, I used TOR to search the Dark Web.'

MacRae smiled. 'Yes, there's not much you can't find there if you look hard enough.'

'Anyway I asked the questions on a bunch of forums and within a couple of days someone got back to me. They said they could take me there, and that they were the only one prepared to take the risk of getting caught, or dying from the shit contaminating the place.'

Elias was getting animated as he told the tale. 'I asked if they'd taken anyone there around the time Crane was in the neighbourhood. They said yes, so I asked which date. They wanted money to tell me, they said nothing comes for free.'

'So what did you do?' MacRae said. 'It must have seemed like a scam.'

Elias shrugged. 'I transferred what they wanted to the bank account they gave me. They told me the date, and it matched when Crane was around.'

MacRae was getting interested.

Elias continued. 'So then I sent them a random bunch of photos, six or eight I think...one of them was Crane, and said if they were prepared to identified the customer that day I'd give them five hundred dollars up front, and five hundred if they identified them correctly.'

He sat back smugly. 'Sure enough they identified him.'

MacRae clicked his tongue. Now they were getting somewhere. 'What did you do next?'

'I wanted more information about what Crane did when he was there, so I asked for their name and if I could get back in contact with them to chat some more. But maybe I came on too strong and it spooked them because they ended the chat and I wasn't able to contact them anymore.'

MacRae cursed under his breath. 'Another dead end.'

'Not quite,' Elias said. 'I was pretty annoyed that they'd cut me off, so I offered another job on TOR, this time to anyone who could identify the bank account holder. Another thousand dollars and a week later and I had a name. Well at least I think it's the right name.'

'And?'

Elias picked up on MacRae's impatience, so made him wait before he spoke.

'Sar Fendi.'

'And you were able to contact them again?' MacRae said.

'No,' Elias said. 'I searched the web and contacted many people of that name, or that were on Facebook at the time, but I couldn't find him.'

MacRae was right. It was another dead end.

The men sat in silence, the only sound the water lapping against the boat.

Then Elias suddenly glared at MacRae, his face twisting into a snarl. 'You don't believe me do you? You think I'm a conspiracy theory crazy.'

The mood between them was cooling as quickly as the air temperature dropping for the storm. Huge droplets of rain started spattering around them.

Elias abruptly stood, hands on hips as he leaned towards MacRae, raising his voice above the rising sound of the downpour.

'You're just like the rest of them. Time for you to get off my boat.'

A final glare at MacRae and Elias ducked into the forward cabin, pulling the door closed behind him, leaving MacRae slightly bemused as the heavens opened and the tropical storm proceeded to soak him through.

~

Nineteen-eighties soft rock music drifted through the room, as MacRae sat back on the vinyl bench in the corner booth of the diner. His damp shirt clung uncomfortably to his back as the last of the storm slowly evaporated in the air-conditioning. The diner had been recommended by his hotel just across the road, but the tired decor or music didn't inspire confidence. His stomach grumbled angrily as he waited for his food order to arrive.

He took a sip of strong black coffee, wincing at the harsh bite of the cheap coffee beans, and looked at the menu again, mildly curious to see if their claim of it being *the best all day breakfast burger in the south*' was warranted.

He reflected on his conversation with Elias. It all felt a bit surreal now that he'd almost dried off after the storm. It looked like Elias walked a fine line between sanity and craziness. The trouble was it was hard to know what to believe about Crane.

He mulled over the name Elias had given him for Cane's guide to Aralsk-7. What was it...*Sar Fendi?*

Elias hadn't had any luck finding the right one years ago and sounded like he'd given up, but maybe it was worth another try with fresh eyes. MacRae set to work on his phone, scouring Facebook, LinkedIn, and using Google and another couple of more obscure search engines. The name wasn't too common and he quickly came up with a short list worth further scrutiny. He checked out the first three based on age and location before he realised that the name Sar could possibly be short for either the male name Sardor, or the female name Sarvinoz, in that part of the world. Elias had said the guide was male, but was that just an assumption?

The diner and his damp wet clothes faded from mind as he looked into the potential matches. Most of them seemed to live pretty average lives with jobs and families...life seemed pretty tough in that part of the world...until a Facebook page full of spectacular images jumped out at him. The page owner, according to the personal information, was a woman in her late thirties. And her life was anything but average. She described herself as *"A Professional DJ, available to run the best party you've ever been to...anywhere in the world."*

The claim was ambitious, but as MacRae scrolled through her photos he started to believe it. He recognised a lot of the locations she'd performed in, dazzling beaches in Bali, the unmistakable sights of Goa in India, and many he didn't know, mountains and forest in the South America, possibly Peru?

The party photos all had common features: beautiful locations, big crowds of beautiful people caught up in a dancing frenzy, spectacular lighting. And always up the front of the stage, gold headphones atop her head, spinning the disks on the turntables of the mixing desk was Sar Fendi, or *Hellfire Angel* as she called herself professionally, the name emblazoned in letters of flame on a banner behind her.

MacRae sat back and smiled. It looked like she had a great life. He left the reality of his world behind as he checked out more of her photos, soaking up the fun and adventure of her world. She obviously took the opportunity to explore when she travelled for her work, many of the photos showed her in hiking gear surrounded by forest or jungle, and it appeared she also had a taste for danger as she free-climbed sheer mountain cliffs, snorkelled in pristine blue tropical water, or was speeding through the desert on a hybrid motorcycle.

But one photo stood out from the others, at least to MacRae. This one showed her dressed in dusty leathers and leaning against her motorcycle, framed underneath a metal archway topped by writing in Russian. Behind her, slightly out of focus, were decaying buildings and rusted trucks.

MacRae smiled. He instinctively knew where she was...it must be Aralsk-7. And he knew in his gut that he'd found the mystery guide Crane must have had hired years ago to take him there.

He put his phone down and gazed out the window, wondering what Crane had been doing on his trip to the old Soviet Union. The possibilities were endless, and as much as he tried MacRae couldn't think of anything that didn't fill him with a terrible sense of foreboding. Then his phone pinged with a string of new message notifications. The first that flashed up was from Schneider. Good news hopefully. He opened the message, quickly scanning the few lines. Schneider was still following up the medical flight to the US but hadn't managed to track it to its final destination yet. MacRae felt a pang of disappointment. He'd been hoping to hear of some progress.

He closed the email and checked the other notifications, skimming through the majority. There wasn't anything that really needed his attention. He paused on the last one, a list of events in the area advertisers thought he might be interested in. MacRae worked in the security business and went to considerable lengths to keep his digital footprint, personal details and movements private, but the way pretty much everything anyone used on their smartphones was linked, from the GPS using maps, to social media and internet searches, everything was stored, analysed and usually on-sold without you even knowing it. So whether he liked it or not the events were uncannily relevant to his tastes and recent interests, even where he currently was. A jazz singer performing in a secret bar caught his eye, then nothing else until the last one on the list.

The Prepare, Defend, Survive Expo.
SALT LAKE CITY, UTAH

Tickets selling fast!

Almost without thinking he clicked the link and was taken to a slick website promising days of family fun learning about bunkers, guns and how to live through the end of the world if necessary. He smiled. It seemed extreme, but in uncertain times maybe some of it had merit.

The list of exhibitors was huge. Obviously there was big money in this event. And he couldn't help being drawn to the information on how to eat, provide electricity, purify water...all simple but essential things when society collapsed. Not so far-fetched given how much of the world's population still lived at a subsistence level, or in places like New Orleans or Haiti when natural disasters struck and the structure of society disappeared within hours.

He flicked through more exhibitors, then paused at an ad for a book stall specialising in survival manuals. Something about it was vaguely familiar. He tapped the table then remembered. He'd seen the man running the stall in an image he'd found of Crane when he'd been researching him previously. The man had been launching his latest book and had his arm around the shoulders of a smiling Magnus Crane holding a copy.

It didn't take MacRae long to find the image again, and the article accompanying it. Both men looked a decade younger, and the article described Crane as an ardent supporter of the self-sufficiency movement.

'Here you go sir.' A grey haired server smiled as he placed a huge burger in front of MacRae. Egg yolk oozed down the side of a hash brown, and the mountain of fries struggled desperately to stay on the plate.

MacRae pulled the plate in closer and grinned. 'I might need more coffee with this please.'

He took a bite of burger, then went back to work, finding an online copy of the book and opening it for a preview. The chapter list covered a lot more than just survival, with whole sections devoted to lethal measures used to protect a property from intruders. Then he saw Crane's name in the foreword. He was thanked as a great support in the survivalist community.

The server returned and topped up his coffee from a steaming glass jug, finishing just as his phone rang. It was Marion.

MacRae waited until the server had left before answering, then spent a couple of minutes filling her in on his meeting with Elias.

'So there are more connections and coincidences around Crane that we didn't know about, but nothing that really takes us anywhere,' Marion said.

MacRae washed a mouthful of hash brown down with coffee before answering.

'I'm afraid so. I was hoping for something more concrete, but I just don't know about all this stuff about medical trial cover-ups years ago, and trips to Soviet bio-warfare labs.'

'I think we're at a dead end again,' Marion said. 'And there's not much happening for me here at the moment either. There's some contracts coming up in a few months for vaccination programs in India, but nothing concrete until then, so I might head back to Europe for a while.'

MacRae was silent. Surely he wasn't at a total dead end? And he couldn't help liking the idea of spending more time with Marion...if he could persuade her.

'I was thinking of heading home too,' MacRae said. 'But there's an expo this week that might be useful for my work, so I might check it out first.'

'What's the expo about?' Marion said.

'The areas that interest me are aid and survival planning in disaster zones, the same kind of thing that applies to your work. And there's a chance I might get some more insight into Crane while I'm there too.' MacRae smiled to himself, giving Marion time to let it sink in before he continued. 'Do you feel like joining me for some professional development before you leave the US?'

Marion chewed it over, then spoke. 'It might be a good opportunity whilst I've got time on my hands. What's the connection with Crane?'

MacRae filled her in about the survival manual and the picture of Crane, then threw in another sweetener.

'I'll cover the travel and accommodation expenses.'

Marion made a decision. 'Sure, why not? Count me in.'

~

CHAPTER 25

PREPPERS

Marion's face clouded over as she read the enormous banner hung across the front of the exhibition centre. MacRae couldn't help comparing it to the grey storm clouds gathering around the hills in the distance.

'It's a preppers expo?' She planted her hands on her hips. 'You've tricked me into keeping you company at a preppers expo?'

MacRae grinned sheepishly. 'Well to be fair it does cover emergency aid and survival in disasters.'

'Along with what are the best weapons to kill anyone trying to join you in your bunker. I'm very tempted to leave you to it and head to Europe you know.'

She swivelled on her heel to see the taxi that had delivered them accelerating away across the enormous parking lot. MacRae was glad to see that option disappearing...for the moment at least.

Her face softened when she saw MacRae's grin waver.

'But then I suppose you've already paid for it, and the accommodation. Okay let's just go and have a quick look.'

~

The exhibition centre was divided into sections based on themes, each colour coded in a thick brochure handed out as they entered listing the exhibitors. They spent five minutes in the foyer surrounded by an excited throng of visitors having their entry passes scanned, while they debated what to see first, then headed into the main hall. They stayed close to avoid losing each other in the crowd, aiming for the Survival Section, but an accidental turn to the left instead of right at a huge stage and they found themselves in the Home Defence section.

Marion was shocked by the seemingly endless range of assault rifles, hand guns and other technology on display designed to deter or kill anyone that came too close.

'Is all this stuff legal for civilians to buy?'

'Depending on where you live, where you purchase it, that kind of thing,' MacRae said.

Marion shook her head, then paused to watch a stall attendant in body armour, weapons hanging from webbing, as he chatted enthusiastically to potential customers, enthusing about the ease of use for anyone, pointing out the benefits for families, women and anyone else who cared to feel the weight and balance of a particular piece.

Marion had had enough. 'I spend my life working to clean up the mess made by people wielding weapons just like these. Let's go and see the non-violent ways to assist human survival?'

MacRae hesitated. 'You go and I'll catch up with you...' He glanced at his watch. '... in an hour?'

He saw Marion sigh and stepped in close, touching her arm.

'This is still part of my life. I need to keep abreast of what's available out there to the military and the public, the weapons I might come across in my work. From either end of the barrel. Do you understand?'

Marion forced a smile. 'Sure.'

MacRae went back to the exhibits as Marion walked away. She paused at the exit, turning to watch him for a few seconds from afar before she left the section. He was engaged in an animated conversation with an exhibitor, checking out options for magazines and telescopic sights for a gun that looked designed for soldiers, not civilians.

Flashes of their past came back, the refugee camps and war zones, MacRae as a counter-terrorist officer kitted in black from head to toe, wearing a Kevlar vest, machine pistol slung across his chest. The mental image of him was so strong. She smiled as she remembered that was how he was when they first met, how she'd seen him as yet another adrenaline junkie tough guy out to make his mark. Then she'd got to know him and realised he was genuine and caring, truly there to try and make a difference, and when she pictured him kitted out ready for an operation she saw him as tough and capable. And she remembered how back then, when she was around him she felt safer than anytime else.

It was that exact moment MacRae looked around, straight at her. It was like they were still connected. She blushed as he smiled and threw her a wave, then he turned back to the exhibit.

Marion shook her head. It was over a long time ago and reminiscing like this did no good for anyone, especially her. Time to go and see what was the latest for nutrition in disaster zones.

On the other side of the room MacRae had felt the connection too, the unconscious feeling that she was watching him. That was why he turned when he did. And he too knew that thinking like this wouldn't help their situation.

'So you were in law enforcement did you say?'

MacRae snapped back to the present. The attendant had come around to stand next to MacRae.

'Something like that.'

The man was young, broad chest, tattooed arms. And he grinned at MacRae with a smart-arse know-it-all look.

'Didn't they train you to stay focused, not lose your attention on a piece of ass?' The attendant shot a glance at Marion as she left.

A couple of people stopped by to watch the exchange. The attendant's colleague behind the desk grinned at them both, egging his friend on.

MacRae looked into the man's eyes. He could see he was being set up as a side show. It seemed like this was a game he liked to play.

MacRae held his gaze, waiting for it, as he stepped back.

'You should be careful how you speak to people you don't know.'

Then MacRae saw what he'd been waiting for. The man's eyes flinched ever so slightly a millisecond before his hand flashed to his hip, pulling out a side arm and swinging it up into MacRae's face in a well-rehearsed move.

At least that's what he intended to happen.

Instead, MacRae twisted his torso to move out of the path of the gun, grabbing the man's wrist and the weapon as he hooked his leg behind the man's knee and pushed him to the ground backwards.

Before the man could blink MacRae ejected the magazine and opened the breach then pressed the gun back against the man's forehead.

The man pushed back against MacRae's hand for a second then gave up, sitting on the ground.

Then he grinned. 'I guess I should sir.'

MacRae released his grip, and helped the man to his feet, noticing that he was getting a round of applause from the small crowd. They must have thought it was part of the show.

He leaned in to the pat the man's shoulder before he left the stall, and whispered in his ear.

'Remember this and it might keep you alive one day. It doesn't matter how good you think you are, sooner or later you'll meet someone better.'

~

MacRae found Marion as she was about to leave a stall with a sample bag of freeze-dried emergency survival rations. He waited behind her as the conversation finished.

The stall holder raised an eyebrow as he spoke. 'Really? Peanut butter?'

'Yes, really.' Marion smiled. 'I'm looking forward to trying your meals, and they do have amazing nutritional value. But if you just want people to survive in extreme circumstances you can do a lot worse than ship in a ton of peanut butter. It's an amazingly complete food.'

'Maybe I'll stock up in my bunker.' The stall holder smiled. 'Just in case.'

'Unless you happen to have a peanut allergy of course,' Marion said as she turned, bumping straight into MacRae.

'Looks like you've got us lunch,' MacRae said, nodding at her samples. 'Ready to move on?'

MacRae led the way, threading through the crowds, scanning the stalls for the one he'd linked to Crane. Then he saw it, the author, smiling as he signed a copy of his latest book for a giant bearded man in camo pants. He'd aged, but it was unmistakably the man sharing the publicity photo with Crane years ago. There seemed to be a bit of a rush on the stall so MacRae and Marion waited to one side for things to settle down a little.

'There's some amazing stuff at the expo,' Marion said.

'Useful information for your work?' MacRae said.

'Well there's some great ideas for disaster survival but it's definitely targeted to the domestic preppers market.'

'Not suited to your kind of disaster relief?'

'The trouble is,' Marion said, waving a hand around. 'This tends to be more suited to how western aid agencies think they should provide aid, rather than necessarily how locals need it in a disaster.'

'How do you mean?' MacRae said.

'Well often aid money might be better spent locally, helping the people affected rebuild their own shelters and housing, rather than spending it in the west to buy expensive shelters that don't suit the local conditions or the culture of how local people live. That way they get what they actually need, and the aid money raised overseas helps the local economy.'

'That makes sense,' MacRae said.

Marion shrugged. 'Typical well-meaning arrogance of the west I suppose.'

She looked over his shoulder. 'So what do we have here?'

MacRae lowered his voice. 'This is the guy who thanked Crane for his support for one of his earlier books.'

The last of the crowd at the stall wandered on, books clasped in their hands.

'Okay,' Marion said, squeezing past him. 'Let's have a chat like good preppers would.'

Marion smiled broadly as she approached the stall, then spoke loudly to MacRae.

'See honey, this is the book I was telling you about, the one from that survivalist forum.'

MacRae slid up next to her, checking out the display. 'They reckoned it was pretty good?'

'The go-to book for the basics. It was rated eight point five out of ten.'

MacRae selected one from the front of the display, turning it in his hands, then looking inside the front and back covers.

The stall holder watched with curiosity. 'So my book is still getting good reviews? I was worried it might be getting a bit dated.'

Marion spoke. 'Maybe, but anything endorsed by that business guy.. What's his name?'

MacRae shrugged. 'Don't ask me baby doll.'

'I've got it. Crane. Is it Magnum Crane?'

The stall holder was suddenly more interested. 'Magnus Crane? Is that who you're thinking of?'

Marion nodded. 'That's him. People like him, You know, rich, successful, they know what's going on way before the rest of us. So if he's smart enough to plan ahead for the worst, then that's good enough for me.'

'How did you know he supported my book?' the stall holder said.

'Old publicity photos on the internet,' Marion said. 'When I was looking up your book online.'

The stall holder nodded. 'He was smart enough to know that you should plan for the worst to protect your own, long before he was famous. He used to be real involved in the movement back then.'

MacRae placed the book back on the table. 'Any chance of a signed copy? And maybe a photo of you and my wife holding your book?'

The stall holder puffed his chest with pride as he picked up the book and looked for a pen. 'Sure, It'd be my pleasure.'

Marion messed with her hair, preening for the photo. 'He's not involved anymore?'

'Nah, I guess he just got too busy as he got richer. Maybe it didn't fit his new corporate image neither.'

Marion frowned. 'How do you mean?'

The stall holder poised his pen over the inside of the cover.

'What would you like me to write?'

Marion waved her card over the terminal, waiting for the ping signifying the sale was approved. 'I don't know, how about *to Marion a new friend?*'

The stall holder scribbled the words, finishing his signature with a flourish, then came around the front of the stall and stood next to her. They each took a side of the book, holding it in front as MacRae stepped back to take the photo.

'How do you mean it might not fit Crane's new image?' MacRae said, flipping his phone from portrait to landscape for the photo.

'Well someone who runs a corporation selling hope around the world with drugs and whatever that he promises will end the suffering of humanity, probably not a good look if he's building survival bunkers at the same time, and putting together an arsenal to keep the hordes out if it all goes wrong.'

'Just hold still for a moment.' MacRae took another couple of photos, then showed them to Marion and the stall holder.

The stall holder waved MacRae over, pulling him in next to them and lifting his phone to take a selfie of the three of them.

'Is that what Crane was doing when you were launching your book, how you met him?' Marion said.

The stall holder went back behind his stall. 'Will you put that photo on the exhibition website? It's good publicity.'

Then he looked from MacRae to Marion curiously. 'Yes, that's when I met Crane. He was real smart and keen to be involved. So what brings you guys here anyway?'

Marion let MacRae answer. 'We both travel a lot for our work... Ian's in the security business and I consult with aid organisations... and like to know what the real world is doing in keeping people alive in disasters. Who knows, we might need to do it for ourselves one day.'

The stall holder shrugged. 'You never know.'

A group of tourists wandered up to the stall, flicking through the books. The stall holder focused his attention on them.

Marion slid the book into her bag as they left. 'Nice talking to you, and thanks for the book.'

The stall holder watched them as they disappeared into the crowd. It had been a long time since anyone had asked about Crane supporting the book. Something didn't ring true about them.

He hadn't contacted Crane for a long time, mainly because he didn't seem to want to be associated with this world anymore. But what the hell, either it was still the right phone number or it wasn't.

He waited until the last of the tourists drifted off, then wrote a brief text to Crane, wishing him well and mentioning the curious visitors with an accent, maybe Canadian, maybe Australian. Then with a press of a button the message and photo were gone, and the stall holder thought nothing more of it.

~

Across the country Magnus Crane's phone pinged as the text arrived. He was sitting in a rather boring meeting. Global finance didn't really interest him. He paid others to be interested in that. He frowned as the sender was an unknown number, then sat upright as he looked at the attached picture. The stall holder, a face he hadn't seen for a very long time, flanked on both sides by MacRae and Marion holding his book. This was starting to get a little bit troubling, the man just wouldn't go away. Time to sort it out, and perhaps this was the opportunity to try something a little innovative.

He thought back to earlier in his career, when he'd been supervising trials of newly developed drugs. One in particular stood out because it had gone disastrously wrong. The intention had been noble...well, as noble as a corporate profit making entities' intentions can be...to bring to market a game-changing drug to stop and possibly reverse the devastating effects of dementia on the fragile mind. He'd been organising the trial, but the implementation had been contracted to a third party, and they'd accidentally administered the wrong dosage to the dozen paid volunteers for first stage trial...

by a factor of ten. Instead of a rather boring but well paid week in a controlled environment being tested for improvements in their cognitive responses, all twelve of the test subjects had within a space of twenty minutes from the first dose descended into a psychosis similar to one induced by the infamous LSD military experiments. The trial administrators had managed to purge the drug from all but one test subject successfully, who never returned to the real world from the delusional nightmare they'd been sent into, dying shortly afterwards from organ failure.

As usual in the corporate medical world, the drug trial contract company had quietly been liquidated, the surviving volunteers financially compensated for their mental and physical injury, and the results of the trial never released publicly. Miraculously Crane had managed to keep his corporate record clean and continued his stellar rise to the top. And with no official record of the drug or the trial, no hospital would ever effectively diagnose or treat anyone who had ingested a lethal amount, almost guaranteeing death, and no chance of identifying the source.

At the front of the room the Chief Accountant, talking in a monotone to a PowerPoint presentation filled with tiny text, numbers and charts, felt energised as he saw Crane suddenly looking alert. He must have finally got the tone of the presentation right to catch his bosses' attention.

Crane tapped out a text. He didn't know exactly where the Russian was, but the man had an uncanny knack for being around when Crane needed him. The instructions were clear and concise, and needed to be executed immediately, otherwise Crane would have to consider alternate strategies. The text sent, Crane mentally moved on, settling into a pleasing mental movie reel of how his India strategy was going to unfold, and his name go down in history as the biggest single factor in saving the planet for future generations.

~

The Russian was expressionless as he read Crane's message. He was just collecting his luggage after landing from a six hour flight, and without a second thought booked another six hour flight departing within the hour. Destination...the Prepare, Defend, Survive Expo in Salt Lake City.

~

CHAPTER 26

TRIPPING

The Russian frowned as a thin layer of fog formed on the window of the diner. Too much cooking with inadequate ventilation on a chilly morning was adding a risk, albeit small, that he'd miss seeing MacRae and Marion leave the hotel.

He shuffled along his bench seat closer to the window and discreetly used his jacket sleeve to wipe the window and restore his line of observation. He checked his wallet, confirming he had enough notes to cover his coffee and flapjacks breakfast. Unlike his targets, he avoided using cards to pay bills as it was exactly that that led him to find them so quickly. You just had to know the right services to access on the Dark Web, and you'd find the location a card was being swiped or tapped almost before the owner finished the transaction.

He stifled a yawn. The back-to-back flights had been a little arduous, and he'd struggled to get his body clock back in sync after crossing the time zones in rapid succession. And it hadn't helped that the last flight disgorged him to fight his way through the many airport security screening requirements at a little after four in the morning.

He'd followed Crane's instructions, arriving in the city centre at the diagnostic services laboratory, no doubt affiliated with one of Crane's many companies, at just on five. As promised he'd been met at the door by a laboratory assistant with a plain wrapped brown cardboard box. The sleepy and dishevelled man had apparently been wrenched from his sleep with instructions to go to the lab and await a parcel delivered by courier. He was then to hand it over to the

Russian and no-one else. It was obvious to the Russian from the man's curt manner that he didn't much like the look of him, and was probably looking forward to going back home to his warm bed and wife for another couple of hours before he started his work day properly.

It didn't bother the Russian that many people he met looked at him with a hint of mistrust or even disdain. He looked at his reflection in the diner window. He wasn't vain, but he'd been told by the few women he'd allowed in his life that he had rugged good looks, edgy and with a hint of danger. He cropped his hair short for practicality, and a constant five-o'clock shadow of beard hinted at his eastern European heritage. Maybe it was how he carried himself, the faint scars on his face, his cold blue eyes. Or perhaps most people were uncomfortable around him because of the unusual requests and circumstances he worked with.

Unlike the sleepy lab assistant, in the Russian's world day or night was neither here nor there. He did whatever was necessary to get the job done. And the vast majority of the population, like the mousy lab assistant, was totally oblivious to the dark, murky and violent world that co-existed around them.

The Russian, glanced around the diner. No-one was watching him, and he'd been careful to select a seat in a blind spot of the security cameras at each end of the room. He carefully lifted the lid of the box and looked at the tiny vial resting in layers of bubble wrap. He was curious about its contents. His instructions were to simply administer the liquid to MacRae without detection, then stand back and watch the show. If he couldn't achieve it within twenty four hours, he was to remove MacRae with a convincing looking accident. He'd killed many people over the years with convincing looking accidents, but the instructions for the vial had him intrigued, so he was really keen to succeed with the first method. He thought of it as professional curiosity. And heaven knows, working with Magnus Crane was never dull.

He glanced out the window again. No sign of them yet. He'd checked the hotel dining room earlier. It would have been a good first opportunity for him...he had a pretty tight time frame...but they were probably taking breakfast in their room. He waved his hand to the server wandering the diner, coffee pot in hand. Another top-up would help pass the time, and many years working in covert surveillance had taught him the virtues of patience.

MacRae and Marion left the hotel at just after eight thirty. By force of habit he checked the street for anything unusual. Their eyes met and he was briefly distracted by the intensity of his feelings for her. That's why he failed to notice the man seated by the window in the diner across the road watching them as they hailed a taxi for the brief drive to the second day of the expo.

They shared the back seat of the cab as it whisked them through the chilly morning air, and whether it was conscious or not their hands touched in the spare seat between them.

The morning at the expo passed quickly. They'd gone through the list of exhibitors again the previous evening, and there were only a couple more either of them wanted to visit, so by late morning they were finished and were heading back to the hotel, this time taking a more leisurely route on the local bus.

They sat near the back, Marion by the window, MacRae watching as she sorted through a blue plastic bag filled with glossy brochures and samples.

'Anything good in there?' MacRae said.

Marion shrugged. 'Not a lot, catering for a different market than me I guess. Do you think it was worthwhile coming along? Not the expo...talking to the author about Crane. I mean that's what this was really all about wasn't it?'

And spending more time with you, MacRae thought.

'It's all part of building a picture of Crane.' MacRae turned to face her. 'The more we learn, the more he seems at odds with his public persona. The world sees a humanitarian, philanthropic businessman. We see someone who treats the world as a place to be feared and protected from. So from that point of view yes, it's telling me we're on the right track, even if we still don't have anything concrete yet. And to be honest it's all we can do for the moment, unless we get a lucky break.'

Marion smiled. 'In my experience with you Ian, you make your own luck.'

'Maybe,' MacRae said, as watched the shops passing by. 'So what's next for you?'

Marion glanced at him, then looked away. 'No sure. It's been nice to have some down-time though. Despite the topic of the expo it's made me feel a little bit normal for once, just out and about doing what other people do.'

She looked around the half-empty bus, a few people dressed for office work, but most more casual. An olive skinned mother in a brightly coloured dress clutched a baby to her chest whilst struggling to keep a wriggling toddler seated next to her.

'This is a nice way to get a feel for the people in a new place don't you think?'

'Yes, and so is having lunch somewhere like that.' MacRae smiled. 'What do you think?'

Marion followed his eyes to the busy cafe bar coming up on their left. A low fence surrounded a dozen tables along the edge of the footpath, diners soaking up the sun as servers dressed in crisp black and white uniforms bustled around them. Wide brick arches spaced along the front of the building provided entry to the Spanish-styled interior.

Marion grinned as she pressed the button, the ping of the bell signalling the driver to stop. 'Sounds good to me.'

They waited at the entrance to be directed to a table inside, MacRae using the time to check out the menu, and the extensive list of the locally brewed beers on tap. He could see Marion was focusing on the food menu, looking for the vegetarian options.

A server approached, a hipster with a long groomed beard and curly moustache, apologising unconvincingly as he advised them there were no empty tables, but they were welcome to sit at the bar.

They took a seat at the quieter end of the bar and ordered drinks. MacRae relaxed as he looked along the line of shiny beer taps, condensation dripping into the silver tray below, then to the hundreds of gin and whisky bottles lit up on the glass shelves from waist height to the ceiling behind the bar.

'I think I like this place,' Marion said, raising her glass of wine to clink gently with his beer.

Behind them at the entrance, a man with shoulder length blond hair and thin rimmed black plastic glasses surveyed the room, spotting them instantly at the bar. The Russian weaved through the diners to the left of them and positioned himself a metre from MacRae, leaning against the bar to order. He hadn't realised how much he'd missed the old days in the Service using disguises.

He'd been taught by the best. His trainer used to joke that even his mother wouldn't recognise him, and on one occasion when working undercover he'd actually run into his mother at the counter of a grocery store, and sure enough she hadn't recognised him as they'd discussed the unseasonably cold weather.

He watched MacRae and Marion talking from the corner of his eye. He knew the guy was good, their previous encounters had shown that, but he was slipping, totally let his guard down, probably because he was with the woman.

He reached into his pocket and retrieved the vial, carefully removing the cap out of sight below the bar. He'd already checked the location of the security cameras and should be able to do this unobserved, but even if it was recorded he'd never be identified.

Then the time was right. The room was buzzing with activity as MacRae put his beer glass on the bar. The Russian dropped his other hand holding a glass of water down in front of him, then threw it back and to the side behind MacRae and Marion. The drink hit the floor at the feet of the hipster server as he walked by, shattering into pieces with a crash. Everyone turned to look, and in a second the Russian's hand waved over MacRae's glass and the vial was emptied, just as Marion turned back to the bar.

She'd sensed rather than seen the movement in her peripheral vision and looked at the man next to MacRae as he stood back from the bar. Their eyes met briefly, and although she didn't know him, there was something chillingly familiar about him. Then he was gone.

Marion realised MacRae was looking at her with concern.

'Are you okay? You look puzzled.'

Marion was silent then smiled. 'No, just thought I knew someone.'

MacRae picked up his glass to finish the dark ale just as their lunch arrived. Marion laughed, snatching the drink from his hand and downing it in one.

'Mmm, the beer really is good here.'

MacRae growled with mock annoyance as he ordered them another rounds of drinks. 'I didn't know you had to watch your drinks around here.'

The Russian waited patiently at an outdoor table. He had a line of sight to Marion and MacRae but he knew they'd struggle to see him with the bright sunlight at his back. He didn't have to wait long.

Marion had just finished her meal when the first wave of the drug swept through her, shattering her relaxed mood and flooding her consciousness with visions from hell.

MacRae was waving to attract the bartender when the relaxed buzz of the bar was pierced by Marion's blood curdling scream. To her, the customers had been transformed into hideous demons, caricatures of violence, decadence and decay, rotting faces glaring at her with hate and malevolence. MacRae was waving his hands at her, fingers covered in spikes, blood dripping from their tips. Dismembered bodies writhed on the floor around her.

MacRae stood and took her shoulders in his hands, looking into her eyes. 'Marion, what's wrong?'

She screamed again at his touch, pushing his arms aside and throwing herself through the crowd towards the entrance.

The Russian looked up as he heard the chaos unfold, and clenched his teeth as he realised it wasn't the man who was out of control. Then he was left with no doubt as Marion ran through the outdoor diners and rushed straight onto the busy road. Instinctively his hand swept behind him to confirm his weapon was firmly nestled in the small of his back, then he rose to his feet so he could watch her.

MacRae brushed straight past the Russian as he pursued Marion onto the road, grabbing her arm and yanking her back from the path of a delivery van, the driver desperately pumping his brakes as he sped towards her. She recoiled in horror as she saw a demonic MacRae next to her. She lashed out with her fists, striking a glancing blow to his chin. Then she wriggled from his grip and was off again, racing along the sidewalk and darting down an alley to the right.

MacRae gritted his teeth as he sprinted after her. He'd seen this kind of reaction before as a young police officer when he'd been called to scenes of drug overdoses, the addicts crazed and paranoid, often with superhuman strength. He had no doubt Marion had been drugged, and given the circumstances knew it was most likely the drug had been intended for him.

The Russian followed at a discreet distance, disappointed that it had gone wrong, although he was impressed at the speed and efficacy of the drug that Crane had arranged for him. The woman was behaving extremely violently so perhaps she would still do the job on MacRae and save him the trouble.

Marion ran with the speed induced by terror, but had entered a dead-end alleyway. In her mind she was now confronted with a wall of fire, the only way forward through the flames leading to a seething pit of deformed animals and demons, faces contorted in agony and intent on devouring her. And fast approaching from behind was MacRae, a bent and twisted figure carrying rusty curved knives in both hands with which to disembowel her.

MacRae slowed to a walk as he got closer to Marion, watching closely as her eyes darted left to right, seeking escape. Then she dropped to her knees, hands scrabbling and wrapping around two discarded beer bottles. She crashed them together, both shattering in half, then with a desperate cry she threw herself at MacRae, thrusting the jagged edges at his face and torso. MacRae was briefly caught off guard by the viciousness of her attack, only just leaping to one side, a shard of glass ripped through his shirt sleeve and grazing his forearm. He swivelled on his heels to face her again as she instantly continued her attack, eyes wide. MacRae was caught between his close combat instincts urging him to deliver a debilitating strike to his assailant and end the attack, and the knowledge his attacker was the last person in the world he wanted to hurt.

Marion rushed at him again, glass swinging at his face. MacRae feigned to the right, then pivoted to the left, staying in close and wrapping his arms around her before throwing them both to the ground, Marion releasing the bottles as she fell. MacRae tightened his grip as she thrashed wildly in his arms, fingers scratching and feet kicking at any part of him. He adjusted his hold, placing an arm around her throat and leaned back, placing a gentle but firm pressure on the side of her neck. It didn't take long before the blood supply to her brain was restricted enough for her struggles to weaken and within a matter of seconds she slid into unconsciousness.

MacRae slowly loosened his grip as he felt her go limp in his arms, and stayed in position until he was sure she was out. A broken bottle was still near her outstretched hand so he kicked it away before releasing her. He rolled up onto his knees and carefully rolled her onto her side and placing her head on her arm in the coma position. He knelt down, checking her pulse and breathing, then gently lifted first one then the other eyelid. Her pupils were hugely dilated, and her eyes flickered as the drug coursed through her body, trapping her mind in a private hell.

MacRae looked around the alley then up to the entrance, the cars and pedestrians passing by oblivious to them. Then a figure entered the lane way, just a dark shape back-lit by the sun.

Marion coughed, a wet choking sound, drawing MacRae's attention. He cupped her head in his hand and leaned her forward to ease her breathing just as she purged herself, depositing the contents of her stomach on the cracked concrete ground in front of them. She groaned as her stomach cramped, determined to expel the poison within her. MacRae's heart ached as he watched her.

The scuff of boots drew his eyes back up the lane way. Light cloud had drifted in front of the sun, and the figure was now part way towards them. As it got closer MacRae could see the shape was becoming clearer as that of a man, and the object held down to one side sent a shiver through his spine as he recognised the unmistakable profile of a gun.

MacRae checked Marion again. She'd finished purging now and was weakly struggling to lift herself on one elbow. Her eyes opened and a surge of relief went through him as he saw recognition in eyes, confusion more than fear.

He pressed her gently back to the coma position, and whispered in her ear. 'Just lie still and get your strength back. I have to go for a minute okay?'

Marion lay back down, and shut her eyes as MacRae stood to face the new threat.

His eyes darted around the laneway. It was empty save for a couple of battered old steel garbage bins. Steel fire ladders reaching the upper floors of buildings offered a possible escape route, but not for Marion. He picked up the broken bottles Marion had dropped, then ran to the cover of the closest garage bin. As weapons they were better than nothing...but not much.

The shadowy figure saw MacRae moving into cover and raised the gun into a firing position, lowering his stance for stability as he moved. He crabbed forward along the far side of the lane way, making sure MacRae would have to come into the open to tackle him. MacRae pressed himself into the corner, listening to the approaching footsteps.

He had two choices: charge at the man as he rounded the bin, or launch himself over the top. Both options would still leave him completely exposed for a crucial few seconds as he closed the distance, and he knew for a skilled operative that would be more than enough. But if he didn't take the risk there was no doubt both he and Marion would die.

The clouds drifted away from the sun, bathing the laneway in harsh light. MacRae looked up. The building next to him had cast a deep shadow over the bin. Maybe it would be enough to hide him for just long enough.

He ducked low and poked his head quickly out past he bin. A soft pop and sparks flew as a bullet skipped off the rusty steel bin just above his head. Fuck. That was way too close. He was out of time. He reached up, grasping the top of the bin and tensing his muscles to throw himself over the top of the bin and at the attacker. He pictured where the man must be and took a deep breath, charging his muscles with oxygen. But before he could launch himself the laneway was filled with the roar of a diesel engine, the whirr and clatter as giant steel forks reached out to lift the garbage bins and empty them into the garbage truck.

The distraction was just what he needed and MacRae hurled himself over the bin in smooth motion landing on the other side of the bin, jagged glass bottle held out in front. But it was too late. The man had obviously considered it wasn't worth the risk to finish the job with witnesses and was disappearing into the light of the busy street at the entry to the laneway.

MacRae tensed. Should he go after the attacker, risking a confrontation with an armed man in a crowded street? Then he realised the operators of the truck were staring at the image of the mad-man brandishing a broken bottle who had suddenly appeared in front of them as they drove up to the bin.

He relaxed and shrugged at the driver, tossing the broken bottle into the bin behind him, then went back down the alley to where Marion was struggling to get to her feet.

MacRae approached warily, then took her elbow to steady her.

'Marion, take it easy. How are you feeling?'

She looked at him, confusion etched on her face, but thankfully no longer panic as she recognised him.

'Ian? What happened? Where are we?'

MacRae forced a smile. 'It's okay, but you've been drugged. I think your...well actually my drink was spiked in the bar, but then you drank my beer. It kinda sent you crazy for a while.'

Marion blinked as the memory of the terror flooded back. 'I remember...faces, blood...'

'You were hallucinating, ran out into the traffic, and tried to kill me when I cornered you back here.'

'Who did this to me?'

Then she remembered back to the bar. 'I saw someone I thought was familiar next to you in the bar. Then the glass broke on the floor and when I looked back he was leaning towards us, that must have been when he did it.'

'I remember him,' MacRae said. 'Long blond hair, glasses?'

Marion nodded. 'There was something about his eyes...'

'I think he followed us down here,' MacRae said. 'Probably planning to finish the job.'

Marion eyes widened. 'He's here?'

'He was, the garbage truck came in and he took off.'

'Has he gone far? Could you catch him?' Marion face clouded over.

'You're my first priority,' MacRae said. 'We need to get you to a hospital.'

Marion squeezed his arm as he looked in his eyes. 'I'm feeling okay now. I think whatever it is has been purged from my system. If you think you can catch him, go for it.'

MacRae squeezed her hand, then sprang to his feet and ran past the bewildered garbage men, covering the length of the laneway in seconds and bursting out into the bright light of the busy street.

He stopped at the edge of the footpath, looking both ways. A splash of yellow in the gutter caught his eye. It was a blond wig. He thought back to the bar, picturing the man next to them, height, build, clothes.

The street was too busy, he couldn't see more than a few people either way, so he ran to a nearby bus stop and leapt up on the seat, searching the crowds for anyone vaguely familiar. Then he saw him, weaving between slowly moving traffic across the road twenty metres away.

MacRae had seconds before he lost him and ran out onto the road. The distance closed rapidly as he approached his quarry unnoticed. Fifteen metres, ten, then the driver of a shiny black Porsche stamped on his brakes as MacRae skipped around the hood. MacRae grinned an apology and was rewarded with the driver pumping his horn and hurling expletives in his direction. MacRae's target turned to look, instantly spotting him. That was when MacRae recognised him. How the hell had the man who'd tried to kill them on the roadside on the other side of the world found them here? The Russian barely hesitated before his hand flicked behind him to retrieve his gun.

Adrenaline coursed through MacRae as he saw the weapon. He closed the remaining distance between them in seconds, throwing himself through the air and hitting the Russian mid-chest, the two men tumbling backwards at the edge of the road.

MacRae pounded his fist into his opponent's face, only landing glancing blows as the Russian twisted and turned, trying to clear the gun from beneath them. With a kick to MacRae's torso the Russian pushed free. MacRae leapt to his feet watching as the gun came around...then flew sideways as a bicycle courier slammed into him, knocking him back to the ground.

Packages of Chinese take-out littered the road around them as the cyclist retrieved his bike, apologising to MacRae. The Russian cursed under his breath, his clear shot to MacRae blocked by the cyclist and bystanders coming to watch the spectacle. He debated whether to move in and take the shot anyway, but it was too risky, so he slid the gun back in its holster and disappeared into the pedestrians crowding the footpath.

MacRae moved to follow but the cyclist wasn't letting him go until he was sure there was no harm done, gripping his forearm as he brushed road dirt from MacRae's shirt.

'Ian.' His name echoed across the street. It was Marion, concern etched across her face.

With a last glance at his disappearing foe, MacRae extricated himself from the courier's grip and crossed back to join her.

~

For the first time since the incident, MacRae relaxed when the door to their hotel room closed behind them. The cab ride back to the hotel had passed quickly without much conversation, as Marion still looked like she was only just hanging on. A long hot shower seemed to have done her the world of good, and now he watched as she moved gingerly across the room to lie on the bed. At least the colour was coming back into her face.

MacRae ordered up coffee then sat next to her, her hand in his. 'How are you feeling?'

'Much better. I'm not getting any visions at all anymore.' She shivered. 'That was one of the most frightening things that's ever happened to me Ian. And I think it only stopped because I was sick and got most of it out of my system so quickly.'

'I think you're right,' MacRae said. 'Sometimes people drugged like that never come back from the hallucinations. I might have lost you forever and I don't know how I could cope with that.'

Marion saw the haunted look in his eyes. She realised she felt the same dread at the thought of losing him. Words formed in her mind, but she forced them away. This wasn't the time.

'And you're sure it was that same guy?'

MacRae nodded.

'I guess that explains my feeling that I knew him.'

'And it means someone is definitely gunning for us, at least me,' MacRae said. 'Are you sure you don't want to go to hospital to get checked out? There may be lingering effects of the drug.'

Marion shook her head. 'I'm sure. I feel a lot better now and I don't want to get drawn into the medical system here whilst this is going on.'

MacRae shrugged. 'Okay. Well, you rest while I see if I can get some assistance for us.'

Marion smiled and laid back on the bed. She was asleep the moment her head hit the pillow.

A knock on the door signalled the arrival of the coffee, and MacRae drank half the pot while he made some calls. There was nothing more he could do for the moment, so he sat in a lounge chair to watch Marion as she slept, shifting positions to get comfortable. The fight with the Russian and the collision with the courier had knocked him around more than he'd thought, and soon he also drifted into a troubled sleep.

Movement in front of him broke through his subconscious and he slowly opened his eyes. Marion was sitting on the end of the bed, hands in her lap watching him, tears streaked down her cheeks. She saw him stir and took a step, kneeling in front of him. MacRae sat up as she reached out to hold both his hands.

'Marion, what's...' MacRae only got the first words out before Marion placed a finger on his lips.

'Ssshh. Let me speak.'

MacRae nodded silently, feeling her warmth and the familiar electricity between them through her hands.

Marion took a deep breath. 'What the hell is this thing between us? We fight it, deny it, I try to push it away...'

'Marion, you don't...'

'Let me finish, Ian.' She placed her finger back onto his lips.

'We've chosen to be apart for years, forcing ourselves to pretend it's impossible between us. But all we're doing is causing each other to live a lonely, painful, empty life. We try so hard to help everyone else in the world live better lives. Except ourselves. And it's taken all the events since I met Hassana to realise if we can't live complete lives ourselves, what the hell are we doing telling other people how to live. You feel it too don't you?'

It wasn't a question.

'I've loved you since the day we met.' MacRae smiled. 'You're part of my mind and soul. There's been a piece of me missing every day since we parted.'

Marion leaned in to kiss him, gently brushing her lips against his. 'Isn't it time we made us the priority, find a way to work instead of excuses for us not to work?'

MacRae's life flashed before him. Yes he was doing important work that filled him with pride and satisfaction, keeping safe the people that risked their lives to help others. But there was always an emptiness at the end of the day, an emptiness that had vanished almost without him realising now he was spending time with her again. But Marion was right, it had come at great cost to both of them personally. And maybe it was time to set that right.

He took her face in both his hands, meeting her eyes, searching her soul. 'Yes it is time for us to figure out how to live our lives together.' MacRae felt a weight lift from his shoulders as he said the words. Maybe part of it was letting go of the fear of loss if they couldn't make it work. But now was the time for them to look for a future no longer alone, but as one.

Marion glowed, relief etched across her face as she now knew they felt the same about each other. She rose to her feet and straddled his lap, eager fingers at first gently undoing his shirt buttons, then ripping it open, hands stroking his toned chest, then moving lower to loosen his belt. MacRae kissed her neck and in one swift move lifted her blouse over her head. Marion squealed as MacRae stood up, her legs wrapping around his waist as he walked her to the bed, gently lying her back to finish undressing her, savouring every moment as if he was unwrapping the most precious gift in the world.

Marion grinned cheekily as MacRae paused to gaze at her, lost in her feminine softness and curves, then with a casual flick of her hips Marion upended him, flipping him onto his back on the bed and straddling him again.

MacRae laughed. 'Hey, didn't I teach you that Jujitsu move to turn the tables on an opponent?'

Marion nodded. 'I knew it'd come in handy one day. I think it's time I took the upper hand for a while, so just lie back and let it happen.'

MacRae knew it was too good an offer to refuse and relaxed back as Marion set to work with hands, mouth and body, taking them on an erotic journey that would live with them both forever.

And that's when MacRae realised that Marion's love, commitment and passion for him was more than most men could imagine or would ever have the privilege to experience, and this time as they slowly joined together in the most intimate of embraces, being as close as two people can be, consumed with love and desire, he knew in his heart that he must honour her.

~

MacRae woke with a start. He'd been dreaming the courier had been shaking his arm, refusing to let go. But it was actually Marion, gently shaking him as they lay slumbering together.

'Ian, wake up, it's Brad calling you.'

They'd been asleep for a while, the light outside the window was softening as the day drew to an end. He took the phone and hit *answer,* placing the call on speaker.

'Brad, what have you got?'

Schneider's voice was calm but concerned. 'I've run some searches but haven't found anything that identifies the guy who's tracking you. Whoever he is, he's not on the usual law enforcement and anti-terror lists.'

'I'm not surprised,' MacRae said. 'He's obviously good at this, which is a concern.'

'Sure is,' Schneider said, pausing before he continued. 'I hope you don't mind but I took the liberty of getting one of the local guys to keep an eye out for you after your call.'

'I don't need babysitting,' MacRae snapped.

'Maybe not,' Schneider said. 'But I did it anyway. The guy's a buddy of mine, we go way back so I trust him.'

MacRae softened. 'Thanks Brad. Sorry I snapped.'

'Well he's been snooping around the place the last couple of hours, and the only thing he could tell me was that he found nothing.'

'That's a relief,' Marion said.

'Not really,' Schneider said. 'Because he also said he has a real strong hunch the guy is still around, waiting for you. Nothing he could pin-point, but his hunch is good enough for me.'

'So what are you saying Brad?' MacRae said.

'Everything that's going on here is unofficial Ian. I can't give you resources or protect you and Marion here, you know that. I think you should get out of town right now, go somewhere hard to track and lie low for a bit. If we get anything on the guy, or Hassana I'll let you know okay?'

~

Marion sat on the bed, watching as MacRae paced the room, thinking aloud.

'I could go after the guy here, but he seems to have all the advantages. And while I'm okay with that, I'm not prepared to risk your safety. So I think I've got no choice but to take Brad's advice and go somewhere hard to track.'

He sat next to Marion. 'And I think you should leave the US too for the moment. You'll be safe back in Europe.'

Marion twisted to face him. 'I'm in as much danger as you. Who's to say he won't find me just as easily in Europe?'

MacRae tried to smile. 'Europe will be safer than where I'm going. And this is my fight.'

Marion's eyes blazed. 'Don't you tell me this isn't my fight. I'm the one who was drugged then tried to kill you. And I'm just as involved with Hassana as you are now. So where are you going? Because wherever it is...I'm coming too.'

MacRae grinned at Marion. He loved her fiery spirit. It was one of the many things that drew him to her.

'Vozrozhdeniya Island.'

Marion frowned. The name was familiar. 'Isn't that the Soviet bio-weapons testing site in Uzbekistan that guy Elias was telling you about? He thinks Crane went there.'

'Sure is. Still want to come? There's no shame in backing out.'

Marion shook her head. 'I'd better pack a face mask and surgical gloves.'

~

CHAPTER 27

ISLAND

M acRae adjusted the climate control in the rental car, raising the temperature a couple of degrees against the chill of the night air outside. He checked his watch and smiled. Their timing should be perfect. It had been a long trip getting here, their flight arriving at Nukus airport well after dark, and then a frustrating amount of paperwork to secure the car before they were on their way. But now after a couple of hours of driving, as they neared their destination of Muynak at the edge of the dried-up Aral Sea, MacRae was feeling excited.

Marion shuffled in her seat, getting comfortable resting her head in the rolled-up jumper she'd placed against the side window.

'I hate to sound like a kid, but are we there yet?'

MacRae peered through the blackness of the moonless night. Had he seen it right? A flash of light shot up into the sky in the distance. Yes, this must be it.

He pressed the button and his window slid silently down, a rush of cool night air flushing through the cabin around them.

'Hey, do we really need the whole outdoor experience?' Marion grumbled.

'Wait for it,' MacRae said, listening hard. Then the sound drifted in from the distance, the deep *boom boom* of a musical baseline.

'What the hell is that?' Marion snapped awake.

'We're about to see our tour guide in action,' MacRae said.

When they were about a kilometre from Muynak the sound of dance music was unmistakable, the sky constantly lit by the colours of music festival lighting.

MacRae glanced across at Marion, her face was alive with curiosity.

'What on earth are you taking us to, Ian?'

'Well,' MacRae said. 'You remember I told you how the Soviets drained the Aral Sea to feed their new cotton industry?'

'Sure,' Marion said.

'The town of Muynak, one of the closest places to Aralsk-7, is on the edge of the desert that was created in the dry sea bed. It used to be a fishing port, but has long been dying a slow death as the jobs and people leave.'

'Okay,' Marion said.

'Apparently,' MacRae continued. 'Tourism is on the rise in the region, and money is coming back. Part of the development effort is a regional arts program, including the Stihia Music Festival. Once a year the demise of the town is celebrated by partying adventurers from around the world at the festival, and...' MacRae paused for emphasis. 'Our tour guide, the one that I think took Crane to Aralsk-7 years ago, is amongst other things, a professional DJ, and playing tonight at the festival.'

Marion looked at him sceptically. 'Really? Our tour guide is a DJ?'

'It takes all sorts,' MacRae grinned. 'So I hope you're in the mood for a party.'

He slowed the car as they neared the edge of town, following the noise and lights, until the streets were blocked off and clogged with parked cars, vans and buses.

MacRae found a space to park, and they stepped into the midnight air, the chill soon forgotten as they joined the throngs filling the streets heading to the festival.

The crowd slowed and split into lines as they reached the entry gates where security staff scanned festival passes.

'How are we going to get in?' Marion said.

MacRae reached into his jacket pocket and pulled out two passes on lanyards, passing one to Marion, and they were in.

Marion couldn't help smiling as they weaved their way through the crowd, heading for the main stage. All nationalities and ages were represented, clothed in anything from Uzbekistan national dress, to hard-core dancers in fluorescent tops, and hippies in kaftans and sandals. Long lines snaked back from food and alcohol stalls, and misting stations sprayed cooling clouds of water on overheated partyers. And everywhere in the background the dance music thumped a tribal beat.

MacRae took Marion's hand as they pushed their way into the crowd nearer to the stage, squeezing through gaps as they opened and just as quickly closed. She leaned in to him and shouted, struggling to be heard above the soaring melodies of the dance music.

'This is amazing, I haven't done this for such a long time.'

MacRae nodded and led her closer to the stage.

The excited energy of the crowd embraced them and as they reached the edge of the mosh pit, staying just outside the packed crush of heaving dancers, MacRae stopped.

'I think this will do.'

Marion grinned as the swaying crowd swung her against MacRae. She shut her eyes and focused on the music. They were so close to the enormous speakers to the right of the stage that she could feel the sound wave generated by the base notes pulsing through her body. Subconsciously she started to sway, and then noticed MacRae was doing the same. Right here and now nothing mattered but the moment. So they danced, embracing the hypnotic rhythm and tribal closeness of being part of something bigger with thousands of other likeminded people.

Almost imperceptibly the tempo of the music slowed. MacRae looked over the top of the crowd at the stage and saw the changing of the DJ's, a young, bearded man in black pants and singlet giving control of the turntables to a woman. MacRae recognised her instantly from her Facebook page and website. Sar Fendi.

He tapped Marion's shoulder and pointed to the stage.

'That's her.'

Marion craned her neck to see around the dyed green hair of a man that was blocking her view, and took in the sight of the woman dancing wildly as she held a set of gold headphones to her ear with one hand, hyping up the crowd into frenzy.

The beat of the music slowed, the dancing of the crowd slowing with it. There was a palpable sense of anticipation then the speakers thumped a new pumping beat and the crowd roared, leaping into the air as one, carrying Marion and MacRae with them.

An hour passed and MacRae could feel the effects of jet lag, his body slowing with exhaustion.

Marion hooked an arm around his and leaned in. 'I think I need a rest. What time are we meeting her in the morning?'

MacRae smiled. 'Me too. She's picking us up at eight thirty.'

Marion pulled MacRae gently back through the crowd, enjoying the space and free flowing air as they left the dancing behind. She kept her arm linked in his as they left the festival, heading back to the rental car for a precious few hours rest before the trip in the morning.

Once in the car MacRae ran the engine and the heater for a while, putting an arm around Marion as she rested her head against him shoulder and started to doze.

Her words slowed dreamily as she drifted off. 'I don't know how she gets the energy to do that for a living, then take us out for a tour.'

MacRae knew how. No-one else probably noticed, but halfway through her set he'd watched as Sar had gestured to a heavily tattooed security guard with a shaved head at the side of the stage. He'd handed her a water bottle, and it was done ever so subtly, but MacRae had seen the pills pass from his hand to hers, and without missing a dance step she'd flicked them into her mouth and washed them down with a swig of water. Seeing the casual ease of the drug use took him back to his days as a police officer, occasionally posted to a festival or rock concert, knowing you were surrounded by drugs and stoned young people, knowing that for some it was a dangerous pastime, and others a one-off occasion, and being arrested could devastate an otherwise promising life or career. That part of his life seemed so long ago as he also drifted off to sleep.

~

MacRae and Marion stepped out of the cosy cocoon of the cafe into the chill of the westerly wind, the warmth of the thick dark coffee quickly fading. A shiver went through his spine as he leaned against the forces of nature trying to throw him from his feet. He often wondered how people could live in these isolated places, what drew them to try and forge a life in extreme climates where just surviving the elements at times was a feat in itself. Although it was cold this early in Muynak, by midday they'd probably be baking in the forty or fifty degree heat of the desert sun.

He checked the time...their guide should be here any minute... and glanced behind him. Marion was leaning against the elements at an angle to match his. She rubbed the tiredness from her eyes. Thankfully, when they woke at first light in the car they hadn't had to wait long for a cafe to open and offer them some much appreciated coffee and breakfast.

'Nice day for a walk eh?' MacRae said.

Marion raised her voice to be heard above the wind gusts. 'And let's throw in a lethal dose of bio-weapons, just to keep it interesting shall we?'

MacRae grinned. 'Stick with me and you'll always have an interesting life.'

A black SUV with dark tinted windows drove slowly past as they neared what MacRae assumed was the local City Hall. The driver craned their neck to check them out, then pulled to the kerb and stopped, engine still running.

'I think that's our ride,' MacRae said.

The window slid down silently as they approached and MacRae recognised Sar Fendi from the stage last night, and her pictures on the internet. She looked them up and down with slightly bloodshot eyes and nodded.

'Are you MacRae?'

'Yes, Ian MacRae. And you?'

'Sar.' She tilted her head at Marion and continued in a thick eastern accent.

'And her?'

'My friend Marion.'

Sar thought for a moment. 'My price was just for you going to the Kantubek.'

'So, how much extra for my friend?' MacRae said.

Sar shrugged. 'Get in, we'll sort it out on the way.'

MacRae got a feel for Muynak as they drove the streets in the early light. Most of it spoke of a small, isolated town, a community, that had pretty much died long ago...old, unloved buildings reflecting the jobs and money long gone. But then there were signs of renewal with development money finally flowing back in, bringing with it new facilities and infrastructure, giving a glimpse of hope and confidence.

The scenery got eerier as they left the town behind. A vast flat expanse of rocks, sand and not much else surrounded them as the kilometres sped by, the SUV powering along the gravel road. Marion dozed in the back seat briefly, then woke with a start as MacRae tapped her leg.

'Check that out. Not what you'd expect to see is it?'

Marion craned her neck, not sure if she was seeing it correctly.

'Ships? What the hell...?'

Sar glanced back at her with mild amusement, then spoke.

'This is...was...the Aral sea until the Soviets fucked it up. It's now the Aralkum Desert.'

'They really did turn a sea into a desert,' Marion said.

'Yes,' Sar said. 'Draining a sea full of life to feed a cotton industry that never should have existed.'

'People still had the attitude that the world's resources were limitless back then.' MacRae joined in.

Sar grunted. 'They were wrong.'

She waved a hand expansively towards the rusty steel hulks. 'The Aral Sea used to have a thriving fishing industry, supported thousands of people...and their families. Muynak was a port. No one believed you could drain the sea.'

'So all the ships were just left to rust,' Marion said.

'That's it, there was nowhere for them to go. One of the worst ecological disasters in history,' Sar said. 'But at least we can drive to Kantubek and check out Aralsk-7 now that it's not an island anymore. Although that mightn't be forever.'

'The government's trying to fill the Aral Sea back up again isn't it?' MacRae said.

Sar nodded. 'The Kazakhstan government up north has built dams and they're slowly filling up the northern sea. I think it's back to about a fifth of its original size.'

'That doesn't sound like much,' Marion said.

'Better than its been for a long time. Maybe we'll be able get some of the old ways of living back,' Sar said. 'So how do you guys make a living?'

MacRae answered first. 'I'm a business consultant. I travel around a lot, get to go to some pretty interesting places, like here.'

'And you?' Sar glanced at Marion.

'I'm a doctor.'

'So why come here?'

She shrugged. 'Where better to contemplate deadly infectious diseases than the site of a secret bio-weapon testing station?'

Sar wrinkled her brow, not sure what to make of them.

Marion beamed a smile at her, then settled back in her seat and before long was dozing again while MacRae and Sar negotiated the additional fees.

They lapsed into silence for a while, then MacRae spoke.

'Do you do this a lot?'

'Take people to the island?' Sar shrugged, shooting him a glance. 'Not so much nowadays, I don't spend a lot of time here anymore, travelling for work. Back when I started I was the only one who'd do it. It had a reputation. People knew bad stuff had happened there, that biological weapons had been developed and tested. Plenty thought it was cursed. Fishermen getting sick and dying, mass antelope deaths on the plains. There were plenty of stories.'

'You didn't believe it though.'

'Idiots.' Sar snorted. 'They don't know the difference between superstition and plain bad people. The Soviets cleaned it up when they left, so it was safe enough for me.'

'You knew what they'd been doing there and it didn't scare you away?' MacRae said.

'I just had to be careful, keep my eyes open,' Sar said. 'Take a shower when I got home.'

MacRae shook his head. 'But you know that the Soviets had run out of money by the time they left, and their cleanup was half-hearted at best?'

Sar shrugged. 'We're all going to die sometime. Might as well have an interesting life while we're here.'

MacRae raised an eyebrow and focused on the view.

'So why did you contact me to take you to Aralsk-7?' Sar said. 'There are other commercial tour operators who would have taken you nowadays, given you the whole local cultural experience, a night in a yurt, traditional dancing. Although you don't seem like the average thrill seeker doing the latest dark tourism experience.'

MacRae smiled. 'We like to do things our way, and we came across your name when we did our research. Figured we'd get a more authentic experience.'

The breeze from the parched sea bed whipped up clouds of dust, sending them spinning in their path, gritty sand scraping across the polished car. MacRae relaxed, letting his mind wander, wondering what they might still find in the abandoned weapons research station after so long.

Movement in the side mirror caught his eye. A dust cloud was being stirred up hundreds of metres behind them. But this was different. It was moving along at the same pace as they were, so unlikely to be the wind. Instinct kicked in and suddenly he was fully alert again, watching as the dust cloud kept its distance but stayed behind them on their journey.

The trip passed quickly and by mid-morning Sar slowed the SUV as they arrived at Kantubek, stopping at the edge of the derelict town.

'This is it. Do you want the guided tour? It'll cost extra.'

MacRae shook his head as he stepped from the car. 'No, we're fine to look around by ourselves.'

He walked around the SUV to join Marion. 'Give us a couple of hours okay?'

'Sure,' Sar said. She reached under her seat and pulled out a fresh bottle of water. 'Want this? It's going to get pretty hot soon.'

Marion took it, placing it in her backpack. 'Thanks.'

Sar leaned her seat back and put on a set of white wireless headphones, searching her phone for something to listen to.

'Good luck, have fun. I hope you find what you're looking for.'

~

MacRae and Marion wandered slowly down what was once the main street of the thriving town. Buildings in varying states of disrepair lined the streets, broken windows and peeling paint blending with faded Soviet-era signs. Rusted truck bodies, long stripped of anything of value, sat forlornly amongst piles of sand swept in by the desert winds. MacRae couldn't see it, but he'd read that there was even the hulk of a Soviet T-55 tank somewhere, once used to test the protection of armour against biological weapons.

He wiped a bead of sweat from his brow with his sleeve. The wind had dropped and the heat of the day was starting to drain their energy already.

Marion held out the plastic bottle. 'Water?'

He took a deep draught, savouring the refreshing coolness of the liquid.

'It's eerie isn't?' Marion said.

'Yes,' MacRae said. A shiver went down his spine as his mind flashed back to his visit to Chernobyl years earlier, a similar Soviet era town, abandoned almost overnight. And he couldn't shake the feeling that, like Chernobyl, Aralsk-7 was the key to something much bigger, more deadly, if that was even possible for the site of hideous chemical and biological warfare experiments.

'Let's start over here shall we?' Marion's voice broke through his thoughts. 'It looks like a laboratory building.'

MacRae followed her outstretched arm to the row of decaying buildings to their left. They had a bit of ground to cover if they were to explore most of the site, once a thriving town for fifteen hundred scientists, soldiers and their families.

It was hard to picture it as a bustling town with cafes, shops, sports facilities and a school. Now it was just full of the ghosts of the men and women who devoted their careers and lives to a failed political system, by developing weapons to kill countless millions of their faceless enemies. Not just combatants though. It was just as much about destroying the enemy's society in such a horrific way that they'd lose their will to fight. And yet rather than war ending the Soviet empire, it had come down mainly to money. The capitalist west had simply drawn the communists into an endless spending war, an arms race that had driven them broke.

MacRae looked around. There was so much to explore and he had to make sure their time was well spent. While it would be fascinating to explore the full site, to see the proving grounds outside the town where animals where once tethered in the path of airborne pathogens and the dump where the genetically modified anthrax from Compound-19 had once been buried, they had to be selective, learn what they could from the town, and from Sar, their guide.

MacRae smiled at Marion. 'Sure, let's start over there. I don't know how much we'll find after years of it being picked over by local scavengers, or the adventure tourism crowd.'

'They've got no idea of the risk they're still taking just by coming here,' Marion said as she passed a rusted out truck. 'The Russians left in a hurry, only taking what they thought was worth something.'

'But didn't the Americans come and have another go at cleaning up the place a few years ago?' MacRae said.

'I think that was some kind of private US trust just trying to kill the buried anthrax,' Marion said. 'People don't realise some of this stuff never goes away, stays dormant in environments like soil for a helluva long time, just waiting for someone to dig it up to take some selfies.'

An involuntary shiver went through MacRae as he looked around. 'I'd rather have talked about Crane with our guide in the comfort of a bar than here to be honest.'

'So why didn't we?' Marion said.

MacRae led the way into a decaying brick building, every window smashed long ago. The smell of mould and something a lot worse hung in the heavy humid air.

'She wouldn't say who else she's taken here when I contacted her initially, and I didn't want to spook her like Elias did. She said she'd only talk about the place when we experienced it. I guess she wanted the cash to take us here.'

Marion kicked a pile of rubble, the glint of broken glass catching her eye. 'So why do you think Crane would actually come here? I mean he's a business man. Surely most of his decisions are just about money?'

'You're right,' MacRae said. It didn't make sense, unless they were approaching it wrong. 'I've been seeing him as a scientist first, but maybe it's not just about the science, maybe for Crane, just like the Soviets, it's about economics.'

'You've lost me,' Marion said.

MacRae spoke slowly, thinking it through. 'Part of what drove the race to develop these weapons in places like this...as much as anything it came down to cost-efficiency.'

Marion frowned.

'Like it or not the world runs on economics,' MacRae said. 'We can all kid ourselves about our benevolent governments, but they all do the same numbers in their budgets, how much is a human life worth? And that shapes the health budget of each country. Every life has a price.'

'I'm with you so far,' Marion said.

'Well it's the same for the military budgets. In the world of economics it's called the Killing Effect.'

'The Killing Effect?' Marion said.

'That's the effect of killing about half the population in a one kilometre square area,' MacRae said grimly, stepping around a rusted steel chair. 'So in a cost comparison it works something like this:

The Killing Effect might be around two thousand dollars using conventional weapons, compared to eight hundred dollars with a nuclear weapon, six hundred dollars using a chemical weapon, and a bargain priced rate of one dollar to achieve the same Killing Effect with a biological weapon.'

'One dollar?' Marion gasped. 'That's it? My God, what are we humans doing to each other?'

MacRae shrugged, then bent to look at a piece of twisted metal at his feet for a moment before moving on.

'That's the economics of it, and why governments have been so interested in developing these weapons.'

'And you think the economics might interest Crane?'

'Sure he's a scientist...but as you said he's also a businessman and that's all about cost efficiency, probably giving the best dollar value to his military clients. Especially if he can come somewhere like this and get the benefit of someone else's research and development dollars for free.'

A flash of movement across the main road caught MacRae's attention through one of the broken windows. Wildlife? He couldn't see anything. Something didn't feel right. He touched Marion's arm. 'Are you okay to keep going through these buildings while I check out some on the other side of the street?'

Marion squatted down and pulled on a pair of thin latex gloves to examine a pile of broken glass vials in the corner of the room. 'Sure. Meet you at the end of this block in half an hour?'

MacRae nodded and retraced his steps to the entrance of the building, before crouching low to run across the empty street and down an alleyway.

He peered around the end of the building and listened. There was nothing but the sound of the wind whipping up mini sand tornadoes. He climbed into a building through a broken window and took a rotting timber staircase to the second floor, then walked silently along a corridor, taking care to avoid stepping on anything that would make a noise, and found a room facing the street. He crossed the room to a window that gave an uninterrupted view and knelt beside it, waiting, occasionally swatting away a persistent fly, then was rewarded as he spotted movement maybe fifty metres from the building Marion was examining. Two men were hugging the wall as they circled around to where MacRae and Marion had been. His heart sank and the brief hope that they were tourists faded as he spotted objects held out in front of them. It looked like they were armed.

He waited a few seconds longer, making sure there weren't others he hadn't seen, then sprinted across the room, down the stairs and out a rear door to the street, keeping close to the wall as he covered the distance to where he'd last seen the men. He stopped at the corner of the building and checked the street. They were gone, presumably inside the building.

MacRae kept low as he ran to the closest door. He paused before entering, and heard the crunch of boots on glass from inside. He peered in and seeing no-one walked quickly across the room, following the clumsy footsteps ahead, gingerly stepping between piles of broken glass. He stopped at the next door, well inside the building. They must be getting close to where he'd left Marion. He could still hear footsteps, but no voices. It must be only one person.

He poked his head through the door and saw the hulking figure of a man dressed in a black jacket and jeans a couple of metres away at the other side of a corridor. The man was motionless, peering through a doorway, arm extended in front of him.

It was a risk not knowing where the other guy was, but now was his chance. MacRae took two steps and tapped the man on the shoulder.

'Hi, looking for someone?'

The man spun around, recognition flashing in his eyes. He snarled and swung a bright red tube at MacRae. MacRae leaned back, blocking the man's arm away, the red tube flying from his grasp and skidding across the floor.

The man rushed across the corridor, ploughing his shoulder into MacRae, sending them both sprawling onto the floor. MacRae was up first, scanning for the weapon, but another second and the man was also on his feet. MacRae closed the gap between them and threw a boxing combination into his face.

The man staggered back, covering his face with one arm then charged at MacRae, using his body weight to pin him to the wall. MacRae pushed back, but the man was too big, raising an enormous fist and driving it at MacRae's face. MacRae jerked his head sideways, the fist striking the wall beside him. MacRae drove his knee into the man's groin, following up with a headbutt to his nose. The man yelped and stepped back. MacRae pushed away from the wall, but the man came back at him, throwing a front kick into his stomach. MacRae jerked back, feet slipping on rubble and fell over backwards, the air knocked from his lungs. The big man grinned, shaking off the pain and flung himself down on MacRae. MacRae pulled his knees to his stomach as the man landed, and grabbing the man's shoulders, pushing up hard with both legs, sending the man sailing over his head, striking the wall behind MacRae with a dull *thud.*

MacRae took a couple of desperate breaths, forcing air back into his lungs before turning to his foe. The man was motionless, a crumpled heap on the floor. MacRae approached him cautiously, rolling him onto his back, checking his vital signs. He was breathing, and the worst injury appeared to be a long cut on his forehead oozing a thick bead of blood. Nothing too serious. MacRae checked his pockets. The first items he found were to be expected...a wallet and phone. The next item, a packet of thick black cable ties, was more concerning. What the hell were they up to?

MacRae went back along the corridor and knelt, retrieving the item he'd knocked from the man's hand. It was a half metre long tube of red plastic, a shaped handle on one end with a press button, two short metal prongs on the other. He held the tube at arm's length and was about to press the button when his body exploded in pain, sending his muscles into spasm and throwing him across the corridor.

He shook his head, clearing his vision to see the other man, just as big as the first, leaning over him holding an identical red tube, a huge grin creasing his face as he moved in to hit him with the electric cattle prod again.

MacRae's pain was fading, *thank God these things weren't lethal.* MacRae looked around. The one he'd been holding was too far to reach. Then his body exploded in pain a second time as he was hit on the arm, the crackle of a hundred thousand volts jumping between the electrodes ringing in his ears.

MacRae felt his muscles spasm again as he scrabbled his way across the floor to escape his tormentor. The first feelings of panic were started to rise but MacRae pushed them back down. A face came into his mind, a distant memory. The scarred face with a cropped orange beard and cold grey eyes was that of an unarmed combat trainer from long ago teaching him the brutal lessons of knife defence. The English ex-SAS trainer had toyed with him just like this with an electric cattle prod, explaining that if you ever faced an attacker skilled with a knife you would inevitably be cut, and if you had no choice but to face them you must embrace the pain and put them out of action in the few seconds before your body went into shock and they finished you.

MacRae stopped moving, waiting for the next attack, this time focusing one thing...when it hit, detach from the pain and disable the attacker.

The electric shock coursed through his body again but this time, to the man's disbelief, MacRae moved in on him, gripping the hand with the cattle prod and twisting it backwards. The man dropped the weapon, and swung an elbow back at MacRae's face. MacRae raised his arm but was too late, the elbow striking his jaw and spinning him around, then the man was on him again, wrapping MacRae in a bear hug and squeezing hard. MacRae tensed his body, fighting the grip but he was too strong, MacRae's vision starting to fade. Then muscle memory from years of combat training kicked in. MacRae twisted his body to the side and raked his heel down the man's shin and foot, simultaneously driving his fist backwards into the man's groin. The man grunted, and his grip loosened slightly. MacRae relaxed his legs and dropped down whilst jerking both elbows up, breaking out of the bear hug, and twisting sideways drove an elbow into the man's solar-plexus, followed up with three knuckles into his throat. The man gasped for breath and collapsed to his knees.

'I can't breathe. I'm going to die.'

MacRae stood next to him watching impassively. 'It might feel like it, but not today, you're not.'

~

MacRae was just finishing restraining both men with their own plastic cable ties when Marion entered the room.

'What the hell? I heard noises up the corridor...who are these guys?'

The first attacker was slowly regaining consciousness. MacRae and Marion watched as his expression went from confusion to a mix of fear and anger as he looked at them and his friend, and tested his restraints.

'Let me go or...'

MacRae stepped forward with a cattle prod, waving it gently sideways as the lightening arced across the electrodes.

'I don't think you're in the position to be threatening me.'

The man scowled.

MacRae flicked through their wallets, reading their IDs, stopping when he came to their names on business cards for an entertainment industry security company. He'd had the feeling that one of them was familiar. He'd seen him the night before on the stage handing water and drugs to their tour guide Sar Fendi.

He tossed the wallets on the ground, and looked between the men.

'Why are two security guards tracking us out here? Why the cattle prods and cable ties? And what's this got to do with our guide? I don't think this is a coincidence is it?'

The men were silent.

MacRae took a step forward, the cattle prod sparking angrily.

'You obviously don't know me, because if you did you'd know I've spent a lot of time in war zones interrogating terrorists. The scientific data from studies of interrogation techniques used by the CIA after 911 suggests that torture doesn't work. That it's far better to build trust...'

The men looked relieved.

'...but personally I'm not convinced, and quite enjoy the old ways. So let's get started, and just to be fair I'm going to shock you both each time until I get the answers.'

He stepped forward, arcing up the cattle prod. Both men scrabbled backwards, then the first screamed at MacRae.

'Stop. I'll talk.'

MacRae paused, cattle prod still arcing. 'Are you sure?' He looked a little disappointed. 'If you're fooling with me I won't stop next time.'

The man nodded. 'She paid us to come after you.'

'Who paid you?' MacRae said.

The man hesitated. MacRae arced the prod again.

'Sar did. She said you were a couple of dumb, rich old tourists, and wouldn't be any trouble.'

'So what were you meant to do with us?'

'She said you'd shit yourself with the sight of the cattle prod, and if you didn't, a couple of shocks would do the job. Then we'd tie you up with the cable ties and get your bank account details and passwords from you.'

'Then what? There's no phone coverage here.'

'She's got a satellite phone in the car so she'd make a call, and someone would clean out your bank accounts.'

'And then?' Marion said.

The man shrugged. 'We'd take off and she'd pretend to come looking for you in a couple of hours, maybe take you to the police to make a statement I guess. She said you'd never suspect her, probably be just glad to get away from here.'

MacRae took Marion's arm, leading her out of earshot of the men. 'I'm going to bring her here for a little chat.' He handed her the spare cattle prod. 'Are you okay to look after these two?'

Marion tested the button, satisfied to see the bright arc.

'Just let them try something on me.'

MacRae approached the SUV from the rear blind spot, and as he got closer he could see Sar with the seat laid back, feet up on the dash, listening to her headphones with her eyes shut. He tried her door, it was locked. She heard or sensed him and sat bolt upright, obviously surprised to see him. He tapped on the window with the cattle prod. Her eyes widened and she fumbled with the keys, trying to start the car.

MacRae sighed, and lifted up the rock he'd held behind his back. She blinked and tried to start the car again, forgetting the correct sequence. A short swing of the rock and the window shattered, the tiny pieces of safety glass showering the floor at her feet. MacRae reached in and jerked the keys from the ignition, then opened the door from the inside and pulled Sar from the vehicle.

He didn't talk as he led her kicking and screaming back to Marion and the two men. She went quiet as she saw them.

MacRae pulled over one of the rusted steel seats and pushed Sar down onto it next to the men.

'Let's not waste any time here shall we? I know who these guys are and why they're here. They've been very cooperative.'

Sar glared at him. 'So what the fuck are you going to do about it then? You know that us even being here is illegal, so who are you going to tell?'

MacRae smiled. 'Just like them, you've totally misjudged me and why I'm here. I'm here about Magnus Crane. Nothing else.'

Sar frowned. 'Who? I don't know what you're talking about.'

MacRae shook his head. 'Why do you have to make this hard?'

He fired up the cattle prod, bringing the electrodes within millimetres of her thigh. 'I could have just asked you a few questions and you answer them. I offered you good money to bring us here, just like you brought Crane. Did you decide to rob him too?'

Sar blinked. MacRae saw her reaction and smiled.

'You do remember him don't you?'

Sar sneered and slapped his face. 'Fuck you.'

MacRae grabbed her wrist as she attempted to do it again. That was when he noticed the tiny scars on the inside of her elbow. Old needle marks from years of drug abuse?

'Is this why the money wasn't enough?' He pointed to them. 'You have some very expensive habits to keep up with your career choice.'

Sar looked away defiantly. 'Think and do what you want. I'm not telling you anything.' Her eyes lit up. 'Unless you pay me more.'

Marion looked at MacRae in disbelief, then spoke to Sar.

'Maybe he doesn't frighten you, but you know I'm a doctor don't you?'

Sar nodded.

'My speciality is bio-weapons.' She reached into her bag and pulled something out and concealing it in her palm stepped around behind Sar, used one hand to press her down in the chair, and before she could react, drove the tip of a needle into the side of her neck.

'Hey.' Sar yelped.

'Don't move a muscle,' Marion said. 'I've just broken your skin with a needle filled with a sample of military grade anthrax from a broken vial in the other room.'

Sar froze, eyes wide.

'...and if I push the plunger you will get a lethal dose that will take days to kill and can't be treated.' Marion leaned in front of Sar, meeting her eyes. 'Do you understand what I just said?'

Sar looked desperately at the two men bound on the floor next to her. They looked away helplessly.

Marion continued. 'So just answer Ian's questions and we'll all just get on with our lives okay?'

Sar nodded. 'Okay.'

Marion smiled at MacRae. 'Now let's talk about Crane.'

MacRae took out his phone and thrust a picture of Crane in Sar's face.

'He paid you to bring him here a while back?'

She squinted, taking in Crane's features, then nodded.

'And this was before most people knew about it, and you were one of the few people who would bring people here?'

'Yes.'

'So how did it happen?'

Sar sighed. 'He came here for work, something about a charity project to fix the Aral Sea. He must have asked around for how to get here and someone passed on my name.'

'And then?' MacRae said.

'I figured he was just another thrill seeker, taking the chance to see something weird and creepy while he was here. It was easy money for me. I was coming here for fun anyway, now I was going to get paid for it.'

'So you brought him here in the SUV?' said MacRae.

Sar went to shake her head, then feeling the pressure of the needle in her neck, thought better of it.

'The first time he wanted to come on the motorbike with me, but that would have been too hard, so yeah we took the SUV.'

'The first time?' MacRae said.

'Sure,' Sar said. 'I took him three, maybe four times, I can't remember. He paid really well.'

'Interesting,' Marion said, swapping hands holding the needle.

'And what did he do when he came here?' MacRae said.

Sar shrugged. 'Different things each time. The first time he just looked around, took a few hours to go over the whole site. I gave him a bit of a tour, then he wandered around by himself.'

'After that?' MacRae said.

'The other times he didn't really want me around so much. I'd wait in the SUV while he went around with a big bag.'

'What kind of bag?' Marion said.

'Like a big black briefcase. But this wasn't for business. I sneaked a look in it one time. It was full of glass bottles and stuff, you know, the stuff you'd see in a laboratory.'

Sar looked from MacRae to Marion. 'Why do you want to know all this stuff about him anyway?'

MacRae answered. 'That's our business. So what did he do with the briefcase?'

'He was like you,' Sar said. 'Just poked around in the buildings and the dirt, filling bottles up with stuff and labelling them.'

She grinned. 'I have to admit it made me a bit nervous the way he did everything wearing white coveralls and with gloves and a mask.'

MacRae looked at Marion. 'He definitely was collecting samples of pathogens.'

'Looks like it.' Marion said.

MacRae turned back to Sar. 'Did he do anything else unusual while he was here.'

Sar raised an eyebrow. 'You mean other than wearing creepy lab clothes and digging up dirt from a secret Russian army base?'

'You know what I mean.'

'Well, I thought he might like a selfie with me here as a souvenir, but when I stood next to him and held the camera up he got really angry. He grabbed the camera and I thought he was going to hit me. It scared the shit out of me. I kept out of his way after that.'

'Have you heard from him since that visit?' MacRae said.

'No,' Sar glared at him. 'He'd paid me really well, and the deal was that I didn't talk about our trip. Ever. And I haven't until now.'

MacRae looked at Marion. 'Anything we haven't covered?'

She shook her head.

'I guess we're finished then,' MacRae said.

'Hold still, this won't hurt...much.' Marion said, as she gently pulled the sharp tip from Sar's neck, then walked around to MacRae and wiped a drop of blood from a shiny silver folding hair pin with a tissue.

Sar's eyes widened. 'You said you had a syringe full of anthrax...'

Marion smiled. 'That would have been far too dangerous for all of us, and very irresponsible of me.'

MacRae gunned Sar's SUV, the eight cylinder turbo diesel roaring as they left the desolate town and Sar along with her two friends in the dust behind them.

Marion cast a worried look over her shoulder. 'Are you sure they'll be alright?'

MacRae squinted in the afternoon sun, pulling the sun visor down. 'They'll soon wriggle out of the cable ties now we're gone, and there's a commercial tour due later today. I'd love to hear their explanation for how they got stuck there. And I'll call the number Sar gave us for her cousin when we're clear of Muynak just to make sure.'

'They won't come after us?' Marion said.

MacRae tapped his phone. 'She knows I recorded the whole conversation with her and the security guys.'

He touched her knee. 'Don't worry, we'll be on a plane out of Uzbekistan in a few hours, unfortunately with even more disturbing information on Crane.'

Marion sighed and settled back into her seat with her eyes shut, hoping to catch up with some sleep after a very long day.

'And where's next on this little vacation?'

'For me, somewhere that you definitely can't go...you don't have the skill set I'll need,' MacRae said. 'As for you, well that's up to you.'

CHAPTER 28

THE BADIA

Thierry LaBruge slapped MacRae's shoulder. 'Ah, the Lone Ranger and Tinto are back together again eh?'

'I think you mean Tonto.' MacRae corrected him as he swung the wheel of the battered Hilux sharply to avoid the enormous pothole... or more likely a crater from some kind of military ordinance.

LaBruge thought about it and broke into a deep laugh. 'Yes, I expect I do.'

MacRae was glad to have LaBruge riding shotgun for him on this trip. Aralsk-7 had been a mixture of unsettling and enlightening, but now MacRae and Marion agreed that Elias was telling the truth about Crane, at least the truth as he knew it, and some of his conspiracy theories were right. The question had then been what to do next?

They still had nowhere to go on the search for Hassana, so Marion had decided to head across to Europe to follow up a couple of potential aid contracts, while MacRae went to put Elias's story to the test while he was in this part of the world.

He'd called LaBruge from the airport before they left Uzbekistan to ask if he was available for a short job. Travelling in this part of the world wasn't something MacRae wanted to do alone, and he wanted someone he could trust in such a dangerous place.

He glanced across at LaBruge. He'd known it was a long shot. They hadn't been in contact since Hassana and her sister had been taken and Holgate murdered, and MacRae had heard on the grapevine that LaBruge had left the contract security world for a quieter life. But when MacRae explained that he hadn't been able to let go of the search for Hassana, and outlined the chain of events leading to Magnus Crane, LaBruge had jumped at the chance to get involved again, even at such short notice. So MacRae and Marion had travelled north around the Caspian Sea together, before heading south to meet up with LaBruge in Turkey.

MacRae smiled as he recalled LaBruge's reaction to meeting Marion. He'd shot discreet glances between then, watching their faces as they spoke, and joked about their friendship. He was far more intuitive than people gave him credit for, and MacRae could see he'd picked up on their chemistry as they shared lunch before seeing Marion off on her flight to Paris.

After Marion had gone, MacRae had explained to him the nature of the job, and the joviality had been replaced with concern. After all, their destination was Syria, and the desert, or Badia, was currently one of the most dangerous places on earth. In a country wracked by a vicious civil war, with the interference of neighbouring countries and a couple of world superpowers, MacRae knew LaBruge would be invaluable.

And he'd been right. It had only taken LaBruge a few hours to find out where the best contracts for mercenaries in Syria were, and therefore what were the places to avoid as they travelled to the village Elias had spoken of...the long deserted place on the edge of the Syrian desert he'd claimed to have witnessed the murder of his father so long ago. LaBruge had also used his contacts to get them discreetly into the country and procure the resources they'd need for the trip.

MacRae yawned. It had been a long drive since they'd met LaBruge's contacts and picked up what they needed. They'd passed numerous tiny villages on their journey, many of them devastated by the lengthy civil war, and no-one had taken much notice of them. The choice of the battered old vehicle had been a wise one, blending in to the war-torn landscape, the rusty bolt holes in the rear tray a tell-tale sign of it once being an improvised platform for some kind of heavy weapon. And the pair of beaten and worn AK-47s that had come as part of the deal with the truck would be of little comfort if they encountered one of the many combatant forces in the region.

MacRae carefully watched a youth tending a couple of skinny goats at the side of the road as they drove past. Out here even the most innocent scene could be disguising an ambush or roadside bomb.

LaBruge saw him focusing on the youth and spoke. 'Good to see you haven't lost the survival skills.'

MacRae shrugged. 'Yeah, it's a shame that I still need them.'

He shot a glance at LaBruge. 'I'm still surprised you took this job. I'd heard you'd had enough of this life, you were semi-retired?'

LaBruge brushed a fly from his face, knowing it was futile and would be replaced in a moment or two. 'I thought I had too. But then after doing the alternative for a while...'

'What was the alternative?'

'Close personal protection.'

MacRae grunted, reaching for a water bottle.

LaBruge winced. 'Not as glamorous as it sounds, believe me.'

'I thought it was a bit of a gravy train?' MacRae said, between swigs of water.

'Maybe. I was under the impression when I signed up that I'd be providing protection for high net worth individuals under threat of kidnap or whatever, business people presumably. But the jobs turned out to be babysitting their rich brats when they were out partying in nightclubs in Goa and Ibiza, trying to keep them from being arrested doing drugs or getting in fights.'

'Ah,' MacRae said.

LaBruge shrugged. 'Then you mix in money and sex and it's always going to end in trouble.'

'Not quite the fulfilment you were seeking.'

'Yeah, that's why I jumped at the chance to make it right with you and Hassana.'

MacRae smiled, focusing back on the road. 'Well I'm just glad you could come.'

The sun was sinking lower in the sky, and it had been many hours since they'd seen any signs of civilisation when LaBruge consulted the map one last time. He held it up to MacRae as he drove, then pointed over to the ridge of a hill on the horizon.

'I think that's it, that's the place he described.'

MacRae shot a glance at the map, noting the narrow track they should take to the right any time now. Then there it was.

He slowed the truck to a walk, steering carefully over a dry riverbed next to the shattered bridge that used to cross the watercourse. This time there was no doubt; the chunks of concrete, rusty steel reinforcing protruding in every direction the obvious result of a powerful blast. MacRae didn't want to be around anything like that while he was here if he could help it.

He poked at the air-conditioning button, the green light shining, but not delivering any cold air, and opened the window again. The blast of hot air pulled his face scarf down, exposing the dirt and grime of time spent travelling through this harsh sand and stone wasteland.

He accelerated up to a running pace, the truck bouncing around on the rough track. It showed all the signs of being unused for a very long time, LaBruge gripping the door handle as the vehicle lurched over huge rocks.

LaBruge broke the silence. 'So you and Marion have a history?'

MacRae swung the wheel hard, throwing LaBruge against the door. 'I guess you could say that.'

'Is that all I'm going to get?' teased LaBruge.

MacRae glanced at the other man.

'Okay, years ago we were close, but it didn't work out. And it was a long time ago.'

He slowed the truck to negotiate a section of road long washed away by a now empty watercourse.

LaBruge pressed again. 'Why not? There's sparks in the air when you two talk.'

MacRae smiled. 'Is it that obvious?'

LaBruge nodded.

'We worked together in trouble spots. Marion was an aid worker, I provided security. And as you said, sparks flew.'

The engine roared as he changed up through the gears, the tyres slipping in loose gravel as the truck climbed back onto the road.

'It got to the point where both of us were wanting to know what happened next. We had a choice to follow the other, or our own career.'

LaBruge shook his head. 'You gave her an ultimatum, didn't you?'

MacRae's smile faded. 'I guess I did. She offered me everything and I let her go. She went overseas, and that was the beginning of the end. She's never forgiven me.'

LaBruge clicked his tongue. 'We all make mistakes. I had a woman like that once...'

Then he slapped MacRae on the shoulder again. 'But we get wiser as we get older don't we? We learn what's important, and don't make the same mistakes twice do we?'

They lapsed back into silence, each lost in their thoughts.

Another hour passed, the main road disappearing into the distance behind them as they broached the ridge and headed down a steep and winding track, barely wide enough for walking, let alone driving.

MacRae's heart leapt when a half dozen fighter jets screamed low overhead. They were too quick for him or LaBruge to identify, but in this melting pot of warring nations it didn't really matter who they were...Syrian, Russian, American or Turkish...they were all a potential threat to a lone vehicle in the middle of nowhere. Then they arrived.

MacRae felt the excitement as he saw the towering sand dunes off to one side, and when they rounded the base of the dunes there it was...the ruins of a village abandoned in haste a lifetime ago, just as Elias had described it.

MacRae killed the motor at the edge of the ruins, he and LaBruge cautiously exiting the truck, AK-47s held loosely to their sides. Neither of the men spoke as they walked, each taking one side of the village. Charred remains of mud and timber huts stood caught in time by the dry desert air, the stone walls of the larger buildings showing signs of the harsh desert winds slowly wearing them down.

LaBruge spoke first. 'Is this what you were expecting to find?'

'It's as Elias described it,' MacRae said.

'Okay,' LaBruge said. 'And what are you hoping it will prove? You were pretty vague back in Turkey.'

'There was a reason for that,' MacRae said. 'The guy...Elias...I've been talking to about Magnus Crane seems solid, there's certainly truth in some of what he's told me about Crane and his past. But other stuff he says seems like conspiracy rubbish.'

LaBruge stopped walking, turning to look at MacRae. 'So why have you gone to these lengths then to see if he's legit?'

'I've just got a hunch we're on the right track. And let's face it, at the moment it's all we've got in the search for Hassana. Either Crane is a wealthy, successful businessman and philanthropist, as his public persona says and it's just a string of coincidences that have taken me to him, or he's got a far darker agenda. That's why we went to Aralsk-7.'

LaBruge let out a low whistle. 'So Crane was definitely poking around the old bio-warfare site?'

'Seems like it, the guide said it was him.' MacRae grinned. 'Although to be fair you could say she was under duress.'

LaBruge raised an eyebrow. 'And that brings us here?"

'Elias's story about seeing Crane here in the eighties just seems to ring true,' MacRae said. 'And if it is, if Crane was here as part of a team conducting a medical trial that went wrong and they tried to cover it up by killing the victims and burning the bodies...'

'...it shows he's capable of doing just about anything.' LaBruge finished the sentence.

'Yes,' MacRae said. 'So were looking for anything that might corroborate his story.'

LaBruge resumed walking. 'Let's see what we can find then.'

MacRae peered through the arched stone doorway of a building, timber roof long collapsed, burnt beams crisscrossing the floor.

'I'm not sure what it tells us though, apart from it being abandoned or destroyed a long time ago.'

'Yes,' LaBruge said, joining MacRae in the doorway. 'Is there any way this can verify what he told you?'

MacRae shut his eyes, recalling the conversation with Elias.

'I'm not sure. Ideally we'd access the records of what happened here, maybe old, archived newspapers in the nearest major population centre. But I doubt there's anything like that left in a war zone, and it'd be way too dangerous to try and track it down.'

A rumble in the distance caught MacRae's attention. He closed his eyes to listen. The sound faded then returned, louder and more constant.

'Thierry, can you hear that?'

He opened his eyes to see LaBruge running up the sand dune.

'Already on it.'

He watched as LaBruge crabbed his way along the ridge on his stomach, then LaBruge froze, before sliding backwards and running back down the slope.

'Tanks, maybe five clicks away, heading over this way.'

'Shit.' MacRae cursed. 'Do you think they know we're here? Maybe the fighter jets saw us?'

'It's unlikely,' LaBruge said. 'But I'd rather not be around when they get here.'

'I'm with you on that. It doesn't look like there's much to learn from here anyway,' MacRae said, glancing around a last time before heading back to the truck.

He slung the AK-47 onto the floor. 'I'm not sure these pieces of junk would be much help to us in a scrap. Not that the M16s that Elias said the murderers had thirty years ago would have been much better.'

LaBruge stopped next to a collapsed wall.

'He said the killers had M16s? They would have been as rare as hen's teeth around here back then. He must be mistaken, they would have had AK-47s'

'No, that was why he was adamant the killers weren't terrorists or militia. He said only westerners would have had access to M16s.'

LaBruge knelt down, peering at gouge marks in the stones of the wall. He ran his fingers over them, moving to inspect the other side of the wall.

'Well how about that.'

MacRae knelt next to him. 'How about what?'

LaBruge stood, hands on hips and shook his head. 'He might just be right.'

'What do you mean? What can you see?' MacRae said.

'Are you up for a quick lesson in ballistics of that time?'

'Sure,' MacRae said. The rumble of the tanks was getting closer. 'I just hope it's a quick lesson.'

'Okay, your friend is definitely right about one thing. Back then, Africa and the Middle East, well anywhere there was trouble really, was awash with AK-47s. They were cheap and easy to get, churned out by the Soviets to earn foreign cash and assist all the insurrections against the west and their puppets.'

'Yes, I get that,' MacRae said.

'And so the only ones that could afford or get access to the more expensive and superior M16s had to be aligned with the US or other western powers, or had access to their resources.'

'Go on,' MacRae said.

'Your source was adamant the killers here weren't local insurgents or terrorists, they were westerners. And he said they were definitely armed with M16s but that there was a cover-up, and the government investigation at the time said AK-47s were used when the villagers were massacred and their bodies burnt?'

'Yes he was sure.'

'Well,' LaBruge said, triumphantly pointing at the stones. 'He was right. The proof is right here.'

MacRae was getting impatient. 'Where? Are there bullet casings?'

'No it's a bit more subtle, and you have to know what you're looking for.'

LaBruge took MacRae's arm, pulling him down to the lower part of the wall. 'See these holes? They're bullet holes. And because of their size and shape I'm almost positive they're from an M16.'

MacRae peered closer. 'How can you tell?'

LaBruge stood back a couple of metres, waving MacRae over. When he'd joined him he swung his AK-47 to his shoulder and fired a round into an undamaged section of wall, sending chips of stone flying.

MacRae winced at the noise of the gunshot. 'Was that wise with the tanks heading this way?'

'They won't hear a thing over their engine noise.'

He walked back to the wall, pointing at the new hole. 'See the difference?'

MacRae put his hands on his hips. 'Sure, but how do you know the other was an M16?'

'The design of the two guns is quite different, and that means so is the impact on their target. That played out in conflicts like Vietnam, where the Americans had the far better designed and built M16. It should have been a real advantage as it was designed to be accurate, and put a bullet through both sides of a soldier's helmet at a range of a thousand metres. Trouble was it was more complicated and sensitive to heat, moisture, well just about everything really.'

'And...' MacRae said.

LaBruge hefted his AK-47 affectionately. 'These things though were an old design, nowhere near as accurate, and a far shorter useful range. The good thing was that they were amazingly robust and you could drag them through mud and they'd still fire, whilst the Yanks were pulling their guns apart to clean them. They also used a bigger heavier round.'

MacRae interjected. 'So what does that tell us?'

'Well the Viet Cong had to adapt their tactics. They knew at long range they were easy targets and couldn't respond effectively, so they learnt to engage the Americans close in wherever they could, to even things out. And because of the AK-47's heavier cartridge it would do this.'

He took MacRae around the other side of the wall.

'Ah, I get it now.' MacRae ran his hands over the wall. There was only one hole on the inside of the wall, and it was far bigger than the entry hole outside.

'So up close, the lighter M16 round doesn't fully penetrate the wall, whereas the AK-47 round punches straight through. Not so good if you're on the other side of the wall.'

'Yes,' LaBruge nodded as he walked along the wall, looking for exit holes. 'So I'm almost positive these were done by M16s not AK-47s, just like your friend said.'

'Which means a lot of the other stuff he said may be true after all.'

LaBruge agreed. 'Well certainly with regard to what happened here.'

The wind changed direction abruptly and carried the roar of a rapidly approaching vehicle. This time it was very close.

'What the hell...' LaBruge exclaimed, then propelled himself back up the sand dune, pausing briefly at the top before running back to MacRae.

'I didn't see it before, looks like an armoured personnel carrier. It must be escorting the tanks, and it's just on the other side of the sand dune, probably checking the path ahead.'

'Can you tell who's it is?' MacRae said.

'Not sure,' LaBruge said. 'But judging from its shape it's Russian made, so it's most likely Syrian army. Although it could be on loan to Russian mercenaries from either the Russian or Syrian army.'

'Either way, no-one we really want to meet,' MacRae said, as he climbed back in their truck, gunning the engine and driving down the centre of the village to pull in behind a large, wrecked building at the far end. LaBruge ran behind him, scuffing away the tire tracks as best he could with his boot.

MacRae killed the engine and leapt from the truck carrying his AK-47. LaBruge ducked in behind a low stone wall and waved at MacRae to do the same on the other side of the road. The two men settled into firing positions and checked the action of their weapons, just as the heavy steel armour at the front of a vehicle appeared around the sand dune and drove slowly up to the edge of the ruined village.

MacRae crouched silently, watching as the armoured vehicle slowed then stopped, a thin trail of smoke curling from the exhaust. A hatch opened in the top and a helmeted head popped up, swivelling to scan the village. MacRae felt his heart beating slowly as his senses heightened.

The man lifted himself partly out of the vehicle, then started talking into a microphone attached to the helmet. He looked down, barking some instructions, then grabbed the grips of the machine gun mounted in front of him, working the action to cock the weapon. The vehicle lurched forward with a low growl of the engine, the gunner swaying forward and back. MacRae tensed, glancing across at LaBruge.

LaBruge checked his weapon and smiled grimly back at MacRae. Looks like this was about to turn nasty.

MacRae guessed how it was going to unfold. Hopefully the vehicle would get within their range before they spotted the truck, then he knew as soon as they had both flanks covered LaBruge would take out the gunner either temporarily or more permanently. They'd then have a couple of precious seconds of confusion to get onto the vehicle and, with any luck, take control of the situation before anyone else got killed.

MacRae counted the metres between them as the vehicle approached. The gunner would see their truck any second. MacRae saw LaBruge sighting his weapon, ready to shoot when they came within range.

Then the gunner spoke into his headset microphone and the vehicle stopped. The gunner looked around, still talking into the microphone, taking orders and issuing instructions? MacRae could see LaBruge's finger still on the trigger of his weapon, waiting silently.

For thirty long seconds nothing happened, the gunner scanning the village. Then the machine gun roared into life, strafing the far end of the village, a constant stream of high velocity steel jacketed rounds ripping into the stone and timber ruins around MacRae and LaBruge as they crouched low into the ground, bullets and fragments of buildings ricocheting around them. The bark of the gun was deafening as it echoed around the confines of the village. Then as abruptly as the gunfire had started, the village fell silent.

Stone dust highlighted in the setting sun floated through the air around MacRae.

The gunner scanned the village again, swinging the machine gun in a wide arc, then spoke into his microphone again. The engine roared and the vehicle reversed into a turn, crashing into a low wall, reducing it to a pile of rubble, before changing gears and heading back out of the village.

MacRae breathed a sigh of relief, then realised he couldn't see LaBruge. Where the hell was he? He jogged across the village just in time to see LaBruge pull himself from under a web of shattered timber and stone.

'Are you okay?'

LaBruge spat dust. 'Yes, nothing a hot shower won't fix.'

He brushed dirt from his shoulder then winced. 'What the...'

MacRae turned him to the side, checking out LaBruge's shoulder, and grimaced.

'Stand still, this won't hurt a bit. Well hopefully not too much.'

'What the...arrghh.'

A sharp tug and MacRae pulled the huge timber splinter from LaBruge's shoulder, grabbing his hand and pressing it over the ripped shirt to stop the slow seep of blood.

'Let's get that dressed.'

LaBruge retrieved his gun from the ground, and they headed around the building corner to their vehicle.

'Damn,' MacRae said, walking slowly around the vehicle to inspect the new bullet holes in the bodywork.

LaBruge knelt down, checking under the chassis for puddles of fuel or coolant. 'No serious damage thankfully.'

MacRae stowed his assault rifle in the truck and pulled out a battered first aid kit, sticking a broad pad over the wound in LaBruge's shoulder.

The thunder of the approaching tanks drifted through the air to them again. They didn't have much time.

MacRae said what they were both thinking. 'Time to go?'

LaBruge jumped into the truck. 'Just what I was thinking. If we keep the ridge between us and them we should get clear.'

The wheels of the truck threw up a low plume of gravel behind them as MacRae sped back past the sand dunes and onto the rough road away from the village and the tanks. His mind was now working through what LaBruge had told him about the old bullet marks in the village, and what it meant. This was getting more complicated the more he found out. And the thought of the tanks entering the village behind them made him very keen to get out of Syria where he could plan his next move.

He reached for the sun visor, pulling it down as the sun set in front of them. LaBruge constantly turned to look out the back window, assault rifle across his lap. It was unsettling to see the mercenary looking uncomfortable.

'Any sign of them?'

'No, but the sooner it gets dark and we have a few more kilometres between us the better I'll feel.'

The first red glow of sunrise was appearing on the horizon before MacRae and LaBruge returned the rented truck and weapons to LaBruge's contact in the small town on the Syrian border. MacRae sat back on a comfortable lounge chair in the courtyard of the large house where LaBruge was negotiating the additional fees for the machine gun damage to the vehicle. He sipped hot sweet tea provided by the host, watching through the wrought iron bars on the window into the house as LaBruge and the owner waved their arms, occasionally shouting as they negotiated. Then suddenly it was all smiles and a handshake as agreement was reached.

A huge man in baggy pants and sweat shirt watched MacRae from a rusty steel chair in the corner of the courtyard, eyes narrowing as MacRae's phone pinged. Unexpected communications made people in this business nervous.

MacRae checked the message. It was only a couple of lines from Schneider, but it sent a flash of hope through him. Schneider's persistence might have paid off.

Identified a probable match between the private medical evac flight departing Germany and an international medical care flight arrival twenty four hours later at a regional airstrip in the US. Call to discuss.'

MacRae hit the international code to make the call under the watchful eye of his minder. Schneider answered immediately and got straight to business.

'Hey Ian, where are you?'

MacRae looked over at the minder, carefully choosing his words before he spoke. 'Northern Syria.'

'What the hell are you doing there? Never mind,' Schneider said. 'So I'm not one hundred percent certain, but after an *exhaustive* search,' He emphasised the word. 'I found a flight that seems to be a match carrying a single patient from a private airfield near Berlin to the US, and a private medical international arrival near San Francisco. It's the same plane, and fits the timeline. There's also a few coincidences that may not be so coincidental.'

'Go on,' MacRae said.

'Well, when we last spoke I'd found a few potential matches for flights taking Hassana out of Europe, but the patient names didn't match, and the passport photos on record were inconclusive. It's easy enough to fake a passport image I guess. Also none of the flight plans gave any indication of links to Hassana. So I dug a lot deeper. This time I ran all the passport images through some new facial recognition software, great stuff, borrowed from the Chinese by the NSA without their knowledge. It works on different identifiers than we've been looking for. They use better metrics for distance between the eyes and whatever, much harder to fake. The algorithm gave a ninety eight percent probability that one of the patients was her. So I looked into the history of the charter flight company, and it does a lot of work for medical research companies throughout Europe and Africa, all of them subsidiaries of or having direct links to Medici-Royal, Crane's corporation.'

'Okay,' MacRae said. 'So his corporation uses one charter flight company in Europe, and it may have carried a patient similar to Hassana to the US.'

'That's it. After a couple of refuelling stops on the way it landed at a regional airfield near San Francisco. And this is where it gets interesting. I checked out the flight lists for planes arriving and departing this particular airfield over the past month, and one of the most common clients using private charter flights was a secure facility, a sanatorium in the hills nearby specialising in exotic disease treatment and research. Guess who owns it?'

MacRae smiled. 'Medici-Royal?'

'You got it,' Schneider said. 'And it looks like the corporation owns a number of facilities in the area.'

'Is there any way we can verify if Hassana is at the sanatorium?'

'Not that I can see,' Schneider said. 'We can't do any kind of search unless we have pretty strong evidence of wrongdoing on their part.'

MacRae thought out loud. 'Maybe we need to use someone who doesn't have to play by the rules to see inside without being there.'

'A hacker? Someone like Ritchie would have been perfect,' Schneider said.

'Exactly,' MacRae said. 'Someone like Ritchie.'

Both men were silent.

Did Schneider know about Ritchie or was it a throwaway thought? MacRae almost asked him outright, but this wasn't the time.

'Give me the details you've got so far Brad, and I'll see what I can find out.'

MacRae was typing notes into his phone and sending a message to Sarah when he felt someone standing next to him. It was LaBruge, looking at MacRae with curiosity. He must have been listening in.

'You've got a lead on Hassana?'

'Well the best lead so far at least,' MacRae said. 'I've got some people doing some digging for me, and I think I'll head back to the US to follow it up.'

'Well we're all done here now,' LaBruge said.

'So you'll be off to your next contract?' MacRae said, still typing.

LaBruge fidgeted while he thought. 'You really think you've got something?'

'As I said, the best lead so far.'

LaBruge made up his mind, grinning at MacRae. 'Another contract babysitting rich kids? I don't think so. Besides you'll need my help.' He slapped MacRae's shoulder hard. 'I'm coming to America with you.'

~

CHAPTER 29

RETURN

Sarah wrapped both hands around her steaming cup of hot chocolate, the warmth melting through her as she sat in the study of her house staring at the soft blue glow of the computer screen. Through the window behind her the breeze swayed the trees hypnotically. It was eerily silent as she communicated with Ritchie. It was all done by text through a website she'd never previously encountered, just as he insisted, and the software ensured any text between them appeared briefly on the screen just long enough to be read before fading to nothing as she watched. He took his security very seriously it seemed, even though they were communicating under the cover of the Dark Web.

She read quickly as he typed, and took screen shots of pictures and photos as they appeared. They'd made a lot of progress in the hours since MacRae contacted her from Syria with an update on his time there and Uzbekistan, and the new lead from Schneider. True to his word, Ritchie had been there for her when she'd asked online, and he was more than delivering. He'd given her a running commentary of how he was accessing information and she marvelled at how insecure most organisation's computer systems were. Sarah watched as a flood of files was loaded onto her computer, more information about Crane and his operations for her to sift through later.

Then she sucked in her breath as she read the next message, reading it again to make sure she'd read correctly.

I think we've found her. I ran live images from every security camera in the sanatorium against the pictures of Hassana you provided using facial recognition software. 99.89% probability it's her in a secure part of the facility.

I'll download stills from the camera feeds to your computer, and summarised background info I've compiled from the facility that may be useful.

The words glowed white at Sarah as she absorbed the news before they faded into nothing. She'd better let Ian know.

~

Soft jazz music played in the background of the Luxoura Airport Hotel Lounge. MacRae and LaBruge sat on opposite sides of a large coffee table in sleek low lounge chairs. LaBruge cradled a neat whisky in his lap, eyelids slowly drooping as he struggled to focus midway through the overnight flight to San Francisco.

MacRae hated the time spent on stopovers between legs of long trips, but at least some were made bearable when you could purchase time in lounges at airport hotels like this. Fifty or so dollars got you three hours in a quiet and comfortable environment with free drinks, free food, and a toiletry kit to freshen up. It sure beat trying to doze with a thousand other people on plastic chairs in an overcrowded transit lounge.

He adjusted his laptop brightness as he swapped between email account, messaging apps, and multiple web browser windows. There was a lot going on to sort through, from Sarah back home, Schneider in the US, and the new information he'd just received from his conspiracy theory friend Elias.

It had been a delicate phone call to Elias an hour earlier. He was obviously still suspicious of MacRae's motives, but when MacRae had described his trip through Aralsk-7 then Syria and what he'd discovered about Crane, Elias had softened and sent him the confidential Medici-Royal documents he'd been receiving. MacRae had only had time to read the first few, but the reports on illegal pathogen development, and haphazard distribution systems around the world had been shocking. Then he'd noticed that all the documents had been whitewashed, stripped of anything that could be linked to the sender, meaning the information couldn't be verified and was effectively useless. MacRae had asked if he could contact the anonymous source, but Elias said all the information had been sent via a VPN and was untraceable.

MacRae arched his back, stretching out tired muscles, then leaned forward to his screen again. Despite all the uncertainties hopefully he now had enough information to formulate a plan of action for when they arrived in the US and reunited with Marion.

He was looking forward to seeing her again, but nervous about what they were planning to do. Part of him wished she'd decided to stay in Europe while he and LaBruge followed up on Hassana. But just like LaBruge, she was stubborn and insisted on being involved, and at this very moment was in a plane or airport lounge on her way to meet them.

MacRae re-read the long message from Sarah. According to her it looked like Schneider's hunch that the sanatorium was the most likely place in the area to hide someone if they were part of a research program was right. The Pine Eagle Glades Sanatorium public website had informed that most of the facility catered for day visit patients for therapeutic mental and physical programs, specialising in exotic disease research. There was also some capacity for more extended visits and treatment programs. It had also proudly proclaimed it's involvement in partnerships around the country and the globe in accordance with the philanthropic and social conscience philosophy of its parent company and the founder, Magnus Crane. MacRae smiled. Crane certainly had created a great public image for himself.

He read on, scrolling through the numerous documents on Crane and his operations around the world Sarah had compiled, comparing it to what he'd already discovered and Elias's documents, and a very disturbing picture started to form. Surely MacRae had got it wrong? He glanced up at the flight information board flashing flight arrival and departure times and gate numbers silently from the corner of the room. He didn't have time to crystallise it now, he'd have to come back to it later.

He returned to the first part of the message.

Sarah had asked Ritchie to delve deeper into the organisation and the sanatorium, and he'd apparently gained access to their entire computer network through an insecure online appointment booking system. Once in, he'd gone through the building, checking everywhere there was an active security camera. And that's when he'd found Hassana, restrained and perhaps drugged in an accommodation suite in the secure research part of the facility. MacRae tensed with anger as he looked again at the images Sarah had attached to the message. It looked like Hassana but could they be certain? Sarah said that Ritchie had run facial recognition software on the images, as had Schneider, and he was positive it was her, so that was as good as it was going to get. Now to get her out.

MacRae skipped further through Sarah's message, sifting through the information, reading out loud to LaBruge anything he thought might help them, site layout, access to the emergency management system, even internal Human Resources memos about staffing issues. LaBruge asked questions and then between them, like pieces of a jigsaw puzzle coming together, they formed a plan.

Now to get some assistance. He called Schneider, LaBruge opening one sleepy eye as he heard MacRae mention Schneider's name, outlining what they were planning. LaBruge dozed again until he heard MacRae raise his voice. A server clearing glasses at the adjoining table glanced over.

MacRae lowered his voice. 'You can't help us with anything? I appreciate there's not enough evidence for the CIA or police to be involved and you can't be implicated if it goes wrong, but can't you at least hook us up with some weapons?'

LaBruge sat up to listen.

'I respect your decision, and I get that you're probably still under some kind of surveillance after the Devil's Breath shit fight, but you understand that we have to give it a try no matter what the risk don't you?'

They talked for a minute or two longer then MacRae ended the call.

'He can't help?' LaBruge said.

MacRae shook his head. 'I know he'd like to. He's always come through for me, but this time we're on our own. At least until the rescue is over.'

LaBruge smiled at MacRae. 'We might not have Brad, but we're not on our own. We've got God on our side.'

MacRae's glanced up the flight information being updated across the room. 'I hope so Thierry. It's time to move.'

~

CHAPTER 30

SANATORIUM

The chatter of small children trotting alongside their parents in the shopping mall car park was muffled inside the shiny black van where MacRae, Marion and LaBruge sat working through the rescue plan for Hassana. MacRae and LaBruge had been in San Francisco for less than twenty four hours, just time enough to pull together the resources they needed before picking up Marion at the airport. After a few hours rest they'd put the plan, such as it was, into action, no-one wanting to wait in case Hassana was moved.

MacRae looked from face to face, reading the reaction of each as they posed questions, looking for the best solutions. By nature MacRae was a meticulous planner. In his line of business the more information you had before you even left home, the more prepared you'd be for the myriad things that could go wrong. And in this case there was very little information, and more than a few assumptions, and that meant they were taking a huge risk.

He was okay with that for himself and LaBruge. But despite her chosen life often putting her in harm's way, MacRae felt this was one time Marion should stay clear. But deep inside he knew she was more than capable of looking after herself, and perhaps what he was feeling was more personal than he would admit.

He watched as Marion and LaBruge chatted. She was calm under pressure, but this would be different as they'd be the aggressors, hopefully controlling the situation. LaBruge always seemed relaxed. He very much thought and lived, even thrived, in the moment. As a soldier for hire, he'd assess the risks before he took on a job, then it was about route planning, situational awareness, and ultimately responding to rapidly changing circumstances and threats, from drunks in a nightclub when he was babysitting the rich kids, to the kind of mess that occurred when Hassana was taken and Holgate was killed.

MacRae pushed away the thoughts. He needed clarity right now, not guilt or melancholy.

'It's a shame this is all we've got...Ian?'

It was Marion, handing him back one of the Taser guns they'd just bought.

'Yes it is,' MacRae said. 'But if we use them effectively we might be able to pick up something with a little bit more punch when we're there.'

LaBruge turned his Taser around in his hand, looking at it with disdain. 'Are you sure you don't want us to just tickle them until they give her to us?'

MacRae grinned. 'Whatever works Thierry.'

He was trying to lighten the mood but he felt the same. They were woefully under-gunned, and if anything went wrong, they'd all be caught, or possibly injured or killed.

He pulled the rest of the gear out of the bright yellow plastic SuperDupaStore bag, spreading it out on the metal van floor then handing it out. In addition to two Tasers each...MacRae and LaBruge had chosen plain black devices in contrast to Marion's bright pink plastic version...they each had 140 decibel personal alarms, guaranteed to cause excruciating, disorienting pain in the ears of anyone within fifty metres. He tore open the packaging on the personal communication ear pieces and fitted the batteries before they checked in with each other. The ear pieces would also hopefully be enough to protect their own ears from the personal alarms. Then he passed around a handful of pepper spray canisters and marine smoke flares.

A couple of minutes to familiarise themselves with the operation of the devices and he felt they were as ready as they could be. Considering their circumstances, MacRae thought they had reasonable capability to control a hostile environment with non-lethal devices. And all available from your local SuperDupaStore.

The last piece of equipment they each took was a ballistic vest. If things went terribly wrong the vests might just keep them alive. They each strapped them on, then pulled on generic white laboratory coats with a red medical symbol embossed on the front. The perfect cover from a fancy dress shop downtown.

LaBruge tapped MacRae's shoulder and nodded out the windscreen. A portly Hispanic shopping mall security guard was sauntering towards the van, chewing gum slowly. Had they done something to draw attention to themselves? MacRae swivelled into the driver's seat, readying to start the van. Then the guard turned to the car next to them, a beaten up Civic, and climbed inside, revving the engine noisily before roaring out of the car park and into the main street traffic.

MacRae rejoined Marion and LaBruge in the back. He checked the time. It was almost visiting time at the sanatorium, and they were about to get a visit they wouldn't soon forget.

A couple more questions from Marion and they fell silent.

'I guess we're about as ready as we can be then,' LaBruge said.

MacRae took the driver's seat and started the engine.

'Okay, let's do this.'

~

The drive out of the city and into the forested foothills was quick and uneventful, light traffic meaning they got to the turn off to the sanatorium with time to spare before visiting hours commenced. MacRae noted the carefully concealed security cameras starting at the stone entrance to the grounds a few hundred metres out from the main buildings. They shouldn't be a problem with the tinting on the windows of the rental van, and the false ID he'd used hiring the van should make them untraceable.

MacRae slowed the van as they drove down a long avenue surrounded by the forest on both sides to approach the entry boom gate. A car in front of them proceeded at snail's pace then accelerated past a guard house as the gate was lifted automatically, MacRae following suit as they too were waved through as expected without scrutiny.

'Ritchie's coming through for us so far,' MacRae said.

'They really need to pay attention to their online security,' LaBruge said.

MacRae nodded. Sarah's notes had said that due to budget constraints at the facility, there had been staffing cuts, and cuts to training. So all vehicles except heavy commercial vehicles were to be passed through the boom gate without stopping, and visitors would be vetted as they entered the building.

But MacRae, LaBruge and Marion had no intention of entering the building.

Fifty metres ahead as they rounded a curve in the driveway the low-slung bulk of the sanatorium was revealed, the white rendered wings of the facility exuding menace in the mottled forest light. MacRae glanced at Marion and nodded as they approached the main entrance, then swung past towards a series of parking bays.

Marion tapped a message into her phone and hit send. MacRae slowed the van to walking pace as they waited. Thirty seconds went by, it became a minute.

Marion looked at MacRae. 'Ian...'

Then the hush of the forest around them erupted into the scream of alarms, as from a location unknown to them, Ritchie accessed the private security firm monitoring the facility, and triggered the poison gas detector alarms throughout the sanatorium.

MacRae veered the van to a loading area to one side.

'Is this the right place?'

LaBruge consulted an aerial photograph and printed site plan. He pointed to the left, moving his finger along the parking lot.

'Yes. These are the emergency marshalling areas for the main part of the facility.'

Then he pointed to their right at the rear of the building.

'And that is where they should go from the inpatient research units.'

The main doors to the facility swung open as patients and staff flooded out to be rounded up in groups by emergency marshals.

MacRae looked anxiously at the rear of the building. Nothing was happening.

Marion spoke. 'Are you sure they'll evacuate her section?'

'Sarah said the protocols are just like anywhere else,' MacRae said. 'When an alarm is triggered the entire building will be emptied.'

LaBruge frowned. 'Even the secure section?'

MacRae nodded.

'And the marshalling area is definitely there?' Marion stabbed a finger at sketch.

'Yes,' MacRae said. 'We'll only have a few minutes when they evacuate and assemble before the alarms are cancelled. But hopefully they'll be like everyone else in an emergency, it'll be total confusion. And that's when they're vulnerable.'

The seconds ticked by as the alarms screamed and people filled the front marshalling areas, then the flow seemed to slow.

'Shit,' LaBruge said.

The air in the van was thick with tension. Then the recessed emergency exit slid open and a stream of staff and patients, many on wheeled beds, filled their emergency area.

The three of them scanned the faces a mere ten metres from where they were concealed in their van. MacRae saw her first.

'Over to the right at the back, blue gown, strapped to a bed. That's her.'

LaBruge waited for an overweight male nurse to step sideways then he saw her too. He smiled as he recognised her. They'd finally found her after so long.

'Confirmed. And she's got security.'

'Well spotted.' MacRae had already seen the black-clad guards hanging back at the building exit.

'Armed?' LaBruge said.

'Not that I can see,' MacRae said.

The marshalling area near them was almost full now with maybe fifty or sixty people milling around, the air filled with the buzz of excited conversation.

MacRae, LaBruge and Marion pulled life-like latex party masks over their faces before MacRae slid open the side door.

'Let's go before we lose her.'

Then he was out, walking quickly through the crowd to find Hassana. LaBruge was out a moment later, taking up a position between the main assembly area and the security guards. Marion stood in the open door watching the crowd and both men.

'All clear so far.' She watched MacRae step to one side. 'Five metres to target at two o'clock.'

MacRae changed direction. He noticed eyes glancing at him as he passed. The masks were lifelike, but there was something about them not quite right, and it was just enough to unsettle people.

Then he stopped as he bumped into a trolley. It was a middle aged man, bald head shining in the sunlight. Abruptly the alarm sirens stopped, as did the hum of conversation, and after a few seconds of confusion a voice called from a PA system.

'*Emergency evacuation is complete. The facility is verified safe. You may return to the building.*'

MacRae felt rather than saw the movement of the crowd as they turned towards the facility. It had been too quick.

'Marion, where is she?'

'Twelve o'clock, three metres, a tall orderly with blond hair.'

MacRae spotted the man and pushed through the crowd, bumping into another trolley. He looked down and his heart leapt as his and Hassana's eyes met.

She looked at him without recognition. Was it the fog of the drugs? Then he realised, how could she recognise him wearing a mask?

'I'm with her. She's restrained and appears drugged.' MacRae spoke softly, the sensitive microphone in his communications set just picking up his voice amongst the crowd.

'Are we ready?'

First the voice of LaBruge, then Marion came through.

'Ready.'

MacRae turned to the nurse pushing the trolley back towards the building and spoke with the practised authority of years in law enforcement.

'I'll take her from here.'

He took the end of the trolley and turned towards the van. The nurse let him go, confusion across his face, then grabbed the trolley back.

'Who are you? Where's your ID?'

MacRae lifted his fake ID tag and waved it at the nurse.

'Patient transport for the Medici-Royal care flights. Don't make me report you...'

The nurse hesitated again, before peering at the ID, reading aloud. 'Nurse Naughty? What the fuck...'

'It was worth a try,' MacRae said, as he slipped a hand in his pocket, pulled out the pepper spray canister and discharged it into the man's face.

The nurse jumped back and screamed, tears streaming down his face.

MacRae shouted above the crowd. 'It's the gas leak.'

The crowd around him panicked, pushing and shoving each other to get away. MacRae grabbed the trolley again and pushed towards the van, the crowd clearing in front of him.

Then he heard his name, drifting up from the trolley. It was Hassana.

'Ian, your voice...is it you? Have you come to save me, or am I dreaming?'

MacRae smiled down at her. 'Yes it's me, we're getting you out of here.'

Another voice drifted above the crowd. A shout.

'Stop. You with the trolley. Stop now.'

MacRae looked over his shoulder. It was a security guard, pushing through the crowd towards him.

MacRae ignored him and went faster. He was almost at the van when he heard a scream. He threw a quick glance over his shoulder. The guard had pulled a gun, the crowd parting in front of him as they saw it.

Then MacRae felt a punch like a metal fist in his back as the nine millimetre round struck his ballistic vest, knocking the wind from his lungs even before he heard the gunshot. He fell to one knee, gripping the trolley for support, then pulled himself up again, turning to see the security guard poised to take a second shot. This time the weapon was aimed at his face.

'Drop Ian.' Marion screamed.

Then as his finger tightened on the trigger to fire a second time, the guard jerked upright, throwing his arms out and dropping the gun, before he collapsing to the ground, a grinning LaBruge standing behind him with the Taser in his hand.

'Get her in the van. I'll watch your back.'

Marion looked over the crowds. More security guards were heading straight for them. She grabbed smoke flares from the van floor, ignited them and tossed them up wind behind MacRae. The gentle breeze quickly laid a cloud of thick orange smoke over the crowd and van, and within seconds the security guards and LaBruge were lost from view.

MacRae pushed the trolley the last few metres to the van, steering it into Marion's hands. She yanked hard at it, pulling it into the van as MacRae pushed from behind, the trolley legs automatically folding beneath it. MacRae slammed the door shut and climbed through into the driver's seat, starting the engine and motored slowly back towards the driveway.

Marion stuck her head out the window.

'Where's Thierry?'

MacRae shrugged. 'I'm sure he's not far away.'

A gust of wind and the smoke parted in front of them Two security guards were running at the van, guns drawn.

'I guess we should have expected them all to be armed,' MacRae said. 'You know what to do Marion.'

She nodded and picked up her personal alarm, holding it out the window towards the security guards. She glanced at MacRae.

'Ready?'

'Yep.' MacRae braced himself, then the ear piercing scream of the alarm filled the air in every direction, sending pain through the unprotected eardrums of everyone within range.

Marion looked on in amazement as everyone, including the security guards, clamped their hands to their ears, trying to block out the pain. Everyone except her, MacRae and hopefully LaBruge.

MacRae turned to Marion and grinned. Their communications ear pieces were muffling the alarm down to a mere irritation for them.

A figure burst through the smoke in front of them and ran to the van. It was LaBruge. He circled around to the passenger door where Marion let him in.

'I was wondering when you were going to join us,' MacRae said, then looked down at the matt-black nine millimetre Glock pistol in LaBruge's hand. 'Where'd you get that?'

LaBruge shrugged. 'The security guard didn't need it, and it seemed such a waste to leave it behind.'

Marion frowned in disapproval and turned off the alarm.

LaBruge slipped the gun into his pocket. 'Let's just call it a souvenir shall we?'

He leaned into the back of the van.

'How's Hassana?'

Marion knelt next to the trolley, loosening the restraints and giving her a quick check over. Hassana lay still, seemingly dazed.

'Physically she seems okay, psychologically....I'm not sure.'

'Let's get her far away from here then,' LaBruge said.

MacRae sped up, and the facility buildings, staff and patients quickly disappeared behind them. He slowed as they approached the entry boom gate.

'The gate's up. That's a bit of luck,' MacRae said.

'Probably raises automatically when the alarms are triggered,' LaBruge said.

The security guard at the entry saw them. He looked undecided then hit the override switch to lower the gate.

'You spoke too soon,' Marion said, as the white painted steel beam swung down.

'Hang on.' MacRae gritted his teeth and floored the throttle.

They shot forward, the hideous screech of metal on metal echoed through the cabin as the beam pressed down on the roof before the van forced its way through and they were free.

LaBruge stuck his head out the window, thrusting a raised middle finger at the scowling security guard.

'Fuck you ass-hole.'

Marion looked at MacRae. He raised an eyebrow, then they both erupted in laughter, the pent up tension melting away.

CHAPTER 31

CONFRONT

The spectacular view over San Francisco Bay from the hotel bedroom window was just as stunning to MacRae as he remembered it from their first visit. But it was only a brief distraction from the harrowing reality of Hassana recalling more details of her time as a prisoner, as her mind cleared from the last of the drugs.

Marion sat on the edge of the bed, checking Hassana's pupils. Three days had passed since they'd got Hassana away from the sanatorium, and Marion felt her recovery was going well. Physically she was in excellent shape. Apart from being sedated a lot of the time during months of imprisonment, first in Nigeria, then various locations in Europe before being taken to the US, she hadn't been harmed. It seemed her captors really did see her, as one had described it, *very special and precious.*

She'd remembered various people running tests on her in hidden medical facilities, an assumption she made because she felt she often wasn't far from the safety of other people, but she never saw anyone apart from her captors.

MacRae realised he was staring at the track marks on Hassana's arms, the lingering reminder of frequently having blood taken and being injected with God-knows-what.

'Most of them didn't talk to me. I was just an experiment subject,' Hassana said as Marion stood up. 'But when they did, I tried to remember everything. Like the woman who said it was a privilege to design diseases that only work on some people, like African women. But if you made the disease you also needed the cure. And I was the cure, or at least not affected by whatever it was they invented, but they had no idea why.'

Marion looked to MacRae. 'They can do that, target diseases?

'It looks like it. I know it's been talked about for a long time, the Holy Grail of biological weapons. I remember seeing a video of Vladimir Putin discussing it. He said he had no doubt every major world power was trying to do it,' MacRae said. 'And if scientists can do it based on race now, maybe they can use all kinds of other markers.'

'Like what?'

'I don't know. I suppose for any government it would be ideal if their military could just kill an enemy without any risk to themselves,' MacRae said.

'But it wouldn't just kill the soldiers would it?' Marion said. 'It would kill indiscriminately, civilians, adult, children. It's abhorrent.'

'And someone thought they'd developed a new one, until you came along.' MacRae looked at Hassana.

She smiled. 'It was little bit satisfying knowing I had them stumped. They didn't know what to make of me.'

Although Hassana seemed to be recovering from her ordeal what worried MacRae was the injuries you couldn't see, the unavoidable psychological scars from the harrowing events she'd endured. She was chatty now but Hassana would often go silent, not wanting to talk about the events, especially any mention of her dead sister. MacRae knew the signs of post-traumatic stress disorder, heaven knows he'd experienced enough of them himself over the years, but so sad to see in someone so young.

They left the room to let Hassana sleep, Marion pulling the door closed quietly behind her.

'I think she's ready for the move,' Marion said.

MacRae nodded. 'Good. I can't help feeling the longer we're here the more likely we are to be found again.'

'I agree,' Marion said. 'I'm glad Brad came through for us on this.'

MacRae nodded. Schneider hadn't been able to help with arming them for Hassana's rescue, but now they had her he'd been able to arrange a secure location they could stay in...MacRae assumed a CIA safe house...until they figured out how to get Hassana out of the country. Not so easy without a passport, and hers was long gone.

He checked his appearance in the bathroom mirror, smoothing down some errant hair and straightening his jacket.

'How do I look?'

Marion smiled, adjusting his tie. 'Pretty good I have to say.'

He hadn't dressed up for a while but the event he was attending this afternoon required him to look the part. Although it was ninety minutes' drive outside San Francisco, he couldn't pass up the opportunity to see Magnus Crane as keynote speaker at the Eco-Science And Global Security Conference in a few hours. It didn't totally surprise MacRae that Crane would risk being near where Hassana was held, he guessed Crane loved living dangerously. And this was the perfect chance for MacRae to confront him, especially as MacRae had purchased the premium ticket, guaranteeing that he'd meet Crane in person at the exclusive post-talk cocktail party meet and greet.

'Well I think you're good to go.' Marion stepped back to admire her work. 'But I wish you could stay and help with moving Hassana.'

MacRae was torn. Schneider had given them a pretty short window to get Hassana into the secure house, and unfortunately it coincided with MacRae trying to confront Crane.

'Me too. But Thierry will be here to make sure it goes smoothly, and I'll meet you there in a few hours okay?'

~

The hybrid rental car whirred almost silently as he cruised along the highway out of the city. He still felt conflicted leaving Thierry and Marion to move Hassana, but if Crane was about to depart the US for the water treatment plants commissioning in India as the media was reporting, this might be his last chance.

He still wasn't quite sure how this was going to go, but the threats to his and Marion's life had continued long after the death of Edison, and the only common denominator was Crane. One way or the other, now that Hassana was safe, MacRae was going to get some answers.

~

A scan of the conference QR code on his phone got MacRae into the building and he'd been directed by a smiling usher to the cavernous conference hall. He found his seat with a couple of minutes to spare and took the time to check out the crowd. It must have been a couple of thousand people, ranging in age from early twenties to retirees, and what appeared to be a mix of business people, tech geeks and alternate lifestylers. Unsurprising, given the proximity to Silicon Valley and the surrounding hills.

The lights dimmed and a huge screen flashed into life behind the stage. A lone figure entered the stage from the left and walked into the centre spotlight to rapturous applause. It was Magnus Crane, and he seemed to have celebrity status, amongst this crowd at least.

MacRae relaxed into the show, watching as Crane, obviously a practised public speaker and undoubtedly charismatic, worked the crowd, pausing at the right moments to emphasise a point then smiling as the audience erupted in applause.

MacRae had to admit the talk was fascinating as well as entertaining, and fitted well with Crane's carefully crafted image. The topic was emblazoned atop every image on the big screen:

A SUSTAINABLE FUTURE...OURS TO GRASP OR LOSE

Crane's talk followed a well-planned arc, from the current state of the planet, to a civilisation in decline, then offering a way forward with hope for a better future. All with the guidance and assistance of Medici-Royal.

A succession of slick videos backed Crane's view that the world was an amazing and resilient planet with bountiful resources but struggling under the burden of an ever-increasing population. He proudly explained the benefits of modern technology and pharmacology in increasing the length and quality of life for billions of people, and how the tradition of raising many children to care for elderly parents was a norm disappearing across almost all cultures, particularly when they realised the benefits and pleasures of increased income without the expenses and worry of raising children. Colourful charts showed population growth slowing, indeed perhaps one day the world population being static or even falling.

'Many western societies are now struggling with falling populations as different lifestyle choices are made.' Crane's voice echoed around the theatre.

Glossy images of tourists and locals lounging at cafes near beaches, children nowhere to be seen, merged across the screen.

'Where will the future tax base come from, the endless fiscal growth we are taught is necessary for our economies? But is it really necessary? Modelling has shown unequivocally that our society and the planet can co-exist with a stable world population of six billion people. That's about one and a half billion people, or around twenty percent less than the world's current population. Our aim, by enhancing quality of life through science and equality, is to achieve that population reduction within the next fifty years. But the question remains...' Crane's voice boomed, 'will that be fast enough for a truly sustainable future for our planet and indeed for us as a species?'

More graphs showing the crossing paths of world population and diminishing resources and increasing pollution. A video faded in of conflict spots around the globe, disputes over water resources, oil, even on the open ocean over fishing rights.

'It's easy to be overwhelmed by the problems and the numbers of overpopulation, but population reduction has been done before, although historically it's been through terrible circumstances.'

Graphic images flashed onto the screen, a charcoal drawing of a hooded figure with a hooked beak from the middle ages stared out at the audience, then grainy photographs of hundreds of patients in tent hospitals.

'The Black Plague and the Spanish Flu, nature's way of population control?'

Then black and white movie clips of German and Russian soldiers fighting on snow covered plains, followed by etchings of Mongol warriors on horseback.

'Then humans at their worst. Fifty million dead in six short years during the second world war. And Genghis Khan's armies were estimated to have killed eleven percent of the world population in their conquest of the known world.'

The graphic images were replaced by pictures of windmills, large scale greenhouse food production and scientists studying marine life.

Crane's voice became calm. 'We all have a choice, as individuals, communities, governments and leaders. Act now or accept a bleak but avoidable future.'

Then came the sell.

'But many of us have a vision of a cleaner, fairer and safer world, where wealth is distributed across societies, where everyone can access the health care they deserve, where people don't need to fight, and balance with nature can be achieved. And through the medical advances and philanthropy of Medici-Royal I'm playing my part in striving for this future.'

A map of India appeared, dotted with markers.

'Is the distribution of wealth in our society fair? Maybe not, but in the hands of the right people great good can be done. In a few short days a dream will come true for me, as across the vast nation of India, water treatment plants designed and built by Medici-Royal will be commissioned to provide clean drinking water to almost a billion people. And for the Indian people it will be a double celebration as they travel home to their loved ones to celebrate their national Festival of Lights during Diwali.'

He stood with hands on hips, waiting for the applause to subside, then continued. 'The technology, skills and generosity of Medici-Royal will raise the living standards of almost one-fifth of the world's population, and the state-of-the-art facilities will allow, at the press of a button, the distribution through the water supply of any number of medical therapies to further enhance the health of a nation, with the proven effect of stabilising and eventually reducing their population.'

Crane basked in the applause, bowing his head in a show of humility as his presentation ended. But for MacRae the applause was fading into the background as in his mind everything he'd learnt about Crane came together like the pieces of a jigsaw, the last piece being Crane commissioning the water treatment plants during Diwali. And the picture it made was terrifying.

Abruptly the lights went dark and when the lighting came back up the stage was empty.

MacRae looked around. The room was buzzing with conversation. The next speaker had quite an act to follow, but that was of no interest to him. It was time for the truth.

~

MacRae headed out the auditorium exit and was directed to the VIP lounge for the private meet-and-greet with Crane. Another scan of his QR code and he was in. The room was comfortably full, maybe forty people, and quite a different crowd to the main auditorium, the alternate lifestylers nowhere to be seen in the sea of men and women in business suits. The hundred dollar entry fee for the event probably had something to do with that. MacRae took the glass of champagne offered by a server in a crisp white blouse, and scanned the room for Crane, spotting him on the far side of the room surrounded by eager disciples. By habit MacRae checked the room for security cameras and exits. He quickly spotted the three security personnel in matching suits, but no conspicuous bulges of concealed firearms. He waited patiently but the crowd around Crane just kept growing. The opportunity was slipping away. Then Crane excused himself and headed to the bathroom.

MacRae waited a few seconds, checking he wasn't attracting any attention then followed Crane in.

Crane turned from washing his hands at a white marble sink when he heard the bathroom door open and close behind him.

'Hello Mr MacRae. Another coincidence...or have you become a fan of mine?'

Crane was expecting him.

'You don't seem surprised to see me,' MacRae said.

Crane rubbed his hands under a dryer. 'I always check the guest list for these events.'

MacRae scrutinised Crane's face. He hoped there would be some sign, a giveaway when he was in the presence of evil, but it was always the same, the monsters amongst us looked just like everyone else.

'I wouldn't say I'm a fan, but I've got to know a lot more about you since we last met, and I think we both know that the image you've presented to the world hides someone very different.'

Crane's smile wavered. 'That's very dramatic. How so?'

'Ever since I started investigating the murder of a friend of mine in Nigeria, your name and your companies have kept coming up, from the Tasmanian Devil research program with Dr Edison, to a medical trial cover up in Syria thirty years ago. And whenever I get closer to finding out what's going on someone tries to stop me.'

Crane frowned, mentally linking events. 'So Dr Edison's death wasn't an accident. Have the police connected you to her?'

MacRae was impassive. 'Dr Edison and I had an interesting chat. She told me about your history together, what happened to your daughter, and your shared vision for the future.'

'Dr Edison and I did go back a long way,' Crane said. ' She was brilliant but was letting her vices get the better of her. You've saved me making a difficult decision about her, but I'm not sure what she meant by our shared vision for the future. I think you're finding links that don't exist. Why are you here Mr MacRae?'

'I came here because at first I thought all the previous events were linked to Dr Edison, but then she was out of the picture and that left just you as the common factor. I know you're directly involved in the facial cancer program, and I've seen photos of you with a man that's tried to kill me.'

For the first time Crane couldn't mask his surprise.

MacRae continued. 'I also know you went to Aralsk-7 and took samples of Soviet bio weapons.'

Crane snorted. 'You know you're starting to sound like a conspiracy theorist, just like one I already sued and won in court. Sure, we do research for the Defence Department, but that helps us develop vaccines against diseases never previously encountered, like SARS, and yes I went to Aralsk-7, it's called adventure tourism, particularly for someone in my field of work.'

'Maybe,' MacRae said. 'But put that with the fact that you manufacture bio-warfare agents for the government that somehow end up being sent across the world, your links to survivalists and your dream to depopulate the world, it's not too hard to see where it's going.'

Crane didn't look amused anymore. Where the hell had he got this information from? Obviously someone who had extensive access to the computer network for Medic-Royal and its subsidiaries. Very few people had that kind of access to records across the network. Maybe a hacker? Then a face popped into his mind. Surely not Jake Welsh, his medical statistician?

'I've got it right haven't I? You sick bastard, you're planning to use your water treatment plants in India to infect the population with a pathogen your company has developed, then spread it throughout the countryside when everyone travels back to their home towns to celebrate Diwali...'

Crane stared at MacRae in silence.

'...and the pathogen is genetically modified to target only Indian DNA, with a high infection and mortality rate. This is the real research you've been doing isn't it? All for some delusion about saving the world from overpopulation.'

Crane didn't need to answer, the truth was in his eyes.

MacRae stabbed his finger hard into Crane's chest. 'I'm not going to let this happen.'

Crane stepped back. 'You've got no proof of any of this or you would have acted already.'

'I've got enough to get the right people interested and maybe delay the commissioning of the water treatment plants, at least until there's greater scrutiny on you.'

MacRae turned to go just as the bathroom door swung open behind him, then the world turned upside down.

~

MacRae was surprised just how clean the bathroom floor tiles were, even the white grout between them was spotless. It wasn't something he'd normally notice, but his body position as he slid along the floor face down was anything but normal.

It took him a long second to realise what was happening. He recalled the sound of the door opening behind him, then Crane nodding his head ever so slightly. It must have been a security guard come to check on Crane, then the sledgehammer *thump* in his back as he'd been kicked from behind, sending him sprawling across the room.

He stopped with a dull *thunk* as his head hit the cabinet below the sinks, then he heard footsteps closing from behind.

In one motion MacRae rolled to the side and swivelled on one arm, swinging his foot out and sweeping the legs from under the security guard. MacRae regained his feet at the same time as the security guard hit the floor. Crane had been watching the fight, but now bolted for the door. MacRae threw himself across the room, slamming into Crane's back and propelling him into the door. Crane's face crashed into the solid timber and he staggered backwards, falling to his knees. The security guard was struggling back to his feet so MacRae stepped behind him and locked an arm around his neck, applying pressure to the carotid artery. It only took thirty seconds for the guard to slump into unconsciousness at his feet.

MacRae turned back to see Crane was up and almost at the door again. MacRae took a couple of quick steps and pressed a foot against the door, jamming it shut.

'You're not going anywhere until I get answers.'

'Fuck you MacRae.' Crane snarled. The men glared at each other, until the deadlock was abruptly broken by banging on the bathroom door, muffled voices calling for Crane from the other side.

Crane smiled. 'Looks like you're out of time.'

MacRae weighed up his options. He might keep security out for a little longer, but could he get anything from Crane? Probably not.

'It's your move Mr MacRae.'

MacRae pushed Crane away from the door. Time to get out of here. 'This isn't over. I'm going to stop you getting to India.'

Crane shrugged. 'You know I could have had you arrested as a stalker as soon as you arrived here.'

'I'd have been out on bail within hours,' MacRae said.

'That's true,' Crane said. 'But aren't you curious why, if I knew you were coming I didn't arrange another meeting with the man you encountered previously in Tasmania, then again in Salt Lake City?'

'It makes no difference to me,' MacRae said. 'He hasn't stopped me yet.'

'Well maybe you should be more focused on looking after your own, rather than chasing shadows.'

'The people I care about are safe. I know how to look after them.'

'Really? Aren't you curious where he is?' Crane stepped forward, his face centimetres from MacRae's. 'You know, he was quite a find as an employee. Ex Russian special forces or something, kicked out because he doesn't like to play by the rules. Perfect for my needs. He's a hunter by nature and the most dangerous time for the hunter's prey is when they leave their den and are out in the open.'

A cold sense of dread crept over MacRae.

'I know where you took her after the sanatorium. San Francisco is a small place when you know what you're looking for. And I know she's moving today. And here you are talking to me.'

There was no time to waste. MacRae swung his elbow into Crane's jaw, sending him staggering across the room.

MacRae took a deep breath then removed his foot from the door and swung it wide open, two security guards stumbling past him into the bathroom. They stopped and stared first at MacRae then Crane, and when they turned back MacRae was gone, weaving through the bemused crowd at a run as though Marion's and Hassana's lives depended on it. Because they did.

~

Crane watched as MacRae shot through the door. He'd got much too far with this. The Russian was usually completely reliable. Maybe he, like Edison, was past his prime. But he'd have to do for the moment, there wasn't time to find a replacement. Once the girl was back in their care, he'd give him a last quick job to do before they headed to India. After that, nothing would be the same again.

~

CHAPTER 32

GRAB

The Russian sat in the front seat of the van twirling a pen between his fingers. He checked the time. They should be coming out any minute...if the information they had was good. He looked relaxed, but inside he was tense. And if he admitted it to himself, both angry and excited. But feelings were to be avoided as they clouded judgement.

He checked the hotel forecourt again using binoculars from their parking spot on the opposite side of the busy street. No sign of them yet.

The brazen raid by MacRae and whoever had helped him to rescue the African girl from the facility, had come as a shock to both him and Crane. They'd underestimated him. He was extremely resourceful, and receiving help from unknown sources. He wasn't going to let this go.

He checked his phone again, re-reading Crane's last message saying that MacRae had turned up at his lecture as expected. Not that the Russian was concerned if MacRae had been at the hotel, it would have given him a chance to settle the score once and for all. But he couldn't deny it would make this go a little easier if they only had to contend with the woman doctor, the African girl and the mercenary MacRae had hired as additional security.

'Anything happening yet?' A deep voice with a Brooklyn accent boomed from the back of the van.

The Russian twisted in his seat to talk to the big man, dressed in a black suit with a balaclava over his face. Just like his companions.

One of them tapped his assault rifle impatiently. A little bit of apprehension before an operation was good, but he wanted them calm and professional.

'Patience my friend. Our intelligence is good, they'll be out soon enough, and it'll go like clockwork.'

He rehearsed the operation in his mind. A combination of phone triangulation, credit card usage and facial recognition from city security cameras had led them to the hotel they'd been using as a temporary refuge for the girl.

The Russian had to admit he was impressed by the resources Crane was able to access. Surveillance and a few bribes had confirmed it was MacRae, a foreigner called LaBruge, the African girl Hassana, and the female doctor staying there. A background check on LaBruge quickly revealed his professional history.

When the Russian had found out they were checking out today he'd figured they were moving to a more secure location, so this might be the last opportunity to get the girl back. It had only taken a day to put together the operation to retake the girl. MacRae and LaBruge were just obstacles to be removed. Now there was nothing to do but wait.

He raised the binoculars again as a stream of cars entered the hotel forecourt, disgorging passengers before being whisked away for parking by the valets. Then he saw them, LaBruge leading the way to a waiting cab, followed by the two women, their bags on a trolley pushed by a bellhop.

The Russian zoomed in on LaBruge, watching as the mercenary scanned the forecourt and street for threats. The man was definitely a professional. But he hadn't noticed the nondescript van with its engine idling across the street.

The Russian scanned his body, looking for the shape of a concealed weapon. He couldn't see anything, but he was doubtless carrying.

A squeal of laughter drifted over from the girl. She seemed relaxed and happy. Not for much longer.

'They're out, it's game time,' the Russian called over his shoulder. 'Let's keep this short, sharp and professional, minimal casualties okay?'

A grunt of agreement from the back, then he spoke to the driver. 'You ready? Any questions?'

The driver shook his head as he pulled his balaclava over his face and readied to move the van.

~

MacRae threw his phone to the passenger seat of the car. Why the hell weren't LaBruge or Marion answering? And even the hotel number just gave a sickeningly polite voice informing that *all the reception staff were currently busy, but his call was important to them...*

He threw the car into a left hand turn, tyres screeching around the corner as he raced back to the hotel using all his high speed pursuit skills from his police training so long ago.

The image of Crane smiling at him as he revealed they knew where they were staying burned into his brain. And the thought that something may already be underway...

His phone GPS had advised him that it was still a twenty minute drive to the hotel, obeying the speed limits, and if the traffic was light.

MacRae slowed for a line of cars at traffic lights, then swerved around them accelerating hard down a side street onto another route. The torque of the electric engine as he hurtled through the speed limit was extraordinary. He was going to do it in ten.

~

The cab bumped over a pothole in the road with a thud, bouncing Hassana in her seat.

'We almost disappeared into that one,' Marion said with a smile.

LaBruge said nothing. He looked relaxed, but constantly looked around the street for anything unusual that might indicate a threat.

Hassana and Marion sat close, sharing the back seat, while LaBruge rode up front. Marion looked fondly at Hassana. They were becoming quite attached to each other. Maybe Hassana was starting to see Marion as some kind of mother figure. Marion wasn't quite sure how she felt about that, deciding so long ago to follow her career over family. Or perhaps that was just how life had panned out for her and MacRae.

Hassana had recovered so quickly from her imprisonment in the facility. She had remarkable resilience, the true spirit of a survivor. But then she'd had no choice with the events of the last few months. Adapt to survive.

LaBruge noticed the van following them after about fifteen minutes of driving, halfway to their destination. He didn't know how MacRae had arranged the use of a CIA safe house until they got out of the country, but then MacRae often surprised him.

Up until now they hadn't seen any real risk in moving from the hotel to the safe house. But now LaBruge felt a creeping unease, growing with each passing moment. He pulled out his phone and noticed MacRae's missed call. Shit. Maybe they should have waited until MacRae got back before they checked out of the hotel.

The traffic was lighter in this part of town as LaBruge looked over his shoulder to check the traffic. Marion saw his eyes widen as the van sped past then swerved to a stop in front of them, blocking their path.

The cab driver threw his arms up. 'Freakin idiots, what the hell they think they're doing?'

The side panel of the van slid open and three men leapt out brandishing assault rifles, faces hidden by black balaclavas. A fourth man stepped from the front passenger seat, pistol held in front of him. LaBruge knew with a terrible certainty that this was the assassin MacRae had described.

The cab driver froze. 'What the fuck?'

LaBruge snapped into action, barking instructions at the driver. 'Reverse the car, NOW!'

The driver slammed the gear shift into reverse and stamped on the throttle with a screech of tires.

The lead attacker didn't hesitate, training his weapon on the front of the car to pour bullets into the tires and engine.

The car swerved briefly then came to a stop against the kerb, engine revving wildly, the driver shaking in terror and raising his hands in surrender.

LaBruge spoke calmly. 'Marion, Hassana, get down right now.'

Then he leaned across the driver, jerked the shift into drive, twisted the wheel and flattened the throttle.

The car jerked forward again, forcing the advancing men to jump out of the way, before it collided with the rear corner of the van in a spray of plastic and glass. The engine stalled.

LaBruge cursed, reaching into his jacket and pulling out the Glock he'd taken from the security guard at the facility.

One of the men raised his weapon and poured a stream of bullets into the front of the cab, shredding the chest of the driver, a round entering LaBruge's side.

He grunted with the pain, then as he always did when he needed to kill, he asked his God for the strength to do what he needed to do.

Marion held Hassana down in the back seat as the bullets hit the car. Then she saw LaBruge open his door and roll out onto the road, hitting the ground and hugging the side of the car. He located the attackers to one side, firing two shots at each.

The first fell to the ground silently as a round passed through his throat. The second flung himself sideways, a round hitting the body armour under his jacket, another grazing his arm. The third dropped to a crouch and unleashed a dozen shots towards LaBruge. Eleven missed their mark, ricocheting off the car into the street. The twelfth hit LaBruge's hand, shredding his fingers, the gun clattering onto the road behind him.

A voice rang out. 'Stop shooting at the car. We want the girl alive.'

It was the Russian.

An unnatural silence fell across the scene as the Russian approached LaBruge. The two other attackers stood back, weapons poised.

LaBruge climbed to his feet, swaying steadily, blood dripping onto the road from his torso and shattered hand. He stared into the Russian's eyes.

'I've heard of you and what you do. You are a piece of dog shit on my boot, and now it's time to wipe you off.' The words dripped from his lips with contempt.

The Russian's eyes narrowed as he took another step closer.

In the back of the car Hassana raised her head, taking in the scene. Then she noticed LaBruge's gun on the road just outside her door.

LaBruge winced as he coughed a glob of blood to the ground, fighting to stay upright, slowly bending at the waist.

The Russian trained his gun on LaBruge. 'I don't really think you're in a position to make threats.'

Traffic had stopped short of them on both sides, drivers gawking at the scene, some taking photos or videos on their phones, others making calls.

The Russian spoke to the other gunmen. 'Get the girl into the van.' He waved his gun at the dead gunman. 'And him.'

LaBruge had been waiting for an opportunity. It was now.

His hand flashed to his ankle and with a flick of his wrist he flung a combat knife straight at the Russian's throat.

The Russian spotted the motion and flinched to one side, the knife flying past him harmlessly as he fired at LaBruge, striking him in the chest.

Hassana suppressed a scream as she saw LaBruge get hit, then she opened her car door a crack and reached for his gun, her fingers wrapping around the barrel and drawing it towards her.

LaBruge sank to his knees, gasping for breath.

MacRae rounded the final corner to the hotel as he heard the breaking news bulletin on the radio. A carjacking was currently taking place a couple of blocks away, with multiple casualties. There was speculation of a terrorist attack. SWAT and the police had been dispatched, but were some minutes away.

MacRae floored the throttle again. Screeching away from the hotel, hoping desperately that he wasn't too late.

~

The Russian's face was impassive as he approached LaBruge. LaBruge reached down again, pulling a second smaller knife from its sheath against his leg. He lunged towards the Russian but his ruined body refused to obey his commands anymore and he barely made half the distance before the Russian fired more three shots.

Thierry LaBruge was dead.

Marion peered over the seat towards the approaching gunmen, gasping as she saw LaBruge die. She looked over at Hassana, blinking in surprise as she saw the sleek black gun in her hand.

'We have to get out of here right now. Give me the gun and I'll try and buy you some time okay?

Hassana shook her head. 'No, this is all because of me. I'll stay and fight.'

Marion scowled. 'You have your whole life ahead of you, now give me the gun so you can get away.'

Hassana peered over the seat, just as a face in a ski mask appeared at the window. She shrieked, at the same time pointing the gun and firing twice. The sound echoed around the car as the window shattered and the bullets struck the attacker's face.

Marion snapped into action, kicking open the door on her side and dragging Hassana out onto the street, just as another gunman rounded the back of the car.

He almost fell over them, then spotted the gun in Hassana's hand, kicking it free with a steel capped boot.

Hassana cried out, watching as Marion threw herself at the gunman, fingernails clawing at his eyes.

She screamed at Hassana. 'Go now, they don't care about me. I'll follow you in a second.'

Hassana froze. She could see the Russian approaching around the car. Memories of her imprisonment at the facility flooded back, the fear, the degradation of the tests, not knowing if she'd ever get out. So she ran.

Her legs pumped as she zig-zagged across the road, charging for the nearest car. Then she heard the Russian shouting.

'Leave the doctor, get the girl.'

Hassana glanced over her shoulder. Marion was lying motionless on the ground next to the car, and a gunman was running after her. He was gaining so fast, but struggled as his gun swung around his body.

Hassana dodged between two more cars, then she was at the shops on the other side, darting into the first open doorway. In an instant she was surrounded by the startled jewellery store staff and security guards with guns drawn.

The wail of police car sirens echoed down the street as they wove through the stalled traffic.

The gunman stopped, looking back to the Russian for instructions.

He stood over Marion's unconscious body, weighing up the options. Fuck, it had gone pear-shaped quickly. Who would have thought the women would fight like this? It was time to cut their losses.

His voice boomed across the street. 'Let's go, time to get out of here.'

He looked down at Marion. She was more trouble that she was worth. He aimed the gun at the back of her skull, pressure increasing on the trigger. Then released. Perhaps it wasn't a complete loss after all. She might be useful leverage over MacRae and the girl.

The other gunmen helped the Russian carry Marion to the van, and with the roar of the engine they were off, pushing their way back into the traffic seconds before the police, and MacRae, arrived on the scene.

~

The police officer still had his pistol drawn as he stood over LaBruge's body. The other officers kept the crowd back, cordoned behind plastic police tape stretched between three patrol cars. A SWAT van was parked further up the street where heavily armed officers awaited instructions. To MacRae's experienced eyes they looked disappointed to have missed the action.

Sirens wailed in the distance as more patrol cars converged on the area, tasked with locating the offender's van.

MacRae waited until the officer's attention was drawn away, then slipped under the tape and approached the shot-up taxi. His heart leapt when he saw the shattered windscreen and bloody body in the front seat, a sigh of relief and guilt when he realised it was a male. Then he saw LaBruge on the road.

The officer at the car turned as he noticed MacRae.

'Sir, what are...'

MacRae dropped to the ground at LaBruge's side, reaching out to his friend, sadness washing over him.

The officer stood next to him. 'Who are you sir? Do you know the victim?'

MacRae nodded. 'He was my friend.'

He rose to his feet, mouth set with anger. 'Where are the others? There should be a women and a girl here too.'

The officer shrugged. 'There's no-one else here. The offenders took off in their van. I guess they took the women.'

MacRae felt the crush of despair. Marion and Hassana taken, and LaBruge was dead. What now?

The officer spoke. 'Your accent sir...are you a US resident? I'm going to need a statement from you regarding your involvement in this incident.'

MacRae moved to leave. 'Sorry, I haven't got time for this. I need to find my friends.'

The officer placed his hand on MacRae's arm to restrain him.

'I can't let you do that sir.'

MacRae paused, assessing the scene. Could he escape the officer, maybe take his weapon and go after the van? It was worth a try...

'Mr Ian, Mr Ian they took Marion.'

It was Hassana, pushing past the police barrier and running towards him. An officer tried to grab her, but she was too quick, and barrelled into MacRae's arms, tears streaming down her face.

'I'm so sorry, they were coming for me. Marion made me run away then they took her.'

MacRae held her tight as she sobbed.

'It's not your fault Hassana, I should have been here.'

The officer released his grip, then turned away as he took a call on his radio.

'...responding, will join the pursuit.'

MacRae's ears pricked up.

'They've found the van?'

The officer nodded, holstering his gun.

'Yes sir, it's been located driving in traffic about five blocks from here. We're coordinating a cordon around the area before we approach them.'

MacRae glanced at the officer's ID and took a huge gamble.

'Officer Ryan, they've got my wife, and they killed my friend.'

Hassana shot a confused look at him, mouthing the word *wife?*

'I've served most of my life on local and federal police forces. I know the work you guys do. Please let me come with you.'

Ryan clicked his tongue. 'I totally shouldn't do this...'

He looked between Hassana and MacRae.

'What about the girl?'

MacRae touched Hassana's arm.

'Stay here with the other officers. You'll be safe. I'll arrange for my friend Brad Schneider to get someone to look after you until I get back okay?'

Hassana searched his eyes, then looked down.

'You find her and bring her back. You promise me Mr Ian.'

'I promise Hassana.'

Then he and Ryan were gone.

~

MacRae adjusted his knees, trying to stretch out his muscles. He felt a little cramped in the passenger seat of the police cruiser. It seemed a million years ago that he was a uniformed police officer back home in Australia. The memories came back of going on patrol when he was a rookie, just he and his partner out there keeping the citizens of Hobart safe. Subconsciously his hand went to his side and touched the scar, the souvenir from being stabbed attending a domestic violence incident.

MacRae dialled Schneider's number and he answered almost immediately, listening in silence as MacRae explained what had just happened. MacRae tried to be discreet with the police officer next to him in the car, but there was no other way than to tell it as it happened.

Schneider thought it through, then spoke.

'It seems Crane's access to information is greater than we thought, and he's not afraid to pull shit like this in the US.'

'I should never have left the women to go after Crane,' MacRae said.

'Maybe,' Schneider said. 'But we'd done the risk assessment, and LaBruge is extremely competent. Dammit, was. He would certainly have gone down fighting.'

'So, Hassana?' MacRae asked.

'Don't worry Ian, I'll get her looked after. You just get Marion back okay?'

MacRae's face was grim. 'I'm on it.'

He ended the call and smiled as Ryan looked at him curiously.

'I have some good friends here in the US.'

Ryan nodded. 'Sure sounds like it.'

MacRae changed the subject. He'd noticed Ryan's wedding ring. 'You're married?'

Ryan nodded. 'Going on eighteen years. Two teenage kids.'

'How does the wife feel about the job?'

Ryan shrugged. 'She knew that was part of the package when she married me.'

MacRae looked at Ryan's face. Smooth olive skin, he guessed he was early forties.

'The job can be tough on relationships,' MacRae said.

'Yeah. But she's my greatest supporter,' Ryan glanced at MacRae. 'That's why I let you come with me. I know how I'd feel if my wife had been taken.'

They didn't use the siren or lights as they sped through the city. The strategy was to surround and isolate the offender's vehicle before they even knew they'd been found, then stop it and engage the offenders in a controlled environment.

MacRae spoke. 'I'd forgotten what it was like on patrol.'

Ryan nodded. 'I love the streets. I don't think I'll ever be suited to a desk job.'

MacRae took in the interior of the patrol car. It looked like an aircraft cockpit. A lot had changed since his days in the force. There was so much technology now for communication and law enforcement.

Ryan followed MacRae's eyes. 'Yeah we've got a lot of assistance now, certainly makes things easier.' He flicked his head down to under the seat. 'And when we need it, we've got the firepower.'

MacRae nodded. 'What do they give you?'

Ryan swept the road at an intersection, before accelerating hard into a right turn into the traffic flow.

'It depends where you're assigned, and what you prefer to use. You can get assault rifles, but my preference is a pump action shotgun. I want to just point it in the right direction and know it's gonna stop the bad guys, know what I mean?'

MacRae knew exactly what he meant. The path he'd chosen in life had meant he had to make those kind of choices far too often.

'I really appreciate you giving me the chance to help to find my wife.'

Ryan shrugged. 'Maybe you'd do the same if our situation was reversed.'

Ryan wasn't totally sure why he'd let MacRae come along, and the phone conversation he'd just overheard asking for protection for the girl and a safe house had been deeply concerning. There was a whole lot more to this than he was letting on.

The radio crackled into life.

'All units in the vicinity of Roma and Huston, suspect van involved in the carjacking has been sighted heading south. Identify and follow, but do not intercept.'

The radio operator followed up with a detailed vehicle description, including the smashed rear corner, and registration.

Ryan checked his GPS then spoke into his microphone. 'We're only a few minutes away, re-routing to intercept at Roma.'

He spun the wheel, sending the patrol car screaming around a corner and accelerated hard. MacRae relaxed back into the seat, checking his seat belt tension as Ryan expertly weaved the car through the city traffic.

Then the radio erupted in chaos, voices of officers and the dispatch room tumbling over the top of each other.

'…truck has been positively identified, but I think they've spotted us.'

'Copy that. Fall back and keep in sight. Do not engage.'

'…suspect vehicle has left Roma, turning left at high speed. In pursuit.'

MacRae and Ryan listened to the radio calls, the sound of sirens wailing in the background. Then a chilling call from the pursuing cars.

'…the van has mounted the footpath, colliding with pedestrians…'

'…multiple casualties…'

'…my God they're killing people…'

'…set up roadblock at…'

'…all vehicles converge on…'

Ryan swung the wheel again, sending the patrol car skidding down a side street, before crossing a main road at full speed, darting between the cars, then diving into another narrow laneway.

'This should take us almost to them.'

He turned left at the end, just in time to see the van disappear into a driveway a hundred metres ahead, a patrol car hot on its tail, lights flashing and siren screaming.

'Now we've got them.'

MacRae's heart leapt as he imagined Marion being thrown around the back of the van during the chase, and the risk to her as a hostage if the kidnappers were cornered.

Ryan called their location into the radio as he drove, accelerating into the driveway to close the distance, then entering straight into the gloom of an old warehouse, needles of light spearing to the ground from the rusted steel sheet roofing.

The drop in visibility caused Ryan to brake hard...just before he hit the rear of the first patrol car.

It took a moment for MacRae and Ryan to take in the mayhem in front of them. Muzzle flashes from weapons lit up the warehouse as two police officers engaged the gunmen. He could see the officers hugging opposite walls, firing their pistols as they tried to flank them. MacRae counted at least three separate muzzle flashes from the far end of the warehouse, but these were from assault rifles, the gunshots echoing around the cavernous space as dozens of rounds searched for their targets. MacRae saw the officer to their left jerk to the side and fall to the ground as he was hit.

The gunmen saw their chance and advanced towards the patrol cars, crouching low and firing in short bursts at the other officer, chunks of the concrete wall next to him bursting into the air until he also fell. Then they turned to MacRae and Ryan's car.

Ryan unclipped his seat belt and drew his pistol, snapping at MacRae. 'Stay here until backup comes...'

Then he was out of the car and running...straight into a spray of bullets and stumbling a few more steps before crashing to the rough concrete floor.

The gunmen turned their attention to MacRae in the car, his eyes meeting the cold eyes of the killers. He felt rather than saw their muzzle flashes as they unleashed their weapons at the car, high velocity rounds peppering the front of the vehicle, splinters of glass spraying the interior as the windscreen and windows shattered around MacRae. But they fell harmlessly on his back as he was lying flat on the front seats, reaching down then fingers wrapping around the familiar shape of a combat shotgun.

He brought it up to his waist and worked the action, confirming a shell in the breech, and waited. Then it came, the brief silence as the gunmen paused to either reload or check their handiwork.

Now it was his turn.

A hard kick flung the door at his feet open, the sound distracting the gunmen for a vital second...as MacRae flung himself out of the opposite door, lying prone on the ground at the feet of two gunmen who were looking in the wrong direction.

He swung the weapon around and pulled the trigger, discharging the shotgun at close range into the closest man, killing him instantly, his assault rifle spinning away to one side. MacRae tried to line up the second gunman, but he was too close and too fast, his boot kicking the shotgun out of MacRae's grip.

The gunman swivelled on his heels to train his assault rifle on MacRae and fired, but MacRae had already moved, swinging his legs and leaping to his feet, the bullets punching chips out of the concrete floor harmlessly.

Ten metres away another gunman tried to get a clear shot, but MacRae kept moving, making sure the two gunmen were aligned. Then he charged at the closest man, feigning to one side then darting in close and swinging a hook punch to the centre of his face. The man's gun became a liability as MacRae was too close and had both his hands free, throwing a flurry of punches. The gunman staggered back, blood streaming from his face but MacRae followed with one last punch, a brutal hook to the man's temple, felling him instantly.

But now MacRae's cover was gone and the other gunman had a clear shot. MacRae was too far away to tackle him. The gunman fired from the hip, spraying bullets in an arc, the *zing* of a bullet frighteningly close to MacRae's ear.

MacRae dived into a roll, coming up at the left side wall, then sprinting for the van at the rear of the warehouse, the sound of the assault rifle firing close behind him. A pull at his jacket from a bullet brushing his skin then he was there...the van between him and the gunman. He listened for footsteps but there were none. Where the hell was the guy?

MacRae dropped to the floor and looked under the van, seeing the gunman's feet walking slowly around the other side of the van. MacRae sprinted the opposite way round the van, coming up on the man from behind. The gunman heard his footsteps at the last moment and swung his weapon around but MacRae was already on him, throwing a front kick hard into his back. The man slammed into the side of the van, his weapon dropping to the ground under the van. MacRae kicked him hard again, this time the gunman fell to his knees...before springing back up and lashing out sideways at MacRae with a combat knife.

The gunman took a moment to regain his breath, then went into a slight crouch, his left hand swaying in front of the knife to stop MacRae attacking it. MacRae partially turned to one side. He had nowhere to run, no weapon, and this guy seemed to know how to handle a blade. There was no room for error.

The two men circled each other, sizing each other up. MacRae bunched his jacket sleeve on his left arm and extended it out in front of him. This would be his shield, where he was choosing to be cut to give him the chance to win the fight.

The gunman leapt forward, slashing the knife quickly left to right in front of him as he closed the gap. MacRae jumped back, keeping his attacker at a distance. They circled again, this time the man steered MacRae back towards the van, then he leapt again. MacRae jumped back again, but this time slammed his back into the van. The knife slashed towards his throat, MacRae deflecting it to the side at the last moment with his wrapped sleeve. The razor-sharp blade flicked up pieces of cloth tinged with blood from MacRae's forearm.

The man sensed victory as he lined up MacRae again.

MacRae moved away from the van. And then he saw a narrow shaft of light across the room from a tattered hole in the wall sheeting. A slim chance, could it be enough?

He backed away from the man, drawing him nearer the brilliant sunlight, feeling it warm the back of his head. Then he taunted him.

'Come on motherfucker, give it your best shot.'

The man's lip curled as he flung himself forward again slashing the knife across in front of him, but not as focused as he'd been...and straight into the shaft of light, blinding him for a crucial second.

MacRae darted to one side, then used his jacketed sleeve to flick the knife hand sideways again, leaving the man exposed. MacRae stepped into the gap and pounded his palm repeatedly into the man's nose, eye sockets, and jaw, shattering his face. The knife clattered to the ground, followed by the man. MacRae wasted no time, finishing him with a swift kick to the jaw.

The warehouse was silent as MacRae retrieved the man's assault rifle from under the van and cautiously approached the rear doors, heart pumping with a mix of apprehension and excitement at seeing Marion again. He checked the gun was cocked, grasping the chromed door handle, and with a sharp twist pulled the doors open.

Nothing. The van was empty, except for smears of blood on the floor.

MacRae ran back to the unconscious man, slapping his face until his eyes flickered open.

'Where's the woman?'

The man mumbled a few words, eyes slowly closing again.

MacRae found a pressure point in his elbow and pressed hard. The man's eyes shot open again and he yelled with pain.

MacRae repeated the question, this time pressing the barrel of the gun into the man's forehead. 'Where's the woman? Or shall I kill you now?'

The man glared at MacRae defiantly, then shrugged, spitting blood on the ground. 'She's gone.'

MacRae pressed the barrel harder into his forehead. 'What do you mean? She escaped?'

The man grinned at MacRae. 'She was never here. We dropped her and the Russian in a side street before the police found us.'

He coughed blood. 'You'll never find them now.'

MacRae's heart sank. The Russian again. But now he was more determined than ever to end this.

A punch to the jaw sent the man back to sleep. MacRae stood, assault rifle by his side. What now?

336

The warmth of his blood trickling down his hand drew his attention back to his own injuries. The burning pain of his wound from the slashing knife pushing back through the dropping adrenaline levels. He gently pulled back the thickly wrapped jacket from his arm, grimacing as he saw the long, but thankfully shallow wound, then re-wrapped the jacket back over his arm. He needed to get it cleaned and dressed.

A moan drifted through the air. MacRae followed the sound back to the patrol car, finger on the trigger of the assault rifle. Then he relaxed. Officer Ryan was alive and struggling to sit up.

MacRae knelt by his side and started to check him for injuries, his hands gently probing the blood soaked clothing, finding multiple bullet entry holes in his trousers. Ryan's eyes cleared, focusing on MacRae's as he tried to speak, but the effort was too much. MacRae moved in close to hear, not noticing the three patrol cars approaching them slowly in the gloom.

MacRae patted his shoulder, and turned to get up. 'Wait here mate, you're going to be alright. I'll call the cavalry.'

The front car turned on its headlights, dazzling MacRae as he stood over Ryan, assault rifle in his hand.

Officers jumped out, weapons levelled at MacRae, voices yelling over each other.

'Put the weapon down...get on your knees...move and I'll shoot...'

MacRae slowly knelt, placing the gun gently next to him on the ground. An officer ran up, taking in the scene, the bodies of the gunmen and police across the floor.

'You son of a bitch.' He planted his boot in MacRae's back, sending him sprawling on the ground, before kneeling on his spine, pulling his arms back to handcuff him.

Then he pressed his pistol in the back of MacRae's head.

'I should end you now.' His finger tightened on the trigger, until a voice cried out.

It was Ryan, weak at first, then stronger. 'No, he's with us.'

MacRae breathed a sigh of relief as the gun was taken off his head and he was allowed to stand.

~

The room was silent save for the gentle rhythm of his breathing as MacRae dozed. He snapped awake, instantly alert as the door to the police interview room opened. It took a moment to orientate himself, then it came back to him. He glanced at his watch. Fourteen hours since he'd been escorted to the police headquarters to *'assist with their enquiries'* into the incident the day before.

To be fair he'd been looked after as well as could be expected considering he wasn't under arrest, and being ex-police himself he knew what had to be done. But there had been no news of Marion or the man or men that had been dropped off from the van before it'd been cornered, and he knew that in this situation every minute counted if there was a chance of finding her alive.

A weary looking middle-aged man placed a tray of coffee and pastries on the table between MacRae and himself. He opened a grey folder and pulled out a sheaf of printed documents. MacRae recognised the text as his statement, detailing as much of the events as he felt he could reveal without making things more complicated.

As far as the police were aware this was simply an abduction attempt gone violently wrong, and that's how they'd pursue it. MacRae had seen the looks between investigating officers when they'd questioned him, particularly regarding his association with the US government and Brad Schneider. But they seemed to accept that was because Marion was involved in international aid projects.

MacRae's stomach growled. He chose a croissant, tearing a piece off to dip in his coffee before eating it. Damn it was good.

'Well Mr MacRae, this is the last of it.' The man slid a pen and sheet with a dotted line at the base. 'If you can just sign your statement here you're free to go.'

MacRae spoke as he scrawled his name then pushed the paper back to the man.

'How's Officer Ryan...and the other officers?'

The man slid the paper back into the folder, toying with the pen for a moment before answering.

'He's had surgery overnight but it looks like he's doing okay now.'

MacRae nodded. 'Glad to hear it. Your officers were very brave.'

The man shrugged. 'Yeah, the others were brave but not so lucky. They didn't make it.'

'Sorry to hear it.' MacRae murmured.

The man scooped up the paperwork and stood, waving MacRae to the door.

'Oh, and Officer Ryan's asked me to personally thank you. He said you're the only reason those guys didn't finish him off.'

MacRae followed the man back through the building and through security to the front entrance, glad to be in the throng of the city coming back to life on a work day, the morning sun warm and welcome on his skin.

MacRae tried one last time, hopeful that there would be something.

'Any developments on the men that left the van before we caught up with it, or Marion's whereabouts?'

'We're chasing all the leads up, but there's nothing new so far.' He extended his hand to MacRae. 'We'll be in touch. And Officer Ryan said anytime you're back here he'd love to buy you a beer, and introduce the Aussie who saved his life to his family.'

MacRae smiled. 'I might just take him up on that.'

~

MacRae watched as the man went back into the building, then headed across the road to a diner and took a seat at a booth in the corner, out of earshot of the other customers. He ordered a coffee from a cheerful server in a neat black and white uniform, then called Schneider.

'I've been expecting your call.' Schneider's voice was calm and professional. Just what MacRae needed when he thought about Marion.

Two cups of thick black coffee loaded with sugar later and the men had debriefed. Schneider was true to his word and Hassana was well and truly in the murky world of witness protection. He'd pulled a few strings, and eventually questions would be asked about who she was and why the CIA was babysitting her, but for the moment both Schneider and MacRae were sure she was beyond the reach of Crane.

When it came to Marion though, the news was more bleak. The police were following their procedures but there were few leads to follow up.

Schneider pressed MacRae. 'So you're one hundred percent sure it was Crane that took her?'

MacRae tried to keep his voice calm. 'He's been all over me since I came to the US, and when I confronted him he more or less told me it was happening.' He glanced around. A server walking past with a stack of dirty plates gave him a curious look, then went to the kitchen.

MacRae continued. 'The primary target was no doubt Hassana because of her value to his research programs, but I'm sure he wanted Marion as leverage against me.'

There was silence on the other end.

'Listen Brad, I know it's all circumstantial, everything I've told you. I know I can't prove anything but in two days he's going to be in India as an invited guest for the official opening of the most significant health improvement project in India's history. And when he does he's going to commit the biggest genocide ever by wiping the population of India from the face of the planet.'

MacRae heard Schneider working on a keyboard, then he spoke.

'I believe you Ian. But we both know we haven't got enough to convince anyone about this...anyone that can do anything about it at least.'

MacRae waved the waiter back over and ordered more coffee. The diner was filling up, mostly office workers getting an early breakfast, a couple of families with kids tucking into the house special hotcakes, piled high and dripping with molasses and ice-cream, happily oblivious to the frightening reality of the world they lived in.

'So Brad, what have you got that might help me? Do you have any idea where I can find Crane now?'

'Well you're not going to like this, but it's all I've got. I've been keeping tabs on the flight plans logged for Crane's corporate jet, and just got the latest ones sent through.'

'And...' MacRae said.

'The flight plans take him from the US to Delhi, getting him there a day before the official opening ceremony.'

Schneider paused, then continued. 'The flight plan included a number of additional passengers. They're recorded as a female being transported with a medical condition, and a male personal assistant to Mr Crane.'

'Yes,' MacRae exclaimed. 'We've got him. Can the flight be delayed?'

His heart sank as Schneider replied.

'I'm sorry Ian...the plane departed three hours ago.'

MacRae drummed his fingers on the side of his cup, then his decision was made.

'Looks like I'm going to India then doesn't it?'

~

The elevator door opened with a soft *ping* as it stopped on the eighth floor of the apartment building. The Russian was uncomfortable in the slightly too small AirEx Delivery jacket, but it was the best he could do on short notice to get past the building security. No one bothered to check delivery workers now half the world's commerce was online. He was about to step out when a man stepped in next to him and pressed the button marked *Lobby*.

Jake Welsh was feeling a lot better about life since he'd compiled and sent the files to that conspiracy theory guy. Although he'd probably never know if anything came of it, he felt his conscience was clearer now, and was going to make some, no, lots of changes in his life now. It was time to stop living miserably for the sake of money. That's why was he was going to sit in on the travel forum tonight to hear about crewing on sail boats around the Caribbean. An adventure could be just the fresh start he needed.

The Russian recognised Welsh as the door slid shut again. Damn, he was going out.

The Russian reached across and hit the emergency stop button as the elevator started to descend, bringing it to a shuddering halt.

'What the...' was all Jake Welsh managed to say before the Russian tossed the empty package to him, Welsh catching it instinctively, at the same time as the Russian fastened both hands around his neck, cutting off the supply of blood and oxygen to his brain. For Jake Welsh it was a surprisingly short journey into unconsciousness.

The Russian sent the elevator back to the eight floor, checked the corridor was empty and carried Welsh back into his apartment. No alarms had gone off in the elevator so the Russian took his time to finish what he had started, by strangling Welsh with his dressing gown chord, and then looping it around the top of the bathroom door. There would be an investigation of course, but this type of death had gained enough publicity nowadays that the authorities would most likely write it off as another suicide.

He spent the next ten minutes searching the apartment for anything that might lead to Crane, then checking that everything looked more or less as it should, locked the apartment on the way out, and headed directly to the airport for his flight to catch up with Crane in India.

CHAPTER 33

BOOM

MacRae stood patiently in the line at the non-resident immigration counter at Delhi Airport, then he was next, smiling and chatting to the serious looking official carefully scrutinising his passport and the sheets of visa documents he'd printed out the day before.

Normally a procedure that took weeks to assess, he'd asked a lot of favours, and spent a lot of money ensuring he could get into the country within twenty four hours, because he was sure that was all the time he had to find Marion and stop Crane.

MacRae had worked in the murky world of private security for a long time, and basically pretty much anything could be arranged if you knew the right people and had enough money. Fortunately for him at this point, the world was a dangerous place and his professional expertise was in high demand, so his business was booming and money wasn't a problem. The nature of his business also meant that many of the things that would raise eyebrows with officials in different countries were almost seen to be expected from him in his line of work.

However there was always the chance that someone had slipped up when forging his approved visa application and ensuring everything would stand up to scrutiny. MacRae didn't relish the prospect of being deported, or possibly arrested and thrown at the mercy of the Indian legal system, when every minute counted.

He realised his mind was wandering and the official was holding out his passport to him and waving him through the gate. MacRae nodded and thanked him. A final security check as he left the airport with his bags and he was into the heat and organised chaos of India, made all the more chaotic by the mass movement of the population heading home, crammed onto the already crowded buses and trains for possibly hundreds of kilometres to celebrate Diwali.

India gave little time for acclimatising to the culture, and after a vigorous negotiation with a taxi driver who promised to look after him like a son and take him to the best hotel, the best restaurant, and find him the best women in Delhi, MacRae persuaded him that all he needed was a fast trip to his hotel.

The room was clean and modern, and being on the seventh floor had a great view. He cranked up the air-conditioning and took a cold shower to wash away the grime of the travel. A quick call to reception and a light lunch of bread and dips with coffee was sent up. He inserted the Indian phone company SIM he'd bought at the airport into his phone, then got down to business, calling up local contacts in the security world. He was going to need on-ground resources very quickly, some of them legal, some of them definitely not. This was a risky game...when you crossed this line you could never be quite sure who you could trust.

It was early evening before he was satisfied he'd done what he could for the moment. He'd tried to stay objective when planning and making the calls and arrangements, but he couldn't forget that this was personal. Marion's life depended on it, and he had a score to settle with Crane and the Russian for LaBruge.

He headed down to the hotel bar overlooking a small pool surrounded by palm trees, and ordered a beer and a variety of curries for an early dinner. He relaxed as the alcohol coursed through him. The bar was getting busy, mostly businessmen. Cricket played on a screen at the back of the room, and lanterns representing the Festival of Lights flickered on shelves behind the bar. A couple of unaccompanied women at a table chatted and laughed over their cocktails, seemingly oblivious to the curious looks of many of the male patrons. To MacRae the bar seemed like a haven from the frantic pace of life outside the hotel, the only hint of reality the constant noise of vehicle horns drifting over the hotel walls.

MacRae mentally worked through his plan, such as it was.

It had taken a couple of phone calls to journalists to confirm the location for the commissioning ceremony for the new water treatment plant that would service Delhi, and MacRae had guessed right when he'd assumed there would be a practice run the day before. He'd then arranged for a small local security firm to watch out for Crane arriving and leaving the practice session, sending them a recent media photo for ID, and instructions to follow Crane unobserved back to where he was staying. They were then to report back to MacRae.

The rest was a bit more complicated and apparently had to be arranged in person. His phone pinged. His ride was out the front of the hotel.

~

The stony silence of the driver of the black SUV was in marked contrast to the exuberant friendliness of the hotel reception staff MacRae was used to, and he felt a pang of unease as the car abruptly turned off the crowded main road and started twisting down the maze of streets and alleys as they headed to the edge of the city. A blindfold would have been unnecessary as within minutes he was hopelessly lost. He checked his phone, the signal dropping in and out as they drove, and the GPS bore no resemblance to the streets they were taking anyway.

Men and women wandered the streets, eating at open cafes and food stalls along both sides. Cows wandered along the road amongst the traffic, and scrawny dogs loped along the broken footpaths looked for a shady spot to sleep.

The car slowed at a tall wooden gate, then squeezed between stone walls and into a courtyard. The gates were closed by a couple of young men, then MacRae was out of the air conditioned comfort of the car and being directed to sit opposite a well-built man in a suit in the shade of a concrete veranda. He was smiling but even in the shade MacRae could see his eyes were cold, perhaps even cruel.

'Tea?' The man poured two cups of a steaming brew, the scent of spices drifting up. His hands caught MacRae's attention, both bearing scars from old injuries.

MacRae smiled and took the ornate china cup. 'Thank you.'

The man sipped the drink, savouring the flavours before continuing.

'I understand you have requested some rather unusual items and services. Not the things we would normally expect from a tourist in our country.'

MacRae sized the man up. On the surface he looked like one of the countless successful businessmen forging ahead in the dynamic economy of India. But the security contacts who had arranged the introduction for MacRae had advised him to not be deceived by his looks, and tread very carefully. He had risen from poverty in the slums by sheer force of will, and although he could put his hands on pretty much anything for a price, his loyalty was given strictly to the highest bidder, whether that was the police, politicians, or rival criminal gangs.

'No, my needs are a little unique. But I have an important job to finish here, and I'm happy to compensate you as you see fit.'

The man sat back, pondering MacRae's words. He looked him up and down, then focused on the hardness in MacRae's eyes.

'You come highly recommended, so I'll give you the resources you need. I don't want to know what you're planning, but if you interfere with anything in my jurisdiction your life will be mine. Do we understand each other?'

MacRae extended his hand. 'I greatly appreciate your kindness and generosity.'

The men shook on the deal and negotiated the use of a vehicle and driver. Then MacRae was taken into the sparsely furnished house to select his weapons.

~

Sun streaming through the curtains woke MacRae early the next morning. He checked his phone. No messages or missed calls.

He felt sluggish, the change in time zone knocking him around. He stretched his arms, arched his back, then dropped to the floor and started counting the push-ups out loud, changing hand position with every tenth one to exercise different muscles.

Finally he grunted, 'Fifty,' and jumped to his feet.

His pulse was racing as he expected. Why didn't push-ups ever seem to get any easier?

He took a quick shower before going to the hotel dining room for breakfast. He ate heartily, a mixture of European and Indian dishes, and pondered how to fill the morning. The practice for the opening ceremony wasn't for another couple of hours and he hated waiting around, so he headed out for a walk...always the best way to experience somewhere different. That certainly described India.

The streets were buzzing with activity as he wandered...but then in Delhi, they were pretty much twenty four hours a day. The aroma of food cooking at dozens of open food stalls drifted through the air, and street hawkers and beggars vied for his attention. His skin colour was not common in this part of town, and that usually meant a tourist or businessman with money.

The hours passed quickly, then, as he was admiring yet another ornate and beautiful shrine by the side of the road, his phone rang.

He listened intently as the security company manager reported the morning's activities in English with a strong Indian accent. MacRae was right, Crane had attended the opening ceremony practice, staying for around half an hour at the glistening new water treatment facility.

The security company described in great detail how their operative had observed unseen from the roadside, despite the high levels of security, particularly when the government minister responsible for the opening ceremony had arrived with his personal security escort. Then they'd discreetly followed Crane for almost an hour through the countryside back to his villa in a gated compound on the edge of the city.

MacRae asked for a detailed report to be sent via email, giving the accurate location of the compound, the route they took, how long to the various landmarks along the way. Finally he asked if the security firm could keep Crane under observation and advise when he left the compound the next day for the opening ceremony.

He was about to end the call when the manager offered him a couple of additional and unexpected services.

'Would you like to purchase video footage of the compound from above? We have a drone available for your use at a small additional cost if you require it.'

MacRae negotiated the fee and described what would be helpful. The manager assured him that the drone would be at a sufficient height to be unobserved.

The manager spoke again. 'And would it be helpful for you to drive the route your subject of interest took this morning? I can arrange for my operative to pick you up within the hour.'

MacRae didn't hesitate.

'That would be extremely helpful.'

Now things were coming together he allowed himself to think that perhaps there was a chance this could succeed and he just might find Marion and stop Crane.

~

The heat and humidity was passing its peak as the afternoon drifted by. It had taken a couple of hours for MacRae's driver to retrace the route taken by Crane earlier that day, starting near his gated compound.

They'd driven the country road past the front of the property twice, taking care to not draw attention to themselves. MacRae had no doubt there would be various security and surveillance measures in place to watch for unwelcome visitors. To the casual observer the masonry front boundary wall and steel double gates looked no different to most of the other large properties appearing unexpectedly throughout the countryside, grand gestures to a promise of wealth to come, but the tired paint and crumbling mortar in places hinting that maybe the vision was greater than the reality.

But MacRae noticed the details that mattered...the steel work of the gates was thicker than you might expect, the fresh grease on the hinges and runners showing regular maintenance, hidden surveillance cameras strategically placed along the wall, and the lack of vegetation near the inside of the walls suggested clear zones for observation. This was what he'd expected to see in a hardened compound, and he couldn't shake the feeling that perhaps he was only a few hundred metres from Marion.

MacRae pushed the thought from his mind. For this to work he needed to be totally focused and dispassionate. This was simply an operation he had to execute perfectly, because one way or another he knew he'd only get one shot at it.

His driver had kept a respectful silence, only responding when MacRae had asked to stop in a couple of locations, or queried him about the traffic conditions at different times of the day, noting that traffic would be hard to predict with community feasts and parades in the streets to be expected for Diwali. Everywhere they went MacRae assessed the route for opportunities and risks, making mental notes and planning how he might execute his plan, such as it was. By the time they'd reached the water treatment plant, MacRae had prioritised the locations and was satisfied that he'd done what he could to prepare under the circumstances.

MacRae had a few more questions for the driver, then they headed back to the hotel, MacRae marvelling as they weaved through the traffic, surrounded by the constant honking of vehicle horns. At one point MacRae found himself smiling at the wide-eyed face of a baby half a metre away from his window, strapped to the back of her mother as she sat perched side-saddle on the back of a motorcycle behind another child and their father.

Then they were back outside the hotel. The driver waited patiently while MacRae extracted a handful of tattered notes from his wallet, his eyes widening in appreciation as he realised the tip was a week's wages. MacRae knew that what to him was a couple of nice meals out back at home would feed this man and probably his extended family for a week.

MacRae took a moment to relax in the refreshing air conditioning of his room, stripping off his shirt and shoes before he laid back on the bed. He grabbed the TV remote control and scrolled through the channels, pausing to watch a couple of star crossed lovers in traditional Indian clothes dancing around each on the side of a hill and declaring their love for each other in song, whilst Bollywood dance music pumped rhythmically in the background. He drifted into the entertainment, letting himself get caught up with the innocent romance of the movie, an escape for him just as it was for many of the Indian population whose lives were a much harsher reality than the colourful playfulness being played out on film.

Another ping on his phone he snapped back to the present. It was a text message from the security company with a link to a cloud account for the video of Crane's compound shot from the drone.

MacRae took his time poring over the clip. They'd done a great job, with every detail of the compound and it's surrounds picked up from various angles.

From above, the building was basically a huge cube. It looked like it was hewn from a solid block of concrete, except for the architectural touches of steel and timber along the edges and what appeared to be the fittings and pipes for the building's services. The first thing that came to MacRae's mind was that it looked like a huge military bunker. There was a main entry facing along the concrete driveway, and high level windows faced the other three sides. Huge folding glass doors opened out to a courtyard featuring a kidney shaped swimming pool and hot tub.

MacRae went back to the zoomed-in shots from above, looking intently at the lines along the edge of the building. Were they gutters? He referred back to the lower angles of the walls, noting where things aligned, and then it clicked. The structure was built like a Chinese puzzle. The exterior surfaces were designed to move, sliding over each other to cover up the windows and doors, making the entire structure a smooth and impenetrable monolith.

MacRae sat back on the bed. This was some pretty serious technology, and the only way to gain entry would be by invitation. He smiled grimly. That was fine with him, because tomorrow Crane was going to invite him in whether he wanted to or not.

~

MacRae rose early again the next morning, this time feeling a little better as his body adjusted to the time zone, and he'd slept soundly. He followed the same routine as the previous day, exercise, shower then breakfast in the hotel restaurant, the pattern of discipline helping to reduce the tension he could feel rising in him.

It was a surreal feeling eating breakfast surrounded by so many people oblivious to what could befall the country if MacRae was right about Crane and couldn't stop him. The restaurant was decorated with the traditional lights and flowers of Diwali and everyone was simply focused on the celebrations that were getting underway, and where they would spend them, many people planning last minute trips back to family across the country.

But for MacRae today was the only day that mattered. He had moments of doubt about what he was planning. Had he misread the events that had led him here? Was the commissioning of the water treatment plants actually just a huge humanitarian gesture for a wealthy and successful benefactor? Even if it wasn't, how could MacRae, one man, stop the chain of events that were about to be put in motion? Then there was Marion. Perhaps he was just following a hunch and she was still being held somewhere back in the US? Perhaps she was already dead.

His logical mind kicked back in. This was far more than just an educated guess. He always trusted his intuition and it had held him in good stead. This time was no different. One way or another he was going to stop Crane, and do everything he could to find Marion, no matter what the cost.

He checked his phone. No messages yet. It was still early so he took the local speciality coffee, a sweet milky brew known as filter coffee, out to the pool deck, choosing a table in the shade as the heat started to rise for the day.

He could see a TV inside the restaurant crossing between a local soap opera and news bulletins. The opening ceremony for the water treatment plants across the country was big news, even during a festival period such as Diwali. Then the first of the messages came through. Crane was on the move, just as MacRae had expected. He checked the time just as a second text came through. His transport was waiting for him in a side street just around from the hotel. A last mouthful of coffee and MacRae left the hotel, squinting as he walked through the bright morning sun. The streets were already busy and he was conscious of the stares of the locals as he headed into the side street.

A man waved to him from a driveway. It was the same driver that had taken him to make his arrangements yesterday, although today there was no sleek black SUV. Today's transport was a slightly dirty but otherwise nondescript white van.

The man seemed a little friendlier this time, nodding a greeting to MacRae. They climbed in the van, and with a quick glance to the side the driver thrust them out into the traffic. MacRae looked over the driver, wondering quite what his instructions would have been. The man was the same height as MacRae, around 180 centimetres, but slightly more heavily built, probably lifted weights, MacRae guessed. He had short cut jet-black hair and was wearing jeans and a short sleeved shirt. He certainly gave the impression he could look after himself.

MacRae had considered driving himself, but quickly realised that negotiating Indian traffic would've added an additional layer of risk in an already very risky plan.

The driver saw MacRae summing him up and spoke.

'So where are we going?'

'Just head east, out of the city. We're going to intercept another car so I'll update the directions as we go okay?'

The driver shrugged. 'Sure.'

He flicked his head towards the rear of the van.

'The items you ordered are in the back. You can check them out while we drive if you like.'

MacRae unbuckled his seat belt and clambered between the seats to the cargo area. A large crate was strapped to the side wall.

MacRae braced himself against the crate as they negotiated a roundabout, then undid two latches and swung the lid open.

A smile creased his face as he scanned over the items inside, mentally ticking them off one by one. The choice was a little more limited here than say the US, but it would suffice.

He took out a polished brand new AK-203 assault rifle with a folding stock, balancing the weight in his hands, then working the action. He opened a box of bullets, filling the magazine and working a round into the breech, before flicking on the safety.

MacRae called to the driver. 'Do you know what's back here?'

'Sure, I helped pack it,' the driver replied.

'How the hell did you get one of the Indian Army's newest assault rifles?'

The driver laughed. 'In India everyone knows someone. That's just how it works.'

He quickly worked through the rest of the crate, checking the Sig Sauer P229 Legion Compact nine millimetre pistol, and trying on the body armour for fit. He tested the charge on the Tasers, then pulled out the two steel petrol cans, noting that one had a small piece of blue electrical tape around the handle as requested. He checked off the last items then closed the crate before rejoining the driver up front.

The driver spoke. 'Looks like you're planning a bit of a special Diwali celebration for someone?'

MacRae looked out the window. 'Sometimes there are things you just have to do.'

The driver grunted. 'In my world we do what we're paid to do. Nothing more, nothing less.'

MacRae noticed a packet of water bottles on the floor.

'May I?'

The driver nodded. 'Help yourself.'

MacRae emptied half a bottle then spoke.

'And you're being paid to drive today?'

'Just to drive. That's it.'

MacRae finished the water, crumpling the empty bottle and tossing it in the back.

'Well I'll let you know when your driving is finished, then I'll do the rest okay?'

'Sure,' the driver said as he slowed to negotiate a huge pothole in the road.

The two men lapsed into silence, apart for discussing the route as MacRae guided them to where he wanted to intercept Crane's vehicle.

The security company had sent through photos and a description of the car, and advised it appeared there was just Crane and his driver when the vehicle left the compound that morning.

MacRae had studied the photos carefully, and by the way the BMW rode, sitting low on the suspension, he had to assume the vehicle was armoured.

The landscape started to look familiar to MacRae as he recognised the route he been driven along yesterday. They were almost at the interception point. He directed the driver to head to the south another kilometre or so, then pull up next to a hedge on a side road. Crane should be passing by within a couple of minutes, it was just a matter of waiting.

He climbed back into the rear of the van to prepare, pulling on the body armour and filling the pockets with spare magazines for the guns, gaffer tape, handcuffs, cable ties. He tested the cigarette lighter, and recharged the Tasers.

He felt the familiar mix of tension and adrenaline as the moment of action approached. It was unsettling that despite the changes to how he lived as the years went by, he continued to find himself in situations not unlike those he'd sought to leave behind in his former life as a police officer and in counter terrorism operations across the world.

When he was satisfied he was fully prepared he clambered back into the front seat, placing the assault rifle on the floor in front of him and turned to speak to the driver.

'Okay, I'll take it from here.' He held out his hand to the driver. 'And thanks for your help today.'

The man didn't move. 'I think I know what you're planning to do with the van and this car you want to stop.'

He waved his arm at the busy road, the usual mix of cars, trucks, motorcycles, pedestrians and cows competing for road space. A flurry of explosions came from firecrackers igniting alongside the road as a group of revellers celebrating Diwali went by. A small crowd in colourful costumes danced to traditional music in a vacant space between shopfronts.

'You'll never do it by yourself. One mistake, anyone, or anything local gets hurt and you'll find yourself surrounded by an angry and unsympathetic mob. Not a good place to be for a foreigner.'

MacRae tapped his knee as he thought, then spoke.

'I have no choice. This is the one chance I'm going to get to prevent this guy from hurting a whole lot of people, and maybe I can rescue a friend of mine at the same time.'

The driver nodded his head. 'So you will pay me, and I will help you use this van to stop him okay?'

MacRae considered his options. He could refuse, maybe have a nasty disagreement, maybe even have to kill him. But then it might not be MacRae who won the fight in this confined space. He couldn't afford the risk.

'Okay, this is what I need to do...'

The men spent the next few minutes discussing MacRae's plan, the driver explaining the best chance he saw to make it succeed. Then they were ready, watching the world go by in a tense silence.

MacRae checked the time against the reconnaissance run he'd made the previous day. They were running out of time. Maybe Crane had taken another route? That would've made sense from a security point of view, but it would have introduced a variable into their schedule and MacRae was sure they wouldn't risk it.

The driver reached forward and started the engine.

'Here they come.'

MacRae reached down and retrieved the assault rifle and checked the action one last time.

A loud honking of a horn as Crane's BMW pushed its way past an overloaded truck in front of them and then they were off, MacRae's driver following from behind a mini-bus full of school children.

They shadowed the car for half a kilometre...another kilometre or so before they'd reach the interception point...when a truck swung in from a laneway between shops, grinding to a halt in front of their van to avoid hitting a cow, crates of vegetables tumbling on to the road next to them.

'Shit.' MacRae cursed. 'We can't lose them. Can you get around it?'

The driver grinned. 'No, but I can still get in front of the car before the interception point.'

He slammed the van into reverse, turning the van and darting up a side street, then onto a dirt path along the side of an industrial estate.

'They're too far ahead. We won't catch them,' MacRae said.

'I wouldn't give up just yet,' the driver said as he slammed the throttle to the floor.

MacRae was pushed back in his seat as the van rocketed forward.

'What the hell have you got in this thing?'

The driver chuckled. 'We might have upgraded the engine a little bit from what it originally came with. In our line of work a little bit more power never goes astray.'

He flicked a glance at MacRae. 'I love seeing the face of people who think this is just a delivery van...until it leaves them in a cloud of dust.'

MacRae settled in to enjoy the ride as best he could, the driver swerving around huge potholes and half-built storm drains along the roadside, until off to his left he saw the familiar layout of the interception point.

The driver swung off the dirt path and back onto the road, through another laneway and then pulling over on the footpath next to an electronics shop, the BMW coming into view two hundred metres away as it approached them.

MacRae unclipped his seat belt and checked his weapon, before turning to the driver.

'Last chance to change your mind. Are you sure you want to do this? I'm happy to do it by myself, and you can just walk away.'

The driver grinned, pulling a huge revolver from his belt and cocked it. 'I wouldn't miss it for the world.'

~

Magnus Crane was outwardly calm and relaxed in the rear seat as the BMW whisked him to his destination in an almost silent cocoon. The car thumped a little harder over the rough patches of road than you might expect, but that was due to the stiffer suspension required to cope with the weight of the armour plating hidden in the bodywork.

However, inside he was feeling the pressure. His was truly an appointment with destiny. Initially he would be portrayed as the greatest mass murderer in the history of mankind. But then over time, he would be given the recognition he deserved, as the man who gave an overwhelmed planet a chance to adapt and survive the effects of an exploding human population...albeit a population around one billion people less than it was a matter of months earlier.

Up front, the Russian was driving, negotiating the country roads in silence. Crane always felt secure with him around, that was why he kept him on despite his somewhat violent tendencies. And the fact that he sometimes overstepped the mark and challenged Crane's judgement. Like this morning when, according to *a feeling in his gut* as he'd described it, the Russian had suggested they take an alternate route to the commissioning ceremony.

Crane admitted it was a little unexpected that they'd heard nothing from MacRae since the incident at the hotel back in the US when his friend Marion had been taken. That hadn't been part of the plan. Hassana with her fascinating immunity to the devil cancer was the one of real value, but it had been better than nothing, and the threat of Marion coming to harm appeared to have had the desired result of keeping MacRae off his back whilst he finished his work.

Besides, Crane knew that if MacRae turned up he'd be no match for the Russian, so he'd firmly insisted they take the proven route as previously agreed. After all what's the purpose of a trial run if you then did something different?

For the first time in many days Crane allowed himself to relax and indulge in a daydream of the unfolding of the spread of an unstoppable, cleansing disease throughout the population of this hugely overpopulated nation. He didn't even see the white van as it came out of nowhere, charging through a gap in the crowds and traffic to collide with the front of the BMW, pushing it into an open storm water trench at the side of the road.

MacRae gritted his teeth and braced his hands against the van dashboard as the vehicles collided, watching with satisfaction as the BMW stopped with its front nestled in the bottom of the open drain. He hit the seat belt release and was out the van door in an instant, assault rifle in both hands as he ran to the BMW.

The front airbag had inflated, tangling the driver. MacRae couldn't see their face but they were obviously disorientated. He went to the side of the car where Crane was looking down, struggling to release his seat belt. Then he was free and looked up at MacRae. Crane's eyes widened in disbelief. How the fuck had MacRae done this? Then they narrowed in anger as he leaned forward and shook the driver's shoulder.

MacRae tapped the passenger window with the assault rifle barrel, motioning for Crane to get out. Crane ignored him, shaking the driver again until he stirred, leaning back in his seat and opening his eyes. Now MacRae recognised him. He felt his body tense. This man must be treated with great caution, but for the moment at least he wasn't a threat.

MacRae hit the passenger window again, this time with the butt of the rifle, testing the glass. It was tough as hell. Inside the car Crane smiled and took out his phone, dialling a number and waiting for it to answer.

MacRae knew he must act quickly before whoever Crane was calling responded. It didn't matter if it was the police or other security Crane had on tap, it would be trouble.

MacRae stepped back and collided with a local man. He saw the gun and rejoined the curious crowd...maybe twenty or thirty people so far...that had gathered when the cars had collided. MacRae knew this could get out of hand very quickly.

He flicked off the safety catch on the weapon, swung it to his shoulder and fired off half a dozen rounds into the other rear passenger window. The bullets gouged the armoured surface but didn't penetrate the glass. Inside the car Crane grinned as he spoke on the phone. In the front seat the Russian was coming back to life.

He saw MacRae and snarled, pulling an automatic pistol from his jacket and working the action as he talked to Crane. He went to exit the car, but Crane restrained him. Obviously he was expecting help to arrive soon.

MacRae heard the murmur of voices behind him. The crowd was getting restless as they watched the action. He raised the weapon again and loosed off another half dozen rounds into the air. The crowd stepped back. A couple of young men yelled at him in Hindi. He walked back over to the van, pulling open the side door and grabbed the two petrol cans, heading back to the BMW and jumping onto the hood.

Crane and the Russian looked at him curiously. MacRae stared back as he unscrewed the cap from the first can and splashed the contents over the roof of the car, trails of liquid spilling down the windows on all sides and onto the ground. MacRae didn't know whether Crane could smell the fumes inside the car, but just to make sure he got the message MacRae opened the second can and poured a litre of fuel over a pile of rubbish next to the car, and with a flick of his wrist lit a lighter, tossing it onto the rubbish. A soft *whoop* punched the air as the vapour erupted in flame. MacRae watched Crane carefully, noticing with satisfaction as his eyes widened in fear as he realised what MacRae was going to do.

MacRae caught movement in the corner of his eye and swung to his left. The crowd was moving forward again, a young man brandishing a thick stick like a club leading the way.

This was getting out of hand.

MacRae swung the weapon in their direction.

'Keep back and no-one will get hurt.'

The man screamed abuse at him again in Hindi and kept moving forward, breaking into a run, the crowd now doubled in size, following closely behind.

MacRae levelled the gun to aim just above them. Could he scare them off?

The boom of a handgun echoed from the side of the crowd.

The mob stopped in their tracks.

'Who wants to be the first to die?'

It was the driver of the van, towering over the mob from the top of the van, pistol swinging casually from person to person, stopping on the leader, aimed right between his eyes.

'Drop the stick and get back or I'll send you to join your ancestors.'

A murmur went through the crowd. The leader looked from MacRae to the driver, and realised he was looking at his own death if he moved forward again. A snarl escaped his lips and he threw the stick to the ground and stepped back.

MacRae smiled at the driver and nodded his head in thanks before focusing back on the task in hand. He lit another lighter, hovering it close to the car, then tapped the windscreen with the barrel of the assault rifle motioning again for Crane to get out. Crane's eyes shot pure hate at MacRae as he opened his car door and stepped out into the drain, his shoes sinking into a pond of stinking mud.

'Up here now and on your knees.' MacRae kept the weapon trained on Crane.

Crane scrambled up the side of the drain, shiny black shoes slipping in the mud, filthy water splashing on his immaculate business suit.

MacRae kept the gun trained between Crane and the Russian in the car as Crane approached him, stopping a metre away to stare defiantly in MacRae's face.

'On your knees and hands behind your back.' MacRae's voice dripped with menace.

Crane didn't move, the men locked in a battle of wills, then he slowly dropped to his knees and placed his hands behind his back.

MacRae darted behind him, whipping out a couple of cable ties and wrapping them around Crane's wrists and pulling them tight.

And that few seconds when MacRae was using both hands gave the Russian the opportunity he'd been waiting for. In an instant he was out of the front passenger door, keeping the car between him and MacRae.

MacRae heard the car door open and spun around to see the Russian jump up beside the car, pistol held out in a double-handed grip. MacRae cursed, and kicked out to push Crane over onto his side on the ground, then swung the assault rifle around at the Russian. He cursed again. There were people everywhere. He couldn't afford to hit anyone else.

The Russian had no such reservations and fired three rounds, the bullets a hair's breadth from MacRae's face as he twisted around. Now he had no choice, and aiming low fired a burst at the Russian, peppering the car with bullets, making him duck for cover.

A sound behind him and MacRae turned back to see Crane had jumped to his feet and was sprinting away from him.

He let the assault rifle go from one hand, plucked a Taser from his pocket, aimed it at Crane and fired. Crane was quick but the twin electrodes of the Taser were quicker, piercing through his trousers and hooking into his right leg to deliver a fifty thousand volt shock.

Crane froze for a second, shook violently, then collapsed to the dirt roadside.

MacRae dropped the Taser and turned back to the Russian knowing he was too late as the Russian had run around the car and had adopted a solid shooting stance, pulling the trigger another three times.

This time the rounds found their mark, punching into MacRae's chest, the hammer blow of each one knocking out his breath. But the ballistic vest under his shirt stopped their penetration. MacRae staggered three steps, fighting for breath as the Russian ran forward to finish the job.

MacRae struggled to lift his weapon, but the Russian was too quick, closing the distance between them in an instant. Another three booms punched the air as the van driver shot from the top of the van again. Two rounds flicked up the dirt, but the third caught the Russian in the back. He lost his footing and tripped, then knowing he was between two attackers, rolled to one side and sprinted into the crowd.

MacRae's breath came back. 'Did you see where he went?'

'I lost him in the crowd,' the driver replied.

MacRae glanced at his watch. He was running out of time, he'd have to let him go.

The crowd were moving forward again, undeterred by the gun shots.

MacRae called to the driver. 'I've got to go right now. Can you help me?'

'Sure.'

The driver jumped to the ground, waving his gun in the faces of the men at the front of the crowd, clearing a path back to the van for MacRae.

MacRae slung the assault rifle across his back and walked to Crane's prone figure, just as he struggled back to consciousness.

MacRae knelt beside him and slapped his face a couple of times, until Cranes eyes flickered open, confusion etched across his face.

MacRae unhooked the Taser electrodes, dragged him to his feet and spoke. 'Yes this is real, and you're coming with me.'

Crane stumbled to the van alongside MacRae, then MacRae bundled him in the side door and handcuffed him to a side rail.

MacRae slammed the door shut and turned to the driver, who was engaged in a yelling contest with the crowd. The gun making it quite clear who was in charge.

MacRae paused and listened. Sirens in the distance... and they were coming closer.

'Okay, I'm out of here. Are you coming?'

The driver grinned. 'No, I'll stay and keep the crowd under control, and maybe have a word with the police when they arrive, try and make sure they head in the wrong direction when they go looking for you.'

'Won't they arrest you?' MacRae asked.

'No-one's been hurt as far as they can see, and everything is open to negotiation out here.'

MacRae climbed into driver's seat and started the engine.

'Well if you're sure...'

'Besides,' added the driver, yelling above the crowd. 'I want to see if I can find our other friend in the crowd, before he finds you.'

MacRae put on his sunglasses. 'Good luck with that.'

He threw the van into gear, revved the engine and headed off along the road back to Crane's compound, his heart pounding at the thought of finding Marion.

The crowd stepped back as the van pulled away from them, losing their appetite for a fight, and focused their attention on the crashed BMW, swarming over the car to see what they could salvage.

The van driver grinned as they lost interest in him, and turned to await the arrival of the police. He didn't notice the man crouched down in the crowd as it brushed past, only seeing the hand extended with the pistol in the millisecond before the Russian shot him twice at point blank range.

~

It didn't take MacRae long to cover the distance to Crane's compound. He'd memorised the route description and landmarks he'd seen the previous day and the drive was uneventful, except for the stress of adapting to the intensity of the traffic on Indian roads, and avoiding the occasional cow lying contentedly in the middle of the road.

Crane had started the trip fighting his situation, yelling abuse at MacRae and kicking the side of the van, then threats, and trying to persuade him to let him go, before finally accepting that MacRae wasn't going to deviate from his path.

MacRae stopped the van at the front gates, and using the van to keep Crane hidden from prying eyes, dragged him over to the keypad entry lock. Crane typed in the code and stared at the eye scanner, then with a muted click the gates slid silently open.

MacRae bundled him back into the van, handcuffing him to the side wall again for the short trip down the drive to the house, the gates sliding silently closed behind them.

~

The Russian drove quickly but carefully down the same route as MacRae and Crane. The taxi wasn't the fastest car he could have chosen, but it was easy to obtain, the driver eagerly letting the westerner in, before just as easily being persuaded by the huge pistol the Russian had held to his head, to get out and let him drive off. The driver had no idea how lucky he had been to live, given the Russian's enjoyment of killing people.

The Russian had absolutely no doubt where they'd be heading, unlike the local police who'd bumble about searching the local area for Crane. And with what he planned to do to MacRae and the woman Marion, the Russian didn't want the police, or anyone else for that matter, anywhere nearby.

~

MacRae looked over the facade of the building as they approached. It was far bigger than it looked in the drone video footage, and MacRae noted the lines of the cladding that must slide across each other to cover the windows and doors, enclosing the structure in an impenetrable concrete layer. Just the thing for any forward thinking survivalist billionaire.

The driveway terminated in a turning circle wrapped around a grey granite Indian religious statue mounted as a fountain in a small pond. The trickling water flowing from the elephant god's trunk gave a calm and peaceful air to a place with a sinister purpose.

MacRae, assault rifle slung over his shoulder, followed as Crane walked to the front door and typed in another security code, then spoke into a wall mounted microphone. The voice identification system confirmed his password and Crane led the way into the cool air-conditioned interior.

MacRae scanned the layout as they passed through a spacious entry foyer. His eyes were drawn up, to where a slot in the ceiling concealing what appeared to be a wall.

Crane followed his eyes. 'It slides down to provide a hermetically sealed isolation and decontamination room.'

'Perfect protection in a biological war?' MacRae asked.

Crane shrugged.

The rest of this floor opened into a huge open plan space, kitchen area to one side and dining and living to the other. Partition walls at the back perhaps led to sleeping and bathroom areas?

A staircase curled up to another level above.

Crane turned to MacRae, hands still cuffed behind his back.

'Okay we're in. What now?'

MacRae checked his watch again. It was getting tight, fifteen minutes until the official commissioning of the water treatment plants, and then it would be too late for millions, perhaps a billion of the Indian people. He glanced around. There were TV screens on most walls.

'Turn these on. I want to see the live coverage of the commissioning ceremony.'

He recalled the security cameras he'd seen throughout the compound and building. 'And I want to see live vision of the compound security cameras.'

Crane twisted around, holding his cuffed hands out to MacRae. MacRae unlocked the cuffs and used his pocket knife to remove the cable ties. Crane rubbed his wrists then spoke instructions out loud.

'Turn on living area screens. Show live news channel on main screen, and scrolling security cameras on other screens.'

The voice recognition operated computer system silently followed the instructions, screens flashing into life.

MacRae watched as news readers discussed the pending opening ceremony, cutting between images of the city and countryside, then the government minister and his entourage entering the water treatment facility for the opening ceremony. A banner of text scrolled across the bottom of the screen, describing the statistics of how much the population would benefit from the amazing improvement to water infrastructure to be commissioned today.

MacRae noted there was no mention of Crane, the guest of honour, failing to arrive, and the panic that must be ensuing behind the scenes.

He waved Crane to a long white leather couch, keeping his hand on the butt of the pistol in his belt. The lush green gardens were a beautiful backdrop through the massive plate glass windows behind

Crane. The sense of serenity a contrast to the monster MacRae was threatening with the gun.

'You can probably guess why we're here can't you?'

Crane smiled. 'It's not hard with someone as predictable as you.'

'We'll see who's predictable won't we?' MacRae replied, sitting on the coffee table opposite Crane. 'So you understand there's only two things we need to achieve for you to stay alive?'

Crane sneered. 'Save the world and save your woman. The only question is which is more important to you?'

MacRae flicked the gun out with twist of his wrist and fired at Crane, the bullet tearing through the couch next to his shoulder.

Crane's face went white. 'You think you can frighten me?'

'Whether you're frightened or not doesn't concern me. Just know that I really don't care whether you live or die. The choice is yours. But the water treatment plants are not going to be commissioned, and I'm taking Marion back unharmed or you die here today, right now. That's all you need to understand.'

'And what if I think that what's about to happen, the single most significant human act ever to protect the planet and our species, is more important than my own survival?'

MacRae knew this question was coming. It always did with egomaniacs like Crane.

'I guess that's your choice. Are you really the champion prepared to die for a noble cause?' He leaned forward. 'Or are you just another self-interested psychopath who's prepared to risk anyone's life except their own?'

Crane spoke defiantly. 'What if I were to tell you that it doesn't matter what you do to me, I can't stop the commissioning of the plant? It's all been automated.'

He waved an arm at the screen, sneering at MacRae. 'Look at them. Do they seemed panicked because I'm not there? You think you can run around with your tough guy attitude and make things happen. Maybe it's worked in the past, but not this time. You're just going to have to sit here with me and watch the show.'

For a moment MacRae believed him. But then he leapt forward and whipped the butt of the pistol across Crane's face.

Crane fell sideways, spitting blood and teeth on the white leather.

MacRae's voice was expressionless. 'Everything I've learnt about you in the last few months leaves me with no doubt that you're obsessed with your own power and control over the destiny of others.' He sat back on the coffee table. 'So I have absolutely no doubt that you can control everything about the operation of this plant from wherever you are.'

Crane glared back at him, wiping blood from his mouth with the back of his hand.

'So now you answer me two questions, while you can still talk. Firstly, how do you stop the commissioning of the plants? And secondly, tell me where Marion is right now.'

MacRae casually pointed the gun at Crane's right kneecap.

'You can tell me before I destroy your body, one bullet at a time. Or you can wait until you're barely recognisable. Your choice, but we both know you'll tell me eventually. Isn't it better to live to fight another day?'

There was silence between the men, until MacRae lifted the gun to adjust his aim, finger tightening on the trigger.

Then Crane smiled, wincing with pain from his damaged teeth.

'Okay. Let's get this done.'

He stood then led MacRae across the room to a bench stretching along a side wall.

'Now what?' MacRae said.

Crane bent slightly and placed his right hand under the bench, stepping back as the patterned wall flashed into life as a monitor, and the section of bench illuminated as a touchscreen keyboard.

MacRae smiled. 'Impressive.'

Crane pulled out a stool from under the bench and sat, tapping away at the keyboard. 'This place is full of surprises.'

A complex series of control panels appeared on the monitor in front of them, Crane entering passwords as he went deeper and deeper into the system.

MacRae checked the time. Five minutes to go.

'You'd better get this right before the plants are commissioned, or this is where you will die, right here and now.'

Crane slowly shook his head. This wasn't the first time he'd been threatened with death, and he had no intention it would be the last.

MacRae stepped back and checked the other screens still playing live TV. The official opening seemed to be continuing without disruption. Surely Crane hadn't been telling the truth and they could proceed without him?

He looked to another screen with a news banner scrolling along the bottom. The text was all about the water treatment plant, and the vision above showed crowds of revellers parading through the street to celebrate Diwali. MacRae noted there was no mention of a kidnapping incident or a missing western businessman, although he felt sure the police would be ramping up their efforts to find Crane by now.

Crane's increasingly frenetic typing on the keyboard snapped MacRae away from the screens. Which is why he didn't notice the live security camera vision showing a crystal clear image of the Russian entering his security codes at the compound front gates.

'How's it going?' MacRae pressed the gun into Crane's back for emphasis.

Crane struggled to keep the tension out of his voice. 'I'm getting there okay? It's very complex to break through and overwrite the onsite automated control systems.'

'But you can do it?'

'Sure. As you said, I like to be in control.'

'So what happens when they press the button or cut the ribbon or whatever at the official ceremony?'

Crane chuckled. 'Well apart from being a bit surprised that nothing happens, they'll be flooded with messages on their control software saying that they've been hacked, and if they pay a ransom they'll get control back.'

'So a win-win for you then?'

'Let's just say I like to cover all the bases.'

Crane hit the enter key hard to emphasise progress and turned to MacRae.

'It's got to run some algorithms to coordinate the shut downs, then I'll finish it off.'

MacRae's eyes flicked from the program scrolling down the computer screen and Crane expressionless face.

'Don't you feel any sense of guilt about wanting to inflict death from facial cancer on countless innocent people?'

'Cancer?' Crane looked up wrinkling his brow, then he understood. 'You think I'm using the variant of the Tasmanian Devil facial tumour?'

Now MacRae was confused. 'Isn't what this is all about?'

Crane frowned. 'The facial tumour research was just a side project.' He leaned back, warming to the subject. 'Well, a pet project for Dr Edison really. I think she was hoping it would win favour with me actually.'

'I don't understand,' MacRae said.

'This kind of research into modifying diseases...'

'Gain of Function?'

'Yes,' Crane snapped at being interrupted. '...has been going on around the world by everyone for a long time. Discovering the devil facial tumour disease could infect humans was just luck. Good or bad luck depending on who you are.'

'It wasn't planned?'

'No,' Crane said. 'A scientist at the Merton working on trying to find a cure for the disease before the devils became extinct somehow got infected.'

'I can't recall seeing anything being reported about that,' MacRae said.

Crane shrugged. 'You wouldn't have. We made a deal with her before she died. She agreed to be our secret lab rat and in return her family got a big insurance payout and never had to deal with the way she was actually going to die.'

'Dr Khan? That whole story of her disappearing in a maritime accident was false?'

Crane shrugged. 'I think that was her name.'

'Her family had a right to know the truth.'

'Would it have made any difference?' Crane said.

'A lot to your reputation, and the Merton's obviously.'

Crane looked away.

'So then Edison worked on developing it?' MacRae said.

'Yes. She got the transmission rate for humans right up, very impressive work, and also was able to target it by ethnicity. And it had an almost one hundred percent mortality rate,' Crane's voice rose with excitement. 'It was extremely promising.'

'Until Hassana in the field trials in Nigeria,' MacRae said.

Crane nodded. 'The disease was useless unless it was totally lethal. And the results were skewed male to female. Early results indicated it was effective against males...'

'But it's the females you need to eliminate if you want to stop future breeding isn't it?' MacRae said.

Crane nodded. 'You're smarter than you look.'

'So if the facial tumour disease isn't suitable, what are...' MacRae corrected himself. '...were you putting into the Indian water supply?'

'Does it matter?' Crane said. He checked the progress of the algorithm then turned back to MacRae. 'It's actually just a simple variant of the tried and tested killer, the Spanish Flu, quite unexceptional really. So you stumbled across me because of Edison's pet project trial in Nigeria then? Ironic because her work has ended up providing extremely useful data in the control and treatment of cancer in humans.'

'Too late to help your daughter though,' MacRae said. 'It's different when it's someone close to you dying isn't it?

Crane's eyes blazed. 'Fuck you MacRae.'

MacRae smiled. Now Crane displayed emotion.

⁓

The front gates at the compound entry slid silently closed behind the Russian as he accelerated the taxi down the driveway to the house. He'd also been watching the time and knew MacRae would be inside doing his best to get Crane to stop the plant commissioning, and whilst his duty was to protect Crane and his interests, he was relishing the opportunity to kill MacRae and the woman. The house loomed up in front of him, the blank concrete wall increasing his sense of excitement. He slowed the car as he approached to minimise noise, and pulled off the driveway before he got to the house, parking behind a low bush.

A jolt of pain shot through his neck as he exited the car... whiplash from being run off the road by MacRae in the van. Yet another reason he wanted to watch MacRae die. He stretched it out then checked his gun. The magazine was full, so he worked the action and slipped off the safety.

He wished he'd had time or the opportunity to retrieve something more lethal from the crashed BMW than the 9mm automatic he was carrying. But the crowd had been getting out of control and he couldn't risk trying to get to the MP5 machine pistol in the trunk.

He checked the gun a final time as he approached the front entrance. Although he was totally confident in his abilities, he was smart enough to treat MacRae with respect.

Inside the building, MacRae trained the gun between Crane's eyes as he waited for the computer to finish it's algorithms.

'So now to the second question. Where's Marion?'

Crane grinned. 'About three metres below us.'

'What do you mean?'

'This place is fully protected above ground as I guess you already know. But there's another layer of security in a basement shelter, and amongst its other functions it includes facilities for restraining personnel if required.'

'So why did you go to the trouble of bringing her here to lock her up?' MacRae asked.

'Keep your friends close, but keep your enemies closer, as the old saying goes.' Crane glanced over MacRae's shoulder, suppressing a smile as he watched the Russian silently operate the entry security system.

'I figured I'd have more leverage over you if I had her with me. Besides with her knowledge of disease outbreaks in third world countries she might yet turn out to be useful in the pandemic to come.'

'You mean the pandemic we're stopping,' MacRae corrected him.

'Maybe not after all.' Crane smirked as the entrance door opened with an electronic swish and the Russian rushed into the house, firing three shots in quick succession at MacRae's back.

Not for the first time in his chosen career MacRae saved his life by acting on instinct, a sixth sense that he could never conjure up on demand, but had always been there when it mattered most. Subconsciously MacRae had seen Crane's eyes glance over his shoulder and for a fleeting moment a smile play at his lips. That's when MacRae had thrown himself sideways, rolling up from the floor into a crouch, gun in firing position and finger already pulling the trigger.

The Russian's gunshots echoed around the room as his first two bullets flashed past MacRae's rolling body and into the armoured windows behind Crane. Spiderwebs appeared in the glass in a tight pattern. By the time the Russian had pulled the trigger the third time he'd reacted and started to track MacRae as he moved, the third bullet striking the assault rifle still slung over MacRae's shoulder and ricocheting into MacRae's left forearm.

MacRae grunted as shattered pieces of bullet ripped through his flesh, a crimson stain spreading across his shirt sleeve.

Then it was the Russian's turn to dart for cover behind a dividing wall as MacRae's bullets whistled past his head.

MacRae didn't move, training his gun on the wall near the Russian, waiting for him to reappear, when he heard the sound of running behind him. He kept low and swivelled around to see Crane had run to the back of the room and opened a concealed door to an elevator. Crane flung himself inside and turned, grinning at MacRae as the door slid closed.

MacRae knew that he couldn't cover the distance to the elevator before the doors closed, taking Crane to the underground bunker and Marion.

MacRae glanced back. No sign of the Russian yet. He fired two quick shots in his direction to keep his head down, then as the door closed the last few centimetres MacRae pulled the assault rifle from his shoulder and flung it at the elevator.

Crane's face went from curiosity to anger as the rifle slid into the last of the gap in the elevator door. MacRae smiled. It seemed even private bunker elevator doors had pressure sensors to stop people being crushed as the door closed.

Crane leapt forward to dislodge the rifle but was too slow as the door bumped the weapon, pausing before sliding back open.

MacRae jumped to his feet and sprinted across the room, throwing himself into the elevator next to Crane just as the door started sliding closed again. He scooped up the rifle from the floor, and looked back into the room to see the Russian running at him gun held out in front...but not daring to fire as Crane was too close to MacRae to guarantee a clean shot. Then the door slid shut.

The elevator rattled as the Russian slammed his boot into the door. Crane made a grab for the assault rifle, trying to wrestle it from MacRae's grip. MacRae twisted sideways and slammed his left arm still holding the rifle across Crane's throat, pushing him against the elevator wall, then punched him hard in the face with his right fist.

'You fuck with me again and I'll kill you and worry about the other stuff later. Do we understand each other?'

Crane's vision swam, and he released his grip on the rifle before he answered, face seething.

'Yes, we understand each other.'

MacRae felt the elevator slow as it reached the basement. For the first time he felt the pain in his arm from the bullet fragments. His shirt was sticky from blood, and a thin trickle dripped down his fingers to the floor. Not much he could about it right now though. He checked the time. Was it too late?

'Can you finish shutting down the water treatment plants from down here?'

Crane wiped blood from his nose. 'Sure.'

The doors slid open. MacRae pushed Crane out first, then quickly followed, sweeping the corridor with his gun. They were alone, but he didn't want to be surprised again.

'Is there another way down here, or is it just the elevator?'

Crane shook his head. 'Just the elevator.'

'What about emergencies?'

'There's an emergency exit in the utility room, but it's one way, and that's out. You wouldn't want the bad people to come in uninvited, would you?'

'Can you lock the elevator down here?' MacRae said.

'Yes,' Crane said, looking at MacRae. He decided he didn't want to be hit again, adding, 'But it can be unlocked by anyone with the security codes.'

MacRae nodded, considering his options, then laid the assault rifle back in the door of the lift, preventing it from closing. He turned again to Crane, 'Old school security over-ride.'

He nudged Crane with the pistol.

'Okay, you've got work to do. Lead the way.'

Crane headed along the corridor, opening a door at the end and taking them into a space that looked more like an up-market apartment than a bunker.

Back on the ground floor, the Russian gave up trying to call the lift. He went to the keyboard Crane had been using and scrolled through the security camera locations, stopping at the exit to the lift in the basement. He watched as Crane and MacRae left the corridor, and cursed when he saw the assault rifle holding the elevator door open.

He holstered his pistol as he ran across the room, pressing on a hidden panel in the rear wall. A concealed door swung open, giving him access to a small room. He slid panels on the left side wall open, revealing floor to ceiling shelves lined with weapons. It only took a minute to find what he was after, then he shut the panels and ran his fingers along the top of the door, stopping when they found a small button. He moved his feet to the edge of the room, leaving a pattern of four tiles clear, and pressed the button. A muted click came from the floor, and a dark line appeared around the edge of the four tiles. He bent down and pressed hard in the centre, the tiles moving down fifty millimetres, then slid sideways to reveal a small shaft lit with blue LED lights.

He carefully lowered his legs into the shaft, feeling with his feet for the ladder fixed to the side, then silently climbed down the three metres to the basement. A pinprick of light speared across the shaft from the peephole in the basement. The Russian checked out the room, then satisfied it was empty slid open the concealed door and stepped into the utility room.

Switches and control equipment for the various building control and life support systems covered the walls, except for two doors; the one directly opposite led to the main living area of the bunker, the door to his right had a keypad lock on the outside and a glass panel in the centre. He grinned as he saw Marion's face appear in the window, hatred burning in her eyes.

~

Crane sat typing instructions into a laptop at a sleek black office desk in the corner of the apartment as MacRae watched over his shoulder.

Three screens flickered into life on the wall next to them. One was divided into multiple views scrolling sequentially through the compound's security cameras. MacRae noted with concern that there was no sign of the Russian. Where the hell had he gone?

He checked his watch. Fuck, they had literally minutes to go before the water treatment plants were commissioned.

The second screen showed the live vision of the commissioning ceremony. It looked like they were ready to proceed, with or without Crane. The government minister was speaking to the crowd of invited guests, journalists and selected workers from the construction of the plant. A huge control panel behind her was wrapped in a golden silk ribbon, shiny stainless-steel scissors sat in a timber frame on a display stand next to her.

MacRae moved in front of Crane, pressing the barrel of the gun into his throat for emphasis.

'What's taking you so long? You said the override was ready to go when we were upstairs.'

'It was.' A bead of sweat formed on Crane's brow. 'But the command sequence timed out when we were coming down here. If we'd stayed up there it would have been done. Now I have to re-run the algorithm.'

He tapped out more instructions then hit *enter*.

'There, it's almost finished.'

'Maybe you'll live to see another day after all,' MacRae said, watching the screen.

A grey dialogue box flashed silently on the screen.

COMMISIONING OVERIDE READY.
DO YOU WISH TO CONTINUE Y / N?

Neither of the men moved.

MacRae spoke. 'What are you waiting for?'

Crane snarled at MacRae. 'This has been my life's work. You want to destroy it? You press the button.'

MacRae leaned forward to press the key. And that saved his life, as at the same time MacRae heard the gunshot, the Russian's bullet zinged past his head and into the screen behind him, spraying glass across MacRae and Crane.

MacRae dropped to his knee and levelled his gun across the room at the door to the utility room. But he didn't shoot, as the Russian was holding Marion in front of him, gun at the side of her head as he walked slowly across the room.

MacRae's eyes met Marion's and his heart sank.

Her hands were tied together in front of her with black cable ties, a rag jammed in her mouth. Her eyes blazed with a mixture of despair and anger.

MacRae leaned in close to Crane, the only reason that the Russian didn't take another shot. MacRae marvelled at the man's loyalty to his employer.

The Russian spoke first. 'Move away from Mr Crane and the computer or I'll kill her.'

MacRae didn't move, keeping his gun trained on the Russian as he approached.

'You know I'm not going to do that. I'm not going to let millions of people die for this maniac's ego.'

'You're prepared to watch your woman die in front of you then?' The Russian hissed.

MacRae stared at the Russian. He had no doubt he would kill her without a second thought.

'You'll kill us both anyway.' He moved his gun to Crane's forehead. 'And you know I'll do the same to Crane.'

The Russian kept walking. 'Looks like we have a stalemate then, doesn't it?'

Then Crane spoke, his voice breaking into a laugh. 'I don't think so.' He pointed to the screen. 'There's only one loser here MacRae.'

MacRae shot a quick glance sideways. The news vision was panning back from a smiling government minister as she held the scissors, the golden ribbon fluttering down to her feet. The crowd applauded as the control panels behind her showed lights flickering from red to green across a map of India, each light reflecting one of the dozens of water treatment plants coming online and releasing Crane's deadly pathogen into the water supply of hundreds of millions of people, just as they relocated across the country to celebrate Diwali, ensuring the spread of the hideous and unstoppable disease across the entire country within days.

Despite all the years of discipline and training in his career, the Russian couldn't help but watch the screen for a second either. And that was when Marion felt his grip on her shoulder momentarily relax and she let her body drop to the floor at his feet.

The Russian tried to grab her as she fell but he was too late and suddenly he was exposed.

MacRae didn't hesitate, correcting his aim before firing twice at the centre of the Russian's torso. The bullets struck home, but instead of falling he staggered backwards as his ballistic vest took the impact.

MacRae swung his gun to follow him, adjusting his aim to the man's head and firing…just as Crane lashed out, knocking the gun sideways out of MacRae's hand.

The Russian regained his balance and lined up to shoot at MacRae. Marion swivelled on the ground and kicked the Russian's knee. The Russian roared and swung with his pistol, striking Marion in the side of her face. She collapsed to the ground.

MacRae threw himself across the room, covering the distance to the Russian in an instant and barrelling heavily into his chest, the two men crashing to the floor. Both reacted quickly, the Russian swinging his arm around to get a shot, but MacRae clamped his hand on the Russian's wrist with the gun, and drove his other fist into his face.

Crane scrambled across the floor behind them, going for MacRae's gun. Marion's head cleared as she spotted him from across the room. She climbed to her feet, and wrists still bound, ran to the gun, stamping on Crane's hand as he reached for it, then kicking it under a sofa. Crane swung his fist at Marion, catching her shoulder and throwing her onto a low table. The table overturned, tipping Marion onto the floor, her head striking the polished concrete floor with a dull *crack*.

MacRae looked over as Crane scanned the floor for the gun, but couldn't spot it. Instead he ran at the men fighting on the floor and swung his fists at MacRae's face. One connected, the second brushing off his back as MacRae twisted sideways.

The Russian felt MacRae's weight shift and tried to flip him over whilst bringing the gun closer to MacRae's torso, Crane moving around throwing punches at MacRae's head.

MacRae knew he couldn't hold them both off for long. The Russian felt MacRae weaken, and sensing victory threw everything into getting a shot at him. MacRae resisted with all his strength, then as he felt the Russian slowly swing the weapon towards him, stopped his resistance. The Russian sensed victory and squeezed the trigger… just as MacRae rolled his body away, the bullet instead entering Crane's chest dead centre and exiting behind his left shoulder.

Crane's eyes widened in shock, then he slumped to the floor next to the men, a pool of blood spreading beneath him.

The Russian snarled, but MacRae had momentum and slammed the hand holding the gun once, twice, three times into the concrete floor. The third time the gun flew free, bouncing into the middle of the room.

MacRae and the Russian both released their grip and leapt to their feet, circling each other. The Russian charged at MacRae and his hand darted behind his back to pull out a curved short-blade knife with a knuckle duster grip. MacRae saw it just in time, leaning back as the knife swung through the air where he had been. He stepped in quickly and slammed a front kick into the Russian's side. The Russian lashed out behind him, MacRae jumping back to avoid the blade.

They circled again.

'I'm going to enjoy killing you both.' The Russian grinned. 'Just like I enjoyed killing your mercenary friend LaBruge.'

MacRae's eyes narrowed.

The Russian lunged again, this time following MacRae as he twisted sideways, the blade of the knife slicing through his shirt and leaving a shallow cut across his ribs.

MacRae waited until the Russian's arm was fully extended and stepped in, gripping his wrist, pulling the Russian's forearm against his body. The Russian pulled back, but MacRae kept him turning, driving his other fist into the Russian's face as they moved.

Marion stirred on the across the room and seeing the fight tried to get to her feet, but half-collapsed back to the floor.

The Russian turned and bent, hooking his leg behind MacRae's, flipping them both backwards onto the ground.

MacRae's back thumped onto the concrete but he managed to drive the Russian's knuckles onto the floor, the knife freed from his grip and spinning across the room and coming to rest at Marion's feet.

The Russian climbed to his knees, and then he saw it, the gun under the sofa, mere metres away. He kicked out at MacRae's chest and pulled himself free, scrambling across the floor on his hands and knees to retrieve the gun.

MacRae looked for the other gun, but it was simply too far away.

'Ian, take this.'

It was Marion, and she was holding's the Russian's knife.

MacRae reached out his arm as she slid the knife across the floor, MacRae scooping it up and straight into a throwing grip. It was too late though as the Russian was aiming his gun at MacRae's face.

'I win, you lose MacRae.' The Russian paused briefly to enjoy the victory then he pulled the trigger.

Nothing. He looked down at the weapon and realised that after a lifetime of professional killing he'd made the error of an amateur. The safety had been knocked on.

The glint of steel in the artificial light was the only movement in the room as MacRae flicked his wrist to send the knife flying through the air and with a dull *thunk* it found it's mark, embedded up to the hilt in the Russian's throat.

MacRae and Marion froze as the Russian scrabbled at the gun's safety for a moment longer, then dropped the weapon and clasped both hands on the knife handle, staring in disbelief as he sat gently on the floor against the sofa and closed his eyes for the final time.

MacRae climbed to his feet and went to Marion. She tried to embrace him, then realised her hands were still bound. MacRae looked across at the knife still embedded in the Russian, then the monitors on the wall, and his heart sank. The news showed cheering crowds and smiling politicians shaking each other's hand as they celebrated the commissioning of the most significant infrastructure project in India's recent history.

Marion followed his eyes.

'We were too late. We failed, and so many people are going to die.'

A flashing cursor caught the corner of MacRae's eye. Crane's over-ride program was still active and waiting for confirmation.

'Maybe it's not too late,' MacRae said.

A grey dialogue box was still flashing silently on the screen.

COMMISIONING OVERIDE READY.
DO YOU WISH TO CONTINUE Y / N?

MacRae sat on the office chair, shot a glance at Marion then took a deep breath and pressed *Y*.

For three long seconds nothing happened, the cursor flashing silently at them. Then the screen was filled with scrolling lines of text as the program executed, sending coded instructions directly to every water treatment in the network across India.

MacRae let his breath out with a grin.

'We're on.'

Marion nodded, and held her bound hands up.

'And now, if you have a moment...'

MacRae chuckled. 'Oops, sorry.'

He knelt down at the Russian and carefully extracted the knife from his throat, wiping the blade on the Russian's shirt out of sight of Marion. She didn't need to see this.

A quick stroke upwards with the knife and the cable ties were off, Marion gratefully rubbing her bruised wrists.

'Is it working?' Marion said as she looked from monitor to monitor.

Everything seemed to be continuing as normal at the commissioning ceremony from the look of the news footage.

MacRae frowned.

'Maybe Crane wasn't as clever as he thought, after all.'

Marion reached out for MacRae's arm, as the significance sunk in.

'Then within hours, millions of people will have drunk the infected water, and be travelling across the country back home and spreading the disease. Crane will have got his wish and this will be the biggest genocide in history.'

MacRae winced as she gripped his forearm, the wound sending shards of pain spearing through him.

'Maybe not,' MacRae said. 'Look.'

Suddenly the scene on the live news was different. Confusion was spreading from the government ministers, to the technicians and plant operators, as behind them the screens showing the plants in operation around the country were one by one blinking from green to red as they shut down.

'Yes, we've done it.' MacRae clenched his fist as it sunk in.

Marion threw her arms around his neck, her lips meeting his.

'You are indeed a remarkable man Ian MacRae.'

He grinned at her. 'We couldn't have done this without each other, could we?'

She nodded, and stood back, still holding his hand. 'Do you think there's a lesson in that for us?'

MacRae shrugged. 'I think there probably is.'

Marion gently lifted his arm, peeling back his shirt sleeve to inspect his wound. 'First things first though. Let's get this cleaned up.'

MacRae's eyes sparkled as he laughed. 'Good thing there's a doctor in the house. But let's get out of here first.' He shot a glance from Crane to the Russian. 'I don't like the company down here.'

MacRae led the way back into the corridor to the elevator, the door still vainly attempting to close against the assault rifle on the floor. MacRae bent down and retrieved it, and it took the opportunity to slid shut before he could stop it.

Marion laughed. 'You might be able to save the world...but you're still outwitted by an elevator. Not sure this is the kind of man for me after all.'

MacRae looked above the door. The elevator had returned to the ground floor to answer the call from the Russian what seemed like a lifetime ago. He pressed the call button, and the elevator prepared for its journey back down.

Marion let herself relax for the first time in what seemed forever. She leaned back against the wall, holding MacRae's hand, and gave herself the luxury of closing her exhausted eyes for just for a moment.

MacRae smiled and let his shoulders slump. 'We did it sweetheart, we actually did it.'

He moved closer, reaching out to touch her arm. He felt a strange feeling, something he wasn't used to, something that he thought perhaps he'd grown too world-weary to experience any more.

It was hope.

Hope that maybe good people can make a difference in the world. And hope too that perhaps after all these years he and Marion had a real chance of making it together.

Marion opened her eyes, searching deeply into his. MacRae could sense that something had changed. For the first time in so long when he held her gaze, looking into her eyes, her soul, she was no longer shielding her love for him behind an impenetrable wall.

They held each other's gaze for a long moment, MacRae closing the gap between them. He knew everything was going to be alright.

MacRae took his phone from his pocket, smiling when he saw three bars of signal. He dialled a number, waiting, hoping he'd take the call. Then there it was, the cheerful but concerned voice of Schneider on the other side of the world.

The elevator door slid open next to them. Marion moved to step in but MacRae held her back, motioning at the phone.

She smiled, crossing her arms, looking at her watch and tapping her foot in mock impatience. The elevator door slid shut silently.

'Ian is that you? You're still in India? What the hell's going on over there...there's reports in the media that the launch of the India water treatment plants project has been sabotaged.'

MacRae grinned at Marion. 'Yes, I'm here with Marion. And we might have had something to do with it.'

Schneider was silent for a moment, then spoke. 'Jesus, you really pulled it off then?'

'Yes Brad, just like I said,' MacRae's voice was serious. 'But I think Crane might have been able to at least partially commission some of the treatment plants before we were able to stop him.'

'Shit.' Schneider's voice was a whisper.

'You understand what that means don't you?' MacRae said. 'Some of the pathogen might have been released already.'

'I'd better get our people in Delhi talking to our Indian contacts real quick,' Schneider said. 'So fill me in on how it happened so I can get it rolling.'

MacRae recounted the events of the last two days in succinct detail, giving Schneider all he needed to know. Then Schneider grilled him for more information where he needed it.

Marion stood watching as the men talked. This was the MacRae she remembered, purposeful, focused and deadly efficient.

MacRae finished by explaining where they were, sending GPS co-ordinates of the armoured compound.

Schneider sighed. 'I can't believe you did it Ian. I'm just so sorry that you had to do it alone. But I'm sure it'll be recognised that you've saved the lives of hundreds of millions of innocent people.' He chuckled. 'Even if you've shut down the most significant infrastructure project in recent Indian history.'

'I'm sure the spin doctors will find a positive way to tell the story,' MacRae said.

'No doubt they will. Now get yourself out of there and contact me when you're safely in the best hotel you can find, and we'll get a cleanup operation underway and everything formalised okay?'

MacRae ended the call. 'The best hotel we can find Marion? Sounds good to me.'

She smiled at MacRae, moving closer to wrap him in her arms.

Then she frowned, a look of confusion flashing across her face as she glanced over his shoulder down the corridor behind him.

Then confusion was replaced by her voice screaming.

'Ian...'

MacRae spun around, instinctively jerking the assault rifle up into a firing position. The Russian had dragged himself upright and was sitting in a pool of his own blood. He swayed as he struggled to focus on MacRae and Marion from fifteen metres along the corridor. He was holding something aloft, both hands fumbling with it.

MacRae struggled to see what he was doing. The shape in his hands was vaguely familiar. What was it? Then one hand pulled away, holding a ring of steel. The other hand moved back to throw.

Too late, MacRae recognised the hand grenade. He tried to aim his weapon as he pulled the trigger, spraying bullets along the corridor, some ricocheting of the white painted walls.

The Russian wrenched his shoulder forward and threw the grenade...just as the first of MacRae's bullets struck him, shredding his face in a spray of blood. A brief scream and he slumped sideways to the floor for the final time.

Time stopped for Marion and MacRae as the grenade sailed through the air and then bounced with a dull *clunk clunk* on the concrete floor, skidding towards them.

MacRae desperately scanned the corridor. There was nowhere else to go. He stabbed at the elevator call button. Maybe it would open in time? He mentally counted down the seconds to the inevitable detonation, the distance between them and the grenade closing.

10, 9, 8...

It was still ten metres away. Would it be far enough?

Marion's eyes met his, her terror reaching into his heart as she realised what was about to happen.

MacRae moved in front of her, shielding her face and smiled.

'Don't worry sweetie, it'll be alright.'

Then he wrapped his arms around her, trying to cover as much of her body as he could and held her tightly against the wall. All he could do now was pray that his body armour gave them some protection.

He felt her cheek soft against his as he heard the last scrape of steel on concrete of the barely moving grenade.

Marion whispered in his ear. 'I love you.'

Then the world exploded in noise, light, smoke and a blizzard of deadly shrapnel.

MacRae jerked forward as the jagged shards of steel ripped into his legs, arms and neck. The body armour providing vital protection to his torso.

Then it was over and all was silent except for the ringing in his ears.

MacRae clenched his teeth and tensed his body against the searing pain of the shrapnel. He felt the warmth of his blood running from his wounds down his body, the clammy wetness soaking his shredded clothing.

But they were alive.

He winced as he relaxed his arms around Marion, gently pushing himself away from the wall. Moving made his head swim. His vision was becoming blurry. He must have been injured more than he first thought.

He tried to concentrate on Marion, her face moving in and out of focus in front of him.

She was smiling at him, he was sure of it. A sad whimsical smile.

MacRae could see that she had been grazed by some of the shrapnel, a red gash oozing blood down her cheek. She was okay though.

He could feel the strength leaving his legs. God, was he going to pass out now? He struggled to keep holding onto Marion, he needed both hands to stay upright himself.

Was he sliding sideways as he went to the floor? No, it was Marion. She was falling sideways, leaving a crimson smear across the wall as she fell.

MacRae's mind swam as Marion closed her eyes and collapsed to the floor. Then his legs gave out and he too fell in a crumpled heap.

~

CHAPTER 34

ALOHA

MacRae stretched his arms over his head as he lay on the sun lounge overlooking the beach at the US military rehabilitation hospital. He winced as the tightness and pain of the fresh scar tissue down his torso reminded him of where he was and what had happened. The late afternoon sun and humidity of the Hawaiian island warmed his skin, but not his heart. Something inside him had been lost. Maybe it would never be found again.

Five weeks had gone by since the commissioning of the treatment plants in India, but for MacRae it had only been five days since he'd woken from the coma. He was still feeling vague about what had happened...he'd been assured that was normal...but slowly it was coming back, detail by painful detail.

Within hours of his call to Schneider from Crane's compound that day, Indian and US intelligence assets had secured the facility, and the records of Crane's operations around the world it contained. And that's where they'd found MacRae and Marion collapsed on the floor, still in each other's arms.

MacRae had spent the next few weeks unconscious in a private hospital in India, but when it was apparent his would be a long and slow recovery, he'd been evacuated to a US army hospital at the huge Pearl Harbour naval base in Hawaii. But not with Marion.

His mind reeled yet again, refusing to believe it was true. His last memory was the sweet smile on her beautiful face when they knew it was over, they'd survived and could now take the chance with each other they'd both realised they'd been waiting for.

But he'd woken up in a hospital, alone and under guard in an isolation ward, and no-one would tell him anything. Until Brad Schneider had arrived twenty four hours later to debrief him. Twenty four hours of uncertainty and doubt that became hell when Schneider told him that despite MacRae covering Marion's body when the grenade exploded, a piece of shrapnel had grazed her neck, and she'd bled to death within a matter of minutes, MacRae unconscious next to her, helpless to save her.

MacRae still struggled to believe it was true. One minute she was alive, then she was gone. In the intervening time her body had been flown home to her distraught parents for burial.

MacRae had contacted Marion's father from the hospital with a phone number provided by Schneider, and encountered a bitter coldness and resentment. Marion had often spoken of how her elderly parents worried about her chosen life, but accepted that was her choice, living to help others.

Her grieving father's words still rang in his head.

'If you hadn't come back into our beautiful daughter's life our only child would still be alive today. We'll never forgive you.'

Lying in his hospital bed MacRae had searched desperately online for Marion, trying to cling on to her memory through her digital fingerprint, but in their grief her parents had closed all her social media. The only tributes MacRae could find were on the Medecins a Travers Les Frontiers website, recognising her years of dedicated service to the organisation, and a funeral notice in her hometown newspaper. In many ways it was like she'd never existed, and because he hadn't been able to mourn her death part of him refused to accept she was gone.

MacRae squinted in the sun as he saw a figure approaching. It was Schneider striding across the lawn, laptop bag slung across a shoulder.

MacRae leaned forward and the two men shook hands warmly.

MacRae took in Schneider's dark suit and polished black shoes. The only nod to the tropical weather a pair of gold rimmed sunglasses perched on his nose. He waved his arm to the lounge next to him.

'Pull up a sun lounge, it's the perfect time to catch some rays... although aren't you a little overdressed?'

Schneider laughed. 'Not all of us can spend our days sunning ourselves you know. Some of us have jobs to do.'

He glanced at his watch, and pointed at the huge glass bowl of orange liquid with a bright paper umbrella, on the table next to MacRae.

'A bit early for cocktails isn't it?'

MacRae shrugged. 'Not for this kind unfortunately. It's only the finest quality one hundred percent alcohol-free navy issue mocktails around here I'm afraid.'

He took a sip, the ice sloshing around the glass.

'So what's the news today?'

Schneider opened the laptop on the table, turning up the brightness to counter the bright sunlight, tapping in the address of a news website.

'More of the same I'm afraid.'

MacRae scanned the article. The new disease outbreak in India was still spreading on the outskirts on Delhi, although the authorities assured the population that the total lock-down of the region over the last four weeks was starting to take effect, and the spread of the disease was slowing. But for the thousands already infected there would be no cure and a quick death was inevitable.

The Indian Prime Minister had no doubt that a vaccine would be available soon, although international cooperation in developing a vaccine was limited as the disease only seemed to be infectious to those of Indian heritage, leaving foreign tourists and business people unaffected.

MacRae shook his head. 'They could have done better if they'd shut down the region immediately you know, rather than leaving it for a week.'

Schneider loosened his tie to get some air to his neck. 'Yeah I know. But no one takes this stuff seriously until they see people around them dying. Thank God the disease was only released to such a small area though. They have you and Marion to thank for that.'

MacRae looked away, eyes drawn to the surf breaking on the reef.

'She didn't die in vain Ian. You believe that don't you?'

MacRae nodded. 'She'd devoted her life to saving others.'

'Absolutely,' Schneider said. 'And this time it's measured in the hundreds of millions. And there really was nothing you could have done to save her. No one could have.'

MacRae frowned. There was something in Schneider's tone, something he wasn't telling him.

'What don't I know Brad?'

Schneider sighed, watching the sun shimmering on the water.

'I'm so sorry Ian. You couldn't have known. We conducted an autopsy on Marion, standard procedure in the circumstances.'

'Go on.'

'The pathologist discovered the early signs of leukaemia, but it was an unknown, extremely aggressive variant, something we've never encountered before.'

'What?' MacRae sat upright.

'It looks like when her drink was spiked in the bar, it didn't just contain the hallucinogen that induced psychosis, it also contained some kind of isotope. We haven't identified it yet, maybe polonium, like that used to poison the Russian dissident a while back. Anyway, from the moment she drank from that glass Marion was dying.'

MacRae held his face in his hands, then looked up.

'That drink was meant for me. I'm the one who should be dead. Her parents are right. I am responsible for Marion's death, when I should have been protecting her.'

The two men sat in silence, Schneider sharing MacRae's pain.

A couple of marines, weapons shouldered, wandered past on the beach and gave them a cursory nod.

MacRae snapped out of it. He'd have to deal with this in his own time and way.

'How are the investigations into Crane's operations going?'

This time it was Schneider who looked uncomfortable.

'The reach of his organisation is extraordinary. No-one seemed to know what anyone else was doing. And so much work was being done for the US Defence Department that suddenly everything seems to be classified information.'

MacRae shook his head. 'It's always the way isn't it? All the research will quietly be incorporated into other government programs, and no-one will care about how it was developed or why.'

'That's the way of the world buddy,' Schneider said. 'It's no different from the US and the Russians spiriting away the Nazi nuclear physicists and missile scientists at the end of the second world war for their own weapons and space programs.'

MacRae lapsed into silence, lying back on the lounge.

Schneider shut the laptop with a snap. 'Come on, let's take a walk on the beach. I think I can break you outta here for a while.'

~

The sand was warm and soft underneath MacRae's feet, the crash of the surf soothing as they walked. Voices of the children playing in the water mingled into one. Then a squeal of delight broke through. MacRae looked up. Surely not?

Running along the beach arms outstretched was Hassana, Sarah running full tilt trying to keep up behind her.

The girl barrelled into MacRae, throwing her arms around his neck. MacRae grunted with pain, but hugged her anyway.

Sarah joined them, planting a kiss on MacRae's cheek.

MacRae looked across at Schneider. 'Did you have something to do with this?'

But Schneider was already walking away. 'I thought you deserved some visitors. And for some reason there are a lot of grateful people in various governments that seem very happy to pull strings for you at the moment.'

He waved at Sarah. 'Just make sure you have him back by dinner time.'

Sarah linked her arm through MacRae's as they walked, Hassana skipping up the beach ahead of them.

'I'm told they're going to release you in the next week or two, send you back home?'

MacRae nodded. 'That's what I heard.'

'Brad arranged for Hassana and I to visit you on compassionate grounds, apparently I'm your carer on the flight back home.'

MacRae smiled. 'Based on our previous travels together I guess that means we'll be enjoying a few in-flight complimentary beverages?'

'If you insist.' Sarah laughed mischievously. 'Do you know what's been happening at the research institute with the devil facial tumour program?'

MacRae shook his head. It all seemed a world away right now.

'The institute's been temporarily shut down, pending an investigation into systemic corruption and unethical research practices, whatever that means. At least that's what the local media is reporting.'

MacRae pulled her gently over to the water's edge, feeling the warm water splash over his feet. Was this what being normal felt like?

'I guess everyone's rushing to tie up the loose ends now,' Sarah said.

'Yes,' MacRae said. 'And there's a few loose ends I need to tie up when I get home too.'

Sarah kicked the water as she walked. 'Murdoch, the wildlife photographer?'

'Yes. His wife refused to give up hope, but we know he most likely crossed paths with Crane and his hired gun in the central highlands so I suspect he's dead, although I doubt a body will ever be found. Brad thinks it'd be best for the government to declare him dead, maybe get a memorial plaque in the National Park recognising his work in raising awareness of the devils and their plight. Hopefully that will give her some closure.'

Sarah looked at MacRae with concern and spoke. 'I'm not sure people can ever fully accept a death unless they've seen a body, or attended the funeral. It gives them the time to grieve.'

MacRae knew she was referring to him with Marion. 'It just works out that way for some people.'

'And what about the scientist at the Merton Institute who disappeared, Dr Khan. Shouldn't her family know the truth?'

MacRae stopped walking, turning to face Sarah. 'I don't think it'll benefit anyone, especially her kids, to know what might have been done to her by Edison or Crane do you? And the government is doing everything it can to protect the reputation of the research community and the Merton.'

'I guess it's the journalist in me looking for the truth. So it's going to be the usual cover-ups and lies to protect vested interests?'

'It sounds like you're getting a bit world-weary Sarah,' MacRae said.

'Well, if the truth doesn't come out, doesn't it mean we keep making the same mistakes, everyone keeps getting away with this stuff? Let me guess, Crane will still end up being lauded as a philanthropist and a visionary for his work with the new water treatment plants?'

MacRae kept walking. 'Ironically you're partly right...as it turns out Crane will have a huge impact on controlling and possibly reducing India's population over time. Just not in the way he planned.'

'How so?' Sarah said.

'Well, now the treatment plants have been belatedly commissioned without Crane's pathogens, the improvements to the general health of the population and extended lifespans will almost certainly lead to a reduced birth rate, and a more efficient use of the world's resources. Exactly what Crane was trying to achieve.'

They walked in comfortable silence for a while, Hassana running in and out of the surf, kicking up sprays of white foam, then MacRae spoke.

'How's Ritchie?'

Sarah shrugged. 'I don't know. I've tried to contact him a couple of times, he must know what's been going on in India, but it's like he's disappeared again.'

MacRae looked down at the sand. 'I'd like to thank him for what he did for us, Hassana, let alone the people of India.'

He looked at Sarah as she contemplated her next words.

'You don't think Brad knows anything do you Ian, about Ritchie helping us? You mentioned he said it'd be great to have a hacker like Ritchie to help. Was it just coincidence?'

'Surely he would have told us if he knew Ritchie was alive, working for the US government,' MacRae said. 'He knows how important that would be to us.'

'But he'd also know Ritchie was contacting us, breaking the deal he'd made with government,' Sarah said. 'And there would no doubt be consequences.'

MacRae sighed. 'Brad wouldn't lie to us after all this. Would he?'

A wave broke, splashing white foam up MacRae's and Sarah's legs. They jumped sideways in unison.

There was still so much to sort out, so much to worry about.

But today, right now, was just for feeling alive.

~

CHAPTER 35

EPILOGUE

The man's walking boots slipped briefly on the craggy rock at the edge of the cliff to his left. His heart raced as the twenty five kilogram pack on his back swayed him dangerously close to the brink of the sheer drop to the valley two hundred metres below.

'Careful Dad,' came the voice of his sixteen year old son from behind him, as they traversed the narrow ridge between the peaks of the mountain in the Tasmanian central highlands.

They were both experienced bushwalkers, something they'd bonded over for many years, and this walk was one of their favourites.

The man steadied himself, taking a moment to enjoy the view, his eyes following the mountain ranges in the distance, and then peering down to the base of the cliff next to them. A flash of coloured material caught his eye, there was something familiar about the shape.

'What the hell...'

He pulled a worn map from his shorts pocket, found their location, and traced his finger to a thin line marking a track to the base of the cliff.

'Leave your pack here, we're taking a detour okay?'

The young man laid his pack on the ground next to his father's and within minutes they we're scrambling down a steep slope of gigantic boulders and scree to the bottom of the valley.

It took a while before the man found what he'd seen from above... the crumpled body of a man wedged between two massive slices of dark grey granite...a place so inaccessible that even the wildlife hadn't managed to consume it.

He held a hand back at his son. 'Wait here, you don't need to see this.'

But it was too late, the young man already sliding down the rock face. He landed with his feet either side of the body, his father sliding down next to him. Much of the body had decomposed, but his essence remained, the utility jacket full of expensive camera equipment, the machete strapped across his chest. But what the man hadn't expected to see, in fact he hadn't seen since his time as a journalist in war zones many years earlier, was the unmistakable bullet entry and exit wounds.

Three thoughts immediately went through his mind. Who was the poor bastard and how did he end up here? Better get out of here and call the police. And which sensationalist media outlet would pay the most for the story?

The murder of Kane Murdoch wouldn't be a secret for much longer.

~

Twenty kilometres off the coast of Miami, Elias adjusted the tension on his tuna fishing rod as his cruiser rocked gently in the southerly swell. It was hot and humid, but with a gentle breeze. Just as he liked it.

He sat back on the padded vinyl seat and read the latest news article on his phone about the tragic death of medical entrepreneur and philanthropist Magnus Crane recently in India. Death should always be a tragic thing, but this death bought Elias a profound sense of relief and justice. Speculation was rife as to the reason for Crane's kidnapping and murder. There had been no ransom demand or negotiations, and authorities were at a loss to identify anyone who would want Crane's death.

Elias was pretty sure he knew one man who was involved. Ian MacRae.

A huge tug on the rod and Elias leapt to his feet. The battle with the magnificent fish was on, and for the first time since he was fourteen years old, Elias felt at peace.

~

The little girl pretended to play with her doll as she sat on the carpet in the living room with her parents. She watched the news on the TV from the corner of her eye, listening as her parents discussed the outbreak of the new disease in a war-torn part of Nigeria. Only she knew that the disease wasn't new, because she'd seen a horribly shaped face just like on TV once before, through a telescope one night in a hotel in Hobart, Tasmania. And in many years time when she was a mother herself she'd read fairy tales to her children, and explain to them that the scary stories about giants, witches and monsters were meant to teach the children of the time to be wary of strangers and not to trust everyone, but that the giants and witches weren't real. Except to her, monsters were very real, because she'd seen one, and the image would haunt her forever.

~

Doctor Sanita Balodis loved her work at the innocuously named Integrated Research Facility at Fort Detrick, Maryland. Officially she was attached to the National Institute of Allergy and Infectious Diseases laboratories team. But in actual fact her recent work in the highly classified and secure bio-hazard level BSL-4 laboratory hidden below the ground in an isolated concrete building was far more interesting. She was researching death. And today she felt she was the Queen of death.

Raised in a strict Catholic family, she'd always been acutely aware of the moral conflict between researching for the good of humanity, and the opportunities to exercise her intellectual curiosity, no matter where it took her. For most of her career she'd been able to justify the decisions she made and the work she did.

She could find no moral justification for what she was doing now. But it was the opportunity of a lifetime.

She still marvelled at how she'd been tasked with leading a team to collate and extend a vast amount of research that had apparently suddenly fallen into the hands of the Department of Defence. And this wasn't ordinary research. This was the most extreme form of Gain Of Function genetic modification she'd ever encountered. Whoever had been conducting this research had found the way to create the perfect diseases, all highly contagious and lethal, basically unstoppable. And able to be tailored to only target exactly who the scientists wanted them to.

Her fingers fumbled on the computer keyboard as she typed in instructions to the automated robotic laboratory equipment. Was it nerves, or was it simply the clumsy gloves built into the positive air pressure protective suit she was wearing? The robotic arm reached into a huge, chilled storage vault, soft clouds of mist drifting off the liquid nitrogen filled containers inside.

It skimmed past dozens of stainless steel and glass containers then abruptly stopped, picking one up carefully and taking it back into the laboratory.

A scanner flashed over a QR code printed on the side, confirming the contents. Bubonic plague, caused by the bacteria Yersinia Pestis. It sounded so innocent.

She tapped more keys on the computer, eyes flicking across the screen, then nodding in satisfaction. The work on this agent was almost completed. It had already been tailored to individually target seventy five percent of the specific ethnic groups in the world. Another few weeks work and this, like all the other deadly diseases in her care, would be perfected to wipe out any race on the planet the US government felt necessary.

Today was a little more chilling than usual though. She was modifying the genetic code to target only Hispanic DNA. Her DNA.

She pushed the thought from her mind, and focused back on typing, oblivious to the fact that an injury she sustained as a child was, thirty years later, to have a profound effect on the world. A broken bone in her wrist resulting from a roller-skating accident had left her with a slightly bent wrist. This created pressure on the inside of her hermetically sealed suit and had caused a tiny tear that opened and closed as she typed. The tear was so small that it was undetected as a pressure loss in the suit. But big enough to allow the entry of a handful of spores from the plague sample she was working on.

A tickle in her throat and she coughed, drawing the pathogen deep into her lungs as she inhaled each time, where it would grow undetected for weeks, before spreading amongst her extended family attending a christening party the following month.

Although he was long dead, Magnus Crane's terrifying vision was about to be realised.

THE END